She Rises at Night

Jae El Foster

DCL Publications, LLC
www.thedarkcastlelords.net

© 2021 Jae El Foster

First Edition April 2021

DCL Publications
1033 Plymouth Dr.
Grafton, OH 44044

ISBN 978-1-7362178-6-3

Cover design by Jae El Foster

Cover Model: Julian Christian

PUBLISHED IN THE UNITED STATES OF AMERICA

"We grew to know the meaning of love."

~ Martin Lawrence ~

Dedicated to the Keepers of the Book.

Navigate the
HOUSE OF HORRORS

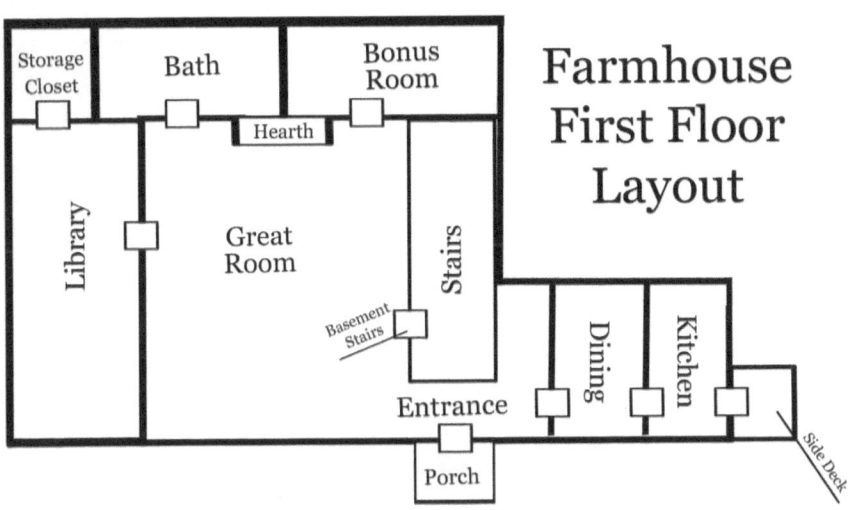

Farmhouse
First Floor
Layout

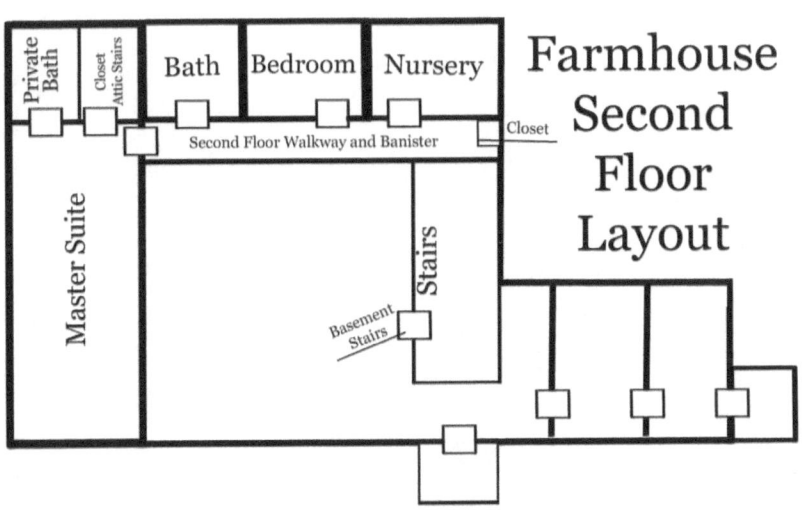

Farmhouse
Second
Floor
Layout

Prologue

2009 – The Old Owners

Lightning struck the hill outside and Marybeth cringed in her seat near the fireplace.

"Every time it storms here, something bad happens," she noted in a quivering voice as her husband Henry stoked the fire. "We've been here four months. I don't know how much longer I can last here."

"I wish you would calm down," Henry told her as he stood from his crouched position. "You're going to stress yourself out and induce labor before the baby's ready."

"That's a good part of my point!" she added in a raised voice, standing from the Victorian period sofa. "I don't want to have our baby *here*, Henry! This house… it's cursed!"

"Cursed?" he scoffed, chuckling under his breath. "Have your pregnancy hormones driven you insane?"

She didn't want to respond – not while she was scared and angry all at once. She had to calm down, and she couldn't do it with Henry pacing the room. Finally, he walked to the door of the library and opened it, stepping inside.

"I'm going to do some reading," he told her and shut the door behind him.

She wished she didn't feel like she did, but as the rain began and she could hear the waves from the sea crash against her land, it was hard to forget why she wanted to leave.

Walking to the large staircase, she began up the stairs, considering how much she and Henry had lost since purchasing the house. It had been a joint purchase, she recalled – a four-person deal with herself and Henry and their best friends, Charlie and Rachel. As Marybeth stepped into the nursery and shut the door, she thought of her dear friends, of how Charlie was now buried in a cemetery ten miles away and what had been found of Rachel was now in an urn, shipped back to the States to her parents' house.

The purchase of the house…the move across the ocean…it had all been intended as a change – an escape from the tragedies and struggles they'd all faced back home. The house had been cheap and purchased online, and when they'd all arrived, it had seemed less like the fixer-upper that the listing had called it and more like a dump that needed to be leveled. It was still a dump – one they were stuck with.

Marybeth sat in the rocking chair near the crib and held her swollen belly with both hands, stroking it. There was a little girl inside of her, just waiting to be born, and Marybeth couldn't imagine letting her come into the world here – in this house of tragic despair.

The nursery was the only part of the house that she and Henry had furnished new. It was her safe-space – a place where the demons of the past were removed with hopes of a better future.

Yet, the reflections of a grim future tainted her mind instead. She couldn't understand why Henry wouldn't take her away from here – why he just wouldn't let her leave and have the baby safely in the city, with doctors and a hospital. He said when the time was near that they would rent a room in the city until she needed to go into the hospital, but Marybeth was aware that babies were rarely right on time. What if this little girl decided to break out early? Marybeth simply would not allow her child to be born here... she *couldn't*.

She wasn't sure exactly what had killed Charlie or Rachel. Much of Charlie's head had been eaten – savagely – and had it not been for his tattoos, he would have been unidentifiable. He was found on the road, just a half mile or so from the house. He had gone out for a nighttime walk in the rain, and never returned.

Rachel's death had been similar. She'd walked down the hill to retrieve something from the shed. It had been nighttime and storming then also, and the moment Henry and Marybeth heard her scream, they rushed out to her. They found only the shoes she'd walked out in, until the next day when bits and pieces of her were found scattered within a mile radius.

The storm grew worse outside and Marybeth shivered. She knew that it was silly of her to relate the storms, the house, and the deaths of her friends all together. Neither of her friends had been killed inside of the house; both had been outside, at night, in the rain. Perhaps the house was a safe place, but the reality was that whatever was outside could get inside if it really wanted to. Not that anything would really want to…

If the house had not been in such cruddy shape, it would have been rather charming. It was large, with three bedroom spaces and a bathroom upstairs, plus a bathroom, a library, a great room, a kitchen and dining room downstairs. There was also a bonus room near the basement door. The basement, itself, was spacious but dark, and it had another door that led into a cellar. Marybeth had not yet stepped foot into the cellar. It just sounded downright scary to her.

Henry spent most of his time in the library. He said he found the research within it intriguing, but Marybeth was not one for reading or research. She left Henry to his library, and he told her nothing of what he learned or read – just as she preferred it.

She heard a boom and thought it was thunder but quickly

recognized it as the front door slamming shut. She couldn't imagine company at this hour. Not even the property's caretaker came by after dark.

Leaving the safety of her rocking chair, she stepped from the nursery and into the hallway. Walking to the railing, she looked over, down to the great room and front door below.

"Henry?" she called, wondering if he had gone outside or if someone else had come in.

When her husband didn't respond, she walked down the stairs and stood at the foot, taking in her surroundings. Aside from the storm, it was quiet and it appeared that Marybeth was alone. She walked to the library door and knocked on it... opened it. Henry was not inside.

She shut the door and walked to the front entrance, peering through its window. She couldn't see a thing for the storm, and so she opened the door and braced herself as she stepped out onto the porch. The wind was cold and the rain was heavy, but the porch roof managed to keep her mostly dry as she looked around the hill, searching for her husband.

"Henry!" she shouted, hoping that her voice would travel over the roar of the storm. She called him two more times, but all of her calls went unanswered. Finally, feeling the rain sting her cheeks as the wind changed its course, she stepped back inside.

Henry stood in the great room, looking at her with a beer in his hand. Marybeth screamed from the surprise.

"What is wrong with you tonight?" he asked her and took a swig of beer. "You're awfully jumpy."

"Where were you? Just a moment ago."

"In the kitchen," he noted, raising his bottle of beer as proof.

"Didn't you hear me call for you?"

"Are you kidding?" he laughed, shaking his head. "You can't hear anything in that room because of the storm. With the windows and the door... it's a little booming."

Marybeth looked around the room. The lights began to flicker from the storm.

"If you didn't slam the front door," she asked, "then who did?"

"I didn't hear any door slam," he told her as he drank. "I'm going back to my book. Why don't you come pick out something to read? It will take your mind off of the storm."

"Go read," she replied, shaking her head. "I'm going to make some coffee."

"At this hour? This... *pregnant*?"

"One cup isn't going to push the baby out of me."

"One cup," Henry repeated, holding up one finger for emphasis. "Our little girl's going to grow up to be a rocket scientist, and we don't want her overexerting herself in the womb."

"Whatever you say, Dr. Kevorkian," Marybeth replied.

"Hey… he wasn't a –!"

"Enjoy your book!"

Before he could respond again, Marybeth – along with the new smirk on her face – stepped through the dining room and into the kitchen, where she began the prep for coffee.

Henry had been right. The storm *was* booming. She could barely hear herself think as she filled the maker with water, a filter, and fresh grounds.

The longer the storm lasted, the more nervous she became, and as she poured a cup of the fresh brew's first strong drops, she sipped and wished the storm would stop. The longer it rained, the worse her chances were of leaving this house any time soon. Heavy rain brought about higher sea-levels, flooding, and the fine art of being stranded.

Considering once more how she did not want to give birth inside of this house, she picked up her cup, took one step away from the counter, and felt her water break.

"No…" she whispered, almost in disbelief. This couldn't be happening. Surely, her baby knew there were more appropriate places to be born than here, in this drafty, damp house in the middle of nowhere. "Stay where you're at." She clenched everything she could as tightly as she could. "Just hang on another day or two."

The arrival of labor pains came as a response to her suggestion. Nearly floored by the sudden and sharp pain, she steadied herself and felt it subside.

"This can't be happening," she said, setting her coffee cup down and slowly crossing to the doorway of the dining room. There, once inside, another contraction came. They were close together. Her baby did not want to wait another day or two – or another hour or two.

She had to make it to Henry. Storm or no storm, she knew he'd help her to the car, load her up, and drive her to the hospital. He'd save her, despite his blatant, irrepressible stupidity.

"I love him," she said through a heavy breath, "but sometimes I hate him so much…"

Just as one pain left her, another took its place. This time, she fought through it, leaving the dining room and stepping into the great room. There, she saw the library door open and the light on.

"Henry!" she called, fighting against the pain as she neared the room. "Henry, please! She's coming! Our little girl is coming!"

Something felt off to Marybeth as she approached the open doorway. She paused just before she reached it, listening for Henry's response. Nothing but silence projected toward her. Stepping into the threshold, she looked at the desk. Henry was not seated at it. Instead, he was on the floor beside it. His stomach…

his neck... his face... something – something *horrible* had eaten him. Just like with Charlie and Rachel.

First, she screamed. Then, she quieted herself. Marybeth felt sick. She felt weak. The labor pains were worsening and her husband was dead on the floor in front of her, missing half his face. She wanted to scream again, but she knew that was the worst thing to do. She wished she hadn't screamed the first time. Whatever had done this had slammed the door earlier – she'd heard it – and she was certain it was still in the house. Any sound she made would alert it to where she was.

Barely able to move and fighting against the pushing and pains of the child within her, she knelt down beside Henry and fished his keys from his pocket. She had to escape, even if she had to do it without him.

As quietly as she had entered, she left the library and hurried to the front door. She opened it wide, stepped out onto the porch, and shut the door behind her. It was raining harder than before, but she could still see the car, parked in the driveway. She swallowed, felt another contraction, and then sped down the porch steps like her life depended on it – which she was certain it did.

She was barefoot and she slid the moment her feet touched the muddy ground. Like a boulder from a mountainside, she fell hard, landing with a thump and a roll. She felt the pain from the fall collide with that from the latest contraction, and it seemed crippling to her. Tears welled in her eyes as she tried to stand – one hand holding her heavy belly while the other pushed off the ground.

Sliding a bit down the hill set her off her course to the car, and it was a fight to push her way back through the heavy wind and torrential rain. Determined, she edged closer to the car – closer to her escape from whatever was inside that house… and from the house itself.

Looking to the house, Marybeth saw the door was wide open, when she knew beyond a shadow of a doubt that she had closed it behind her.

"No…" she whispered with the realization that whatever had killed Henry was now outside with her, hidden by the shadows of the night and the violent storm.

With the car not too far away, she began to run as fast as her weak legs could carry her. She held the ignition key in her hand, ready to cram it in and start the car the second she reached it. She had to escape; she had to save her baby. Twice, her feet threatened to lose their footing again, but Marybeth pushed through, refusing to fall again.

She reached the car, only to find it locked. Fumbling, she hunted for the smaller car key and worked it into the lock. Once the lock released, she opened the door and climbed inside. With a bit of urgent force, she shoved the ignition key into its slot and turned it.

Nothing happened. Not even an attempt at cranking. She tried again. Fooled with the lights… the radio… The battery was dead.

"No…" she whimpered and refused to believe her luck. "Please start… Please!" She tried to crank the car one more time before conceding defeat, and through the rainy windshield, she looked at the open front door of the house. It seemed more looming – more impending – than before, but she knew she had no other choice than to return to it.

Another contraction came as she left the car. Panicked, she rushed back toward the house. The wind and rain beat her with every move, stinging her skin and fighting to once again set her off her course. Still, she persevered, seeing the porch just mere steps away.

Marybeth took hold of the railing and pulled herself up the first step. Then, looking at the front door, she paused. She wasn't certain that whatever had killed Henry had actually followed her outside. Perhaps it had opened the door to confuse her – to throw her off so she'd return and it could eat her too.

She didn't know what to do or which way to go. Either way tasted of death. The pain in her gut reminded her that her baby was coming, and so she had no choice now. She had to go inside, as she couldn't give birth to a child in the storm.

As swiftly as she could, she climbed the steps and hurried to the open door, slamming it shut behind her and locking it instantly. With soft steps, she backed away from it.

The howling of the wind was the first sound that greeted Marybeth in the great room. It roared with ferociousness – threatening… intimidating. She could hear it all through the house, as if the storm was somehow hitting it from all four directions.

The sounds of the storm grew louder by the moment, and as she held her ears, Marybeth turned in circles, trying to block it out.

She had to ignore it – the storm and its sounds. She had to block everything out – her dead husband on the library floor, the contractions that grew worse with each passing moment… the car that wouldn't crank and the flood waters that were quickly rising… She had to focus on finding a place to hide. Somewhere that she could safely have her baby.

Bam! She heard the slamming of a door come from the kitchen. She'd forgotten about the side entrance, and she'd likely left it unlocked earlier. It could have been the storm that opened and slammed the door, she considered as she walked toward the stairs, but when she heard the door between the kitchen and the dining room open and shut, she no longer questioned it. Someone – or something – was in the house with her.

Marybeth had to hurry, as she could hear the doorknob from the door joining the dining room and the great room begin to turn. Unsure of where else to go, she opened the basement door and stepped down onto the top step, shutting the door behind her. Deciding it best to leave the light off, she blindly took each wooden step with caution, letting her hand graze along the wall as she ventured down.

The labor pains were so intense that she wanted to collapse when she reached the bottom, but she held steady, knowing that she had to continue on. It was too dangerous here. She had to go somewhere deeper – somewhere that she'd never bothered going before. She had to go down to the cellar, a place so deep in the house that nothing would be able to find her or her baby.

By the time she found the cellar door in the dark, she was crowning. She could feel it. She had to be careful going down the stairs. She had to take easy steps, or else she was afraid the baby would just fall out as she walked.

With the cellar door shut behind her, she felt safe enough to turn on the dim light. Its glow from the cellar below made her feel somewhat more secure, and as she hurried down to it, she thought of how she would have to deliver her baby with swiftness and then immediately return to finding a way off of this hill and away from this house.

At the bottom of the cellar, she felt a knot grow in her throat and her skin became clammy. There, standing and facing her, were four… people… or things that looked like people. They stood in the middle of the room atop of what appeared to be a chalked-out pentagram on the floor. They each had eyes so pale that they were nearly white – a compliment to their skin tones. One had a slit throat; another had a stab wound to the gut. The third had a gunshot wound to the heart, and the fourth just looked plain dead.

Marybeth screamed in terror. As the four creatures began to approach her, she turned to flee back up the stairs, only to find a fifth creature awaiting her – a little girl with wide white eyes and a mischievous grin.

"No…" Marybeth whispered, but the little girl did not oblige. Instead, she leapt onto her, tearing into Marybeth's flesh with her claws and digging into her cheek with her teeth. Marybeth screamed again and felt the other four creatures grab hold of her from behind. They forced her onto the ground, pinning her down despite her struggling efforts to fend them off. Then, as the little girl began to tear into her gut and eat her child from within her, the others began to devour Marybeth, silencing her screams.

Part I

Day 1 – Karen

"I don't know how I let you talk me into this," Karen told her husband as she looked out the window of their "new" car. The car was a 90's model, and it had been a required purchase for their transition.

"How many times do we have to go over this?" Bob asked her. "I lost my job. You haven't had one in *years*, and we were going to lose the house. You said you always wanted to live in England. You said it was on your bucket list. You said..."

"I know what I said!" she shouted. Then there was silence.

Bob and Karen had been boiling through this fight ever since their plane landed. They fought over what car to buy. They fought over who would drive. They fought over every little bitty thing that they could find, and this ferocious bickering was caused by their unhappiness. They had not been happy in Connecticut.

They had only moved there because – A – Bob could afford it at the time and – B – they had planned to raise a family and had wanted to do it in a calm, serene, neighborhood environment.

Truth be told, they had not been happy since marrying and leaving Chariot, Tennessee, for Bob's job transfer and their *fresh start*. They had only known each other for five weeks before Bob popped the question, and Karen had been all-too swift with her acceptance of it. She had also been pregnant too, and that had a lot to do with it.

"I said I wanted to live *in* England," she whispered, breaking the silence, even if barely. "This farmhouse is not in England. It is way out in the middle of nowhere, and it's on a marsh. A *marsh* for crying out loud!" She no longer whispered.

"I thought you liked being near water," Bob countered, keeping his eyes on the narrow road.

"Every time it rains… every time the tide comes in… every time it *fucking rains* and that marsh rises, you realize we'll be trapped in that house, right? The road will be impassible." She still stared out the window. Everything was brown and wet. There was some green in the trees and there were some greenish weeds, but the land was poorly taken care of.

"Maybe this is what we need," Bob replied. "Everything was so stressful in Connecticut. Things will be a lot simpler here. I'll find a new job much easier here. That reputation… it didn't move here with us. We can get back on our feet, and after a few months – if you still want to – we can sell the house and get a better one if you're not happy."

She didn't know how to respond. She wanted to yell at him again, but she was so tired of yelling. Purely put, she was tired of Bob. The last couple of years, he had proven to be all talk and no action. No... she took that back. It was his actions back in the States that had gotten them into this situation to begin with.

"Anyway, we're almost there," Bob continued. "Honestly, if you give it a chance, I think it will really grow on you."

"Like mold from the eternal dampness of it all?" she chided, albeit without humor in her tone.

"We'll get a second car in a couple of weeks. That way, even when I'm gone, you'll be free to drive to town."

"We can't afford a *second* car, Bob, and besides that, what happens when I do go to town? Must I leave at the crack of dawn every day, just to get the shopping done and make it home before the water rises and floods the marsh? We can't afford for me to stay in town on occasions when I can't get back home – just because we live in Bumblefuck, Nowhere."

"What part of *give it a chance* did you not understand?"

Back and forth. Jab after jab. This was how they carried on until Bob turned off onto an even narrower road that seemed lower than the prior one. From here, there was silence. Karen could smell the stench of the water and see the air filled with gray from a rising fog.

"They say the marshland is the most beautiful place in the world during the morning," Bob said, but he failed to break through the wall of ice that surrounded Karen's silence.

I could fucking kill him right now, was the thought that itched Karen's brain. It was not a passing thought. It was not fleeting. It was a thought – a cognitive aspiration – that stuck in her mind all the time. On a daily basis (sometimes many times a day) it appeared, and she was forced to recognize its existence. Then, she would tuck the thought away – let it subside – and that would be that.

They passed the drives for two other farmhouses, but Karen wondered if they were inhabited. The roof was half-off on one and the other appeared to be leaning and sinking.

It was another mile or so before Bob began to slow the car down. Through the thick of the fog and the gray of the late afternoon, through the stench of the water and the sourness of feared anticipation, Karen could see it – the farmhouse… their new home.

It was gray and dismal, almost black, and it was in dire need of repair. It sat up high on a small hilltop, which served to keep it safe from the marsh water and the cresting sea and its tides. There was a large stone foundation that raised the house off of the ground, and a heavy flight of thick stone steps led the way up to the porch. There were shutters falling off the hinges, and the roof lacked several shingles, which Karen supposed meant that the roof leaked when it rained.

There were two trees in the front lawn – if it could be called a *lawn* – and both trees looked dead. The yard was mud primarily... or muddy grass. She couldn't really tell, and she wasn't sure she cared. Looking down toward the water, she saw two small sheds – one a boat shed with a rowboat inside, and another with a closed door.

Perhaps, Karen thought, *perhaps maybe I should just kill him. Knock him out and throw him in the sea and say fuck this place.*

Bob had given Karen practically no say in this purchase. Their house in Connecticut had been under his name, and when they were moments away from losing it, he put it on the market. It sold in under a week, and they made enough off the sale to pay their debts, with enough left over to buy a shithole somewhere else. Bob found this particular shithole online and bought it without consulting Karen on the decision. For this and so much more, Karen hated him.

"Here we are, *honey*," Bob said with such thick sarcasm that Karen refused to acknowledge it. "Home sweet home."

She hoped that the stare she gave him let him know how

much she wanted him to die.

"Let's give it three months," he told her as he drove up the hill and parked beside the massive house. "Like I said, if you're not happy here in three months, then we'll sell it and find somewhere better."

Three months, she thought. *He'll be lucky if I make it three days here.*

Stepping out of the car, she looked at her surroundings. The land was growing wetter from the cresting sea as it began to fill the marsh. Soon, in just an hour or so, it would be completely covered.

She heard the popping of the trunk and walked around the car to grab her suitcase and duffel bag. She was assured that the rest of her things would arrive within the week, but she was just as uncertain of that happening as she was of anything at this point.

When the trunk lid closed, she looked up at the house. *Massive* had been an understatement. It appeared to be more *overwhelming* or *terrifying*.

"I wonder how many people have died here," she mumbled as they approached the impending steps up to the porch.

"The house was built in the eighteen-fifties," Bob told her in a matter-of-fact way. "There's no telling."

That's not comforting at all, she thought, and she walked behind Bob as he climbed the steps to the porch. The porch was constructed of wood, but the thin remnants of paint that remained showed it had been quite some time since it was last maintained. The boards creaked beneath her feet as she stepped upon them, and several areas seemed to sag from moisture damage. She wondered if she would fall through while Bob unlocked the entrance.

Bob opened the front door and stepped inside. Karen watched him feel the wall for a light switch. She was marveled by the fact that, in a brief moment, a light did turn on.

"The place was wired with electricity over three quarters of a century ago," he said. "It's outdated, but at least we have power."

"Is there running water?" she asked him.

"Of course, but I spoke with the former caretaker after our purchase went through and he said we need to let the water run for a while to let the pipes clear."

"*Former* caretaker?" Karen questioned. "The last owner should have kept him on staff. It doesn't look like anyone has taken care of this place for quite some time."

"The old man retired when the last owner passed away. The house was on the market for several years before we got it."

"And they kept the power and water on all this time?"

"The realtor may have kept it on for showing the house, but I don't know how many showings it's actually had."

The house was completely furnished, but not with her things. Her things, she prayed, would be arriving at the end of the week. The house also needed a good dusting… or just a plain old hosing down.

"I could open an antique shop with this shit," she said, looking at the dated furniture and the layers of dust and cobwebs that covered it. Aside from being dirty, the furnishings appeared to be in good shape – Victorian period, but gently used.

"I'm sorry about the dust," Bob said. "I was told everything was covered up."

She didn't respond. What could she say? The place was disgusting. Dirty… no, *filthy*. She sneezed. Twice. A third time. After the third, Bob offered her a *bless you*, but it did nothing but aid in the irritation of her fourth sneeze.

"I'll help you clean tomorrow," he said, running his finger along the wall and looking at the dirt that had gathered.

"We'll need to go into town for supplies."

"The water will be down by morning. We'll get an early start." Bob smiled at her as he said this, like he thought it would be a fun project they could do together or something, but Karen did not see the fun in any of this. She was distressed, angry and bitter.

"This place will be impossible to clean," she told him. "How many rooms are here?"

"Honestly, I don't know," he said, "but it has a full attic, and a full basement and cellar as well. The house is pretty fucking huge."

Karen's eyes began to wander. She took note of the cryptic

staircase. Without a second-floor light turned on, the stairs seemed to go up into nothing. The stairs were directly in front of the entrance and beside a large room, which served as the house's main living room. It was too large for the type of living room that she was accustomed to.

To the right of the stairs was an open doorway leading into a dining room. Across that room was a closed door. She suspected it entered into the kitchen. Walking into the great room, she noticed a closed door on the side wall. Along the far wall were two more doors, and another door was on the wall under the stairs.

Even with the light on, the great room was dim. There were a couple of windows, and even though the curtains were open, they did nothing to help light the room. The windows were filthy to the point that she could not see out of them.

"The bedrooms are upstairs," Bob said from the doorway to her right as he stepped from it. She hadn't even realized he'd gone in there. "There are three of them, I know that much. Kitchen's through there," he added, gesturing over his shoulder to the door behind him. "The dining room's quaint."

She had been right– it led to the kitchen. Being silently right on a thought she had never voiced made her feel a little bit better. There was nothing better than being right on *anything* that involved Bob.

Karen walked to the door nearest the fireplace and opened

it. It was a bathroom. Not huge, but adequate. She was thankful to see it. Part of her had worried that they would be using an outhouse to shit in and a metal tub to bathe in. The next door over was a small guest room – or if she got her way, a crafting room. She then moved to the door under the stairs, which opened up to the basement.

She shut the door and walked across the great room to the single door on that wall. There, she found a study-slash-library. It was half the size of the great room, but it was still large – double the size of her bedroom in Connecticut. It was also fully stocked with shelves of old dusty books – that, she assumed, could be worth a fortune – and a nice oak desk and a dusty leather chair in front of a large picture window. There was a map of the world on a wall and a globe on the desk. She wondered how outdated they were, as they looked ancient. A part of her was surprised that the globe wasn't as flat as the map.

"If we sold some of this shit," she yelled so that Bob could hear her, "we'd make more than enough money to buy a decent place in the city!"

"That can be your job," Bob answered. "I'm attached to nothing here."

This somewhat pleased Karen. She had prepared herself for another fight, but the fact that Bob was as turned off by the antique décor as she was made her feel better. If she was stuck here, at least she could make the place feel like home – like *her* home.

No, she thought as she stepped from the library and shut the door behind her. *This is not my home. This is my worst fucking nightmare.*

She needed that mental check – that reminder of her distaste for the situation. At twenty-eight years old, this was the last thing that Karen had ever expected to happen to her. She could see being broke; she could see having to move to a shitty apartment. But *this*? This was much worse than any shitty apartment. This was being stranded on a deserted island, surrounded by nothing but water and marshland. No neighbors. No pets.

A farmhouse without land suitable for planting…

Everything was wrong with this house.

"Absolutely everything."

"What?" Bob asked her, and she wasn't aware until then that she'd spoken.

"Nothing," she said, shaking her head. She walked past him and through the doorway on the right. The dining room was big enough to hold the table and four chairs that occupied it, but there was little room otherwise. The kitchen was through the shotgun door straight across from the other one. It was a slightly larger room, more open, and had plenty of windows. They, too, were dirty though, so they would need to be cleaned before sunlight would ever see this kitchen. Obviously an add on, she was thankful she wouldn't be cooking in an outbuilding somewhere on the property or some weird prehistoric shit like that. There was a door on the same long wall as the appliances. It was another entrance – or exit, if she preferred – to the house.

The stove was an old gas model from the fifties. The refrigerator looked like it was from the seventies. Karen walked to the sink and turned on the faucet. It made a sound, and the counter vibrated, but no water came out. Then, in a gurgling splatter, a greenish-brown blob of gunk shot out into the sink. Karen nearly puked – not only from its appearance, but from the foul stench that accompanied it. She watched as it continued to pour out a thick sludge. She didn't move – she didn't blink; she just watched it. The sludge eventually began to thin, turning to fluid, and it soon ran *like* water – albeit brown and stinky.

"Let it run for a bit," Bob told her, coming up behind her and scaring the shit out of her.

She jumped and turned around at the sound of his voice.

"I didn't mean to scare you," he said and he tried to hide the fact that he was smiling.

Karen said nothing. She let the disgusting faucet continue to run – as requested – and breezed by Bob, into the dining room. From there, she stepped back into the entrance way and looked at the staircase. The darkness intimidated her, but she wanted to know what the bedrooms were like, so that she could decide which one would be hers. She and Bob had not shared a bed in quite a while, and she had no intention of changing that any time soon.

As she climbed the stairs, she thought about divorcing him – a thought that appeared in her mind almost as much as the one about killing him. She had threatened a time or two, but each time Bob would make a temporary *grand effort* to improve and she'd forget about it, giving him another chance. But *this* – this was becoming nothing more than staying together in a marriage filled with hate and spite. Wouldn't it have been a blessing to simply part ways and build new lives? That's what she really wanted – a new life, and this moldy house on a hill overlooking the sea was not the new life she had hoped for.

Blinded by the darkness of the upstairs, she trailed her hand along the wall until she felt the switch. The light was dim and dull and it offered very little to help guide her way. She could see though, and that was what mattered. She put a hand on the banister and took in her surroundings. To her immediate right was a door smaller than the rest she'd seen in the house. It was just about her height and thin. To her left were three doors along the wall and then a door at the very end, facing the hallway. She peeked inside the door to her right. It was an upstairs closet for extra sheets, blankets, towels and the like. It was stocked with old linens and everything smelled musty. *Just more junk to clear out*, she thought as she shut the door.

Turning to her left, she opened the first door along the long hallway. It was the first of three bedrooms, and it was small and drab. Darkly colored – perfect for a man, she thought. That would be Bob's room. The second door opened to a room that was a similar size but brightened up with yellow – albeit faded – wallpaper. It was a nursery – or had been – and a dusty old crib was centered beneath the window.

Karen stood in the doorway for a moment and took it all in. A furnished nursery. She had hoped so hard for a baby back in her old life, but twice, that hope – that dream – was shattered. The first miscarriage had been hard, but she'd survived. The second one had been devastating.

After that, she and Bob gave up. They eventually stopped having sex, and over time, they stopped sleeping together. She always felt that having a child would have made their relationship work, and that was a thought that often saddened her.

Another part of her knew, however, that a baby would have only made life harder. Bob still would have lost his job. They still would have had to sell the house. Who knew what amount of misery having a child would have brought to them?

Or… would it have been worth it?

She shut the door to the nursery and poked her head through the third door. It was the upstairs bathroom. It was an okay size, and she imagined soon that the floor would be littered with Bob's clothes and towels. Shutting that door, she opened the door on the sidewall and turned on the light.

This was the master bedroom – large and eloquent. Despite the old-fashioned style, Karen found herself forced to admit that it was beautiful.

It had such a grand feel to it that Karen immediately walked over to the oversized bed and plopped down atop it. A thick layer of dust rose into the air and she coughed as she waved it away. Abruptly standing, she turned toward the adjoining bathroom, partially visible through its open door. Walking to it, she turned on the light and took a gander. It, like the rest of the house, needed a good bath, but it was so old fashioned and pretty that she didn't even care. The ornate claw-footed tub... the Victorian style mirror and mosaic-tiled sink... This, plus the size of the grand bedroom, almost made this house worth it.

Karen stepped from the bathroom and gazed at a door she hoped was the closet. Opening up, she discovered she was right. It was a spacious and roomy walk-in closet that had another door within. Curiously, she opened this peculiar door and discovered a set of ascending stairs that likely led to the attic.

"No question about it; this is my room," she said as she left the closet and walked to the bedroom door. Careful to not make a sound, she shut it, remaining in the room. This was where she stayed for the remainder of the night. She pulled off the top cover from the bed and threw it to the floor, lay down, and shut her eyes. Although she would have sworn it impossible, she managed to fall asleep in a matter of minutes.

* * * *

Because of her slumber, she did not hear the door open as Bob came in to check on her. She did not see him approach and look down at her sleeping face... her sleeping body and the soft rise and fall of her breasts as she breathed. Her shirt was on, but the top three buttons were undone, exposing her cleavage and her white bra. Because she slept, she did not know that Bob masturbated over her as he watched her, and she did not feel it as he reached orgasm, sputtering into her disheveled blond hair.

She did not hear him say, "Fuck you, bitch," as he came on her, and she did not see him rub it into her hair, spitefully – angrily.

She did not watch as he zipped himself away, back into the concealed safety of his jeans, and she did not notice as he turned her bedroom light off, stepped into the hallway, and shut the door behind him – sealing her in the darkness of the night.

Day 2 - Karen

She woke with a yawn, a stretch… bleary eyes and a stiff body. The mattress felt like it was fifty years old, and it probably was. She ran her hands through her hair, felt the tangles and the matting.

"Fucking moisture," she said, blaming the dampness that was ever-present in the air.

She was sweaty… sticky. She must have sweated in her sleep. She always did that when she dreamed, but she did not remember a dream, if one had occurred. She remembered quiet – blackness. There had been no sounds to disturb her – no neighbor's cats knocking over the trashcan outside… no kids getting yelled at by their parents for being out after hours… no anything. Silence – a silence that was disturbing to her. Perhaps there had been sounds. Perhaps she had been so exhausted that she simply had not heard any.

There was no way of knowing, and Karen was too groggy to know the difference. She stood from the bed and routinely reached for her robe. It, of course, was not there. She had forgotten that she'd slept in her clothes, but none of that mattered. She would unpack her suitcase and bag after breakfast, and then she would shower and the world would seem a lot better.

Shower...

She walked into the adjoining bathroom. There was no shower – only the tub – and she turned the water on to let it clear. It, like the sink in the kitchen, spewed out its nasty muck, but she was too tired to give a shit. It did not disgust her as miserably as it had yesterday.

When she opened the bedroom door, the distinctive scent of fresh coffee hit her square in the face.

"Oh, my," she whispered, stepping into the hallway. "He's human after all."

She followed the pleasant aroma down the stairs, through the dining room, and into the kitchen, which had been cleaned spotless.

"Good morning," Bob said with a smile larger than she'd seen on him in quite some time. "I made coffee, and I got a head-start on cleaning this place up.

In a state of amazement, Karen looked around the room. The floor was clean. The walls and ceiling had been wiped down... the light fixture... even the windows. The counter was as sparkling as it could be. What threw her was the coffee pot that had not been there yesterday. It was brand new.

"Where'd that come from?" she asked, pointing at it.

"I brought it with us, along with a plug converter for the outlet. I know how you feel about your morning coffee."

At least he knows something *about me*, she thought.

"It looks great, Bob," she said, deciding he'd earned the praise.

Bob poured her coffee – black, just like she preferred it – and handed her the cup.

"This place cleans up pretty well, huh?" he asked, sipping from his cup.

"It's definitely a start," she acknowledged. She tasted the coffee. He'd made it strong. It was delicious.

"I heard the water start upstairs," he noted. "The water here in the kitchen and in the downstairs bathroom is fully usable now."

"I can't wait to take a hot bath," she moaned through a muffled yawn. "This place is just so dusty. I can feel it crawling on me."

"I know what you mean."

Karen watched as Bob poured himself a fresh cup of coffee. He smiled at her as he left the room and disappeared from view.

"More to do!" he said. His voice trailed off as he walked away. "You'll love it here!"

"That will never happen," she replied, but low enough to

where he couldn't hear her. She was not in the mood for a fight yet this morning. She was thankful for the coffee, and that he'd made the kitchen clean for her, but those were small steps – baby steps – in making up for what this move has done to her, mentally and emotionally.

She wanted to call someone – anyone – just to hear a voice other than Bob's, but there were problems with this. First and foremost, there was no one for her to call. She had no family outside of Bob and his mother, whom Karen found utterly despicable. Also, she had no true friends that she could vent to. Her only real friend in life had betrayed her a few years back, and it had been a betrayal that Karen could not forgive. Aside from this, she had lost cell phone reception on the drive to the house.

"Fuck it," she muttered and took another sip of coffee. The thought of being stranded here trickled into her brain again, and she had to find a way to suppress it. She was here – stuck here for the time being – and she had to make herself feel as comfortable as she could.

After she refreshed her cup, Karen walked to the small entrance way by the stairs and out the front door. On the porch, she looked out at their property, the marshes… the crest of the sea as it splashed against the rocks and murky, sandy dirt. The fenland, she had heard Bob refer to it once on the flight – and she shook her head. The water was in and out. It didn't look dangerous and she could see the road, but Bob told her on the drive in that this part of the marsh had been abandoned long ago when the fenlands were drained and the water was rerouted. Perhaps this was the fault of whoever had owned this property back then. Perhaps they had not wanted the interference of construction and rerouting done here – a stupid decision – and perhaps they had learned their lesson when they realized that their property would never be dry again.

"This water has to go away sometime," she said, draining the coffee from her cup.

"It will take a while," she heard Bob say. Looking down the porch, she saw him cleaning a window. She had not noticed him when coming outside. "That's part of why this place was so cheap. We don't drain well here."

"You told me the water would be gone today."

"I told you we'd be able to access the road today, and we can. They built the road up a while back so it's fine for travel."

"Bob, what the fuck is wrong with you?" she asked him. "Why do *you* want to live in this pit?"

"I just want to have a home with you," he told her as he paused from window washing. "Maybe… maybe we can try for a baby again? I saw there's a nursery here. It's already set up, and it looks brand new, aside from the dust.

A brand new nursery, she thought, taking a deep breath. That meant someone else had lived here with dreams of having a baby that were never fulfilled.

"Let's focused on cleaning the house and making it safe for now," she answered. She wanted to yell at him again, but thoughts of trying again for a baby kept her fighting spirit at bay.

She turned her back to him and stepped inside. How could she even *consider* having a child with him now? She hated him – absolutely, fully hated him. There was no other term for her to use. He had taken her away from everything and everyone she'd ever known and brought her to a place that surrounded her with the appearance of dread and doom. She felt trapped. The water that won't go away… the narrow road that she'd be terrified to drive on – *especially* with water on either side of her… this house of dust and dampness and whatever other horrors that might be lurking.

There were still a basement and an attic to explore, she remembered. Perhaps it would serve Bob well to do the cleaning today alone while she played Indiana Jane and the House of Doom. She considered letting him know this – especially since he'd mentioned taking her to town for supplies today – but there was no way she was crossing that swampy road right now. He could do anything he wanted to do… on his own.

She walked upstairs and into her room, where she unpacked her suitcase on her bed. She opened the dresser drawers, all of which were filled with someone else's garments from long ago. Those, she would check out later. Perhaps there were things she would like or that held financial value. For now, however, they were all pushed aside as she crammed the drawers with her clothes.

She kept out fresh panties and a bra, and a t-shirt and jeans. When she walked into the bathroom, she saw that the water was now clear – a gift from Heaven, she praised it as – and she turned on the hot water and stuffed the plug in the drain hole.

Steam began to fill the chilly room. As she undressed, goosebumps covered her skin. Karen dipped a toe into the filling tub. The temperature felt just right. She turned the water off and then stepped into its warmth, submerging herself up to her chin.

When was the last time she had taken an actual *bath*, she wondered? When she was a teenager? Perhaps younger? Possibly when she had been a little girl and she would be made to take a bath before bed each night. That's the last memory of soaking in an actual tub that she had.

She's *had* bathtubs. The house in Connecticut had one. She just never used it to soak in – always turning on the shower. Quick and efficient. Perhaps that routine had developed in high school, when she switched from bathing at night to showering in the morning before school. There had never been much time – she'd had to run out the door to catch the bus, her hair still wet and in a ponytail.

This was actually nice. The warm water felt good on her body. It helped with the stiffness from her sleep. She had brought in a bar of soap from her suitcase… where was it? She looked around the room but could not see it. Was it still on the bed?

She stood, naked and wet – water dripping from her into the tub. She stepped onto the floor, tempted to grab her towel but deciding against it. This wouldn't take long. Hurriedly, she walked across the bathroom floor and into the bedroom. When she reached the bed, she saw the bar of soap and took it. When she looked up, she saw that she left the bedroom door open and that there was an elderly man standing in the hallway just outside her door looking in at her.

Karen screamed. She rushed from the bed and the view of the stranger and into the bathroom, where she slammed the door shut behind her.

"Karen," she heard Bob call. "Karen!"

His voice was close. He had to be near. Surely, he saw the pervert – the intruder – and certainly he was handling the problem.

But instead, there was a knock on the bathroom door, and Bob's voice followed it.

"It's okay, Karen," he told her as he tried to open the door. She was leaning against it, so it wouldn't budge for him. "That's Mr. McDougal. He's the former caretaker. He drove up this morning to check on the property."

"What was he doing looking in here?" she asked. She was frightened, no matter what that man's name was.

"I don't think he was expecting to see you," Bob answered. "He's pretty embarrassed. Please, get dressed and come meet him."

"Let me finish my bath," she replied through a heavy breath. "I'll be down soon."

She waited until she heard him walk away. Then, slowly, still shaken, she walked to the tub – the steam rising from the warm water. It still looked inviting, but her tranquility had been disturbed. She leaned down to it and pulled the plug from its drain. She stood there and watched as the water slowly emptied out – every last bit, in a swirl through the drain with a bubbling gurgle at the end.

She brushed her teeth and dressed. She was in no hurry to meet this caretaker – the old man that had just seen her naked. The thought of whatever perverted fantasies were going through the man's head made her sick. She didn't believe this *McDougal* character was embarrassed either. He had been smiling when she noticed him. He had been checking her out, and if he *was* embarrassed, it was because he'd been caught at it.

When she stepped out of the bathroom, she saw that her door was closed. At least Bob had given her *some* privacy, she thought, but the damage had been done. She was angry, and *she* was embarrassed. Had Bob known that the old man was coming over today? Had it slipped his mind, or had he just failed to tell her?

Every little thing that happened – whether Bob was the cause or not – made Karen hate him more.

She composed herself the best she could. Ran a brush through her hair, put on her necklace and a pair of silver hoop earrings… She really didn't care how she looked. Today was for housecleaning and house-exploring. She would be filthy no matter what she did.

Take a deep breath, she told herself. *Make the most of it. The worst has happened. You're here. Now, make it okay.*

This was her new daily mantra, she decided. Her old one had been something along the lines of *Bob is an idiot, but killing idiots is still illegal.*

"Fuck," she grumbled as she opened the bedroom door and stepped into the hall. She shut the door behind her. From below the stairs, she could hear Bob speaking with Mr. McDougal.

"I think it'll take some good old fashion elbow grease and a little money, but it's workable, right?" Bob asked. Karen was quiet, so that he wouldn't know of her eavesdropping. If this conversation involved the house, then it involved her, and she had the right to eavesdrop over conversations that involved her.

"It'll take more than some elbow grease to fix the problems here," McDougal told him. "Money, yes – an' a lot of it."

"A lot – as in how much?"

"In American money, somewhere around $500,000 I

imagine."

Karen could have fallen over dead right then and there. *Five hundred thousand*, she thought. She and Bob had never had that much money on hand. Worse yet, no bank in their right mind would be brave enough to lend it to them. Their credit had suffered more than just a dip when Bob lost his job in the States.

"What can I do?" she heard Bob ask. "I don't have that kind of money."

"Well," the old man said in his thick English accent, "Ever since they rerouted the drainage, your water problem is going to grow. It will eventually flood the house. We'll need to irrigate the drainage and build the land up a little, as well as fix any long-term problems with the house itself. Otherwise, I'm afraid your investment in this house will have been worthless."

"How long do you think that'll take? For the waters to rise…?"

"A few months," McDougal said. "A few years. A few weeks, if we get some heavy rains."

Karen had a pair of scissors in her bag. She considered turning around and going back into the bedroom to retrieve them. It would have only taken a second, and then she could have gone downstairs and gouged out Bob's eyes.

No. She couldn't do that. After all, she'd have to kill Mr. McDougal too. He would have been a witness, after all.

Either way, she didn't want Bob to know just yet what she had overheard. So, she opened the bedroom door and shut it again, loudly this time, so that the men downstairs would know she was approaching.

"Karen, is that you, honey?" Bob called.

Honey, Karen thought with a trifle of spite. He had not called her "honey" as a term of endearment in a long time. He only used the phrase when there were other people present, and it sickened her.

"Yes, *dear*," she replied as she approached the stairs. She never called him "dear" either – unless she did it with the thickness of distaste rolling off her tongue.

Karen smiled a bit at McDougal. He, himself, was red in the face – obviously still feigning embarrassment over having seen her naked.

"I'm bloody sorry 'bout before, Mrs. Granger," McDougal said, looking to his feet as he rambled off the words. "I didn't know ya were in there."

"It's okay," she said. And it was true – it wasn't McDougal's fault that he'd seen her in all of her glory. She should have shut the bedroom door. Much more, he shouldn't have been allowed upstairs unaccompanied – no matter who he was or how long he had watched over the property. "It's good to meet you."

"Mr. McDougal said that he might be able to refer some

workers to us," Bob told her. She watched his eyes dart to McDougal's. They seemed to be pleading with him.

"I'll see what I can do," McDougal responded – looking at Bob instead of Karen. Karen noticed that his voice was a bit unsure as he spoke. It seemed to Karen like he didn't know that Bob wanted to keep the house's doom a secret from her. She wondered if Bob would ever tell her, or would he just wait until they floated off into the sea atop their mattresses?

"Well, I'm sure this place will be wonderful when everything is done," she said. Her smile made her feel like a *Stepford wife.* "You would know. After all, you *were* the caretaker here."

"Aye, Miss," he answered. "Through several households and families."

"Interesting. I imagine you saw some pretty *unique* things here?"

"Not really," he mumbled, looking at his feet again. The shiftiness of his eyes annoyed her. "No, just the usual. Families come and go, you know."

"Boy, do I know."

Bob looked at her as she said this, but she did not falter. She still smiled; she still batted her pretty blue eyes and remained polite.

"Well," she continued, nearly curtsying, "it has been

wonderful meeting you, Mr. McDougal. I'll leave you two men to talk. This is a big house, and I have a lot of exploring to do."

"That ya do, Miss," McDougal said and shook her hand as she extended it.

Karen nodded at Bob and turned away from them. As she walked away, she heard the two men engage in general and uncertain casual conversation. She knew they were waiting for her to leave.

She returned to the upstairs and went to her room, venturing from there to the attic.

There were cobwebs —a shit ton of them — and the dust was unreasonably thick. It was obvious that these stairs hadn't been used in a long time, much longer than the rest of the house.

In the attic, she found a world of nothing. There were a few empty trunks, some old moth-worn clothes, and a few pieces of broken furniture, but that was about it. Karen was disappointed. She looked through the clothes. Most of them were turn of the century Victorian, but they were in tattered states of disrepair. There were a few hats, shoes, and random odds and ends that could have been cleaned up and resold or repurposed, but she decided she would think about that another time.

"This is a bust," she said. She still had thoughts of opening an antique shop in the city, but there was not much in the attic that would offer any contribution. "I guess all of the good stuff is being used in the house." This was only momentary, she thought, as what little they had left from their Connecticut house would be arriving in a few days; if it didn't, she swore she would cut out Bob's spleen. There wasn't much coming in the form of furniture, but it would be enough to inspire her to slowly replenish this house with items more along her personal style – not the style of Scarlet O'Hara. Stuff that would work in a new house somewhere else, once they unloaded this dump on some other poor soul. They couldn't afford to fix it. They'd have no choice but to eventually sell it or lose it.

"There's always the basement," she told herself, turning off the light and walking down the stairs. When she stepped into the bedroom, she could feel the dust that had settled on her, even though she'd been in the attic for no longer than ten minutes.

Downstairs, Bob and McDougal were nowhere to be seen. With a shrug of her shoulders, she walked to the basement door. She opened it, found the light switch on the wall, and flipped it up. A dim, flickering bulb barely illuminated. At the bottom of the stairs, she could see that the light was brighter in the basement itself, and that made her feel somewhat more secure.

As she slowly eased down the stairs, she thought of the basement and how low it was, dug into the hill that the house rested atop. How safe was it down here? Surely, the water was slowly tearing the hill up on its way to the house.

The stuff in the basement did little to further inspire her dreams of an antique shop. There were a few old tools, and a washer and dryer from the eighties. There were pieces of lawn mowers, some cleaning products, and the skeletons from a few dead rats.

Karen was about to give up and return upstairs when she noticed another door, almost hidden, on a wall filled with broken down shelves and various household chemicals.

"A wine cellar!" she said, perking a bit. A cellar – definitely – but her hope for a vintage bottle of wine was high. She could use a drink.

She opened the cellar door, which led to another set of stairs, going downward. There was a switch. A dim light illuminated the stairwell. A foul scent hit her and she held her breath for a moment. It smelled like there was something dead down there, and she had to decide if she was brave enough to venture down there and find out. The repugnant smell told her to stay put, while her curiosity pushed her forward.

"More stairs… how deep can this place go?" she questioned as she began to descend.

This area was less dusty – less cobwebs. Perhaps it was too chilly here for spiders to live. Karen could feel the temperature drop as she descended the stairs and stepped onto the hard cement floor.

It was a little hard to tell what was what. The lighting was dim but not too bad. Perhaps the bulb was burning out; it was flickering, like it wanted to blow. She could see a table. There was a lot of stuff on it. She went to it and ran a finger over a few of the items... a little dusty, but not as much as the rest of the house was. Some items held no dust at all, while others showed a thin layer, making her believe it had only been a year or so since being last touched – unlike the stuff in the attic which had been ignored for far longer.

With the flickering of the light, she felt nervous and a little off-put as she browsed the objects. Was it a skull that she saw in the center? It looked like a skull, but it couldn't have been. After all, what would a human skull have been doing on a table, surrounded by – what were they? – vials of old water... old wine... old something? Perhaps the skull had been an old medical prop, like from a doctor's office or something. There were also dusty jars of salt-like substances... and chalk. A lot of chalk.

There was an open book. She ran a hand over it. Its paper was old. It felt leathery to her. Maybe a cannibal lived here and it was made out of skin, she thought as she considered the time an ex-boyfriend made her watch *A Texas Chainsaw Massacre*.

Further teasing her mind with the thoughts of the macabre, she entertained the notion that the book was a special cookbook on how to prepare humans. She saw humor in the thought, but she couldn't imagine ever eating Bob. What an upset stomach that man would give her…

As her hand skimmed the book, her finger touched upon something sharp. It drew blood, and as she dragged her hand upward toward her mouth so that she could suckle the sore wound, she streaked the book with her blood.

"Fuck," she cursed, tasting the fresh blood flow from her finger. Suckling the wound, she took a step back to the center of the small room. At her right was a steel support post. The table was to her left.

Pulling her finger from her lips, she let it hang at her side and felt blood drip steadily from it. She looked to the ground as her blood dripped down to it and saw that she was standing atop a chalked-out circle – very large – filled with lines and shapes and letters and numbers. She tried hard not to laugh.

"Old fashioned witchcraft?" she wondered aloud as she reached over and picked up the book from the table. "If that shit actually worked, everyone would do it."

She looked at the pages of the open book and tried to make out the writing with the aid of the flickering bulb… The writing was Latin, probably. She knew no Latin. She mumbled the gibberish as best she could and added an *Abracadabra* at the end with a flick of her bleeding finger. Nothing happened, just like she knew nothing would.

"I give this shit the same power I give most religions," she mumbled. She looked at the book again – saw where she had streaked it with blood. "Shit. I'm going to stain the page. That affects value." She spat on the blood smear and tried to wipe it off. Instead, she managed to rub it in more permanently. "Fuck."

Karen set the book down on the table, and as it left her fingers, the book slammed shut. "Creepy," she said with a low whistle. Yet, there was an explanation for everything, she knew. Witchcraft was all about intention, and right now, she had no *real* intentions at all… only to rid her mind of this new, horrible place that she lives in and the even more horrible man that she was still married to. She glanced at the closed book one more time and shrugged. Its cover was as hideous as its pages had been. Leathery… scaly. This was a centuries' old handmade book, she felt, and that made it unique and of high value. She worried about the damage her blood had done, especially now that it was smeared in, but she wouldn't concern herself with it any further. If she didn't have to see the stain, then she wouldn't think about it. Out of sight and all that jazz.

"That book was probably worth a small fortune," she griped. "Now, it's worth a slightly smaller fortune."

When she decided she had played enough in this weird little witch's den, she walked up the stairs and turned the light off, leaving the book on the table to be collected later, and closed the door behind her. She took one more look at the basement and shook her head.

"You'd think there would have been more sellable shit down here, but nope. That's okay. Friday, my stuff will be here, and on Saturday, we can go into the city and I can find a space for an antique shop, and then I will at least have some light in this fucking dark nightmare."

She started to move forward, but she began to feel a little dizzy… a bit weak. Her vision started to fade in and out, and her mind began to swirl. Pulling her hand up, she gave herself a sharp slap across the face, stirring her back to the here and now.

"Snap out of it, Karen," she told herself, shaking her head and gathering her thoughts. With the slap, the weakness and dizziness seemed to dissipate rather quickly, and soon she felt normal again.

Chalking it up to the deepness of the cellar and the thinner oxygen down there, she walked up the stairs and turned off the basement lights. Stepping into the great room, she shut the door behind her and sighed.

"Anything good down there?" Bob asked from just a few feet away. He nearly scared the shit out of her, as she hadn't noticed him when exiting the basement.

"No," she said, shaking her head. "Just a bunch of junk. Laundry shit and some mower parts. I cut my finger. Do we have band-aids?"

"Yep," he said, nodding. "I brought a first aid kit. It's in the kitchen under the sink."

Karen almost thanked him, but she decided against it. She owed him no thanks – not even for a band-aid.

She found the first aid kit in the kitchen, but it was not under the sink. It was across the room on a rollout table. She spied it instantly upon entering the room.

"He's such a fucking moron," she griped as she cleaned and bandaged her wound. She put the kit away – under the sink because, otherwise, Bob would have insisted she had put it in the wrong place. She took a glass from the cupboard, filled it with cold water, and walked out the kitchen door, onto a small side deck outside.

The view, she had to admit, was somewhat beautiful, albeit mysterious. It was gray, cloudy. Even though the water was still standing – wouldn't it always be? – she could see some green from the growth beneath. It wasn't too deep yet, she assumed. As long as she could make it to town on Saturday – that was all that mattered. She could check into a hotel, find a place to have her little store, and she would earn enough money to get the hell out of here.

Yes, it was all starting to formulate for her. She would soon be away from this sinking money-pit, but even soon wasn't soon enough.

She realized that Bob must hate her as much as she hated him – perhaps more so. Why else would he have moved her out into a disaster zone in the middle of nowhere? He knew something like this would kill her inside.

Then it dawned on her. Maybe killing her *was* the purpose – the whole intention of this move. Maybe, she thought, Bob wanted her dead, and he had brought her here where no one could save her. No neighbors. No friends or family. No cell service to call for help. Stranded. Deserted.

How would he do it, she wondered as she stared out at the cloud formations in the sky. Would he poison her – maybe with the sludge from the pipes or the old chemicals in the basement? He wouldn't shoot her. Bob hated guns. His grandfather had been a hunter, and he had been told his fair share of accidental shooting stories during his childhood. He wanted nothing to do with guns. What else could he do? Would he hang her? Bob was strong – well-built for a man in his early thirties. He would be strong enough to hoist her body up in the air by a rope.

She sipped her water and wished she had a cigarette. She had a few packs stored away. Bob didn't know that she didn't *really* quit when she gave up smoking. She wore nice perfume and always smoked outside. She'd been sneaking them for years. If he knew, he hadn't let on.

Maybe that was why he wanted to kill her, she thought. Maybe he could smell the smoke on her, and maybe being lied to about cigarettes was the one thing that would drive him to murder.

Ironically, the thought made her smile. Bob was a nut, and for a slightest moment, she remembered him being a nut in the best of ways.

The moment passed. She wanted Bob dead. She needed him dead. Otherwise, she would be dead. That was how it worked, right? Kill or be killed? *Fuck it*, she thought. At least it gave her an excuse.

Another excuse, she corrected.

Bob, if anything, had given her plenty of excuses to kill him. This house was reason enough.

She could not fight the urge anymore and she returned to her room, took a pack of cigarettes and her lighter, and returned to the side porch. Bob was somewhere in the house – of this, she was certain. However, now that she reconsidered her circumstances and lit her cigarette, she really didn't care if Bob caught her smoking. Fuck Bob. Bob was misery, and the nicotine from the cigarette easing her nerves was nothing less than pure bliss.

"Yeah," Karen said, taking a nice, long drag from the cigarette. "Fuck Bob."

From where she stood, she could see both outbuildings. Sheds, one of which was a boathouse with a rowboat inside. As she smoked, she was curious. Was there anything in the enclosed shed? She knew that, with the furnishings in the house, she'd have more than enough inventory to fill her antique shop. Still, sheds often held different types of stuff than houses, and that meant attracting another sort of clientele.

Having an antiquities shop had always been a fantasy of Karen's. In America, they'd neither had the funds nor the stock in order for this dream to blossom, but here – well, that was the one good thing about this place, she imagined. Here, she had the stock – the house was filled with stock – and they had a little money still from the sale of the house in Connecticut, albeit very little money. Working on this house would be pointless. It was eventually going to sink and flood, no matter what they did. So, she would take Bob's little remodeling nest egg and she would spend it on a business – one with a loft apartment above it, or at least she hoped.

She puffed on her cigarette as she walked down the steps and onto the damp, unkempt ground. She stepped on many weeds, but she didn't think that there was one blade of actual grass on the hill.

When she reached the first shed, she flicked her cigarette butt away and lowered the wooden latch from in front of the door. Then, she gave the door a gentle pull and opened it wide. What sunlight was present was barely enough to light the shed, and although she searched for one, there was no lighting fixture here.

She did, however, find something that may have been of value. There was old fishing gear – which, as best she could tell, was still in fairly good condition. There were also a couple of anchors and a ton of buoys. Three or four old trunks lined one wall, but she needed better light before she was willing to dig through them.

The open-ended boat shed contained the rowboat, its oars, and some supplies for maintaining it. There were a few tools hanging and placed on a shelf and a couple of nets and tarps were folded and stacked on a second shelf.

Out of everything she could see in either shed, the piece of antique candy that struck her eye was the old rowboat. It looked like it was made from one solid piece of wood – a huge tree of some sort; Karen did not know one type of wood from another. There were two oars propped inside of it. The boatshed, itself, smelled of fish and dead rodents.

"At least someone was prepared for all of this water," she said as she checked out the boat. She imagined its sale would bring in enough to pay for her new business venture. She would still make Bob help, but that was simply out of spite.

Stepping away from the boat and its shed, she took a breath and began a running list in her head of the things she'd found thus far that she could sell.

Turning around, she saw Bob walking McDougal to his car.

She looked at McDougal, although neither he nor Bob seemed to notice her. McDougal was a strange man, and his answers to her questions had seemed diverted. She could tell he was hiding something and she felt like it was more than just the fact that Bob had bought a money pit. Perhaps it had something to do with the witchy stuff she'd found in the cellar. Did he know about that stuff? Had he been a participant in whatever *rituals* had happened down there?

Karen did not believe in witchcraft or magic. She believed in science, and she believed in nature. The idea of casting spells or contacting demons or spirits – those were things she just couldn't wrap her head around. She had visited New Orleans once, and she'd checked out a couple of those voodoo shops that she'd heard so much about. There had been some really cool and unique things in them, but that was all she had taken away from it. For instance, how could a mummified rat's foot bring someone good luck? Some poor rat had to die for that to be made. How lucky, eh?

McDougal climbed into his car and – albeit slowly – drove off.

She waited where she was until Bob returned to the house. When she saw the front door shut, she walked toward the kitchen porch, climbed the steps, and lit another cigarette. She now wondered what other secrets the cellar held. While the idea of magic spells did nothing for her, the thought of finding more information about McDougal was appetizing. At the very least, she hoped to learn more about whatever cult had lived in this house before her. While voodoo and devil worshiping left her cold, real life crazies entertained her and, all and all, what she'd found in the cellar was the only entertaining thing about this house.

The mystery – the *suspense* of it – entertained her. She wanted to learn more.

When the cigarette was finished, she stepped inside the house and walked through to the great room. As she was about to turn toward the basement door, she noticed the library door ajar and the light on inside. She walked toward it with soft steps, even though some of the floorboards creaked beneath her feet. Just outside the door, she held her breath and listened – hoping to overhear Bob in conversation. Then, the thought occurred to her – who would he be talking too? McDougal was gone and they had no cellular service.

She released her breath and shook her head.

"What are you doing?" she heard Bob say from behind her, and she leapt forward, startled.

"Fucking shit, Bob!" she shouted, clutching her chest and trying to catch her breath. "You scared the shit out of me!"

"What were you doing?" he asked again. He was smiling – it was that shit-eating grin that Karen hated so much.

"I saw the door open and the light on," she told him,

thinking fast. She did not want him to know she was spying on him. "I thought you were with Mr. McDougal and I was afraid someone else was in here."

"That's silly," Bob replied. His smile was lighter now, and he chuckled. "Who else could be here? Try not to let this house make you paranoid. McDougal's gone home, so now it's just you and me. You're perfectly safe."

But am I? she wondered.

"That makes me feel better," she said, smiling a bit. "I'm sorry about earlier. I just wasn't expecting him to be here." If she sounded sweet, then perhaps he would let this whole moment blow over and he'd leave her alone.

"I *was* in the library earlier though," he continued. "There are a lot of old great books in there. I thought maybe we could read one together tonight."

"Read one together?"

"Well, I mean, I know that would be hard, but I could read to you. Or we could take turns. I could read to you, and then you could read to me, and so on."

That was the absolute *worst* idea that she'd ever heard.

"That sounds wonderful," she said. "After supper?"

"After supper," he agreed, patted her shoulder, and stepped by her toward the library. "Speaking of dinner, I'm going to make you a meal to die for. You'll love it!" Then, he shut the door behind him.

Fuck, she thought, with panic growing over her face. There it was. He was planning on killing her at supper. Was he going to poison the food? Maybe her glass? What would he use?

She would make him taste the food first – like they did in powerful families, or at royal suppers. Caesar never ate anything until it was tasted by his flunky. Why should she be any different?

He would never do it, she knew. He'd tell her she was being irrational or silly, and to just eat her damn food like a big girl and enjoy it.

She'd have no choice. She'd have to eat. Unless… unless supper never arrived because Bob was already dead.

The cellar, she thought. Perhaps there was something in the cellar she could use. An old herb, a vial of something or other… a ritualistic blade that she could cram down his damn throat.

She hurried to the basement and then made her way down to the ceremonial cellar, flipping on the light as she started down. The cut on her hand began to thump with pain. Perhaps it was infected. None of that would matter if she didn't live through the night. She promised herself though – once she killed Bob, she'd have the hand checked out by a doctor.

"If I kill him now," she whispered and immediately began rummaging through the items in the room, "then he can't kill me later."

She dropped something. Broke it. A cloud of dust shot up at her, surrounding her face. She breathed it in and coughed. *This sucks*, she thought, worried about her sinuses. She bent down to pick up the broken glass. The graininess from whatever had been inside covered her hand as she gathered the glass. It worked its way through her band-aid to her wound, and it burned.

"Fuck!" she cursed, pulling her hand up and tearing off the bandage. Her wound was now foamy – bubbling like it would if she had poured peroxide on it. "At least it will kill any infection in there."

She let the wound be as she continued searching for something to use in Bob's demise. She knew that there were so many ways to kill somebody, but she'd be damned if any of those ways were coming to her now. Nothing helped – nothing that she saw popped out at her in a way that screamed *this is the perfect way to kill Bob.*

"I want to remember this," she mumbled, still searching. "I want Bob to feel it. I want him to pay."

She realized now that she was no longer *just considering* killing her husband. It was no longer a passing thought. But this was life or death for her. She was without choice. It felt scary, a little sickening, but oddly enough, it excited her beyond anything else she'd ever done or planned.

If Bob were a man that did not speak or think, he would

have been her perfect man. He was beautiful – still handsome after the tiring years they'd spent together. He had a full head of dark hair, mesmerizing brown eyes that were all too often hidden behind his glasses, and his body was still in fantastic shape.

If she were just meeting Bob – if she didn't know him or know his tendencies – then she'd fuck him. She knew that she wouldn't be disappointed either. Bob was very well endowed, and he had a stamina that lasted for hours. For just sex with no emotional attachment involved, Bob was as close to perfect as it got.

As a husband and an actual *lover*, he was the worst. When their attempts at having children failed, he became neglectful to her. He ignored her, and he spent a lot of time locked away in his home office, at the gym, or at his regular office. Karen took it as he grew to hate her.

She hated Bob for that reason and more.

The pain in her hand was miserable. She had to lie down. Suddenly, she was light-headed, a little dizzy. Perhaps she'd over-exerted herself exploring the house or had grown too excited planning Bob's death. Perhaps it was the mucky air. Either way it went, she lay down, which happened to be in the middle of the chalky pentagram, shut her eyes for just a moment to rest them, and drifted off into a dreamless sleep.

It was three hours later when she awoke. The pain in her

hand was gone. In fact, as she stared at her hand, she saw that the wound itself was gone.

"Weird," she said, eyeing it strangely. Perhaps she had imagined the wound. Dreamed it, maybe. Perhaps she had passed out when first venturing to the cellar, and she was just waking up from it. She didn't know. She felt unusual. Almost drained. She looked at the floor beneath her, stared at what she could see of the pentagram, and she stood. There was still broken glass on the floor, but the contents had vanished.

She smiled and nodded. "Okay," she whispered, thinking aloud. "This has all been too much on me, and I've finally lost it. That has to be it. I've gone mad."

She gave the cellar no more thought as she left it, returning to the basement. Hurrying up the basement stairs, she stepped into the great room and shut the door behind her. She noticed that the light in the library was off and the door was open. Bob must have chosen a book, she thought and then shook her head. No, he was planning on killing her. The book had been his version of a romantic cover-up. Something to throw her off. Something to confuse her and make her think that he loved her.

"Bob," she said, wondering where he was. The kitchen, she assumed, and she walked that way.

The kitchen was empty. Nothing was cooking. She ventured back to the parlor and then walked upstairs. His room was empty, as were all the other rooms on that level – including hers.

Downstairs, she opened the front door and went outside. The car was gone. Bob had left.

"What in the living fuck?" she asked, pulling out a cigarette and lighting it. "Where the fuck did he go?"

She walked down the front steps to the driveway. It was dark out now, and although her concern was not for Bob's safety, she had to know where he was – for *her* safety.

Whether he had hinted that he was going to kill her or not, he'd still broken his word by not providing supper, and that irritated Karen further.

She smoked two cigarettes while she waited outside, but it was getting colder and she was feeling weak from hunger. Maybe that was his plan, she wondered. Maybe he'd strand her here in the middle of nowhere and starve her to death.

She returned to the kitchen and opened the fridge. Of course, it was bare.

The sound of thunder rumbled outside, causing Karen to cringe.

"A storm is coming," she whispered and sucked in a breath. "Shit."

Soon, it would rain, and she was alone in this massive house – one that she feared would simply float away, given enough water. She looked for a safe place to relax. Her bedroom? No. She wanted to hear if Bob came home.

Lightning lit up the night sky. It illuminated the kitchen and sent her fleeing from the room. Of all things, Karen was most afraid of storms, and yet she knew that her fear was irrational. She'd never been trapped in one; she'd never had anything terrible or tragic happen during one. But they were loud, had sudden lights and winds, and they caused destruction. In Connecticut, she'd been safe in her house. In *this* house, she felt anything *but* safe.

In the great room, she stood still, facing the library doorway. Even though the light was off, the open door was inviting. She could get lost in a book – any book of *her* choosing; not Bob's – and she could ignore the storm, passing the time until either it ended or Bob returned… one or the other.

She pushed the door open wider and turned on the light. From the window, she could hear the rain begin to fall. It splattered hard against the glass, moving at an angle. That meant it was also windy. She trembled and put her focus on the many shelves, and the hundreds of books that filled them.

The newest title she found was a cookbook, and that was from the seventies. Karen would have to settle for a classic.

She chose *The Scarlet Letter*, a Hawthorne title and one of her personal favorites from school. She figured it would be enjoyable – the tale of a beautiful woman and her affair with a preacher. It was hot, and she needed something hot right now.

Perhaps if she had been as adventurous as Prudence had been in the book, she would have had an affair, and she would have found relief – sexual and emotional – and then perhaps things would have been better between her and Bob.

Every thought she had seemed to lead back to Bob. Karen decided that this was not the book for her right now and she put it back on the shelf. Her eyes and fingers roamed each title of every dusty spine, looking for just the right thing. She was so focused on her search that, even though she heard the loud boom of thunder, it did not terrify her. It shook her, but she held her composure.

There were a few Jane Austen novels to pick through, but Karen was not sure how close she wanted to get to Mr. Darcy tonight, so she passed the titles over. Her stomach growled. She placed a hand over it as if that would soothe it, but she had not eaten a bite all day. She could feel the hunger pains make themselves known.

Karen knew that there would be no food until tomorrow. She would have to suffer through it. Perhaps, with the help of a good book that did not involve romance or sex, she would forget all about her stomach. There was also the option of just going to bed and trying to sleep. The sooner this night was over, the sooner she would be able to focus on food, and on getting off this property.

She opted out of choosing a book and left the library,

shutting the door behind her. She walked to the staircase and took hold of the banister, letting her hand slide up it as she walked. Then, as another burst of thunder shook the house, a heavy knock came alarmingly from the front door.

Karen turned to it with a gasp. She stared – motionless – wondering who was knocking on her door during such a downpour. Had she imagined it? Was it her nerves?

No. *Bang! Bang! Bang!* There it was again. It was not her imagination, and that terrified her. Slowly, uneasily, she walked down the stairs and approached the door. She stared at it for a moment – should she run? Hide? – but Karen was brave and, unlocking it, she opened the door.

She screamed at the image of the man in a dark coat, holding a box, drenched in the rain.

"Finally!" he said, marching inside and kicking the door shut behind him. As he shrugged off the hood from his coat, Karen saw that it was Bob. "It's raining like mad out there."

"Where did you go?" she asked him, thankful to see him and not some *other* killer on her doorstep.

"I forgot to grocery shop, so I drove into town. I tried to find you to see if you wanted to go."

"I had taken a nap."

"I got groceries – they are in the car still – but I also got us pizza."

"Pizza?" she questioned, sniffing the air and looking at the box.

"Remember our first night in our first apartment?" he asked her. "We were too tired to even go out to eat, so we phoned in a pizza delivery."

"At the house in Connecticut too," Karen added, enjoying the moment of reminiscing.

"It seems to be a tradition." He smiled at her and handed her the box as he took off his coat and hung it on a rack by the door. Then, taking the box back, he carried the pizza into the dining room. Karen followed behind. "Shall we?" he asked, extending a hand to the table.

Karen followed his hand and sat in a chair at the foot of the table. She watched as Bob walked by her, into the kitchen, and returned a moment later with two plates, a roll of paper towels, two coffee mugs, and a bottle of merlot.

"Wine?" she asked, knowing the excitement was showing in her tone. "There's wine?"

"I stowed it away," he laughed, popping the cork. "I smuggled it all the way from Connecticut for us."

She watched him pour the wine into the two mugs; one of the mugs had Garfield on it, while the other was a grumpy old woman. He passed her the grumpy old woman.

The poison must be in the cup, she thought, reminding

herself of the true peril of the situation.

"Can I have the Garfield cup?" she asked him, smiling. "It just feels like a Garfield kind of day."

"Sure!" Bob replied, and switched cups with her.

He did that way too eagerly, she noted and looked at the Garfield cup. *Maybe this is part of the plan. Maybe he anticipated that I'd want to switch.*

"You know what, I changed my mind," she said, handing him the Garfield cup. "I like the grumpy old woman."

"Whatever you like," Bob said and handed her the original mug back.

Wait a minute, she thought. *Was that the trick?*

She didn't know what to do. She watched him set the Garfield mug down on the far end of the table, at his seat, and then open the pizza box.

"Take your pick," he told her as he brought the pie and a plate over to her. "It's still warm. I had the heat blazing in the car."

Well, the whole thing can't be poisoned, she considered. *He has to eat too.*

"Any is fine, thank you." She kept her eyes on her husband as he plated two slices of vegetarian pizza and set it down before her. Then, he put two slices on his plate and took his seat. "This looks delicious. It was thoughtful of you."

"Thank you," Bob said. She swore he was blushing. "We

have to eat, right?"

He took a swig of wine. He wasn't coughing or choking or flopping around in a dying state. Kate wondered if she should chance it. She'd been craving a drink, and one was staring her in the face.

Her hand trembled as she lifted the cup. She looked at the rim; there was nothing unusual there. No powder or thin streak of oil. She sniffed it. The scent of the merlot wafted up her nose, filling her with goodness. Finally, she sipped it – tasted it – and after savoring it for just a moment, she swallowed it.

"Good, eh?" Bob asked.

"Delicious," she whispered and took another sip.

Neither her drink nor the pizza had been poisoned, and all she felt after supper was finished was a little drunk and a lot full. Bob was exhausted from the drive to the city and back, and she let him off the hook on his little reading date that he'd scheduled with her. She was thankful for this. She was a grown woman with two good eyes and a functioning brain. She enjoyed reading, but she hated being read to.

"I think I'm going to choose a book anyway," he told her as he stood from the table. "I'll clean up the mess and put the leftovers away, and then I think my book and I will retreat to my room. Would you like to choose one for you to read in bed also?"

What I'd really like is some television and my Real

Housewives, she thought, but instead she said, "That would be nice. Is there anything *light* in there?"

"I saw some Jane Austen," he told her. She rolled her eyes. "There are also some old comic books in a box by the window. I haven't gone through them, but there might be something light in there."

Karen had not noticed the comic books before, but when he led her to them, she found herself thankful. There were a ton of old *Archie Comics*, *A Date with Judy*, *Dick Tracy*, and even some *Tales from the Crypt*.

"Odd," she said, finding a few vintage *Superman* and *Batman* titles.

"What's that?" Bob asked, thumbing through an old copy of *Wuthering Heights*.

"These comics – they're all American. There's not one British title in the bunch."

"Are there a lot of British comic books?" he questioned.

Karen took a moment to think about her answer. Then, she said, "I don't know."

She took the *Archie* comics and two issues of *Tales from the Crypt*. Bob told her she could take the whole box with her if she wanted to, but she was tired, the box was bulky and looked heavy, and she had enough in her stack to keep her entertained. Or, at least, to give her something to drift off to.

She left the library while Bob was still hunting a book. She shut the door behind her – almost closed but still open about an inch or two – an unnoticeable amount, she believed, but one that would let her peek in on her husband if she so desired. Then, she climbed the stairs to the second floor, walked down the hallway to her bedroom, and stepped inside. Closing the door behind her, she set the comics on the table beside the bed and stripped her clothes to the floor. She pulled open the top drawer on the dresser and removed her nightgown. Once dressed for the night, she stepped into the bathroom, brushed her teeth, and ran her fingers through her blond hair.

As she gazed at her reflection in the mirror, Karen was curious about that library. Bob had spent a lot of time in it since they arrived here. How could he not have chosen a book to read by now? With him believing she had retired for the night, it was the perfect opportunity for her to check in on him and see what exactly he was up to.

She very carefully – ultra quietly – opened her bedroom door and crept out into the hall. As softly as she could, she retreated down the stairs and into the parlor. Slow, delicate, easy steps – like a small child sneaking out of her room for a peek of Santa Claus on Christmas Eve – she walked toward the library, and as carefully as she could, she touched the door and looked into the room through the opening she'd left.

There was Bob, sitting on the edge of the desk, his eyes closed, his head tilted up, his pants around his ankles and his cock in his hand. He was jacking off. Karen tried hard not to laugh – she fought the instinct to bust in on him and embarrass him… to cause him to be unable to finish. She took her hand away from the door and backed away, just as softly and slowly as she had approached.

That perv, she thought as she returned to the stairs and ventured to her bedroom.

So, while her husband was downstairs handling his manhood, Karen climbed into bed with her old childhood pals Archie, Betty and Veronica. She had always seen herself as more of the *Betty* type. She was blond, beautiful, and somewhat wholesome – until crossed. Betty had a wicked streak that Karen loved about her. Betty, she thought, was probably insane, and so was Karen. At least, Karen thought she was.

She admitted to herself that she was also a little bit like Veronica. She expected to be treated a certain way – to be loved and to be cherished… the things Bob mentioned when he said his vows at their justice of the peace wedding. Bob was a bit like Archie. He tried too hard at some things, and at others he never tried at all. Like their marriage. He tried too hard when they were working for a child, and he did not try at all once they failed.

He had made Karen feel like less of a woman for it, and for that alone, she would forever despise him.

She put the *Archie* away and opened one of the horror comics. It wasn't light and fluffy like what she had intended to read for a bedtime story, but the artwork was great and she remembered the stories as always being intriguing. This issue featured a tale about a dead woman who arose from her watery grave to extract her vengeance on her murderous husband. She chuckled as she read it. It was a great fantasy, but the last thing she would ever want to do after death was reunite herself with her husband. Certainly, there were greater things ahead for her than that.

She heard Bob's bedroom door open and then shut a moment later. He must have *finished the job*, so to speak. Karen shook her head. She wondered if his orgasm face was the same as she remembered it. It had been so long since she'd seen it… since she'd watched him explode with an ecstasy so strong it would ripple through him and right into her. She could faintly remember the heat between them as they would thrust against each other in orgasmic bliss.

Karen really wanted a cigarette now. Just the thought of one was a trigger for her, and the uneasiness of today had rattled her. It was pouring outside. She could hear the wind howling over the rising waters, and she could hear the rain beating against her window. Again, she thought *fuck Bob* and she went to the bathroom, took the soap dish from the sink, wiped it out, and carried it to the bed to be used as an ashtray.

"This place probably has fifty ashtrays," she said, taking a cigarette from her pack in the nightstand and lighting it.

The fact of the matter was that, if the house indeed had even *one* ashtray, there was no sign of it. Bob would have seen to that. He detested cigarettes. It was his least favorite of Karen's habits, and that was why Karen did her best to hide it from him.

Tonight, like earlier out on the porch, she did not care if he knew or not.

Thunder broke into her thoughts and she nearly jumped out of her skin. She took a few long drags from the cigarette – enough to fill her body with the nicotine that it craved – and she stubbed it out. She could see lightning through the window. It made her tremble, and she abandoned her comic book to hide beneath her covers. Only her eyes and the top of her head remained exposed.

It wasn't precisely the storm itself that frightened her. It served mostly to remind Karen that she was lying in bed in a rickety house that was barely perched on a hill, surrounded with water. And the more that it rained, the higher that water would rise. She was not so much afraid of the lightning and thunder this time – not as much as she was the idea of floating away.

"If I die in this place," she mumbled, "I swear to God I'll kill him."

She turned off her bedside lamp as the storm calmed to a

mere howling. She chose to forget about Bob – to forget about which would kill her first, him or the house – and she closed her eyes. She thought of Archie and his infamous love triangle, and she thought of Hot Dog, Jughead's lovable mutt. She thought about anything and everything *happy* that she could, and with those thoughts, she managed to fall asleep – one that provided her no dreams, nothing but stillness for her mind and body.

Day 3 - Karen

There was a thickness in the air that not even the sharpest of blades could have cut through. It was a tension – high and vigilant – and it built a barrier of silence between Karen and Bob that made each of them seem as frigid as the cold glaciers of the arctic. Karen woke at 6:50; Bob, sometime before that. Neither saw one another until the afternoon, which suited Karen just fine.

It gave her time to work on her plan. No – that was incorrect. Karen had no actual plan, except to stay alive. After a good night's sleep, her paranoia had worsened. The thought of her husband once simply disgusted her. Now, it terrified her. She spent the morning avoiding him at all cost, and in her eyes, Bob had done the same.

Was he planning her death, she wondered? Was he simply biding his time until he struck out at her, like a deadly viper in the sand?

This made her think again of poison. It was probably the cleanest way for him to kill her, unless he used a poison that would seriously fuck with her stomach, causing it to open up while bubbling vile escaped her mouth.

The thought made her shiver. No matter how she imagined it, the idea of Bob killing her made her feel sicker each time.

God, how she hated him. Miserable. He was a miserable son-of-a-bitch. Yes, that was right. His mother was a bitch. Karen knew that the moment she met the woman. Her name was Ethel, and she was as prude a woman as they came. She had hated Karen while she and Bob were dating. She hated her when they married, and when Karen failed to produce grandchildren, Ethel's hatred of her grew further.

If there was one good thing about Bob moving them to Europe, it was that it had gotten Karen away from Ethel. Bob was an only child, and his father had died suddenly in a mining accident when Bob had been in grade school. Karen had not known Ethel before the loss of her husband, but she felt that his death must have had an impact on her, and so Karen tried to sympathize. Yet, from the moment that she met the woman, Ethel had only gotten worst. Karen remembered one instance on Christmas Eve three years ago when Ethel had pulled her aside after supper, only to tell her that – as a woman – she was worthless if she could not produce a child.

From that moment on, Karen hated Ethel just as much as Ethel hated her.

The grandfather clock in the foyer sounded that it was

noon. Its announcement travelled to Karen, bringing her back to the here and now. Bob must have wound the clock, she figured. He was on a roll, trying to spiffy up this house of doom.

She finished a granola bar that she'd stowed away in her suitcase and washed it down with a bottle of water from the groceries Bob had brought home last night. Looking out the window, Karen stared at the car. It was not submerged under water, as she had feared it would be, but she could see where the driveway had become submerged where it connected with what she assumed was the small road.

Trapped.

She was trapped in this house with Bob. There was no escape. It was raining outside. Even if she screamed, who would hear? There was no one.

There was a faint *thump, thump, thump* coming from somewhere in the house. She stood from the uncomfortable wooden chair and walked to the foyer. The sound was coming from upstairs, although she could not pinpoint which room. Then, as she neared the stairs, she heard one of the doors open. A second later, Bob appeared at the railing, smiling down to her.

"There you are," he said with a bit of excitement in his tone. "I've been doing some repairs today."

"Repairs?" she questioned. Her voice did not read *impressed.*

"You know… hammering baseboards back into place, windowsills, screwing the electrical plates back on right. Busy work that just needs to be done."

"Trying to take your mind off the flooding?" she asked. Folding her arms, she stared at him with bitter eyes and a drawn expression.

"It's just a little rain. Things like that will happen, but baby, look. The house is still here. The rain hasn't hurt it a bit."

She wanted to ask him how long until it *did* hurt it, but she did not want him to know that she'd been eavesdropping on him yesterday. Either way, she doubted she'd live long enough to find out. If she did survive Bob though – *if* – she would make sure his death was the worst she could manipulate.

"You're right," she said, smiling a little and diverting her eyes from his. "What room are you working on? Your bedroom?"

"No," he replied with an obvious drop in his tone. Karen knew that he hated sleeping alone and having his own bedroom. "The guest room."

She looked at him again. She was puzzled. "The guest room? You mean the nursery? What do we need a guest room spruced up for? There are so many other things that need to be done."

Bob smiled again and let his hand drag across the banister as he walked toward the stairs. From the top, his smile grew larger and he tucked a hand into a pocket of his jeans. "I was hoping to surprise you. I know how homesick you've been."

"What are you getting at?"

"I'm bringing my mother here to live with us." He shuffled a bit – looked down to the steps.

Karen was speechless. Absolutely without any words – any nuance of comprehension over what he just said to her. Perhaps she misheard. Maybe this was a dream – a nightmare? Yes, that was it. A very poorly understood nightmare. Perhaps if he repeated…

"What?" she asked him – her voice flat and dry.

"Yes, I know!" he exclaimed with obvious excitement. "It will be like back home, except instead of Mom living a few doors down from us, she'll be under the same roof. You two girls can have your tea and cakes and stuff just like old times – but *all* the time!"

Now, Karen prayed the flood would sweep her away. She considered the possibility that it was Ethel that Bob would use to kill her. Perhaps Ethel was his instrument of torture. Yes, that was it. He would use his mother to drive her to suicide.

"When – when was this all arranged? When will she be here? *How* will she get here?" It had to be a joke – a really bad, *bad* joke.

"I talked to Mom before we left. She's flying out this

week."

"But the rain…" she began, seeking excuses to prevent that horrid woman from arriving. "It's flooded. No car can get through this."

"Where there is a will," Bob said with his glimmering smile, "there's a way."

If she'd had a gun, she would have shot him dead right then and there.

"Besides," Bob continued, even though Karen wished he hadn't, "it's not good for Mom to be so alone. She has no other family than us, and you know how reserved and shy she is – she doesn't even know her neighbors. It's such a lonely life for her there."

What about me? she wanted to ask. *What about what I need?*

The truth was, she had never outwardly shared her distaste of Ethel with Bob. She had found it rude and a bit disheartening to tell a man how much one hated his mother. Bob was a *momma's boy* from the basis of the definition, and Karen had been much too mannered to have told him what a bitch his mother was.

That was until now.

"Where do you get that your mother and I are so close?" she asked him. His smile faded.

"Mom came to visit with you all the time when we lived in

Connecticut," he said flatly.

"Yes. To tell me what a horrid woman I was. That woman never gave me a moment of peace. She hated me from the moment she met me, for Christ's sake!"

"Now, Karen, you know that's not true," Bob replied, taking a step down toward her. "Mom loves you very much."

"Your mother is a cunt!" she spat out the words. There they flew... exactly what she thought of the woman, summed up in one phrase. She did not mean to say it. She knew that an insult to Bob's mother would hurt him more than an insult directed at him. Maybe that was what she wanted. She did not know, but watching his expression turn to fully insulted sorrow, she felt herself smile. "Yes," she continued, wondering how deeply she could wound him, "your mother is a fucking bitch, Bob. Every little time she came to visit, it was to tell me how bad of a woman I am. How bad of a spouse to you I am, because I had failed to produce grandchildren for her. And it didn't start there. Oh, no sir, it did not. From the moment she met me, she shot her venom at me. She never wanted me in your life. Not even for a moment. Why, I bet your mom would be happy if it was just you and her, forever and ever. She probably touches herself at night thinking about it."

That last part, she thought, might have been pushing it a little *too* far.

"Stop it!" Bob shouted. Tears were welling in his eyes.

"Stop it, goddammit! You fucking bitch!"

A temper tantrum, she thought as Bob stormed off from her, back into the guest room, slamming the door shut behind him. She felt the vibrations of the slam reverberate throughout the house. She and Bob had been through many fights together before, but she had never seen him run away from one, so hurt – so childlike.

It angered her. She was fired up – ready for a *real* fight – and he had run away from it. The bastard. Couldn't he see that she needed this fight? She needed to stand up to him… to remind him that she was not merely a weak woman. She was anything *but* weak, and she was ready to show him.

How dare he bring his fucking mother here, she thought, turning away from the stairs and walking to the front door. She stepped outside, safe from the rain as it fell onto the porch roof above her. Her cigarettes were on her, and she took one out and lit it. She smoked it fast – rushed without knowing she was rushing – as she let her mind spin in circles around the news she'd just received. Ethel was coming. She was moving here, into this house, and it was the biggest mental and emotional hit that Bob could have made on Karen.

She threw the cigarette butt out into the rain and instantly lit another. This one, she smoked with more leisure.

Karen was angry inside. She was burning. Fuming. Irate

and sad and hurt and betrayed. This European adventure was nothing like what Bob had led her to believe it would be. It was hell – a nightmarish, but very real, hell.

Finally, she cried. If Bob stepped outside and saw her, she could blame the water on her cheeks on rain splattering against her. But they were tears – real tears. An outburst of emotion that she had tried to keep within… that she had tried to bury. Yet, here they were – full blast, full blown tears. She sobbed as she wept – heavy sobs that made her feel as if she were suffering the loss of a parent or a child. But these tears were not for that. She had not lost a parent today. She was gaining the presence of her mother-in-law, 24/7, right here in her *own home*.

Karen needed a drink. Something strong. She needed to escape this newfound reality. She considered the rowboat in the shed. She could use it to escape from here, but where would she go? She knew she would not get too far, and if she did, she would easily get lost.

She just needed away from here – out of the captivity of this *place*… away from Bob.

She could just kill him now. The idea was a strong one – one that appealed to her in every fashion possible. Then, when his mother arrived, she would kill her too. She'd kill them and dump their bodies in the water. Even if the bodies were found, Karen felt like she would not be held accountable. It would have been self-defense, she decided. She would tell the bobbies – she liked that term; she learned it in the airport on their arrival to England – that Bob had brought her here to kill her off in a place that no one could get to, even if they knew she needed rescuing.

As for killing Ethel… well, she did not know anyone who would prosecute a person for killing their mother-in-law. It was every married person's greatest fantasy.

Even outside with the rain, she could hear Bob inside, hammering away. She had to get away from him – away from the sounds that he made. Placing the thoughts of his death aside, Karen decided to slip down to the cellar, where she knew no hammering could penetrate.

Bob, of course, seemed not to hear her as she reentered the house. Karen walked swiftly to the basement door, and as she descended down the stairs, all she could think about was how much she wanted some McDonald's. And she *hated* fast food. Right now though, she could have found comfort in a nice, greasy double cheeseburger.

With bacon.

Oh, yes indeed, with bacon.

Eager to reprise her earlier adventure and further investigate the witchy goods hidden there, Karen ventured straight down to the cellar. She could almost feel that weird book in her hands, and although it made her skin crawl, she was excited for it.

She wondered, when the rain stopped enough for her to leave here, how much it would be appraised for. Surely, something so genuinely handmade and authentically old deserved a bidding war instead of a first come, first served at an antique shop.

The cellar was empty. Completely empty. There was nothing. No pentagram on the floor. No book of spells written in a dead language. No vials or jars or anything else. Cobwebs and dust – there were those – but everything else that Karen remembered being down there was gone.

"What the fuck?" she cursed, shaking her head. "Where the hell did everything go?"

It was a trick. It had to be. A ploy, staged by her husband to make her think she was going crazy. When she mentioned it, she was sure he'd say something like, "What witchy stuff in the cellar? What are you talking about? Maybe this move has taken its toll on you, Karen." Maybe he wasn't going to kill her after all. Maybe he was planning on institutionalizing her instead. It made sense. It was less sloppy. There was no chance on him getting convicted of murder, and he would be rid of her. She would become someone else's problem, and he and his mother could live out their lives happy, together and without her.

The whole thing seemed to have a sort of Oedipus complex developed around it, she thought. It sickened her more than it frightened her.

"Well," Karen mumbled, looking around at the emptiness surrounding her. "Fuck this bullshit! I'm not going to let him win."

She considered going straight upstairs, grabbing him by the ear, and dragging him back to the cellar to explain things. Then, she reconsidered. Perhaps he would have enjoyed that too much, she thought. Perhaps it would have reminded him of how Ethel had treated him when he was young and would misbehave.

She shuddered and left the cellar, back up the stairs to the basement. Turning toward those stairs, she stopped and froze. Her heart skipped what felt like a massive beat.

There he was – Bob – staring at her from the next to bottom step.

"Shit!" she cursed, touching her hand to her chest. "Bob, you nearly scared the life out of me!"

"I'm sorry," he said, obviously trying to hide a grin. "I didn't know you'd be here. I needed more nails."

"Oh," Karen whispered, looking to the floor as she caught her breath. "Well, you know where they are."

She started toward the stairs, but Bob did not step down onto the basement floor to let her pass. "What are you doing down here?" She diverted her eyes again as he looked beyond her, toward the washer and dryer. They were inactive. "I know you're not doing laundry."

"Is that my only job?" she asked him – her tone low and

bitter.

"Do you *have* a job? A hobby? Anything?" He was intentionally picking at her, and she knew it. "You've talked about taking up painting or drawing. There are some pencils and blank paper in the library. Knock yourself out. Be inspired."

Bob stepped down and to the side, letting Karen pass him and start up the stairs.

"You never did tell me what you were doing down here," he added, once again stopping her in her tracks.

"I'm looking for inspiration," she whispered and then continued up the stairs. Shutting the door behind her, she once again separated herself from her husband. She took a deep breath and leaned against the door.

That smile... that horrible, cocky, arrogant smile. He *knew* she had just come out of the cellar. Certainly, he read the confusion that had been on her face. She wondered if it had humored him, but then again – that was a stupid thought. *Of course*, it humored him. He loved seeing her confusion – her anger and her misery, all stretched over her pretty little face.

Karen's breathing turned to a huff and she stepped away from the basement door, her frustration hitting a new high.

In a rush, she went to the kitchen and sorted through the knives. She checked out the scissors and the meat cleaver. Messy. *Too* messy. She already hated the thought of having to keep this farmhouse clean. The last thing she wanted to do was have to clean blood and guts off hardwood flooring.

"I'll wait until he's taking a bath," she whispered aloud. "I'll carry a radio in there, plug it in, and drop it into the water with him."

She could almost see his eyes bulging from his skull as the electricity surged throughout his smoldering, soaked body. It made her chuckle a bit, but she stopped herself, fearing that laughter would only induce suspicions of insanity.

But who would know if she laughed? Looking around, she confirmed that there was no one in the room with her. No one was watching. No one was listening.

Or were they?

Karen had no way of knowing if the house was bugged or under surveillance. Perhaps that was the real reason the caretaker stopped by – to install cameras for Bob to watch her every move. Maybe that was how Bob had known she'd been in the cellar to begin with.

Okay, she had to just stop for a minute. She was beginning to feel paranoid – more so than she had been – and it was starting to make her think that she *was* going crazy.

Besides that, she knew that Bob was too cheap to foot the bill for surveillance. Back in Connecticut, they had stickers on their doors and windows advertising that they had a security system installed, but all Bob had paid for were the stickers. There had been no cameras or alarms. Fortunately, there had been no break-ins either.

Not all of Bob's ideas were completely terrible though. He'd had a point when he mentioned she should have been spending her time seeking inspiration, not skulking around going mad.

But where was her inspiration here? Was it in the rising water that surrounded her ancient farmhouse? Did it lie in the cellar with the cultish echoes of rituals past? Was this inspiration within her husband – within his mind and the madness that churned in it?

No escape. There was no escape here, and if anything, that drove her maddest of all. She had no way to flee from Bob's grip. Nowhere to go. She had to outthink him – outsmart him.

"That shouldn't be hard," she whispered, smiling just a touch. She set the meat cleaver back inside the drawer that she'd taken it from and stepped from the kitchen.

It occurred to her that she had not yet heard Bob return from the basement, but as she neared the stairs in the foyer, she could hear him hammering away upstairs. Had she been that lost in thought, she wondered?

Looking at the upstairs railing, she thought of Bob, hanging from the railing with a sheet tied around his neck.

No, she shook her head. Bob outweighed and out-muscled her. He would have needed to be unconscious for her to have gotten the sheet tied around his neck, and the chances of her being able to lift him over the railing to drop him over were slim. But, if she got the sheet around his neck and dragged him, she could heave him over…

The sheet would rip with Bob's weight and he would drop to the foyer floor, broken but not likely dead. Or, his weight would be too much for the railing, and it would tear it down with him.

"Fucking shit, motherfuck!" she heard Bob yell from the enclosed space of the guest room. His voice brought her back to reality and away from the thought of having to finish off his broken body once he landed from the attempted hanging.

He must have hammered his thumb, Karen thought, and another slim smile stretched across her lips.

She could not help that the idea of Bob in pain made her happy, although there was still a small part of her that hated this fact. She missed the days when she had cared about Bob. She missed making actual love to him, and she missed having real conversations with him. But missing those things was like missing a loved one that had died. It was missing a ghost. Those things, those emotions and ideals, had been gone for a long time. She may as well have been missing her grandmother, whom she never knew.

Nothing could bring back her grandmother, and nothing could return Karen and Bob to who they were.

"Karen!" she heard Bob yell again, distraught. "Karen, I need a rag! And a bandage! Karen? Are you there?"

He was hoping she would respond – she could feel it – but he did not know that she was listening or standing at the foot of the stairs. So, she chose not to respond, to remain silent... to revel in his pain. It filled her with something other than anger, dread or fear for a change. It made her feel good, and she wanted to hold on to that feeling for as long as she could.

"Karen!" she heard him shout one more time, and after checking her pocket to ensure she had a cigarette and lighter with her, she stepped from the entrance way and onto the front deck, shutting the door behind her. She thought of the pain he was feeling – maybe there was blood, too – and she lit her cigarette, inhaling deeply and fully enjoying that first initial drag.

"Ah..." she sighed, blowing out the smoke. "Fuck you, Bob."

Karen decided to put Bob at the back of her thoughts and she focused on the scenery. Sure, the water was rising, but the rain was settling down to a mere sprinkle. There was a bit of light beaming in from the sun, and a few birds darted in the sky, flying from tree to tree in the distance. If she removed herself from the situation, Karen could actually see the beauty of the nature that was around her.

When her cigarette was finished, she flicked it to the muddy ground and stepped inside the house, letting the door slam shut behind her.

"Where were you?" she heard Bob ask. She turned to see him approach her from the dining room. He'd been in the kitchen. His hand was crudely bandaged. "I've been calling for you."

"I went outside for a bit of inspiration."

"Well, while you were outside doing whatever it is you do, I was bleeding like a stuck pig. I hurt the hell out of my hand."

"It looks like you've got it taken care of." She pointed at his bandage and smiled.

"Just once I wish you'd say something like, *oh Bob, I'm so sorry that happened,* or something like that. Don't you have any compassion?"

"I've heard the word before," she began, feeling frustration once again riddle her nerves, "but the news of my mother-in-law's eminent arrival seems to have stripped my compassion away."

"Aw, Karen, have a heart. She's a little old lady."

"She's the devil incarnate."

"When I asked her once what she thought about you, she told me you're her favorite daughter-in-law."

"I'm her *only* daughter-in-law," she noted, "unless you've got a slew of sister-wives hidden away somewhere that I don't know about."

"That's ridiculous and you know it."

"Is it, Bob?" She was mad again, and she'd just calmed down. She wanted to bring up the past – *his* past – and throw it in his face, but that would have only escalated their already growing fight. What began as bickering usually ended in a brawl of words. She didn't want that right now - her need for an actual fight had subsided. She wanted him to go about whatever *repairs* he'd been attempting, and she wanted to be left alone.

Bob was quiet for a moment, and Karen hoped he was choosing his words carefully. Then, he grinned, lightened his expression, and asked, "Do you want to help me upstairs?"

Is he serious? she wondered as she looked at him through blinking eyes of disbelief. *He is insane!*

"You go on doing what you're doing," she replied, deciding it was time to end the spat before she worsened it instead. "I'm going to walk the grounds for a bit and try to get my bearings."

"It's wet out there," he countered. Bob was still grinning like the devil he was. "Plus, there's really not much to see. A hill. A shed. A boathouse. Wow! How exciting…"

"It beats being jumping to command every time you start a sentence with *can you pass me…*"

Bob once again went quiet, obviously considering what she

said – or at least the tone in what she said. His smile seemed plastered onto his face, but it lessened as he nodded his head and took a step toward the stairs.

"Okay, then," he continued, shrugging his shoulders. "Enjoy your tour of Casa de la Granger and the grounds that encompass it."

A farmhouse in England, she thought as she opened the front door, *and he gave it a Spanish title.* "Only Bob…" she muttered and stepped outside, shutting the door behind her.

She really didn't give two shits about touring the grounds any further than she already had. She just wanted another cigarette, and it had seemed like a good excuse to go and smoke one. Karen pulled the cigarette free from its pack and lit it, blowing out the first drag and inhaling the second. She relaxed for a moment while she smoked. She was free once again to rid her thoughts of her good-for-nothing husband and focus on the saltwater-laden landscape around her.

Even with the bit of sunlight poking through, there was a thin layer of fog separating the water from the horizon's skyline. It reminded her of a scene in one of those zombie movies she'd sat through when she and Bob had been dating. She could almost see the living dead rising up from the foggy water, dragging their limp, decomposing bodies toward the muddy hill, the deteriorating farmhouse, and the flesh that resided within it.

"Zombies," she said, shaking her head. "The ridiculous things that people will come up with…"

She finished her cigarette and sat on the porch floor. As sunset began, her scenery changed. Allowing herself to forget where she was and why she was there, she took in the ethereal nature of the sky and the sea, enjoying the beauty of the moment.

She smoked one more cigarette before going inside. She had been able to lose herself in this serene moment with nature, but now that was done for the day. It was time to return inside and retire to her room – or to the kitchen if she could think of something to eat. Bob had brought some food back with him from his trip to town, but it hadn't been much of anything. She could not prepare a meal with any of it, but she could munch and nibble and snack, and so that was how she would survive.

Flicking her cigarette into the night, Karen stepped back into the house and kicked the door closed behind her as she looked toward the staircase. She could hear Bob cursing upstairs again. The pounding of a hammer – *smack, smack, smack* – blended with his shouts. Bob was not the handiest around a house, and Karen figured that he was likely learning this first hand for himself. Still, as much as his pain pleased her, the hammering was drilling a metaphorical hole into her brain, planting a headache there to grow and prosper. She could feel it beginning.

"Could you shout more quietly?" she yelled at the guest

room door as she walked up the stairs and to her room. Once inside, she slammed the door shut. Her newly forming headache was cascading itself over her also-growing hunger, and it wasn't pleasant for her.

Karen climbed onto her bed and closed her eyes, rubbing at her temples to help soothe the escalating ache. She tried to focus on more pleasant things – fashion, films, the great literature in the library that she'd ignored for a stack of comic books. Yet, no matter what she did to try to forget the pain so that it would leave her, it stayed and grew.

Smack, smack, smack!

There it was, plain as day – Bob's pounding, blaring more loudly than before. What the fuck was he hammering that took so much force? Karen tried to block it out; she tried to refocus her thoughts, but every time Bob's hammer slammed onto something, the headache in Karen's skull splintered out like shrapnel, spreading across her brain.

"Bob!" she yelled, hoping her voice would travel over the sound of the hammering. "Please! I have a headache!"

Yes, she did have a headache – one that was spreading beyond her temples and was etching between her eyes, nearly touching the sinuses in the bridge of her nose. It was misery – an insult to the brief moment of bliss she had earlier enjoyed. She stood, walked to her purse on the dresser, and took out a bottle of pills. They were valiums and not really for headaches, but Karen decided they would do the trick. They'd *have* to. She'd run out of actual aspirin after their flight had landed. She'd had only a slight headache then. This one raged.

Bob seemed to have heard her pleas for silence, as she could no longer hear the hammering. Once more on the bed, she laid back and relaxed.

She tried to justify the headache by allotting the amount of stress she'd recently been through, but as her headache grew, the effects seemed to move to other parts of her body. Soreness. Aches. Pains. More than a headache – or at least it wasn't like any other headache she'd ever had.

It made her stiff. She had to stand – to stretch; she couldn't just lie there. There was still some wine downstairs in the refrigerator. It would help. It would loosen her up.

Why haven't the valiums kicked in yet? she wondered.

She stood, tried to shake off the headache, and left her room. Bob was at it again. *Smack! Smack! Smack!* As she crossed by the closed door of the guest room, the loudness of the hammering intensified, and so did her headache. Quickly, she descended the stairs to get away from it.

She reached the kitchen and hurried to the refrigerator. She pulled it open, took out the bottle of wine – maybe a third left – and chugged it. It felt good. Cold. Fruity and bitter, and it swam down her throat and into her stomach where it churned. Then, along with the undigested valiums, it came right back up.

There was no humor in the moment, but as it was happening, it reminded her of the vomit scene in *The Exorcist*; blood-red wine sprayed everywhere. Along with the wine, the three valiums came out in one mushy, lumped chunk that landed right beside her foot.

"What the fuck?" she asked, looking down at the valiums and the dark wine. The mess was everywhere.

She was dizzy... her eyes were blurry. Karen didn't know what was up or down. She moved again, away from the refrigerator and back toward the foyer, but it felt like she was drifting – not running. Not walking. This was something else – some other movement that she either did not know or did not remember. Had she experienced anything like this before? No. She thought perhaps she'd been poisoned, but how? She had not accepted anything from Bob all day. She had felt fine until the headache hit.

Yes, the headache. It was still there, ever-present, pounding away at her head like a hammer to a nail. *Smack, smack, smack!* She could hear it; it was so loud that she may as well have been in the same room as Bob and his fierce hammering.

No... this was a different smacking, she considered. This wasn't the hammering. It was the smacking of her pain against the roof of her skull. That was what it was. *Smack, smack, smack!*

"Fucking shit!" she heard Bob shout from his project in the guest room. Karen hurried to the foot of the stairs. "Goddamn it!" Perhaps the smacking had been Bob after all and not just in her head. She wished he would shut up. His shouting made her pain worsen. "Goddamn this fucking thing!" he yelled again. There was no hammering now. There was still smacking though... yes, it was her headache after all. Still, looking up the staircase toward the guest room, she had to wonder. If Bob wasn't hammering, then what *was* he doing? "Shit!"

"Shut up, shut up, *shut up*!" Karen shouted, covering her ears, clenching her eyes closed and stomping her foot to the ground. Every word he said worsened her headache. She needed silence. Quiet. He was driving her over the edge. "Will you ever just shut the fuck up?" Her shouting was, perhaps, louder than she intended, but she could barely hear it over all the other noise going on inside her head.

He was still cussing, cursing up a storm, slinging profanities as loudly as he could. Karen grabbed hold of the stairway railing and took her first step up. The step made her skull feel like it was going to implode. *Fuck, that hurts!* Then another. *Holy fucking shit!* On the third, she felt like she'd tumble backward and fall, but she held her balance. It was like, with every step up, the pressure was steadily escalating – like a plane ascending into the sky. She'd hoped to just sprint up the stairs and burst into the guest room, catch Bob off guard, and give him a good talking to.

Well, *that* wasn't going to happen.

Instead, one grueling step at a time, she pulled herself upward toward the second floor. It seemed an impossible challenge. Gritting her teeth... sweating massively... her eyes clenched into little slivers, as too much light increased the pain that beat into her skull.

"Come on, you fucking piece of shit!" she heard Bob shout, but his words were more muffled this time. Still, the tone of his voice – the fact that he was speaking at all – made her cringe and the pain in her head worsen.

"Shut up!" she shouted again. She was almost to the top. Almost to the landing. Almost to the second floor and to the guest room door, where she would tear into Bob as if all of hell had broken loose.

She saw the door – it sort of flickered in her vision and faded in and out, but she saw it. Fighting against the worst agony – the most horrible pain she'd ever known – she forced her way to the door, finally reaching it. Just the effort to grab hold of the knob and twist it made her eyes feel like they would pop right out of their sockets. She didn't know what was happening, but this was more than just a headache. It was worse than any migraine she'd ever experienced. This was different, and it was terrifying.

The door opened. Light from the hallway spilled in and helped to light the otherwise dimness of the room. Bob was across the room from her, near the window and lit by a lamp on an end table. He held a screwdriver in his hand as he attempted to repair a crumbling, deteriorated window sill and the baseboard below. Even as she looked at him, he continued to shout and curse at the screw that he toiled with.

She stared at him for a moment. He was hazy – an apparition of himself. In fact, everything she saw around her seemed like this. The pain from the headache made her stiffen. It felt almost like she was having a stroke. It straightened her, like a plank. Her eyes grew wide. Her mouth tried to open. She wanted to scream, and with all of her might, she managed one sentence.

"Shut up, you goddamn asshole!" she shouted, and then she couldn't speak anymore. She could still somewhat see even though the haze was taking over, and despite the pain, she could think, but she could not move. Everything hurt too badly.

"You shut the fuck up!" Bob yelled, looking at her. He stood and straightened. She watched as he pulled at his hair and smacked his forehead, dragging his hand down his face. His other hand clenched the screwdriver as if it was his life support. "Will you stop? Will you ever fucking stop with your goddamn bitching?" His eyes were angry; even through her dizziness and the fading in and out of her vision, Karen could tell this. In a huff, Bob began to shout again, throwing both of his hands up in the air.

She saw it – the release. Was it intentional? Was it accidental? It seemed to happen in slow motion, or maybe it was the fact that it happened so fast. Either way, her eyes left Bob's face the moment the screwdriver slipped from his grip and flew with the force of his movement. She could not blink in time; she certainly could not move. Once more, she wanted to scream, but this time it was from the pain and fear that surged through her as the screwdriver struck her eye and impaled itself into her head.

"Karen..." Bob whispered. His eyes were wide; his voice – shaky... nervous.

The impact of the screwdriver polarized Karen's balance and pushed her backward. She fell back, having no control over her body or what was happening. She could feel the force and the tumble as she reached the banister, and when she fell over it and landed, her head smacked hard against the floor. The last thing she saw was darkness growing over her until everything was black and all of her pain had numbed.

Part II

Day 3 – Bob

Bob's eyes were wide, shrouded in shock and disbelief. He didn't mean to let go of it. It slipped… the screwdriver. He was upset. His hands were flailing and it slipped. But the force – oh my god…it had such force.

He watched her tumble back – the handle of the screwdriver poking out from her eye.

"Karen…" he whispered, watching her as she started to stumble back. He wanted to rush to her – to help her – but he was paralyzed with fear. He could feel the tears start, but he tried to hold them back. He tried to do something – to breathe… maybe – but anything he did would be too late. Bob knew this. He knew it the second he watched her fall backward over the railing, down to the floor below. He was assured of his inability to help when he heard her hit and something on her body snap. The sound broke through the otherwise sudden silence of the farmhouse.

"No, no, no, no, no..." he said. He tried to scream the words, but they came out as whispers. Like a child cowering from a bully, Bob fell to his knees. Tugging on his hair, he broke into sobs – shaky, intense sobs that made him feel like he was about as big as a penny. He'd killed her. He'd thrown the screwdriver – although he hadn't meant to – and he was why it was impaled in her head. He had killed his wife. He was a murderer.

His sobs grew heavier with this realization. But the term *murderer* was a little strong, wasn't it? After all, he hadn't *meant* to throw the screwdriver. It had slipped. He was on edge and she had been screaming at him. All he had wanted to do was fix the fucking window so his fucking mother wouldn't bitch when she arrived. That was all he had wanted.

"Karen," he said in sort of a crackly moan. "Karen..."

Holding onto the edge of the nightstand, he lifted himself up onto unsteady legs. He felt dizzy and had to steady himself. Everything was spinning. He was burning up. His blood pressure, he imagined. Something like this was certain to shoot it up.

Timidly, Bob managed to walk to the doorway and looked at the railing across from him. In front of the door was blood on the floor. It must have squirted out when the screwdriver hit her.

He walked to it, looking down at it with big, terrified eyes – hoping that by approaching it, it would go away... appear less real.

But no, it was still there, real as ever. He knelt down and touched it. It was warm. He stood and touched the railing, closing his eyes as he did. With his eyes shut, he tilted his head down. When he opened his eyes, he was looking at Karen's dead body, sprawled out on the floor with a pool of blood forming around her head.

"No!" he cried in a squeaky voice and turned away. He felt like he would be sick. No; he *knew* he would be sick. There was no stopping it. A gagging, thick lump in his throat had formed, and before any preventive measures could be thought about, his mouth opened and he covered the floor in front of him. His vomit was not thick; it was watery and tan, like the water that came from the kitchen sink. It tasted of disgust and heartburn.

"Karen..." he whispered, trembling with such greatness now that he feared he would leap from his own skin. He tried to steady himself as he turned back to the railing and looked down.

He was crying now – little bursts of gasps and choked words. Tears began to streak down his cheeks, and he was shaky. He looked at her again and once more felt the need to puke, but this time he was able to stop it with a hand over his mouth. Whereas one of Karen's eyes was impaled by the screwdriver, the other was wide-open and staring up at him. Even though its stare was obviously lifeless, it terrified him. He felt as if Karen was looking into his very being – into his soul, but that was impossible. She was dead. He had killed her.

"Fuck!" he shouted, and his voice echoed through the rickety house, haunting him. "What did I do?" He cried again and began to pace nervously. "They're going to blame me for this… they're going to hang me for killing her. God, please! I didn't mean to kill her! I didn't mean it…"

Bob ceased his pacing and walked to the stairs, edging down the first few steps rather clumsily. Halfway down, he paused and looked again at the body of his dead wife. Tears still streamed down his cheeks, but he was not sobbing or huffing anymore. He had to think – he had to use his brain and come up with a solution to this morbid and tragic situation.

Thunder rolled again outside. Another storm was building, and that meant more rain was going to flood the land of their new home… no. *His* new home.

He would no longer be sharing this residence with Karen.

"She hated this place anyway," he thought aloud and finished his trek down the stairs. When his feet hit the hardwood floor, he froze again. He looked at his wife – the expression on her face… the blood surrounding her. The fall had busted open the back of her head and had likely broken many of her bones. "Geez, Karen, even dead, you're a mess…"

He knew the comment wasn't funny the second he said it, but he was willing to try anything – even humor – to stop his tears. He had loved his wife, but over time, he knew that she had stopped loving him. Still, even if she had hated him, he had never wanted to kill her. He hadn't even wanted to divorce her. He had just wanted to find a way to make it work – to make her fall in love with him again, and this house had seemed like the only option left. Now, she was dead and his chances to win her back were over.

Again, the thunder rolled, and this time Bob was startled by it and backed away to the wall. He could hear the rain– pounding on the roof, slapping against the windows. It was just a storm; he knew this. There was no reason for him to be nervous or afraid of a storm. He *was* nervous and afraid though. The storm itself had little to do with it.

Once he regained partial control of his nerves, he walked toward Karen and looked down at her. The screwdriver – the horrible, despicable screwdriver – was staring up at him, tormenting him with threats and reminders of what he had done. He had to pull it out, get rid of it, throw it away… maybe bury it so that no one could ever find it. But right now, during this rainy season, he could bury nothing. Not the screwdriver. Not his wife. There was too much water standing outside.

"I'm so sorry," he whispered to her as he knelt down beside her. "At least you're finally rid of me. You never have to see my mug again."

His hand was shaky as it reached for the screwdriver; his fingers wrapped around its handle. Then, placing his other hand on her forehead to hold her in place, he jerked the screwdriver free from Karen's eye socket. He looked at the end of it – gore. Pure, bloody, pulpy gore.

Once more, he was sick. He vomited to his side, careful to not cover Karen in his bile.

"Fuck…" he groaned, hoping this would be the last time he would be sick. The taste of it was thick in his mouth and it made his throat burn. He looked back at Karen, at her eyes. One was wide open and staring; the other was a shallow, bloody hole with no eyeball to be seen. He remembered learning in school that eyeballs were bubbles of fluid, and he assumed the bubble had popped from the impact of the screwdriver. "This fucking sucks."

The sound of the thunder roared ridiculously from the heavens. For a moment, Bob was certain that it was God, angered and throwing threats and obscenities at him. His mind was havoc. He had to gather his senses somehow.

Getting the body off the floor would be a good start, he figured.

"What do I do with you, baby?" he asked her, brushing his fingers over her unscathed eye and closing it. Then, as he thought more of the rain and the rising water and the sweep of it out to sea, his plan came to him. "You always loved swimming," he told her. "All I know to do with you is give you a burial at sea."

He had to move the body. He had to face the storm. He had

to hold her one final time in his arms – something Karen had not let him do in ages. Kneeling down beside her, he reached beneath her with both hands and rolled her into the bends of his elbows. She felt heavier now than he remembered her being, although she still had the same lovely figure she'd kept for years. When he tried to stand with her, his knees were wobbly. Perhaps, he thought, his strength was gone because of the situation – or, perhaps it was because he had not visited a gym in months. Either way, as he stood up with her, her body rolled in his arms and pressed against his chest, causing him to collapse back. He did not fall, but his arms gave way and Karen dropped free of his grasp.

"Jesus!" he shouted as she hit the ground. Her head bounced in a fashion that looked painful, but Bob reminded himself that she could no longer feel pain. Karen was dead. She could no longer feel *anything*.

Carrying her would not work. He had carried her around many times in the past, but she had never seemed this heavy. He assumed this was what people meant by *dead weight*. He just never took the phrase literally.

Taking both of her hands, he dragged her across the floor, watching the blood smear and streak with every movement. At the front door, he let go of her hands, letting her arms fall down beside her. They made a thumping sound that nearly stopped his heart. He had to control his nerves; they were getting the better of him.

He propped the door open with a stone from the front porch and then dragged his wife outside. He left the door open as he pulled her across the porch, down the steps, and onto the wet, muddy ground. His body was soaked within seconds from the freshly falling rain, and he watched as it cleansed the blood from Karen.

"I don't want to do this," he told her, pulling her toward the sheds. Water squished from the ground beneath his feet as he walked. "You know I don't. You know I love you. I've always loved you. I'm so sorry that it ended like this."

He knew that she could not hear him, but talking to her somehow made him feel better – as if she was alive and still mentally present. But, he knew, she may as well have been a rock or a lump of coal. There was no mentality left in her. No emotions, cares, fears, worries, or even love. All of those things were gone. The only thing that remained of his wife was her corpse.

He laid her body on the ground near the boathouse, and using most of his remaining strength, he pushed the rowboat out and heaved Karen's body into it. Bob gave the boat a slight push and, following behind it in the water, he pulled himself inside. He sat on the middle seat of the small boat with Karen flopped over on the front seat. Taking the oars, he began to row.

Maybe it was an hour or two... maybe it was only a few minutes. He had no way of telling how swiftly or slowly the time passed, and with the darkness of the night, he could not see anything but water, occasional lightning, and rainy blackness. Because of the heaviness of the rainfall, there was additional urgency to get this over and done with. Not only did he have to dispose of the body, but the boat was already gathering water. When he believed that he had rowed far enough out to sea, he released the oars and caught his breath.

"I wish I had dressed you," he began, touching a finger to Karen's cooled cheek, "in that pretty blue dress you got a while back. You know the one. You look beautiful in it, but it's too late now. I'm sorry."

With a pull, a push, and a shove, he toppled Karen into the water. He was not sure if he was crying or not – perhaps it was the rain wetting his cheeks – but his heart felt more broken than it ever had before.

"Had you not hated me so much," he added, sitting back on his seat, "none of this would have ever happened. I hope you know that, Karen. I love you, but you hurt me every chance you got. I never wanted to kill you, but maybe now – just maybe – I can start my life over again and be happy."

Soon, he thought, she would be fish food... and at rest. With those notions on his mind, he said a quiet goodbye to his dearly departed wife and rowed back toward the house.

It was hard for Bob to find his way back to his hill due to

the darkness and the rain. A fog had grown with the hour and it made his journey all the more difficult. Eventually, however, his rowboat touched upon the bank of his watery hill, and he climbed through the swampy wetness until he was up a few feet onto dry land. The rowboat was no longer a concern of his. He never wanted to see it again, and so he let the storm take it where it pleased. Momentarily, as he stepped onto his porch, he thought about his fingerprints and of Karen's blood on the boat, but the rain would have washed all of that away by the time anyone found it.

With a quick glance back, he saw the boat was already beginning its descent into the sea.

Bob considered himself lucky to have disposed of the body so quickly and so relatively easily. Granted, he did not consider Karen's death something easy, nor did he consider the fact that *he* had killed her to be easy. None of that was easy, or even close to being easy. What *was* easy was the disposal method. The rain, the water, the venture into the sea. How convenient that the rowboat had come with the house. He counted his blessings for it.

Walking back through the open door, the smear of red on the floor that led to the pool of Karen's blood caught his eye. He would have to clean it up before it stained the floor. Bob had never had to clean up blood like this before, and he was not sure where to begin. Paper towels? No; what idiot would clean up a pool of blood with paper towels? There was a mop in the kitchen, and there was a bathroom just a door away. That was his best option, he decided, as he could let the tub run with the drain unplugged and continuously rinse the blood out of the mop there.

"Genius," he said with a slight smile. "Why don't they ever think of this stuff in the movies?"

His quick cleaning plan still took Bob nearly an hour to complete. No matter how hard he mopped, the blood smeared and streaked – albeit a little less each time. Eventually, the floor was cleaned and there were no remaining traces of Karen's life fluid to be seen.

Exhausted, Bob crept up the stairs to the second-floor bathroom, stripped, and showered. As he lathered his body with soap, he considered handling himself – a tribute to Karen, he thought… a last blast for her memory. But as he felt it and squeezed and groped, it did nothing but hang limp and fat, weighing down against his testicles.

So, with his shower being quicker than he'd hoped for, he dried off and walked to his room where he pulled on a pair of fresh boxers and a t-shirt. He looked at his bed – small, uncomfortable, disheveled. It was nowhere near as nice as the one Karen had chosen for herself during her room-picking greed.

A small smile twitched over his lips and he left his room, closing the door behind him. With soft, almost excited steps, he walked to Karen's room and opened the door. Stepping inside, he looked around at its spaciousness, at its tidiness, and at its adjoining bathroom. Bob's smile grew as he crossed the bedroom into the bathroom and looked down. A pair of Karen's panties lay on the floor beside the bathtub.

Reaching down, he picked up the panties. He closed his eyes as they reached his face, and burying his nose deep into the soft crotch, he sniffed in long and deep – taking in the scent of Karen's vagina. He let his tongue protrude from his lips and he tasted it, tasted her, and he felt his member finally grow beneath the light cotton of his boxer shorts.

He stepped from the bathroom with Karen's panties steadily held to his mouth. His tongue continued to lick at them as he walked to the bed and climbed onto it. He brought his knees up and pulled his boxers from his body, kicking them down to the ground. Then, as he orally molested Karen's panties and focused on the memory of her perfect puss, Bob satisfied his erection, covering himself in his spillage and using the panties to clean it up.

Relaxed, he shut his eyes, drifting off into a quick but restless slumber.

* * * *

Two hours later, his bladder stirred him. He could hear the

rain outside as he sat up in the bed, and the feeling of pressure on his bladder made him wonder if there was enough time for him to make it to the bathroom. Then, he realized it was his grogginess that had made him think like that. Of course, he could make it to the bathroom. What was he? Ancient?

When he reached the toilet, Bob noticed that Karen's panties were still wrapped around his penis. He began to peel them away, but an *oh shit* moment caused him to stop. While he slept, his spillage had dried, gluing the panties to his member.

"What the fuck?" he whispered. Nervousness filled his voice, body and mind all at once. There was only one thing to do – only one option that didn't involve a pair of scissors. Closing his eyes and turning his face away, he took hold of one corner of the panties, and after a long deep breath, he ripped them away. "Fucking shit!" he shouted from the quick and stinging pain that swelled over his best buddy. Opening his eyes, he looked down and saw that it was red but not bleeding, and it was still intact. He leaned forward and pressed a hand against the wall, letting his pained pecker dangle above the toilet. Closing his eyes, he began to pee, hearing it stream hard into the water. A deep sigh of relief escaped in a long breath.

"I should have used warm water..." he muttered, wishing he'd thought of that *before* yanking the stuck panties from his pained dick.

When his bladder was empty, he flushed the commode and walked back toward the bed. Now that his orgasm was over, and now that he'd had a moment's rest to relieve his mind, he looked at Karen's bedroom and shook his head. It was more than double the size of the room she'd given him. In retrospect, he thought of how he should have killed her then, even though then the idea of killing her had been the last thing on his mind.

Smack! Smack! Smack!

The sound nearly scared Bob out of his skin. He jumped with a start and turned toward the bedroom door. He could hear it – a somewhat steady smacking of something downstairs. He had locked the door after returning from disposing of Karen's body, so it couldn't have blown open with the wind.

Wait, he thought, shaking his head. *Had* he locked the front door? Everything seemed like a hazy, questionable memory, as it had all happened so fast. Yes, he concluded with a nod of the head. He *had* locked the door, just in case someone showed up while he was cleaning up her blood.

Even that, he thought, had been ridiculous, as no one could have reached his house in this weather.

Smack! Smack!

"Fuck!" he shouted and hastily put his boxers back on. In a rush, he stormed from the bedroom and into the hall, down the stairs and into the foyer. The door was indeed shut and locked, and the persistent smacking sound was coming from the kitchen. He turned into the dining room, and as he crossed into the kitchen, he saw the door to the side deck smacking against the wall from the force of the wind.

Rain sprayed at him as he reached the door, and pushing against the wind, he managed to close the door and lock it securely.

"Karen, you fucking cunt," he said, shaking his head. He knew that she was the only reason that door was open. He hadn't used it even once since moving in, but he knew she had snuck out of it to smoke cigarettes. Bob considered how she had been terrible at locking doors, even in Connecticut. Careless, he decided, turning away from the door and leaving the kitchen.

Despite the small quantity of sleep he'd received before his bladder decided to wake him, he was alert and awake. He looked at the clock on the fireplace mantel in the foyer. It was nearing two in the morning. He walked to the library and sat down at the desk, pulling open the bottom drawer. A bottle of liquor stared up at him and he took it, unscrewing the cap and taking a long swig. He'd discovered the bottle only a day ago; it had been untouched when he found it, but now it was nearly half gone. For a scotch, he thought, it wasn't too bad, although he would have preferred vodka.

When he'd had his fill and could feel the effects of the

alcohol warm him and encompass him, he put the bottle away.

"Karen," he whispered, wondering if he was going to cry. No; there would be no more tears. "Karen, what a damn mess you've made of everything this time."

He stood from the desk and walked to the library's furthest shelves. They were the dustiest of anything in the room, untouched for generations. Most were notebooks, Bob saw, and some of the oldest hardcover books were so aged and worn that their titles could no longer be read on their spines. Others were so untouched that, aside from the dust and cobwebs, they were pristine. Perhaps someone with the right eye would have been able to build a fortune out of this collection – someone like Karen – but he was not that person… and neither was she. After all, Karen didn't have a right eye at all anymore. A screwdriver had seen to that.

On the top shelf, just out of reach, he saw a thick series of old journals, all with *Private* written on their spines. This intrigued Bob, as he knew that whomever they had belonged to was long dead. They were private no more. They had come with the house, and they belonged to Bob.

Leaning up on his tiptoes, he was able to finger one of the journals loose. It fell toward him and he caught it, raising a small cloud of dust from the commotion. He waved the dust away and carried the journal to the desk, where he sat down to study it.

"The Private Journal of Doctor Wilfred Longfellow…" he

whispered, reading the hand-printed name off the front. Lifting the cover, he looked at the first page – an entry marked March 22, 1884.

> *Life was granted to Mr. Potter, but something is wrong... horribly wrong. The life, it is only present at night, when the sun is lighting the moon in the sky. I am saddened to say that these results are similar to those of Miss Wells and Mrs. Collard.*
>
> *I fear that I may be reading something inaccurately... pronouncing something incorrectly. What am I doing wrong? There has to be an explanation. Currently, Mr. Potter is in the cellar, chained to a post, but I fear the worst. He shows no sign of these terrible side effects decreasing and he will have to be incinerated, like with Miss Wells and Mrs. Collard.*
>
> *I wish I had never been given that damned book. I only pray that God will have mercy on my soul for what it... no... for what I have inflicted on my acquaintances.*

Bob shook his head, smiled, and closed the journal,

pushing it away a few inches.

"Fucking nutcase," he said, finding it hard to hold back a chuckle. "What the fuck? Doctor Wilfred Longfellow, you, sir, were fucking nuts! Nuts, I say!" Bob laughed again and stood from the desk, popping his back in the process. "Jesus, this house... I bet he had a case of cabin fever. That's easy to get in a place like this, cut off from the world just because it rains." He looked at the structure of the library room – the old wood, wallpaper, the original red and white checkered floor. It was charming, but he could feel its age, its history... its loneliness.

Despite all of this, Bob was still intrigued by one thing in Doctor Longfellow's journal entry – his mention of the cellar. Bob had spent very little time in the basement of the house. He'd ventured down there a few times to retrieve tools and to hunt the house for Karen, but he'd never noticed anything unusual or out of place. As for the cellar itself, he knew it was there but had never visited it.

"Sounds like adventure time," he said, stepping from the library and shutting the door behind him. He looked at the basement door near the stairs and took another step toward it, but the scotch had mixed with his empty stomach, and that next step he took sent him tumbling to the floor, passed out in a dreamless slumber.

Day 4 – Bob

Sunlight drove through the windows and into the great room, shining its beams to brighten Bob's sleeping face. It hit directly onto his shut eyelids, and it stayed there for minutes, burning through the thin layer of skin and into his resting eyeballs. Bob yawned and stretched, but he did so without waking. He rolled over instead, letting the light shine onto his back. Slowly, as a few minutes turned into a few hours, the light moved off his back, down the floor, and then disappeared from view – blocked away by the walls of the house.

When Bob finally woke, he did so in a small puddle of sour drool and the waste from where he'd gotten sick in his sleep. He stood, feeling dizzy and watching the room spin. He was wobbly and tried to stand perfectly still in order to steady himself. With a deep breath, he nodded. There was a headache – a pounding that served as a reminder of drinking too much scotch last night. He had to pee; his bladder was full and pressing.

What time is it? he wondered as he looked around the room to the clock. It was just after one in the afternoon. He couldn't hear the rain anymore. It had stopped at some point, and for that much he was thankful. He could smell it though – the fresh dampness that came after a new rain. It was musky – soiled. It was strong.

He looked at the front door – at where the scent seemed to come from – and saw that the door was wide open. The fresh aroma of a damp day swarmed in from it. He walked toward it, touched it, and remembered that it had been closed and locked last night – he'd checked and ensured it. But here it was, unlocked and wide open. He stepped over the threshold and onto the porch. There was an unfamiliar boat docked at the bank of his hill.

"Who's here?" Bob called out. His voice was raspy; his throat, dry. When he turned to reenter the house, he stopped with suddenness and nearly stumbled back. An old man stood before him, with his derby hat clenched in his hands. "McDougal."

"I do hope that I didn't startle ya, Mr. Granger," McDougal said softly. He stood still and proper in his suit and bowtie. His small round glasses rested on his fleshy nose, just above his white caterpillar mustache. "Please, forgive my intrusion. I assure you that I did knock."

"How did you get in?" Bob asked as he stepped inside.

"Well, with a key, of course. As former caretaker, I have held one for generations." McDougal removed his keys from his pocket and showed Bob. Bob, in return, sighed and slumped, shutting the door behind him. "I can return it to ya now if you would like. I've always held onto one in case of emergencies."

"Where were you just now – when I woke?"

"I had gone into the bathroom. I was going to bring you a warm damp towel. I saw you on the ground and feared you'd fallen and injured yourself. When I stepped back into the room, you were gone."

Bob looked at McDougal through his hangover-affected vision and grimaced. "Where's the towel? The warm towel that you were bringing me?"

"There, sir," McDougal said, pointing to the small table beside the sofa. "It should still be warm if ya need it."

"Is that boat out there yours?"

"Well, yes. It's a bit muddy on the road up here, and the road to your house is just impassible. So, I came the only way I could be certain to get here. My trusty boat."

Bob mumbled a slurred *fine* and nodded his head. He crossed the room and took the towel – indeed, it was damp and warm – and draped it around the back of his neck.

"I called for your wife," McDougal said, walking up beside Bob. "I had hoped she'd have been available to help me move ya."

"Karen went out," Bob said as he swallowed through a knot in his throat. His eyes shifted to McDougal and then to the wall to his right. "By boat, of course."

"You mean that little rowboat that was in the shed?"

"Yes, that's it," Bob whispered. Suddenly, he felt like he was being interrogated. "She left in it sometime this morning. I guess she just wanted to get out for a while."

"Well," McDougal continued, "she must have had her fill of the watery outdoors because that rowboat is docked beside the shed. At least your wife tied it up, even if she didn't put it back in the shed."

Impossible, Bob thought and rushed from McDougal with such intensity that the towel fell from around his neck to the floor. He opened the front door and hurried onto the porch where he looked toward the duo of sheds. There it was, tied to the docking post beside the boathouse. The very boat that he'd ridden out in – that he'd dumped Karen's body from – was back and secured, as if he'd tied it himself.

"Impossible," he repeated the word, this time whispering it in a tone so low that only he could hear it. In a state of confusion, he shook his head.

"Is something the matter?" McDougal asked as he stepped up beside him once more. "Why, you've gone white, Mr. Granger. Ya look as though you've seen a ghost."

"I'm, uh, just amazed that she tied it right. That's all." He could not steady his nerves, knowing that he was trembling as he turned from McDougal. He stepped back into the house and sat in the chair nearest to the fireplace.

"The reason I am here, Mr. Granger," McDougal said, closing the front door behind him, "is that I wanted to see if you've had a moment to consider my offer."

"I'd be taking a loss from what I paid for it," Bob answered, albeit somewhat automatic. Truthfully, he had not had a chance to consider McDougal's offer. After all, he'd just killed his wife. Who had time to consider business transactions after killing their wife?

"You'll lose everything if you stay," McDougal added, breaking Bob's thoughts and drawing his full attention.

"If this land is so worthless, why are you interested in it so much? I understand that you were the caretaker here and that you have memories and attachments and shit, but like you told me – the water will eventually destroy this house. How will owning this land still benefit you?" Bob looked at the old man, who had lowered his head in thought and consideration. In truth, Bob felt bad for McDougal. The man was certainly nearing his death, and he seemed to have his heart set on owning this farmhouse before that dark day came.

"If I own this house," the old man spoke through calm words and quivering lips, "then I can prevent anyone else from ever trying to live here again. There is a curse here, ya must understand. Too many people have gone missing, or worse, from this farmhouse. Now, ya might not believe an old man, and ya might not believe in curses, but I know what I've seen, and over the years, I've seen so many people go and not in ways they would have preferred. There is something dark here, Mr. Granger, and it feeds off those that live in this house. If ya don't leave, I fear the worst for you and your wife."

Nothing about McDougal's story added up to Bob. In fact, Bob believed the man had possibly developed a touch of dementia in his old age – or more than a touch. There was more to McDougal's desire for the house that Bob knew he wasn't being told, and he hated being fed an outrageous lie, one of evils and demons and people disappearing. They were nightmarish fairy tales, taken straight from the journal that he'd read in the library. McDougal had been the caretaker here for a long time, he knew, and so it was certain the old man had at one point or another stumbled onto the journal entries and read about the sick, dark delusions of Wilfred Longfellow.

"I'm not one for ghost stories," Bob told McDougal and stood from his chair. He opened the library door and stepped inside, walked to the desk, and pulled out the bottle of scotch. "Hair of the dog," he said as he drank a long swig and then put the bottle back in its place. "I don't know why you want this house. I don't know if you have some buried treasure here, or if you're just some crazy old kook that can't let go of the past. Either way, I don't care. I could not give two fucks for your reasons for wanting to own my house, but no matter if it's for demons or diamonds, the price is not going to be cheap."

McDougal looked at him quietly. He took off his glasses and pulled them away from his face, staring into them at a distance as if he was checking the lenses for spots. Then, he put them back over his round nose and stiffened in his stance.

"I do not think ya know what you're getting into with this place," McDougal said. His voice was less scary and more matter-of-fact.

"Look, old man, I don't want all your money, but I refuse to sell this place for anything less than what I paid for it plus ten percent. If you had wanted it so badly before now, you should have bought it before me. Now, either pay me what I want or I'll wade it out until the waters drown this place into the sea and then I'll sell it as a fishing port. Either way, I'm not budging." Bob was infuriated. McDougal was wasting his time, and there were more urgent things that he needed to tend to. For instance, he still had Karen's belongings to get rid of. There was also the mystery of how the rowboat became tied to the dock pole. That, he figured, was likely McDougal's handiwork.

"How is your wife?" McDougal asked him, causing his blood to run cold. "I assume she's not feeling well, if she managed to slip in without you knowing she was home and hasn't been seen since."

"My wife is fine," Bob said in a voice that presented sheer hostility in a terrifyingly low tone. "I also think it might be time for you to leave. Now, I considered your offer. It's time you go, and consider mine before you think about coming back here again."

"Hostility is not an attractive color on anybody, Mr. Granger," McDougal told him as he stepped to the front door and opened it. "When I see you again, I will have considered your offer. I also believe you will have reconsidered mine by then. Good day to ya."

Bob was boiling over with anger as he watched McDougal step outside and close the door behind him, separating the two men. A barrier to Bob's inner outrage.

He took a deep breath and calmed himself to some degree. He was not sure what degree that was, only that he no longer wanted to rip McDougal apart with his fingers.

"He knows something," Bob whispered as he began to pace the room. "He knows something about Karen. I know he's the one that tied the rowboat up. He's the one that pointed it out. Surely… surely, he can't prove anything though. There's no body. Karen's just *gone*. She left me. Yeah… that's it. That's what happened. The bitch left me. Apparently, I just wasn't good enough for her anymore."

He smiled and nodded his head. It seemed pretty solid and sound, and who could say anything differently happened? No one saw her die, and no one saw him dump her body. There were no witnesses, and thusly any accusations made by McDougal would have been unfounded.

Bob was pleased with himself once more. He let his heartbeat slow back to normal and his mind relax. He thought of peaceful things: birds... butterflies... puppies... rainbows... cellars... demons... evil presences haunting the pages of a journal and an old man's mind.

He laughed, thinking of McDougal's scare tactic – his wild ghost story. Reality—now *that* was scary. But dark entities or things that would go bump in the night? Those were the stories told by children around campfires. To have heard them come out of a grown man's mouth – that was senility. No doubt.

However, Bob reflected on what he'd read in the journal last night in the library. He had thought the author – Doctor Longfellow – had seemed senile also, but his mention of the cellar had intrigued Bob then, and McDougal's remarks heightened that intrigue now.

Karen had spent some time in the cellar, he thought as he walked to the basement door. She hadn't changed a bit from being down there. She had remained the same rotten bitch right up to the very end. He grinned. She had been a shit to him, but even his nasty reflections of her made him feel kindly toward her memory.

Turning on the basement light, Bob started down the

rickety stairs. "Anyone down here?" he asked loudly, chuckling as he did. "Anyone wanting to eat my soul or do dark things to me? No? No one? I don't do anal, so get that out of your head." He continued to laugh at his remarks, even though he knew he was the only one that could hear them.

When his foot reached the basement floor and no response to his crude jokes had been received, Bob took another breath and looked around. Everything was very still… quiet. To him, it looked just like it did the last few times he'd been down here – just like a basement.

Now, the cellar – that was something different completely. He'd not been in the cellar before, and he was excited over what he would find. Despite the journal entry, he sort of expected to find wines or canned good. Wines would have been preferred.

The first thing Bob noticed as he opened the cellar was the heavy weight of the door. A few times before, he'd been in wine cellars and he wondered if the doors in those cellars had been similarly weighted. He turned on the light after hunting a bit for it and then started down the stairs. Moving slowly, he was cautiously fearful of one of the stone steps breaking beneath his weight. He'd seen it happen in the movies before. Some John or Nancy would hear a strange noise down the stairs and start to walk down, only for the step to crumble or break beneath them. Then, they'd tumble, injure themselves, and then – BOOM! There's the killer, right there.

Nope, Bob intended to be more careful on his journey down. He wasn't worried there would be a killer in the cellar, but he knew if he injured himself, it would be a long time before anyone came looking for him.

Midway down the steps, his bladder hit him, reminding him that he had not yet emptied it. His stomach also felt heavy – a sure sign that he had ignored his morning *rituals*. His stomach rumbled and he cringed as he heard the gurgle.

"Fuck," he said in a sigh. "McDougal got me so worked up I forgot to use the fucking commode."

He decided that, once in the cellar, he could piss in a corner if he had to. The *other* could wait until he was near a toilet again.

"It's my fucking house," he chimed, stepping off the stairs and onto the cold cellar floor. "I can fucking piss wherever the fuck I want!"

The cellar, albeit severely unfurnished, was not completely empty. There was a table off to one side, although it had nothing on it. On the ground, he could see some kind of old writing or drawing that had since been mostly wiped away. He smiled as he looked down at it – right there in the center of the room. He assumed that it had been the handiwork of Karen – a way for her to release pent up tensions or relax… a way to escape her life with her husband.

Bob pulled out his little friend and released his bladder all over what remained of the drawings and words on the floor – all over what he thought were his wife's personal reflections.

"Piss on you, bitch," he said as he shook the last few drops out and tucked his member back into his boxers. "Piss on you."

There was nothing else in the cellar that intrigued him. Yet, as he turned toward the stairs to retreat from this space, he stopped and recalled what he'd read in the journal. Then, he looked the space over once more and noticed a steel post coming out of the floor and stretching up to the ceiling. It had scrapes all over it, as it someone had been chained to it. Perhaps many more people than just poor Mr. Potter, Bob thought.

The more Bob looked, the more he began to see. Scratches on the walls and floor that looked like they could have been made by fingernails. Concrete stained such deep red in areas that it had to have been from blood. It was true, he decided, slowly stepping toward the stairs. Longfellow had kept people imprisoned down there, just as he had written – chained to this steel floor-to-ceiling post, left to rot and die because of an old man's hallucinations.

Bob shook his head and looked down to the floor, trying to take all of this in. Then, he noticed the most intriguing thing yet. The floor was clean where he'd pissed. There wasn't a drop of urine to be seen. He bent down and touched the area; it wasn't even damp.

"What the fuck?" he questioned as he stood up straight and backed away. "I *know* I just pissed there. Where the fuck did it go?" He looked around and studied every inch of floor space that he could see. His pee was just gone.

Deciding he had seen too much *weird shit* for one afternoon, he hurried up the stairs and shut the cellar door behind him, leaning against it as he caught his breath.

"Nope," he said, shaking his head. "I must have imagined I'd pissed. Hallucination. Maybe it's something in the air here, or the water. Must be what made Longfellow snap."

He knew one thing for sure; he didn't want to snap. But, aside from brushing his teeth, he'd not had the water from the plumbing anywhere near his mouth. The air, he thought, smelled a little damp and moldy in the basement and the rest of the house smelled... well, like old houses smelled, but outside the air was clean and fresh.

Heading up the basement stairs, he thought again of McDougal. McDougal had ranted about the evils in the house. McDougal had also been caretaker here for a long time, which meant that he'd breathed the air inside the house for that many years.

"The mold," he whispered, stepping into the great room and closing the basement door. "As soon as this water recedes, I'll have something done about the mold. No big deal. Just more money that I can't afford to spend; that's all."

Once Bob shat, showered and shaved, he dressed in sweatpants and a t-shirt and settled down in the library. He considered taking a snort of scotch from the bottle in the drawer, but he figured that was where he had gone wrong last night. He hadn't been able to think clearly afterward, and perhaps his imagination had run away with him when reading through the journal. So, to further satisfy his curiosity, he returned to the high shelf with the dusty journals and pulled another one down. He sat down and opened it to an entry from April 19, 1884 – just a few weeks after the entry he'd read last night.

> *I believed that I had it right this time; I honestly did. I performed every piece of the ritual just as I should have – as slow as I could have to ensure that my words were not slurred or mispronounced. Inspector Anderson has shown the most improvement from all of my subjects, but he, too, has the hunger. I do wish he had not come to look for the others. He was a good man. Now, he is an animal and I've had to restrain him more securely than the others. He is strong.*
>
> *I worry what the latter effects will be with Anderson. What amazes me, however, is that*

Inspector Anderson is the only one so far to have retained his vocabulary. He is able to hold entire conversations, and his mobile skills are quite human – very much alive. Perhaps this is because I killed him after performing the ritual on him, sedating him for that purpose. While this method shows improvement in the subject, there is an uncontrollable rage in him that I cannot seem to subdue. The rage... and the hunger. While I study him, I must feed him, but I find it difficult to sacrifice possible subjects as a supper or a dessert. Nothing else will fill him. Only the flesh of a fresh human.

Bob slammed the journal shut. He felt queasy. "Disgusting!" he said, pushing the journal away from him. "What the fuck...? That's fucking cannibalism. He was keeping people locked up in that fucking cellar and making them eat other people. That's some seriously fucked up bullshit."

Returning to the shelving unit that held the journals, he looked to the three old boxes at the bottom. He'd not yet thumbed through those, and he wondered if they held more information about his new house. If they did, he hoped the information was a bit more pleasant. He took one of the boxes – it had a little weight to it – and carried it to the desk, setting it down on top. Bob did not sit in the chair; instead, he hovered over the box as he lifted off its lid.

The first thing he saw was a stack of enveloped letters, tied together by a yellow ribbon. They were postmarked during the time of the First World War and appeared to be correspondences between a soldier and his lady in waiting. Bob untied the ribbon and read through the first letter, finding it to be filled with nothing more than mushy loving sentiments and updates on relatives or friends. A glance at a few more of the letters showed him that they would likely all be the same.

Setting the letters to the side, Bob continued to dig through the box. He came upon trinkets, faded photographs, a dried rose pressed between two pieces of glass, some old military metals, and a letter of death about the young soldier with whom the lady in waiting had corresponded.

The box was a tragic box, Bob decided, filled with a woman's most dire and saddened memories. Whoever that woman was, her heart was in the box, and Bob wanted to know no more about her. If – he glanced at an envelope to check the name – Louise was anything like Karen, then – one more glance – Nathan had been better off dead.

Bob dumped everything back into the box, put the lid on, and tossed the box to the floor. It was all trash, he decided and returned to the shelves to choose another box. This one, he sat on the floor with instead of carrying it back to the desk. When he opened the lid, he was much more intrigued than he'd been with the one before.

This box was full of newspaper clippings, covering decades of history. Every clipping, however, was over a missing person, or over a body that was discovered – dead, mutilated, missing pieces… One such clipping dated back to November of 1921 and told of a man found with his cheeks cut off, floating in a boat out at sea. The man was said to be Sir Anthony Humphreys and was the then-owner of Bob's farmhouse. That article continued to state that Humphreys purchased the house in June of 1919, at an estate auction following the death of Doctor Wilfred Longfellow.

"Cannibalism," Bob whispered, shaking his head and setting the news article aside. "But, Longfellow was the one feeding people to his prisoners. If Humphreys was the owner and Longfellow was dead, how was the cannibalism still going on?"

Bob stood from the ground and popped his back. He was thirsty, hungry, and he needed to wrap his mind around everything that he'd just read and learned. He left the library and stepped into the great room, crossed through the dining room, and entered the kitchen. He grabbed a pack of hot dogs from the refrigerator – one of the only meats that he bought on his journey into town – and ripped the package open. He ate three rather quickly, cramming them in his mouth one after another and squishing them soft and flat so he could swallow them down. The fourth hot dog, he let lie on his tongue, broken in half, as he sucked out the juices.

He belched, enjoying the relief of the burp mixed with the aftertaste of the hot dogs. He put the rest of the pack back in the refrigerator and took a bottle of water in exchange. As he chugged it, he turned and glanced at the door, noticing that it was not locked.

"What the hell..." he said, setting the water bottle on the counter. "I locked this last night. I know for a fucking fact that I did."

Bob opened the door and stepped out, looking over the grounds. It was turning night now and the fog was rising; he could see no one out there. He took notice of the fact that the water had receded – much more quickly than he had thought it would.

Shutting the door and locking it again, he cursed. "Fucking McDougal. He probably opened it when he was here. That old man is really pissing me off."

Angered again by the little old man who was after his house, Bob returned to the library – not for the box of news clippings or the journals of horrors, but for what remained in the bottle of scotch. He needed a drink.

Seated at the desk, he pulled the bottle out and gazed at it thirstily. Although he remembered drinking more than it appeared he did, the bottle was still nearly half full, and he was ready to remedy that. He opened the bottle and brought its lip to his. Closing his eyes, he tilted his head back as the cool liquor flowed into his mouth and then turned warm as it slid down his throat. When he'd chugged half of what was left, he pulled the bottle away, released a satisfied sigh, and wiped his lips clean with his upper wrist.

"Fucking crazy house," he whispered, looking around at the many old, dusty books that surrounded him, at the box of war and romance memorabilia on the floor, and then at the journal on the desk before him.

Pulling the journal toward him, he opened it closer to its end, revealing an entry from December 25, 1884.

> *I cannot feel the same about Christmas anymore, or any holiday, I should say. My dear wife, she loved Christmas, but without her, it has no meaning. Aside from my current lack of attachment to the holiday, I find it difficult to celebrate anything under a Christian calendar anymore. When one's soul has been compromised, one loses his ability to find solace in God.*
>
> *My nephew, I am sad to say, has met with the fire. I had hoped that the experiment would*

work better on a child, and perhaps it will settle better with my niece once she awakens, but my nephew was not so lucky. Little Thomas's appetite was greater than any of the adults. He seemed fine at first – I thought it had finally worked! I had successfully reanimated someone to a state that seemed very human. He was full of trickery. Although he suffered the same ailment as the others during the day, at night he seemed just like he had before he drank the poison – youthful and exuberant. He wanted to play, and I was overwhelmed by the accomplishment. I allowed him to venture outside.

Thomas returned three hours later, covered in blood with pieces of flesh hanging from the thin gaps in his teeth. He told me of how he had enjoyed playing and that he was excited to play again tomorrow.

I burned him the next morning once the ailment took over.

Charity, his sister, still has not awoken. She should wake tonight. I pray to anyone that will hear me to please – please – PLEASE – let it work this time. Let Charity be a Christmas miracle, if such a *thing truly does exist. She is all that is left of my family. If I fail with her, I have failed everyone I have ever cared about.*

But if I succeed... oh, it will be a wonder, to hold the hands of life and death equally balanced. To be able to take a life and to give it back – to hold that power. I can taste it... smell it... Charity will be the one.

Slumped in his seat, Bob groaned. Longfellow had been crazier than he'd thought. "The man murdered his family... just to try to bring them back." Pushing his chair away from the desk, he stood. Every journal entry that he read seemed to get worse. Bob imagined that it was one of Longfellow's *experiments* that had finally caused the man to meet his end. Still, the news clipping stated the house didn't change hands until 1919, and this journal was from 1884. That added up to thirty-five years' worth of possible other experiments – other deaths, attempts at rebirth, and likely even more cannibalism.

"This is one fucked up house," he said, shaking his head. He walked over to the far, high-up shelf and glanced at the journals. There were a few dozen there, and he chose one of the last ones on the shelf to pull down. "Let's see exactly how fucked up."

Bob stood where he was and opened the journal toward the middle. This entry read May 14, 1911.

It is a lonely existence that I live. I fear that I have caused my own reclusiveness, and it is not enjoyable. I miss the scent of a woman's perfume. I miss a man's cackle when he has laughed at his own remark. Alas, anyone who dares visit my home is nothing more than a meal for Charity. She can smell them before they are even here. She's much swifter and more agile than any of the others – quick and always hungry. I should have disposed of her long ago, but I cannot find it within myself to do it. I must live with the soils of my creation. Perhaps I have been performing this ritual correctly all along. Perhaps this is Lucifer's greatest laugh – creation without perfection. Why, even God could not perfect man, so why should I be the one with that greater gift? This is the life that I have created, and it does not protect me.

It does not ease my fear.

I know that one day my dear Charity will turn on me as well. When there are no more neighbors on the surrounding farms, when no one comes to look in on me anymore – she will grow hungry, and when she awakes as the sun sets, I will be her next meal.

After that, she will be free to leave this land, and she will cause great pain wherever she goes. But she is just a child. She is just a seven-year-old girl that never grows, never ages, and never gets full.

Bob wanted to feel sympathy for Longfellow, but he found it impossible. In fact, he hoped he had gotten eaten by that little girl. Bob couldn't imagine what kind of ritual the man was performing on all of these people. Had he created some crazy concoction for them – an experimental drug gone wrong? He remembered a mention of poison in the entry about burning the kid named Thomas.

"Wow... my house was the home of a sort of Doctor Frankenstein. This is not the sort of thing I should tell potential buyers when I relist it." He closed the journal and put it back on the shelf, taking the last one in its place. "Bedtime reading."

Bob closed the library down for the night, checked to ensure both entrances to the house were locked up tight, and he retreated upstairs to Karen's room – nope, his room now – for bed. He urinated in his private bathroom and kicked his sweatpants to the floor beside the bed. Climbing onto the bed, he propped the pillow up against the headboard and relaxed.

He held the journal in front of him and looked at it. It felt... *less used* than the others. Less handled. Less thumbed through. He flipped through it, noticing the entries ended a third of the way into it. This journal ended on July 15, 1918, and he settled and read.

> *We are a real family now, true and happy. In her old life, Louise was a sad, heartbroken woman, but now – now that I have mastered this magic – she has learned to be doting. Loving. Sensual to me. At my old age, I had feared that kind of life was over for me, but Louise has a way of using her lips... her mouth in manners that I've not felt in decades. With her reanimation, she seems to have forgotten all about her old life, about her beloved soldier Nathan, and about my abduction and kidnapping of her. All I had wanted was her affection, and now I have it.*

As Bob read, he cocked an eyebrow and smiled. "Dirty old man, aren't ya, Longfellow? Creepy, dirty old man."

> *As a mother to Charity, Louise is caring and*

kind. She is able to help her hunt for food, and I no longer have to aid in that practice.

As a lover, Louise is perfection. She uses her tongue on my manhood with such intensity that I cannot resist it. When she swallows me, I can actually feel happiness again, and when I fill her belly with my seed, I feel powerful again.

Bob did not realize it, but as he read, his hand had drifted down to his newfound erection.

I am still fearful, however. I am fearful that, one night while I am inside of her, she will bite into my throat and not pull away. I am fearful that, one night while she swallows me, she will clamp down with her teeth, severing me for a quick bite to eat.

Bob's hard-on disappeared just as he realized he'd been handling one. The words made him shudder with painful disgust. He threw the journal down, letting it fall to the floor, and straightened his body the length of the bed, stretching out.

"Fuck, no, dude!" he shouted, sitting up. "Never get a blowjob from a dead cannibal bitch! Never!"

As that was from the final journal entry, Bob did not need

to read more to learn what happened. Longfellow had met his end – either with his psychotic niece or his cock-hungry girlfriend.

"Louise must have *literally* loved to eat dick," he chuckled, trying to make light of the situation.

When he settled back down, his hard-on had returned, but he chose not to satisfy it. Instead, he turned his focus away from it and worked only to fall asleep. After all, he did not know what had happened with Louise and Charity. Had they finally met their ends also, or were they still somewhere out there, ripping out throats and biting off cocks?

That did it – that thought sent his boner away for the night. From there on, he focused only on more pleasant things, most specifically on how his life used to be – career, stable home, someone to love him. Those thoughts were finally enough to drift him into sleep.

Day 5 – Bob

When Bob opened his eyes, he screamed. He could have swore that she was there – the horrid woman named Louise from the old photos and journal entries, looking at him from beside the bed – but as he threw on his glasses and his vision began to clear, he saw that she was not there. Not that she *hadn't* been there, but that she *wasn't* there. Bob could not differentiate on whether or not he'd just awoken from a dream, if the sudden onslaught of wickedness in the house had corrupted his mind and his eyes were playing tricks on him, or if the reanimated nightmare from Longfellow's past had actually been there. Either way, he was spooked.

It was as if the vision of her was somehow burned in his mind. He could still picture her, clear as day, as if she was right there beside him. Her clothes, tattered, worn… her skin and hair, dirty and disheveled. The blackness of her eyes and bloodstained smile…

He stood from the bed and paced for a moment, hoping to shake off the creepy feeling that he was experiencing. He relieved himself in the bathroom, brushed his teeth, and then went to *his* room – as Karen would have had it – and dressed in jeans and a t-shirt.

In the otherwise abandoned bedroom, for he had no intention of ever sleeping in there again, he looked at the wall clock. He had not wound it in over a day, but the second hand still ticked and the time read 5:47. Much earlier than yesterday, he thought with a touch of self-pride as he realized the sun must have just risen.

Downstairs, he ate breakfast – oatmeal and an orange – and chugged a bottle of water to help with his dry mouth and try and fight the dehydration that had come from the scotch. He did not feel as bad as he had yesterday though, and he saw this as a genuinely good thing seeing that yesterday he had felt like shit. Still this morning, he was not one hundred percent by any means. He needed today to be quiet – without the interruption of McDougal, and without further reading into Longfellow's journals. Bob was still shaken by the image that he woke with – or woke to – this morning. He needed the day to defog his head and just relax.

After breakfast, he walked into the foyer and sat down on the sofa, ignoring the library and its closed door. Ignoring the basement and *its* closed door. Ignoring anything that could have held more horrors to fill his mind or more annoyances to disturb his intended stillness.

Boredom was quick settling in. Bob sat still for a few minutes. After the second minute, he started tapping his finger on his knee. Bob liked to stay active, and although there had been plenty of activity happening at his new home, it was not the sort of activity that he preferred. He would have much rather been at work than home fighting with Karen, or home killing Karen, or home dumping Karen's body, or home doing relatively *anything* with Karen or having to do with Karen.

And there she was…taking over his mind again. He was trying to relax, but his brain was constantly flashing *Karen, Karen, Karen* over and over again.

"Fucking Karen," Bob grumbled, standing from his seat and walking across the room to the downstairs bathroom. He pulled the chain that turned on the light over the mirror and stared at his reflection. Although clean and shaven, he looked tired. There were dark circles under his eyes, his complexion was pale, and his glasses – when was the last time he'd cleaned his glasses? They were dirty and streaked, and there was blood splattered on the…

Blood. Blood on his glasses. It must have happened when he was cleaning up the floor after dumping Karen. Had McDougal noticed it? Was that what he kept hinting about?

"Fucking shit!" he cursed and pulled his glasses from his face, scrubbing them clean under the faucet. When he was sure that the blood was gone, he dried the glasses with his t-shirt and placed them back over his face. Throughout all of the chaos, he had not before noticed the dirtiness of the glasses or the specks of Karen's blood splattered on the frames. There had been much more pressing matters, like the insane former owner that turned his family into cannibals, or McDougal and his methods of persuasion that he'd used to try to buy the house dirt cheap. Or, for fuck's sake, the woman beside his bed early this morning.

"Louise," Bob whispered.

He knew it was too early for a drink, but he didn't really care. A drink would bring him back to life, he thought. Without wasting another moment contemplating the idea, Bob ventured into the library and walked to the desk for the partially filled bottle of scotch... even though he said he wouldn't.

Pulling open the desk drawer, he took out the bottle and looked at it. His eyes grew wide with disbelief, as the bottle was full again. He distinctly remembered nearly finishing it last night. In fact, he still felt some of the after effects from it.

From behind him, on the other side of the library's window, he heard the distinct sound of a car pulling up his drive, spraying water beneath its tires. Setting the bottle down, he rushed to the window and looked. A taxi was arriving.

"What in the name of living Fuckville?" he asked himself, immediately thereafter smacking himself on the forehead with the answer. "Mom."

His throat fell into his gut. He had completely forgotten about Ethel's arrival today, which meant that he forgot to pick her up at the airport this morning. He knew his mother and her temper. He knew that she would be beyond pissed when she saw him.

He hurried from the library to the front door, heading out onto the porch just as the taxi came to a stop. He could see Ethel's silhouette in the backseat and the driver staring at him with a disgruntled expression. Ethel's door opened and she began to step out of the car just as its trunk popped up.

"Pay the man and get my bags," she told Bob as she saw him. Bob cringed at her voice; it was filled with disappointment.

"Mom, I'm so sorry," he told her as he approached, opening his arms for a hug. Ethel waved him off.

"I don't want to hear it," she said, walking past him and up the steps to the porch. "I'll be inside where it is hopefully warm and dry."

Bob watched her disappear into the house, and he turned to see the driver step out to help with the bags.

"That's your mum?" the man asked him. Bob looked him over. He couldn't have been more than twenty-five and was likely still living at home with his own mum, he decided.

"She is," he answered, taking two of the bags from the trunk while the driver took the rest.

"She's a handful, that lady, if ya don't mind me sayin' as

much."

Bob wanted to agree, but he declined to acknowledge the remark. "Follow me into the house. I'll have to grab my wallet."

He walked ahead of the driver and set the bags down just inside the small entranceway. Ethel was seated, poised and proper, on a chair in the great room by a window. Her eyes were slits, her face drawn, and her head was tilted away from Bob and the driver.

"I'll be just a moment," Bob said as he headed up the stairs to the room that Karen had designated for him. His wallet was on the dresser and, fortunately, he had withdrawn some funds when he went grocery shopping in town.

Downstairs, he saw the driver standing in the doorway with his head lowered and Ethel staring at him as if he'd killed her best friend.

"Pay the fool," she instructed Bob in an almost threatening tone.

Bob sighed as he paid the driver his dues and shut the door behind him as he left. Turning toward Ethel, he plastered on a great, fake grin. "Hi, Mom!"

"Where were you? Do you know I had to wait over an hour for you? Do you know what *kinds of people* linger around airports nowadays? It's not safe Robert." She huffed and looked away, rolling her eyes. "I suppose you sent that wife of yours instead. What happened? Did she get lost on her way? Karen couldn't find her way out of a paper bag if someone pointed the way and guided her by hand."

"Karen left me, Mom." Bob said this in a strange, chipper way that caught him off guard just as soon as it rolled off his tongue. "I haven't seen her in a couple of days."

"I told you she would do this, didn't I?" Ethel questioned. At seventy years old, Ethel had the thin, withered frame of a woman nearing a hundred. Her hair was completely white, and behind her glasses, she had more wrinkles on her face than a California raisin. Bob had not noticed how old his mother looked until he had been apart from her for a few days. He hoped that it was jetlag. "I told you she would leave you, Robert," she reiterated. "I told you she didn't love you. I'm the only woman that could have any sort of love for a man like you, Robert. Me. Your mother!" She shouted this last bit, causing Bob to stumble backward toward the entrance to the dining room.

"You're a worse little shit than your father anyway." Ethel continued and stood from her seat as she spoke. "You couldn't provide me with a grandchild, and you couldn't keep a wife. You've always been lazy and a bore, my son. You were never smart. Never. Your father had you beat in that way. He liked the bottle a little too much but he was mentally as sharp as a whip." She walked to the fireplace and touched a hand to the mantle. "But you're not a bad person. You deserve love too, don't you Robert?

You *need* love."

Bob felt that he was on the edge of tears. Every word his mother said cut into him like thrusts from a freshly-sharpened blade. She was digging out his heart, and she was strangling his mind.

"Yes, Robert," she whispered, turning toward him. She looked him dead in the eye and smiled. "A boy needs his mother. His mother's love... There is no love like a mother's love for her son. But, oh, Robert... how you have disappointed me today, leaving me stranded in that horrible airport." Her smile disappeared and her face went stern. "How could you have hurt me so, Robert? Forgetting your own mother? Leaving me to the *wolves*? After I raised you, nurtured you, loved you? After I gave you life and fed you from my very bosom?"

"I'm so sorry, Mommy," Bob said in a quivering tone as the tears began to fall from his eyes. His mother's expression softened and a sad smile appeared as she extended her arms to him. With slow, wobbly steps, he went to her, allowing himself to be wrapped in her embrace. He buried his face into her shoulder and felt her nose as she sniffed his hair.

"There, there," she whispered, stroking his hair and holding him tight. "Mommy's right here, sweet baby." She kissed his ear, his lobe, his neck at the pulse. "Mommy will make sure you're never unloved again."

Bob stiffened with a familiar discomfort. He remembered this feeling – this hold. This was the way his mother used to hold him, before he married Karen… and sometimes after.

Her hand coursed down his shoulder and his upper arm, onto his back and down to his side, resting at his hip.

"Did you miss your mommy?"

Goosebumps rose across Bob's skin. With his eyes locked shut, he felt more tears about to flow. The memories… the moments spent with his mother long ago. She was his comfort – always and often – holding him, hugging him, kissing him… touching him in ways that only someone intimate would. Karen had been the only other person to have touched him with such tenderness, such passion… Now, Karen was dead and this kind of touching reminded Bob of that. It made him terrified.

Ethel's hand began to caress his lower back and he pulled away from her.

"Is everything okay, Robert?" she asked him. Her voice sounded shocked and confused. After all, Bob had never pulled away from his mother before. He'd always let her calm him… please him. Now, however, everything was different.

"It's just… been a long few days," he told her, looking away and walking toward her bags. Picking two of them up, he said, "I'll put your bags in your room and then show you around."

"The payment for the sale of my house hit my account over

the weekend," Ethel added. Bob looked down at her from the middle of the stairs. He watched her eyes as she looked around. "We could use some of it to repair this... *place.*"

"How much did you end up getting anyway? I know your house had the additional apartment over the garage."

"And the pool in the back," she added. "I got just over two million."

Bob nodded at her and continued up the stairs. When he was out of her sight, he smiled – large and happy.

Two million, he thought, opening the door to her room and setting the bags inside. *I could go to a fucking island and live in peace with that much money...*

"Fuck this place," he whispered, shaking his head.

As he went back down the stairs, he caught Ethel checking out the bathroom. She was peeking inside, making a *tsking* sound. She looked back at Bob as the floor creaked from his footsteps.

"This place is filthy," she said with a grunt. "I take it Karen couldn't bring herself to lift a finger around here to help. She never was much for keeping house. I'd have to tidy up your old home in Deerborne every time I stopped by. Why, imagine how awful it would have been if I hadn't!"

"Let's bring your other bags up and I'll show you your room," he said, ignoring her comments about Karen. Karen, in fact, had been a decent house keeper in Connecticut. Things didn't start slacking around the house until things went bad between her and Bob.

"Oh, I hope it has a nice big quilt. You know how I love quilts."

"It does have a quilt," he said, taking her bags and leading her up the stairs. He stepped inside her room, turned the light on, and motioned for her to follow. "I'm glad the road was passable for your taxi to make it through. We've had a lot of rain. The road was flooded over just two days ago. Even yesterday, it was pretty bad."

"It's terribly wet out there," she said, looking around the room with a straight face – one that Bob could not read. "You will have to take me into town sometime this week. I would like to do a bit of shopping. I had to severely downsize to make this move, you know. My life is condensed into these bags and the *few* furnishings and memories that I'm having shipped in."

"I know, Mom," Bob confirmed in a soothing tone, thankful to hear she was having only a handful or two of items brought over from the States. "It's been an adjustment for me too."

"Well, I can see that. Where is the upstairs bathroom? I hope you don't expect me to have to walk down those stairs every time I have to pee at three in the morning."

"Come this way."

He showed her where the bathroom was, and then he led

her downstairs to show off the dining room and the kitchen. Ethel was stone-faced while looking at each of them, but her curiosity brought a thin smile to her tight lips when he showed her the library.

"Ignore the mess on the desk," he said, walking to it to block it. "I'm just going through some stuff the old owners left behind."

"All these wonderful books," Ethel whispered, strolling through the room and running her fingers along the spines on the books. "Great literature is the key to great understanding."

"You have always been an avid reader."

"I don't believe in letting my brain rot with things like television and radio. That was one of Karen's problems. She loved television too much. She let her mind go to mush."

"Well," Bob said as he straightened up the desk, "you may read any book of your choosing. There are more titles here than I can count."

"You could stand to read some too, you know," Ethel continued. "All that work you do – most of it is on a computer. *Technology*. The Devil invented it; I promise it's so. You don't want to fall prey to the Devil, now do you, Robert dear?"

"No, Mom," he said, keeping his eyes from hers.

"The Devil led Karen to you, and we see how that worked out. No… you must steer clear of the Devil and his tricks, my son.

But I'm here now, and your dearest Mommy will help keep you safe and clean."

She walked to him, touched him on his shoulder, sent shivers down his spine.

"Have you cleaned yourself today, Robert?"

He remembered his youth, when Ethel would feel that he'd been a dirty boy. She'd insist on him bathing, and she would scrub every inch of him until she felt that he had been cleansed. There were times when she had been gentle with him – perhaps too gentle – and there were times when she had been so rough on him that he would leave the bath bleeding from her rubbing away his skin. Sometimes his mother would make him feel so good under the bubbles, but most of the time a bath was more of a punishment, one that he had learned quickly to hate and avoid at every given opportunity.

"Just a few hours ago," he said, pulling away from her and walking from the desk. "I'm sad to say that there's not much in the house for food, so supper tonight will be mediocre. Tomorrow, I'll take you into town and we can shop. We'll get more groceries then."

"You don't have to worry about cooking for yourself anymore," she added, grabbing a book from one of the shelves and tucking it under her arm. Bob could not see the title. "Mommy will do all of the cooking from now on. You love my cooking, don't you, Robert?"

"I do," he said, although that was only partially true. He'd loved his mother's cooking when he had been a child, but when you're a kid, if it's fried or cheesy, it was wonderful. Everything his mother ever made for him was fried, bready, or cheesy. It wasn't until Bob was in high school that he tasted broccoli for the first time, and it wasn't until he and Karen had gotten close that he had eaten his first salad. He then noticed a change in how he felt, and in his body, after introducing vegetation to it. A life on his mother's diet was a death sentence, and he knew it.

"No one fries up fresh gerbil like you," he told her, having to force the words from his mouth.

"God would not have given us such delicacies if they weren't meant to be eaten," she said. "In fact, it must be time for lunch. I'll make do with what you have in the kitchen. Lunch will be ready in under a half hour."

Bob watched her walk out of the room, and he immediately knew that it was a mistake moving her in with him. But she needed him. His father – her husband – was long dead, and Bob was all of her family now. She was aging; she was slowing down. He could see it in her movements.

None of this was enough for him to deny that having Ethel in the house was a mistake. What *did* make a difference was the fact that she now had nearly two million bucks in the bank from the sale of the house – not to mention his father's pension. As her only living relative, it was assured that Bob would be the sole beneficiary if anything were to happen to her.

He would ensure her final days were as comfortable as possible, but he also decided that they *would be* her final days, and there would not be many of them.

He spent the time until lunch in the library, putting the items back in their boxes, and putting the boxes and journals back on their respective shelves. There was more here for him to discover – to learn about what was happening, and what had happened, in his home. But now was not the time for further investigation. Now was the time to enjoy his mother's company, while she was still with him.

Bob had never actually plotted a murder before, but after killing Karen, it all seemed so… easy. Yes, he hadn't wanted to use that word before, not when it came to Karen's death. Then, he was guilt-stricken and riddled with grief. Now however, it was more of a matter of money and survival. He needed the money part for the survival part, and although he knew his mother would have been willing to spend the money on him, he wanted nothing more than to spend the money on himself with her six feet underground… or lost to the sea. He had practice at it now. He would dispose of her in the same way that he'd disposed of Karen; it was as simple as that.

As for how to kill her, he had no idea. Did he push her down the stairs? Was it guaranteed that she'd die from the fall, or would she survive? If she survived it, she'd be in terrible agony. Bob would most certainly have to smother her or break her neck at that point. Perhaps even bludgeon her until the last breath finally left her lips.

He thought about requesting a bath with her, and as he was washing her back, he could push her face down into the water and drown her. There would be a slight struggle, but he was much larger than she. Her fight wouldn't last long.

"I could use a pillow," he whispered, putting the last box back on the bottom shelf. "Smother her in her sleep. She wouldn't know what hit her." His smile curled up the corners of his lips. "Or I could gut her like a fucking deer."

"Robert!" he heard her yell from the kitchen. Her voice ripped through his eardrums like the shrill of an angered banshee. "Robert! Food is ready!"

"Coming!" he replied, and stopping at the desk on his way out, he took the bottle of scotch – no longer caring how it had been refilled – and took a long, deep swig. It tasted clean, not tampered with. He took another sip. Once more, he'd made a dent in the bottle. Secretly, as he tucked it back in the drawer, he hoped that it would be replenished again. Heaven knew he'd need it.

"Robert!"

God, how he hated her. He thought of that as he stepped from the library, shutting the door behind him. Part of him loved her, but there was a larger part of him that absolutely despised her. Ethel had *loved* him so strongly that her touch – or even just the thought of it – made his skin crawl.

The dining room table was set with a full plate at both the head and foot with a bottle of water set beside each. Ethel sat at the foot, smiling affirmatively as Bob approached. He looked at her, and then down to his plate of food. Everything was brown, fried – each of the three items indistinguishable from the next.

"Well," Ethel said, pointing to his chair. "Sit down."

"Wow," Bob remarked, doing as instructed. "You sure did make a lunch here." He stared at the food; his stomach churned. Although, he did not know what he was complaining about. Yesterday, all he'd eaten were raw hot dogs.

"I found a few hot dogs in the refrigerator," Ethel continued. "I battered them up and gave them a good frying. I did the same with some pickles and an onion. I know how young boys love fried foods… I found some ketchup in there too. Do you want ketchup?"

"No," he said, waving his hand. "This will be just fine."

"Well," she added, taking a big bite of fried something-or-other. "Dig in. Fried foods get cold quick, you know."

She hadn't brought out any forks. There was no need for

forks, he figured. Everything was fried. Finger-food, as Ethel often called it. He looked at her as she finished off her bite and then suckled the grease from her fingertips, making a horrible smacking sound that made Bob's skin crawl.

He picked up what he hoped was a fried pickle and brought it up to his face. He looked at it for a moment, inspected it, and then – finding that its touch reminded him of his mother's – he popped it into his mouth to get rid of it quickly.

"Good, isn't it? I remember how you always loved fried pickles. I made them all the time for you. Do you remember that, Robert? Do you remember me making these?"

"Yes, Mom," he said, hesitantly taking another one. "You made them often."

"Yes, I did. Anytime you wanted them. I'd even surprise you with them sometimes. You could eat platefuls back then. Now look at you. You've barely touched your food. Karen has ruined you. I'm glad she's gone. If she was here right now, I'd have no choice than to tell her how much she has destroyed you. She took my precious, sweet baby boy, and she turned him into a loathsome, haggard bore. Why, look at yourself, Robert. You used to stay so clean-shaven. I can see you made somewhat of an effort, but look at that stubble. You're an absolute mess."

Bob went cold. His fingertips numbed. He bit his bottom lip and diverted his eyes to the floor. Finally, he pushed his chair away from the table and stood. He smiled and watched as his mother ate another bite of food.

"Robert, finish your lunch," she told him in a stern but confused tone.

"I'm not hungry right now, Mom," he said. His voice quivered a little but he quickly controlled it. "I have things to do. I appreciate the effort, but this house needs work." He touched his face and the few spots where the razor had missed. Then, he decided he liked it. They were *his* whiskers... *his* stubble. "More so," he continued, "right now, I *want* this stubble. And you know what? I want my chest hair too. And my pubes, Mom. I want my goddamn pubes."

"Where are you going?" she questioned, standing as he turned away from her. "What are you going to do?" She started after him, but it only took one glance from Bob to make her stop.

"I'll be in the library. I need some peace. Please, take the book you chose and enjoy it. Just, give me a few hours."

He did not wait for her to answer him. He needed to be away from her for a while. Every time she spoke, she filled him with memories of his past – memories that he had long tried to escape. She had shaved him before, he recalled as he opened the library door, stepped inside, and shut it behind him. Yes, she had shaved him when he was thirteen. Up until that moment, he had been her *precious baby boy*, but when Ethel walked into the bathroom and caught him in the shower with hair in a place she felt like it did not belong, she shaved off every bit of it. Bob had thrown a fit – crying and screaming. Ethel had not been gentle with him. When she had finished, he had cuts and blood all over – something that would scar him more emotionally than it would physically. After that, Bob spent an extra ten minutes a week in the shower, shaving off any hair on his crotch, stomach and chest to avoid having his mother do it again. This went on until he moved out after graduation.

Near the desk on a small table by a file cabinet was an old record player. Bob decided that music was exactly what he needed to drown out any further noise or comments from his mother. There was a record already on the player; he didn't bother to check and see what it was. He lifted the bar and placed the tip of the needle at the start. Then, turning a dial, he powered the player on. The music was lively, loud. Big Band era. Trumpets, tubas, horns of all kinds. He dug it.

He sat at the desk and kicked his feet up. He considered another drink of scotch – he truly wanted to see if it had replenished again – but he decided to wait. This house had a distinct way of playing tricks on his mind.

He closed his eyes, relaxed in the chair, and let himself become absorbed in the music. Although it was fast and upbeat, it calmed him. In his mind, he could picture himself there, in that Big

Band era, surrounded with great musicians dressed in nice black tuxedos. Back then, he thought, musicians created outrageous symphonies with their music, not like musicians today. Most modern musicians were jaded and formulated. Half of them, when they sang, had to auto-tune their voices. If you couldn't sing without electronics, Bob believed you just couldn't sing... period. He, himself, had no singing talents, and so he didn't try to prove otherwise to the world. He couldn't understand why anyone would want to claim a talent they didn't possess, and yet he believed that so many of them did just that.

Absorbed in his personal debate over vintage greats and modern pretenders, his mind drifted further than he'd intended – into a nap. It was a dreamless nap and didn't feel like a very long one, likely brought on by the exhaustion of having to deal with his mother's arrival. When he opened his eyes again, the music was finished and the record had ceased spinning.

It was still daylight, as the sky outside his window was still bright. This helped to confirm to Bob that his nap had, indeed, been quick and that there was a possibility that his mother had not commenced with too much *damage* throughout the house.

Standing from his chair, he stretched and popped his back. He sighed, groaned, and focused his thoughts to deal with the fact that – yes – his mother was there and – yes – he'd made this bed and now he had to lay in it. It was his fault Ethel was with him;

he'd been the one that had talked her into selling her house and moving there with him – with *them*… him and Karen. Still, it had not taken much convincing. She had jumped at the opportunity, and in her own sly way, she turned it around on him and made it sound as if it was her idea.

When he'd initially invited her, he had done it out of greed – fear of not being close to his mother, fear of not feeling her touch again even though her touch made his skin crawl and his gut hurt. He did it to provide a bridge between him and Karen, as he knew that the move would cause the rift between them to grow. He and Karen had already formed an imaginary brick wall between one another. He had not wanted that wall to expand. Had he known exactly how much the two had hated one another, he might have reconsidered… maybe.

Now, Karen was dead, and the only purpose Ethel served to him was through her demise. He would be well over two million dollars richer as soon as her frail little body slipped going down the stairs.

Yes, that was it, he decided. He'd wait a day or two and then wax the stairs as she slept. When she woke in the morning and began down the stairs, she would slip and tumble to her death. There was no way that she would survive such a fall; Bob knew it with all his being. She would be dead, he would inherit, and then he could put this place – this life – behind him.

As he approached the library door, he heard the distinct sound of laughter coming from the great room. It was Ethel, chuckling up a storm with another person – a man, perhaps. The voice sounded aged but chipper.

"Who in the fuck...?" Bob whispered, opening the door and stepping from the library.

Upon his entrance into the room, he saw Ethel look up at him from her seat – a grand, happy smile plastered over her face... her eyes kinder and lighter than he'd seen them in years – and an old man in a black suit with a matching derby hat atop his lap and a cup in his hand. McDougal.

"Robert, how good of you to join us," Ethel said. Her voice was exuberant, lively. "Please, do have a seat."

"How did you get in here?" Bob asked, staring McDougal in the eye.

"Why, I let him in, of course," Ethel answered. "This kind gentleman came knocking on the door. I imagine you don't get many visitors here, Robert, so I thought I would invite him in. I have most enjoyed his company."

"It's good to see ya," McDougal said, raising a cup of what Bob assumed to be tea. "Your mum is a charming woman."

"Oh, you make me blush!" Ethel chimed, laughing with a cackle that Bob had never heard her make before. "Please... an old lady can only handle so much."

"What's going on here?" Bob continued, ignoring his mother's unusual, flirtatious behavior. "I take it you're here because you considered my proposal on the house?"

"I have thought it over," McDougal said, smiling in a way that made Bob more uncomfortable. "Right now, however, I don't think is the time to discuss matters of business, chap. Why, I am having a delightful time with your mother, though. Where have ya been keeping this woman?"

Bob shook his head. He wondered if his face showed the amount of anger that was fueling his body, or if his natural good looks had somehow managed to conceal it.

He hoped that the anger showed.

"I'm sorry, Mr. McDougal, but Mom, if he is not willing to purchase this house for what I ask, he has no business being here."

"Oh, we have discussed all of that," Ethel said. The expression on her face told Bob that she was up to something, and it scared him. "No need to worry, Robert. With my money from the sale of *my* house back home, we can have this shack repaired and up to code in no time."

Fuck, he thought as he took a deep breath. *She told the little bastard about the money.*

"Mom, I really don't think I want to stay here all that long," he finally said, after having to pause to choose his words with upmost care. "You understand, I'm sure, that this house was meant to be for Karen and me, and without Karen, I don't want to stay here."

"Nonsense, Robert; you're speaking out of grief," Ethel told him, standing from her seat. "Why must you always be such a negative little twit?" She refilled her tea from a kettle on a cart and then returned to her seat. "This kind man has explained to me how he has been the caretaker of this house for generations, Robert. Isn't that wonderful? He knows this house in and out and can oversee the construction. He can see that it is restored to its original glory, but brought up to code with more *modern* conveniences."

"He sure can, Mom," Bob said, smiling coyly, "as soon as he signs the bill of purchase. Otherwise, no."

Ethel looked at McDougal, whose expression showed neither pleasure nor discomfort, and she shook her head.

"Ignore him," she told McDougal. They both sipped their tea. "His wife just left him. He's speaking out of grief, albeit misplaced."

"Ah, yes," McDougal remarked, nodding his head. "Yes, I knew something was amiss. I met the lass. She was pleasant on the eyes but had the personality of a viper."

"That's the one!" Ethel concurred lightly. "I told him this would happen, over and over again. But would the buffoon listen? Of course not. Instead, he just kept trusting her and loving her and letting her walk all over him. Just like I told him she would. A mother is always right about these things, you know."

"Oh, oh yes, I know," McDougal answered kindly. "I do know, indeed."

"Enough!" Bob interrupted, silencing his mother and McDougal. "Don't speak of me as if I'm not standing right here. Now, this is *my* home. No one else's, and I will decide who repairs it, who buys it, who oversees it, *and* who pays for it."

"Robert, now you're just being silly," Ethel murmured, but Bob ignored it.

"Most of all, I will decide who is *in* my home," Bob pursued.

"Oh, come down from that tree before you fall and hurt yourself, Tarzan," Ethel continued, laughing lowly at her own comment. "You're no king. Look at you; you've gone to waste. Piss in a bucket; that's what you are. Be a *man* for a change. Stop acting like a spoiled little boy."

"Ya know, I cannot understand it, my lady," McDougal said, directing Ethel's attention. "If I were out here alone, I would rather enjoy the companionship of visitors." Bob's stare met his. He watched as McDougal's eyebrows fell crooked, his eyes narrowing. "Who knows what I could teach your son about this house, if only given the opportunity."

"Then it is settled," Ethel said, chiming in with a tone that

Bob sorely recognized as the *I have made the decision for the house* tone from his childhood. "You shall be our guest for the next few days as you assess the house, with Bob overseeing of course, and you can work with him to decide what needs to be done."

"Mom, I have made my decision," Bob said, raising his voice a notch higher.

"And I have made mine," Ethel said in yet another tone he recognized, and Bob fell silent. He remembered that tone and what it meant if he were to disobey it. His heart started to race at the memory; he felt clammy… sweaty. He looked to the floor and shook his head. "With Karen gone, there is a spare room, yes? He can stay there."

"Mom, you don't know what you're doing?" he whispered, but he knew his voice wasn't carrying enough for her to hear or understand.

"And surely, I shall decline," McDougal said. His words silenced both Bob and Ethel. "I know I must seem like a sad, lonely man to you fine Americans, but even though I am retired from here, I still have a life away from here. Ya see, I own a boat rental out at the docks. Three fishin' boats – all in use, all the time. Makes a nice retirement fund, I tell ya."

"At least you can stay for supper?" Ethel asked. Her eyes seemed to plead.

"No, me lassie. But once ya be settled in, I'd like to show

ya the town an' maybe buy ya a little bit o' supper." He smiled large and kept his eyes on hers. Bob knew what was happening here. He was asking Ethel on a date.

"Oh!" she exclaimed, blushing. "Why, Mr. McDougal, I would enjoy nothing more."

"Then it shall be," McDougal said, setting his cup down on the table and standing, placing his cane alongside his right leg. Bob had come to realize that the cane was more for show – for decorative purposes – as McDougal had no trouble with his walk or balance, no limp.

"I'll show you to the door," Ethel said. She stood once more and took his offered hand, escorting him to the front door. Bob stayed near the entrance to the library, watching. He watched as McDougal kissed Ethel's hand, donned his hat and tipped it to her, and exited with a laugh and a friendly grin. Ethel shut the door behind him and turned back toward Bob, beaming like a school girl after prom. "Such a wonderful, nice man he is."

Bob was still fuming. He held his silence and shook his head, showing his emotions in his spiteful eyes. He kept his eyes on her as she returned to her seat.

"He said he will be back tomorrow. You know, I think I will have *him* take me into town tomorrow for my shopping. Yes… I think that is a splendid idea. Do *you* think it is a splendid idea, Robert?"

Bob understood why Karen had hated his mother so much. She was a wicked, mean-spirited woman. She was manipulative, she was deceitful, and she was – once again – more valuable to him dead than she was alive. He refused to answer her question. He stood silent, fuming deep within his gut, wanting nothing more than to reach out for her, grab her around her little chicken neck, and strangle her until her eyes bulged from their sockets and her tongue protruded from her lifeless thin lips.

"I asked you what you think, Robert," Ethel continued, pushing Bob's buttons a little bit more. "You know the man better than I do. Well? Speak up already!"

"I think it's a fine idea," he whispered through gritted teeth. He couldn't believe what he was hearing, but if it would get both his mother and McDougal away from him for a while, it would be worth it.

"Fine then," she said, smiling the slim grimace that she seemed to reserve just for family. Standing, she told him, "It is getting late. You can finish your lunch for supper, seeing as you ate so very little of it earlier. It's in the refrigerator waiting on you. Mr. McDougal and I shared a snack together while you were shut away in the library, so I shall forego supper tonight."

"Just what all did you and McDougal talk about?" Bob asked her, following her to the foot of the stairs as she began up them.

"Not much," she said, not looking at him as she walked, ever so slowly. "He is an intriguing man though. I think, in time, you'll grow fond of him."

"In time, he'll be dead and in a grave, Mom!" Bob shouted back through an angst-driven tongue.

"Perhaps you're jealous of him, hmm?" she asked him from the top of the stairs as she stopped to look down upon him. "You don't like the idea of another man having your mother's attention, do you? But have you appreciated my attention while I've been here? I've been in your home less than a day, and all you have done is raise your voice to me. Well, I won't have it a moment longer. I'm going to retire to my room now, and until you have shown me that you appreciate my company, *especially* after having dragged me half way across the globe, I will be spending my time with people who do."

She turned from him and disappeared from view, walking to her assigned room and slamming the door shut behind her. Bob sighed, shook his head, and then grunted. She infuriated him; he reminded himself that this infuriation was only temporary now. She would not survive her stay with him long enough for her to transform this home into the hell he knew before Karen.

Bob was like many people in the fact that he often *thought* 'man, I could kill that person right now,' but he had never been the type of person that would have followed through on it. Yet, since

Karen's tragic but relieving death, the Bob that would never kill had gone away. He could feel the change in him, and he relished it.

Turning away from the staircase, he walked to the front door, opened it and stepped outside. He breathed in a deep breath of the cool, crisp air; it did not seem nearly as damp to him as it had when he had arrived. Perhaps, he thought, Karen had been the cause of all the rain too, because the morning after dumping her dead carcass into the water, the rain stopped.

This could have all been coincidence – Bob knew this – but he liked the idea of blaming Karen for the rain. It made the farmhouse seem like a better investment. Perhaps, he considered, the amount of rain would decrease now and his property value would increase, but that was all fantasy. He knew the rains were long-term, and so was the damage that it had caused and would continue to cause.

Leaving the porch, Bob walked onto the dirty, weedy nub of the hill that supported his farmhouse. The muddiness of it was beginning to dry out, and he wondered if new grass would ever begin to grow.

The boat's return was still a curiosity, he thought as he turned toward it, tied and docked by the shed. Although he was nearly a hundred percent certain that McDougal had discovered it and returned it to him – and that the old man was obviously up to no good, having done this – he climbed down the hill to the sheds and the rowboat. He looked at the knot around the rope's loop. It was skillfully tied – something McDougal was more than capable of doing. Not to mention, had the wind or water somehow magically led the boat back to its home, it would not have been able to tie it to the post.

He untied the rowboat and pushed it into the small boathouse where it belonged. As he placed it, he looked into it. The wood was still damp inside, and the rain water and blood had mixed, leaving the dampness a murky shade of crimson.

"Shit," Bob said, feeling suddenly light headed. He had counted on the boat being out to sea by now, undiscovered, and having plenty of time to have been fully cleansed by nature before anyone discovered it. Yet, here it was, bloody as hell, waiting for someone to come scoop out a vial full of DNA and test it. Then, people would know Karen was dead, and those people would question other people – like McDougal and Ethel. They would tell them that Bob had said Karen left him. Bob would immediately be the prime suspect and placed under arrest.

He didn't want to think any further than that. The thought terrified him. Then, the thought changed solely to McDougal, who had refused Ethel's invitation to stay the night, although he had shown a certain interest in her. That interest seemed forced and fake to Bob, but Ethel had bought it. Perhaps, Bob considered as he stared otherwise blankly into the bloody boat, McDougal had seen the blood and now he was going to the police to tell them of Karen's murder and that Bob had told him Karen had left him instead.

Panic hit him like a baseball bat to a ball, and when it hit, it was full left field. Bob found a bucket and a brush in no time flat and began scrubbing as if his life depended on it – as it likely did. He used dish soap and bleach that had been on a shelf in the shed for untold years, but it was still active and seemed to be doing the trick. Within twenty minutes time, there was no trace of Karen's blood anywhere that he could see... but what if he missed something? A crack in the wood, perhaps, or a single drop of blood on the seat, or on a plank – or anywhere for that matter...

The panic rose instead of decreasing. Bob was white as a sheep as he dragged the boat onto the bank a few feet away from the boathouse. Then, he took an old towel and dried away the water from its bath. He walked into the shed and found a gas can and a box of matches and immediately began to douse the rowboat with gasoline until the can was empty. He took a few steps back and then struck a match. Fire ignited at its tip and he threw the match into the boat. His eyes lit up like a child's on the Fourth of July. The boat exploded into a mass of red, yellow and orange flames, with black clouds of smoke pluming up from the gasoline, wafting high into the evening sky. The smoke gave the sunset a fiery effect.

He watched the rowboat burn until it was nothing but char and the fire had nothing left to roast, flickering out into smoke and faint embers while the sun disappeared and the moon took its place. He doused the charred remains with several buckets of water, washing as much as he could away. Then, he decided he would check the spot again in the morning, under the sunlight, to ensure that no further incriminating evidence remained.

Not wishing to return to the house quite yet, as he was still frustrated with his mother's self-placed entitlement within *his* home, Bob walked to the water, took off his shoes and socks, and stepped into it. It was cool and refreshing. Even though it was fall, it wasn't cold. In fact, he thought it was just right. It felt good – relaxing and relieving. He looked around, glanced back to the house. The light to his mother's room was off; she was likely sound asleep, and there was no one else around.

"Why not?" he asked and took off his shirt, throwing it to the ground behind him. He set his glasses atop the shirt and then removed his pants and boxers. Once stripped, he stepped into the cool water, walking against it for several feet until it came up to his chest. The ground beneath his feet felt a little slimy and mushy, squishing between his toes. He looked up to the moon and closed his eyes, letting it bathe him in its light as the water bathed him in its cool and salty greatness.

Small waves of water crashed against his nipples, teasing

him with an electric sensation that cruised through his body, ending with a throb at the head of his penis. He had not intended to become turned on by his swim, but his old friend had come out to play, and so he began to entertain it.

Bob looked at the moon as he serviced himself, until he had reached the brink of his orgasm, clenching his teeth, sucking in a breath, and clamping his eyes shut as he fired his rifle into the sea.

He smiled and relaxed from the release, letting his body float a bit further into the water. He then wondered if this act was the very reason sea water was so damn salty. Perhaps, he thought, that was how naval sailors got off. Instead of interacting with one another, they just spilled it out over the ship, letting it drizzle into the water, salting it for generations to come.

"Maybe *that's* why they call them seamen," he said in a chuckle.

It was a better thought than the alternative, he thought. He had a few gay friends back home, and he truly appreciated them, but the one time Karen had tried slipping a finger *down there* on him, he thought the burn would never end. He could not imagine making a habit of that.

Pulling himself further into the water, he allowed it to fully submerge him. He held his breath under there for a long moment, enjoying the cool, crispness as it cascaded over him, cleansing him from the trials of the day. He resurfaced, smoothing his hair behind him, and wiped the wetness from his eyes. Now, with his back turned to his home, he looked toward the vastness of water and the night sky. The stars were brilliant, shimmering by the thousands, far away and further illuminated by the glow of the nearly full moon. The vision of the sky was mirrored over the top of the water, rippling with its fluid motion. It was a remarkable sight, and Bob took the time to thoroughly take it in. He had seen immaculate skies back home in Deerborne, but never like this – never with this watery view. With the moonlight and the stars reflection against the water, the effect was doubled, further celebrating the mystification of a universe that he understood little about but appreciated nonetheless.

The burning of the boat and the images of Karen's blood were nothing but dim memories for him right now, and he had filed them away to the back of his mind, impossible to be accessed under such a magical sky.

Keeping his gaze on this mystical reflection against the water, he further relaxed. He was lost in it – lost in its amazement – and he felt himself beginning to grow erect once more. Yet, it felt strange to him. It felt like a pulsating growth, instead of a nice steadily swelling erection. It felt as if something were sucking on it.

Looking down, through the glow of the moon, he could see into the water enough to see a head just below its top, bobbing as it sucked his cock.

Jolting back in terror, he reached down and grabbed the head, pulling it up from the water and off his cock. The face looked at him and licked her lips. It was more bone than flesh, skull showing at the jaw and seaweed blending in with her hair. He recognized the face – recognized *her*. He'd seen her before – in photographs with her old army flame and beside his bed when he woke in the early morning. It was Louise... the cocksucker that Longfellow spoke so highly of in his journals.

"Hey... handsome..." Louise whispered in a raspy, forced tone. Then, she pursed her thin blue lips and tried to kiss him.

Bob shrieked and kicked the creature away, back into the water. Then, turning toward his property, he swam as hard and fast as he could. Through the dark of night, it was faint at first – the dark hill with the dark house, only three lights on inside to help illuminate it. He did not look behind him; instead, he swam as fast as he could, kicking up as much water behind him as possible. He was halfway there now – halfway home. He could almost smell it. Yet, as his land came into clearer view, he stopped swimming and froze. Several silhouettes were at the bank of his property, as if they were looking out at him – still, motionless, awaiting his return. He allowed the water to drift him closer so that he could see who it was. He feared the police, but as he remembered the creature behind him, he feared worse than that.

He put a hand down below and grabbed himself, ensuring that everything was still intact – which it was.

Glancing behind him, he looked for Louise, but he could not see her. With any luck, she was gone. Looking ahead again, as he drifted closer and closer with the soft pushes of the water, he could still see the beings at the foot of his property. They came into clearer view – lit up by the full moon and starry sky. They were all looking at him, just as he looked at them. Only, they were stone-faced, while he knew his face was wretched in terror.

Bob swam to the right, toward the shed and boathouse, where he felt like he had a fighting chance of finding a weapon. This forced him to swim away from the area of ground where he had thrown his clothes and glasses, but even though his vision was impaired, it was the least of his worries. He could still see at a distance; it was close-up that blurred for him.

If he went for his clothes, he would be swimming right to the group of creatures, and that was exactly what they seemed to want. After all, they were waiting for him right beside his clothing.

There were two options here. The boathouse itself was the less attractive of the two, as it was open in the front and the back with no door on either side. There were shelves inside on either wall, and on those shelves were some tools, additional oars, and other possibly useful goodies. Yet, the moment he entered it, he would risk being seen by the creatures, and that felt like a rather terrifying risk to take.

The shed was the second option. It had one door around the front – something he could not safely access. There were also two windows, one on either side of the two walls. Inside the shed were plenty of items that he could use to defend himself, but getting to them would be the problem. As the door was off limits, he could chance trying one of the windows. If the windows were locked, he was screwed.

Deciding the enclosed shed was his best choice, Bob swam to it and stepped onto the murky land behind it. He glanced over toward the creatures; they were still gazing out into the water, as if unaware that Bob had swum on past them. This pleased him and gave him a little hope as he walked to the window and tried to lift it.

It was locked, just as he had feared. He cursed under his breath and then started around to the other window, which he also learned was locked.

Now on land, Bob had an additional option presented to him. He could try and hoof it up the hill, unnoticed, and take shelter safely in his home. The problem with this option was that it would have forced him to run right past the creatures, and they would likely notice him and follow him to the house. Once they knew he was inside, they would surely beat down the door to get to him.

"You were right, Karen," he whispered as he stepped back into the water and waded quietly toward the boathouse. "This place fucking sucks."

He had to chance the boathouse. Even if he could barricade himself safely in his home, he couldn't risk the run up the hill without a weapon. He had to find something to use to defend himself with, and so the boathouse was his last resort. At least without a boat in it, there was plenty of room for him to move around while he hunted.

He entered through the back. There was an upward slope and a docking post ahead at the front entrance. Without his glasses and shrouded in darkness, he found that he couldn't make heads or tails out of the items on the two long, narrow shelves on either side of him. Bob lifted a hand to graze over the first shelf, immediately slicing his finger on a sharp and unprotected hunting knife. He winced in pain and nearly screamed, but he held the urge within as he brought his finger to his mouth and suckled it. Blood was running thick and rapidly, dripping down his hand and into the water around his waist.

This was the second hand Bob had injured in a matter of days, and he was well aware that he only had two of them. Still, as much as the new injury hurt, he couldn't dwell on it. To sterilize the wound – as he had no idea whether or not the blade that cut him was rusty – he dipped his hand into the salty water, wincing from the pain. After a moment of this, he reached again to the shelf and grabbed hold of the hunting knife – more carefully this time – and walked to the front entrance of the boat house.

Peering out to his land and house, he could no longer see the creatures on the shore. Relieved, he sighed. He considered he had imagined them – hallucinated them – but that was unlikely. He knew what he'd experienced on his swim, and he felt lucky to still have his dangly bits.

More so, he knew it wasn't whether or not the creatures were gone. It was a matter of where were they.

Like a bubbling gurgle, he heard the water from behind him splash. Slowly, he turned around and looked down. With wild eyes wrapped in the shock of horror, Bob looked into the gaze of one of the creatures. The creature's head protruded through the water, almost grinning at him as it stared. Then, beside it, up rose another gruesome head, followed by another.

Somehow, he though as he backed out of the boathouse, they had found him. Bob felt the wound on his hand; it was still bleeding. They hadn't simply found him; they had trailed him. Sniffed him out by the product of his own carelessness. Continuing to back away, finally stepping onto his land, he watched more and more of the creatures arise – each appearing more grotesque than the last. Momentarily, he was thankful he wasn't wearing his glasses. He couldn't begin to imagine how hideous they were when viewed through sharper eyes.

"You're some fuckin' *ugly* motherfuckers," he told the creatures, but as one of them growled a reply, he decided against hanging around for further engagement.

As swiftly as his feet could carry him, he left his belongings where they lay and hurried out of the boathouse and up the hill to the farmhouse, pushing his way through the front entrance. Chaotically, he managed to close the door and secure it. With no time to waste, he went to the kitchen and ensured that exit-way was locked tight as well. He set the knife from the boathouse down on the counter as he took a breath.

"This can't be real," he muttered to himself as he left the kitchen, traveled through the dining room, and turned up the stairs. On the second floor, he kept silent, not wishing to wake his mother. He was scared, soaked, and naked, and through the combination of the three, he was freezing. He needed warmth and clothing... he needed a place to hide.

In his bedroom – what was Karen's bedroom – he ventured to the bathroom and took the fluffiest towel in the room, wrapped himself in it, and dried his body.

In his old room, he dressed, found his spare pair of glasses, and sat on the end of the bed, trying to still his shaky hands and calm his frenzied nerves. Sitting did not work. He stood and returned to his wife's old room, where he walked to the far window that overlooked the water and the two outbuildings. Through what light the moon provided, he saw no further traces of the creatures that he'd just encountered. They were either still floating in the water within the boat shed or wandering the grounds – perhaps encircling the house, looking for a way to enter.

Bob stepped away from the window and swallowed. He had to find safety… he had to find somewhere to hide – somewhere that he could barricade himself away from these disgusting beings.

There was one area of the house that did not have a window and was not near one of the entrances. That place was the basement, and so Bob fled the bedroom, rushed down the hall, practically flew down the stairs, and bolted around to the basement door. He opened the door and reached for the light switch. Dim light illuminated the top of the stairs, but a few steps down everything seemed a little brighter.

He pushed forward, shutting the door behind him as he hurried down the stairs and into the basement.

Realizing that he had left his knife – his method of defense – on the kitchen counter, Bob groaned and tugged at his hair. He had to find something else; there was no way in hell he was going back upstairs right now. In a frantic search, he hunted his surroundings until he found a tire iron, a flashlight, and a dark corner to hide in.

Even with a weapon in hand, Bob feared the worst. He knew they were coming for him. He could feel it. They had his scent now – the scent of his blood – and somehow, he just knew they would get into the house and find him. When they did though, he would be ready… he and his tire iron.

There was a sudden noise that distracted him from his thoughts of bravery – a distinct thump from right above him. Surprised by this noise, he stood from his crouched position and swung the tire iron upward toward the sound. Clumsily, the tire iron connected with Bob's forehead, rendering him unconscious and sending him back down to the floor.

Day 6 – Bob

When he awoke, it was by the light piercing into his eyes from the desk lamp. His head was killing him. It throbbed with a headache from Hades.

It took him a moment to realize that he was sitting in the chair at the desk. That he was surrounded by books and journals and was no longer in the basement. *Impossible*, he noted as he tried to stand. The sudden movement worsened his headache and he returned to his seated position, hoping for the pain to pass. After a moment, it subsided enough for him to stand and stay on his feet.

He looked around, surveying his surroundings. The books, the desk, the objects scattered here and there… everything was just as he remembered when he was last here, but he did not remember being in here last. He remembered being in the basement, and he remembered those creatures – those hideous beings – that had come for him during his swim last night.

Something peculiar was afoot, and Bob did not like it at all.

The last thing he remembered… a sound… a thump coming from right above him. That would have been the downstairs bathroom. He remembered hearing the sound and then – like an idiot – swinging the tire iron upward and whacking himself on the head.

So, he passed out – in the basement – and awoke in the library. *Makes perfect sense,* he thought as he shook his head. Perfect sense, like running up the stairs from a knife-wielding killer or locking oneself in a deep freezer just to see how much air could be trapped in there too.

Someone had moved him, or else he had the worst case of sleepwalking he'd ever heard of. Either way, it was unnerving.

As he walked to the door, Bob realized he was also drowsy, on top of having the headache. He needed coffee and aspirin, or at least a shot…

He turned on his heels back toward the desk and opened the drawer. Lying therein was his magical bottle of whiskey. He still could not explain how the bottle seemed to refill itself; perhaps it was enchanted, as it was currently full again. He removed the lid and took a heavy swig. As the delicious liquor swarmed through his insides, he felt the headache begin to ease, and his drowsiness seemed to wane as well. Before he knew it, he had drained the bottle a third of the way and felt so much better than before. He replaced the lid and put the bottle back into the drawer for another time.

"Maybe that magic fuckin' fairy will come fill you up again

for me," he said as he turned from the desk and once more approached the door. Just before grasping the doorknob, he stopped and listened. He could hear voices coming from the great room – the sounds of his mother and McDougal.

Ethel was laughing. It was a laugh that Bob knew so well – exuberating false excitement, likely over drivel that she'd either not understood or hadn't truly found humorous.

"You tease!" she chided, loudly. Bob shivered. "Oh, you wait until I get my hands on you!"

That was when Bob decided to open the door. When he did, he wished he hadn't, as his mother was chasing McDougal around one of the sofas – both giggling like schoolchildren.

All it took to end the commotion was Bob clearing his throat.

"Oh," Ethel said as she and McDougal came to a standstill. "Robert." Her voice drifted from lively to one filled with disdain. "I see you're finally awake and ready to once more join the living."

Bob's mind went immediately to waking up in the library and his suspicions fell on the two people in front of him. He stared at them, wondering which of them had moved him from the basement. They were both older and frail. Bob was a large guy with a good build. It would have taken both of them, especially getting him up the basement stairs. Likely, it was a joint conspiracy, and he wanted a confession.

"So, which of you did it?" he asked them with as calm a tone as he could muster.

"What do you mean, dear?"

"Which one of you moved me into the library? Or was it both of you? A joint effort?"

"Really, Robert, dear... You were up and down all night long. I heard you go to your room, and then down to the basement, and then I heard you go into the library where you finally passed out. You should take it easy on the alcohol. Why, I can smell it on your breath from here."

The goodness that he had felt from that drink of scotch evaporated away. His mother had a way of biting into him, and she was doing a damn fine job of it now. First, she was trying to make it out as if he was drunk, but he wasn't. He was awake. Not drunk. Secondly, she really expected him to believe that he had moved himself into the library, when he knew damn well that he had been unconscious. She took him for a buffoon, and he couldn't wait until she was dead.

"It's good to see ya this morning, Mr. Granger," McDougal told him before he could respond to Ethel. "I've just come to take your mother into town for a bit o' shopping, and then a spot o' tea over some food. Would ya care to join us?"

The look in McDougal's eyes read something; Bob

couldn't tell what it was. He didn't trust it though. McDougal was up to no good; that much was for certain. An invitation from him felt to Bob like a soul-binding contract with the Devil.

"I'll pass," Bob replied. He admitted to himself that he needed time without his mother in the house – time to figure out what the hell was going on and what those things were last night. How was Louise – that horny woman from the journals and photos – still alive after all of these years? He had a good feeling that the answers he needed would be in the library, and he now needed those answers like he needed air. "I have some things I need to take care of around here."

"Well, certainly, but I thought it would be a good opportunity for ya."

"What do you mean?" Bob was curious.

"Ya said your lovely wife has run off to the city. Well, we will be in the city. Perhaps we can find her for ya... patch things up." McDougal grinned and Bob swore it was the grin of Satan incarnate. Goosebumps trickle his skin.

"I'm sure by now she's caught the first available flight back to the states."

"Well... only time will tell, right?" McDougal smiled again. Bob did not like the way the words rolled off his tongue.

"If Bob's been drinking this early too often, I can understand now why she left him." Ethel looked him over. "You're becoming your father right before my very eyes, and it just kills me." She sighed, feigning exasperation, and took her purse from the table by the stairs. "If you need us, we'll be gone quite a while. You'll simply have to make do."

"That's quite a lump on your head," McDougal noted as he led Ethel to the door. "It looks a bit painful. A knot like that could cause delusions if you're not careful. You should rest. Have some tea."

"Sage advice from a caretaker," Bob replied and decided it was time to ask an affirmative question. "Sounds like advice a doctor would give."

"Yes... perhaps a doctor might give that advice."

"You said you've been a caretaker here for a while. Did you ever work for Doctor Longfellow?"

"Doctor Wilfred Longfellow died over a century ago," McDougal told him. "How could I have possibly been employed here during his time? Gracious... do I look *that* old?"

"Robert!" Ethel scolded. She walked up to him, took his hand, and smacked it hard.

"Ow!" he shouted, jerking his hand away.

"How dare you insult this poor man," she continued, walking back to McDougal, where she placed a hand atop his shoulder. "You should be ashamed of yourself." She looked at McDougal and added, "Let's leave this buffoon to his liquor and accusations."

Bob wanted to hurt him – both of them – and they would each have their turn. McDougal was proving to be a problem, and he had to go away. Disappear... owning a dock and three fishing boats could prove to be dangerous work. An old man like him could easily be lost at sea, he figured.

McDougal, Bob thought, had already served his purpose. He'd let Bob know what needed to be done on the house and how much money it was going to set him back. McDougal, himself, was a relic as useless as dinosaur dung and was needed no longer. As for Ethel – a part of Bob loved his mother, but a greater part of him wanted her dead... needed her dead. With her gone, he'd have enough money to kiss this house and its watery surroundings goodbye. Better yet, with Ethel *and* Karen out of the picture, he could truly begin anew – start a fresh, exhilarating life filled with fast cars, expensive hotel rooms, and more pussy than he could eat. He'd be living the highlife; he just needed to put his plans into motion.

Yes, he could feel their times – the times for Ethel and McDougal to meet their maker – grow closer with every insinuation that came out of McDougal's mouth and with every cutting comment that Ethel spewed at him. Suddenly, Bob was riddled with excitement.

"Stay out as long as you want," he told his mother and her

escort as they stepped outside. He heard Ethel say *ciao* as the door closed behind her. She thought the use of the word made her sound cultured, but Bob knew better. She'd never studied the French language a day in her life.

He waited at the closed door, watching them through the small windowpane until McDougal's vehicle was no longer in view. Then, he went to the kitchen and reclaimed the knife he'd left in there last night – amazed that it was still there. He carried the knife up to Ethel's room, where he cut halfway through the heels on each of her shoes. In his vivid imagination, he could see her putting on her shoes tomorrow – likely for some something or other with McDougal – and starting down the stairs when a heel breaks right off. It would be oh so tragic as she tumbled down the stairs, desperately trying to prevent the inevitable – crashing down to her death with a broken neck. The only criminal: a faulty shoe. Perhaps not even faulty. Just worn.

Or carelessness... they could blame it on Ethel's carelessness as she rushed downstairs in anticipation of her new beau's arrival.

Bob stopped fantasizing over it, as he caught himself laughing somewhat like a maniac. He placed his focus back on the sawing of the heels and then made sure to reposition each of her shoes just as she had left them, lined up beneath the raised bottom of the old crib. Although he was no longer chuckling, he was still smiling.

Leaving her room, he considered his plan of action for tomorrow. He would have to be out of range if she cried out for him – in case she survived the fall – and even if he heard her, he'd still need to be far enough away to give her time to finish dying before he could reach her.

Perhaps, he could be outside in the shed, he thought. Then he went pale.

He'd been so distracted with plotting his mother's demise that he'd forgotten about the creatures outside last night. The ones that rose up from the water inside the boat shed. The one that tried to suck him off during his swim. It made no sense to him – especially seeing Louise. She should have been long dead. In fact, according to Longfellow's journals, she *was* long dead… and long alive, too. That would have made her…

"A fucking zombie," he whispered and felt his mind swirl. While it sounded impossible to him, he had no other explanation and the journals only helped to reinforce his proclamation.

At the bottom of the stairs, Bob returned to the library and carried three of the boxes from the far shelf to his desk. He sat and immediately began digging through one of the boxes. He wasn't sure exactly what he was looking for, but when he found it, he'd know it… he was certain of it.

At the bottom of the third box, he finally found something

of interest. It was a newspaper clipping – yellow and brittle. It showed a picture of a boat's remains and held the caption *Doctor Wilfred Longfellow Lost at Sea.*

The article explained that witnesses called Longfellow's sudden disappearance a suicide, and that he had intentionally blown up the boat that he was on – in broad daylight and in front of a crowd of dozens watching from the dock. The reporter stated that Longfellow had become a secluded shut-in following the mysterious disappearances of his wife, niece and nephew. Although it didn't mention when, the article went on to explain how Longfellow – one of the area's most esteemed doctors – had suddenly given up his profession with no explanation to his patients and, more or less, disappeared from the public eye.

The article ended with the news that searches for Longfellow's body had officially ended after three days, and he was pronounced dead and lost at sea. To Bob's dismay, there was no photograph of Longfellow, himself.

In the next box, he found a sale note for the farmhouse. It was dated two weeks after Longfellow's death, and yet something about it caught Bob's eye. He took one of Longfellow's journals and compared an entry to the bill of sale. The lettering of the house's new owner's signature matched perfectly with Longfellow's handwriting in his journals.

While it could have been merely a coincidence, Bob knew

it had to have been much more than that. He couldn't explain it, but somehow – deep inside – he knew Longfellow had purchased his own house, but under an alias.

"But that makes no sense," he whispered, shaking his head and stuffing everything back into their boxes and shelf spaces. "Why the hell would he stage his own death, just to buy his own house back?"

Longfellow must have been in some sort of trouble, he figured as he took the scotch from the drawer and took a deep, long shot. Someone, somehow, must have gotten wind of what he was doing in the cellar, and with his secret threatened, he had faked his own death. Certainly though – if that had been the case – he wouldn't have risked living in his old home anymore.

Every new bit of information he learned from this library seemed to somehow top the previous bit in both mystery and impossibility. Zombies? Impossible. Dying and then buying your own house? Impossible. Magic spells to raise the dead? Impossible. Countless murders in the house you just bought? Downright sobering.

"I need a whore," Bob said plainly and left the library. In the great room, he sat on the sofa and closed his eyes, trying to make sense of what he'd just learned. It was too much... just too much. Secret experiments, burning bodies, staged deaths... *reanimation*. He'd seen *Frankenstein*. He knew how this stuff went. Longfellow probably tried sewing body pieces together at one point or another too. Bob wouldn't have put it past him.

Popping his knuckles, he felt anxious. He stood and paced for a second or two and then returned to the library where he took the impossible refilling bottle of scotch and drank it down until there was nothing left. He looked at the bottle and grinned.

"Let's see you refill *that*, you crazy, fucked up bottle, you…" he slurred. Clumsily, he returned the bottle to its drawer and shoved it closed.

***

Drunk and a little horny in the middle of the day, he missed Karen – or at least certain *aspects* of her. After a good fight, he remembered how she used to let him fuck her brains out. Now, as he climaxed and splattered his chest and stomach, he thought of how he could have literally fucked her brains out now, through that hole in her eye socket from the screwdriver.

While the thought partially sickened him, it also made him laugh.

He took his mother's handkerchief from her bedside table and cleaned the semen from his body with it. Then, folding it just how she'd had it, he placed it back atop her bible and sat upright from his position on the bed.

Bob's clothes were scattered between the bed and the bottom of the stairs. He stood from the bed and began to gather his things, and by the time he reached the bottom of the stairs, he stood naked in front of the door with an arm full. He threw them all to the floor and opened the door, stepping outside.

There was no one around to see him, and the sun felt good against his skin. It was warmer out than he'd expected for a September day, and he was glad for it. He gazed up at the sky, enjoying the mix of blue with the white and gray of dusty clouds. Looking toward the sheds, he thought the water looked almost silver, and it moved in soft ripples that helped to further relax him.

Scratching his ass with one hand and his head with the other, Bob took in this secluded property that he could call his own. Then, he remembered how much he hated it – how much of a dump it was and how much it would cost to fix – and he spat hard to the ground.

He almost wished he hadn't burned the boat. The water looked more inviting to him than his own property… which, he considered, really sucked. He knew he could hop in his vehicle and drive off any time he wanted, and a drive was almost tempting.

Without the boat, he didn't want to go back in the water either, as he did not want to risk having another incident like last time. One blowjob from a zombie was one too many.

"I'm sick…" he thought, shaking his head and tugging at

his hair. "I'm crazy. I'm standing here, thinking about zombie head." He looked around his land, where the creatures had earlier been gathered. His clothes and glasses from his swim were still there, as if daring him to go and pick them up. He did not.

Instead, he looked off at the road, visible and passable, and he looked to the trees beyond. He thought of all of the empty structures and old decrepit buildings that he and Karen had seen on their drive in to this house.

There was nowhere here at the farmhouse for these *living dead* things to hide, but there were plenty of places *near* the farmhouse that would have sufficed as adequate zombie shelter.

Those things had come after him once. He didn't want them to show up again.

He went back inside, pissed, shat, and showered, and then he dressed in jeans, a t-shirt, and a jacket. With a black cap on his head, he put on his socks and sneakers and then grabbed an empty backpack.

In the basement, he took a flashlight, a tire iron, and a handsaw and crammed them into the bag. In the kitchen, he added a bottle of water, a sharp knife, a few large zipper baggies, and an empty coffee tin. Grabbing his keys, he locked up the house and walked to his car. With his bag in the passenger's seat, he cranked the vehicle and backed up, turning onto the road.

He drove slowly, looking in all directions as he passed

through thickets of trees and wetland. Bob was searching for signs of life… at least, reanimated life. He was seeking places to hide… anywhere that one of those creatures might have claimed as *home* when the sun rose.

He wasn't sure why he thought the zombies would hide and rest during the day. In the movies, they were out hunting brains and flesh all day and night long… Perhaps it was the fact that he'd not seen them out on his property during the day, so it at least made sense to him that if they weren't there, they had to be *somewhere.*

There was nothing that he could see through the thickets of trees that he passed. He'd have to venture through them on foot, and so he decided it best to continue onward to the ruined barns, houses and other structures he'd taken note of earlier and check them out first.

Just up the road were a barn and a small house that both looked suspicious to him. He parked the car a hundred feet or so away from the overgrown, marshy drive and hoofed it with his bag thrown over his shoulder. Each step was taken with caution; his breath released with silence.

From the edge of the drive, he looked up at the house perched on a tiny hill, like his house, only this structure was about half the size, missing most of its roof, and was shedding some exterior walls. It also appeared to be sinking. The barn at the foot of the hill down from the house was in even worse shape, although its tin roof seemed to be without as much damage as the house's shingled roof. Either way, both buildings had seen better days.

Instinctively, Bob approached the tiny damaged house first. Although his land seemed to have begun drying out, this ground was still heavily saturated, and his feet sank into the mud as he walked. He found the steps and porch to be made of wood, and the first step crumbled beneath him when he put his weight on it. Quickly, he fast-stepped it up to the porch, which creaked and buckled as he moved onto it.

He stopped and steadied himself, taking a deep breath before continuing. The door was only a few feet away from him, and he began toward it, wondering if he would fall through before reaching it. When he made it safely across, he took a breath of relief and reached for the knob.

He twisted it to the left… to the right. He jiggled it a bit. He shook it and tried to force it. Growing impatient, he pushed on the door while turning the knob… tried to budge it with his weight and shoulder. No matter what Bob did, he could not open the front door of this most certainly condemned house. It was, in fact, locked.

"You've got to be fucking kidding me," he grunted under his breath and rotated his head to pop his neck. "No one can be living here… Why the fuck would the door be locked? There's a fucking wall missing around the side, for Christ's sake."

Bob was dumbfounded, but instead of fighting with the door any further, he decided to walk around to the side of the house, where the missing portion of wall was. The opening was about three feet wide by about five feet tall. Large enough for him to practically just step through, and so he ducked and did. When he entered, he found himself in a dark room, only partially lit from the sun. He set his bag down on the rotted floor and dug for his flashlight. Finding it, he powered it on, took out the tire iron, zipped the bag closed, and hoisted it over his shoulder. With the new light, he looked at the room, seeing the front door just feet away from him. He could see that it was locked with both a twist lock on the knob and a bolt lock above it. It was, by far, the most ridiculous thing he'd ever seen, and he would have laughed had he not been in unfamiliar territory looking for undead creatures that likely wanted to eat him.

"I'm breaking and entering," Bob told himself, as if trying to convince himself to turn around and leave, but he knew that wasn't happening. "Then again… the wall *was* already open. Like an invitation."

He knew he shouldn't be talking, so he shut up and took in his surroundings. There was little to speak of in way of furniture. A couple of broken chairs, an old mud-ridden sofa, a table that was smashed in the center… junk. Trash. Nothing that had been touched in years.

This house was a single-story, and thus it had a hallway off to the right of the main room and a kitchen straight ahead. The kitchen, he believed, was an add-on like his, but it was much smaller and seemed almost claustrophobic. It was also disgusting, with the scent of decay wafting through it. The smell in the main room had been peculiar, but this was like rotting flesh and it made him want to be sick. He choked back his disgust and covered his mouth and nose with his forearm.

There were dead animals in the sink, on the small counter, and cut up chunks of them scattered between the old stove and a small table. At least, he assumed it was all dead animals. Blood, mold, skin, death... everywhere. Bob had to turn away and leave the room, as he could investigate it no further. It repulsed him to a point where it made him lightheaded, and so he hurried back to the front room and turned toward the hallway, which – even with the glow of his flashlight – seemed dark as hell.

There were two doors – one on either side of the hall – that had presumably been bedrooms. There was another door at the end of the hall facing him. That, he suspected, was the bathroom.

He decided to investigate the bathroom first. The moment he opened the door, he closed it again. The stench emitting from within was far worse than that in the kitchen, and he did not desire to see what produced it.

When his stomach felt normal again and he swallowed

down a knot in his throat, he looked to the door on his left and then to the one on his right. He chose the one to his right and, as he wielded the tire iron with one hand, he tucked the flashlight into his armpit and grasped the doorknob with his other hand.

The room was musky and also smelled of rot, but it wasn't nearly as strong as the bathroom or kitchen. Holding his flashlight, he shined the beam across the room, where he saw bodies lined up on the floor, laying as straight as they could be. He shined the light onto each face and each was, beyond a doubt, dead.

Disgusted, mortified, and feeling that sick feeling in his stomach again, he turned from the room and pulled the door to behind him. Leaning against it, he let out a half sigh, half sob as he tried to gather his bearings. He had to control himself. He couldn't be fooled. He knew that those people in the room *looked* dead, but they weren't... not really. Two of the faces he'd glanced had popped out of the water when he was hiding in the boathouse.

He'd found what he was looking for, and now he had to deal with it. Bob shook off the willies and wiped a hand across his face. Then, tapping his foot nervously on the hardwood floor, he looked at the door across from him.

Stepping over to the door, he opened it, now prepared for the worst – prepared to see more of the same.

Inside this room, he found that he was right. There were more undead creatures lying in rest in a perfect line on the floor.

The house seemed to be more than just a hiding place for the zombies. It was like a nest, Bob thought. Or a hive. A hive of brain-hungry bees.

This was his chance to eliminate his zombie problem all at once, he realized as he tightened his grip on the tire iron. He'd lucked out by checking this house first, and he could destroy every last one of them before they had a chance to seek him out again at his farmhouse.

As he wielded the tire iron above one of the sleeping bodies, he considered what would happen if he woke it instead of immediately killing it. Would it scream out in pain, alerting the other slumbering zombies and causing them to wake as well? If that happened, he knew he would be a goner.

But he knew he had to chance it. He couldn't live with the living dead wandering around his property every night. It was creepy and it just wasn't a good selling point for the house.

He set the flashlight down and lifted the tire iron high above his head with both hands. Careful to not conk himself on the head this time, he slammed the tire iron down onto the head of the nearest slumbering zombie instead. The creature's head collapsed from the impact, like a rotted pumpkin, and the zombie did not wake up. Nor did any of the others. He walked to the next body in line and repeated the process, receiving the same response. At the third zombie, he kicked it to see if it would stir. When it didn't awaken, he kicked the one next to it. It, too, stayed in rest. Bob was baffled.

"This is weird as fuck," he whispered, and he believed that Lady Luck was finally shining down on him. Kneeling down, he set his bag down beside him and took out the handsaw, the coffee tin, and the baggies. First, he sawed off the head of zombie number three and secured it inside two of the baggies, as the baggies were just a bit too small for it to fit into only one. Then, he took out the knife and sliced down the headless body, using the handsaw to cut through the bones. He placed the heart in the coffee tin and bagged the hands. He did the same to the fourth zombie, only he took just the brain with the eyeballs still attached instead of the entire head, along with a lung and a foot.

Once he had all of whatever it was that he needed, he continued down the line of remaining zombies and bashed their heads in with the tire iron, just as he had done with the first two. He recognized the last one. She was the one who had given him oral during his swim last night. Louise… He stomped his foot down hard onto her head, feeling it crush beneath his weight. It was satisfying to him.

"Suck on *that*," he told her and then spat on her.

In the room across the hall, he took only from the first one he approached – a male child – and claimed the head, hands and heart. Bob then destroyed the rest of them in the same fashion he had the others.

Once he had bagged his tools and all of the parts he'd collected, he could no longer zip the bag shut. Still, he managed to return to his car without losing a single piece, something for which he was proud.

The house, it seemed, was the mother ship – so to speak – and so he did not bother to inspect the barn. Even if he'd felt the need to, the hour was growing later and he needed to have everything back and hidden away before his mother and McDougal returned from their outing. Plus, he had to clean up. He had zombie goo all over him, and it stunk.

The ride back home went without incident. He carried his bag of goodies inside and straight down to the basement. There, he opened the door to the cellar and moved his collection down the narrow stairs, laying them out across the cold floor. One by one, he placed the heads, the hands, the hearts, the brain with eyes... bits and pieces of this zombie or that zombie. Stuff for him to study as he investigated the remaining journals and boxes of intrigue in the library to learn exactly what he bought when he purchased this house.

Once everything was debagged and organized how he liked, he shut them away in the cellar as he retreated to his room, where he showered and dressed.

* * * *

A knock at the door summoned Bob just as he was about to see if the magic liquor bottle had managed to refill itself. Leaving the library, he went to the front door and opened it. Two delivery men in uniforms awaited him with smiles.

"We have a delivery," the taller, skinny as a rail man said, looking at his clipboard. "A ton o' stuff from the States for Missus Karen Granger." He held his smile as he handed Bob the clipboard and a pen. "Sign yer name an' we'll get 'er unloaded."

Shit, Bob thought as he looked the men over. Part of him thought he'd canceled the delivery. It had been a whirlwind week since he and Karen had first arrived here, and he knew that *something* had slipped his mind. Now, he knew what.

He signed the papers on the clipboard and stepped aside as the delivery men began to unload the belongings from the Connecticut house into this one, cramming the large great room as full of furniture and boxes as it could possibly get. Within twenty minutes time, the van was empty and the delivery men departed. Now, Bob was faced with a disastrous mess – an overwhelming amount of stuff, much of which was Karen's. While they had sold off a lot of what they'd had inside the house in Deerborne, Karen had kept a storage unit full of stuff from her life before Bob. Furnishings, memories, clothing… anything and everything she'd inherited following the deaths of her parents. Bob had forgotten about all of this stuff, but apparently Karen had not, and now, here it all was.

"I think I hate her more now that she's dead than I did when she was alive," Bob noted as he read her name written across many of the cardboard boxes.

The delivery men had offered to carry everything down to the basement and cellar, but Bob hadn't allowed it. He'd insisted that everything would end up being down there forever if he didn't just face it and deal with it. Now, he was facing it and dealing with it just to hide the fact that he had zombie bits in his cellar.

Everything marked *Karen*, he carried into the small bonus room near the downstairs bathroom. He couldn't really consider it a guest room; the space was just too small. There, he stacked the boxes in neat-enough piles. Everything else, he either took to their respective areas of the house, or he dragged them down to the basement, *without* any help from the delivery men.

After dragging two sofas – one, a sofa bed – and a recliner down the basement stairs solo, he began to second-think sending away the help. He could have simply directed them to stay out of the cellar, and everything would have been just fine. But no. Bob was not the brightest when having to think on his feet; he knew this. He was more than aware.

Time passed by more quickly than he'd realized, and the

sound of McDougal's car pulling up the drive distracted him from his duty. He rested his hands on his hips as he caught his breath.

Within a moment, Ethel was at the door, barging in like she owned the place. She directed McDougal, who carried several bags, toward the kitchen, and then she stopped and stared at the mass of stuff in the great room.

"This isn't my stuff," she said and looked at Bob.

Bob cringed. "No... no, it's not. This stuff is my stuff and Karen's stuff from our Connecticut house."

"I thought I recognized that horrible lamp," Ethel told him, pointing at a lamp with green stripes and blue spots, seated on the floor by a stack of boxes. "That is the tackiest lamp I've ever seen."

"You gave us that," Bob replied with a smile. "For our fifth anniversary. Every time I see it, I think of you."

"All of this will have to go. Soon enough, the stuff from *my* house will arrive. My furnishings will look much more attractive here. You can put this junk in the basement, or maybe the attic... anywhere out of sight." She looked at him with the wicked grin that he loathed so much and scratched her chin. "Be a dear and help Mr. McDougal with the rest of the packages. We purchased some groceries, and I did a bit of other shopping as well. There are several items I'm eager to put away, so do hurry."

"You bought things?" Bob asked, suddenly realizing that

she was beginning to spend the money she'd gotten from the sale of her house.

"Oh, yes," she beamed. "New dresses, hats… a slew of new shoes. Out with the old, in with the new, as they say."

Bob felt sick again. All of his hard work, sawing through the heels of her shoes… Now, she was planning on throwing them all away to make room for new shoes that were not sabotaged. His plan was foiled; his efforts, for naught.

"New shoes… how great," he muttered. Then, he tried to divert this new effort by asking, "Don't you have a ton more clothes coming from the States with all of your furniture and stuff?"

"Oh, yes," she admitted. "A great deal of clothing. They would only let me carry so many bags on the flight, you know. But… we'll go through that hoard of stuff when it gets here. Now, quit dawdling, Robert, and go help Mr. McDougal."

Bob rolled his eyes as he walked by her and out the door, to McDougal's car where he gathered as many bags as he could in one trip.

It took him three more trips, along with two extra trips for McDougal.

Eventually, the groceries were put away and all of Ethel's new belongings were carried upstairs to her room. She insisted that Bob bring with him a trash bag, and pair by pair, she chucked her old shoes away. Three dresses, two old hats, and nine pairs of her panties also ended up in the bag – much of the clothing she'd brought with her.

"Are you sure you want to throw all of these clothes out?" Bob asked her, gazing into the bag with bewilderment. "These shoes look like they're still in good shape."

"Good shape or not," Ethel explained, "they reek of my former life in the States, and that's the last thing that I want. Now, go entertain my guest. I believe he's in the kitchen, preparing supper."

"Preparing supper? It's only mid-afternoon."

"Mr. McDougal's eyes aren't as young as they used to be. Why, I imagine he can barely see at all once nightfall comes. Surely, you don't want him driving home at night, blurry eyed and nearly blind?"

Actually, he thought, fighting a grin, *that sounds fantastic*!

"No," he said, shaking his head. "Of course not. I'll just consider it a late lunch and have a snack later."

"Hurry along now." Ethel waved her hand at him and began to admire her new belongings.

Dragging the trash bag full of clothes and shoes behind him down the stairs, Bob cursed his mother through the privacy of his thoughts. He had been so close to being rid of her. Now, because of McDougal and their shopping venture, his plan was a failure.

He'd have to find another way to kill her and still manage to make it look like an accident.

He could always just *push* her down the stairs, he figured, but he knew that would be somehow suspicious – and cliché. It had to be unique, but believable. There were so many ways to kill somebody, but Bob figured there were a lot less ways to kill somebody *and* get away with it.

He'd managed to get away with Karen's untimely death… so far. Her body was lost forever at sea. He didn't have to worry about anybody ever finding her, as by now, she was fish food. Likely, no one would start looking for her either. She had no other family, nor had she any friends that she was close to.

"Would ya mind setting the table?" McDougal asked him as he stepped into the kitchen. Already, three things were cooking on the stovetop and something else was in the oven. McDougal looked like a butler-chef, dressed in his typical suit with a white apron tied around his waist and a chef hat replacing his Derby.

"Nice hat," Bob muttered, holding back a laugh as he took three plates from the cupboard.

"We picked it up this afternoon during lunch at this quaint bistro," McDougal replied with chipper glee. "A lovely lady, Ethel is. What a joy she must'a been raisin' ya."

"Oh, yeah…" Bob shuddered, recalling his tormented childhood with his overbearing mother. "Joyful as shit."

Bob set the table, pulling open the curtains in the dining room to allow some daylight to enter. He took a seat at the side facing the window, intending his mother to his right and McDougal to his left. They would be happy with the placement, he figured, and he could keep an eye on them both during supper. He was finding McDougal less trustworthy the more that he knew him. The man had already shown his dark side to him more than once through shrewd and intentional *slips of the tongue*. Bob wasn't an idiot, and he suspected that the former caretaker likely knew his fair share about the information in those journals and boxes. He couldn't have been a caretaker here for so long and *not* know something about those undead-now-dead creatures. If anyone could answer his questions, it was McDougal.

As for his mother, Bob didn't trust Ethel either. She'd moved in, which he'd invited, but she'd taken over since her first step into the house. Now that she had the money from her Connecticut home, plus what was left in life insurance payouts after Bob's dad's questionable death, Ethel seemed to have an aura about her that claimed to own the world.

Also, she was getting too close to McDougal, and he was showing too much interest in her. Worst of all, Bob thought, she was choosing McDougal over him. Bob had always been the main man in Ethel's life, even as a child. Now, this frail old man swooped in and swept Ethel right off her feet, and she was treating

Bob like crap. It made him more than jealous. It pissed him off.

McDougal brought out a tray of fresh biscuits, warm ham with a cherry drizzle over it, a bowl of boiled carrots, and a bowl of steamed cabbage. It was the first honestly fresh and home-cooked meal in this house, and Bob wasn't sure if he trusted McDougal enough to eat it.

Momentarily, Ethel joined them at the table, taking her seat to Bob's left, as intended. McDougal also did not question his placement at Bob's right. Bob assumed this made both people feel as if they were at the head of this table.

Ethel was the first to fill her plate, followed by McDougal and then, finally, Bob. He waited to taste until his mother and her guest had already taken a couple of bites of the food. When neither began to vomit or die, Bob finally ate. He knew that this had been a silly precaution, as why would McDougal poison food that he too was going to eat?

Still, Bob found it better to be safe than to be sorry.

Conversation was light at the table, covering irrelevant topics of the weather and what was considered fashionable to modern society. Bob wanted to discuss zombies and scientific experiments but decided against those topics while his mother was around. He needed to talk with McDougal in private, as Ethel would only ridicule him over the conversation and call her son a fool, shaming him.

Bob hated when his mother shamed him. He couldn't wait to kill her.

After supper, McDougal served a plum pie from the bakery and fresh tea. Once dessert concluded, McDougal and Ethel retreated into the great room where they shared flattering remarks over white wine. Bob opted out of wine and stepped into the library instead, where he discovered that his bottle had once again somehow magically replenished.

"I'm not even going to question it," he said as he pulled it from the drawer and took a large gulp. It was cold as ice and still burned like fire – just how he liked it. After another gulp, he returned the bottle to the drawer, deciding it best not to get drunk with McDougal still around.

After a moment of alone time, he stepped back into the great room to find Ethel escorting McDougal to the front door.

"Leaving so soon?" Bob asked, still wishing to question the old man in private this evening.

"It'll be dark soon," McDougal replied, putting his usual hat atop his head. He nodded at Bob, kissed Ethel's hand, and said goodbye. Ethel stood in the doorway, watching as he departed. Bob thought she looked like a school girl in love.

"What an exhaustingly wonderful day!" she exclaimed, shutting the door and looking at her son. "I'm simply beat. If you're not going to have any, I'm taking the rest of the wine up to my room and retiring for the night."

"Would you like for me to come tuck you in?" Bob asked her, remembering how she used to insist on it.

"Don't be ridiculous," she replied, taking the wine bottle and heading to the stairs. "I'm a grown woman, Robert. I can tuck myself in." Without another word, she ascended the stairs and disappeared to her bedroom.

Part of Bob was relieved, while part of him was saddened. He didn't want to have to do the uncomfortable things she would often make him do, but he still wanted to be needed. He didn't want to be written off because she'd formed an infatuation with some old kook.

Bob despised McDougal for the way that he had Ethel wrapped around his finger, but he needed him around. He had things to ask him that only he could answer… if only he hadn't run off so early. Bob didn't buy the bad eyesight excuse. Sure, McDougal was old, but as the man inspected the house with him earlier, his vision seemed about as good as it could be. Bob knew why the old man didn't want to be out here at night. It was obvious. McDougal knew about the zombies, and he wanted to escape before they could gobble him up.

Little did he know that Bob had already killed the zombies; there was no reason for him to flee.

With his mother in her room for the night and McDougal

unavailable for interrogation, Bob's thoughts turned toward his new collection of zombie parts in the cellar. He toyed with the idea of going down and collecting one to bring back up to the library. There, he could set it upon his desk and study it under better light.

Glancing out the picture window in the great room, he saw that the sun was setting and, shortly, night would be upon him. Last night, the zombies had played with him. Tonight, it was his turn to play with them.

Before moving into this house, he never would have entertained such a thought. Now, secluded in a money pit of a house on land no one could build or grow on, the idea of zombies was the most entertaining thing he could think about.

"I'm gonna examine me a zombie!" he sang as he practically skipped his way over to the basement door. "Fuckin' zombies…!"

Excited over the idea of examining a chunk of a dead zombie – even *he* had to question that phrase – Bob forgot his worries of jealousy over Ethel and McDougal and strolled down the basement stairs and over to the cellar door.

From all around and most prominently from above, he heard a great boom – the sound of thunder from outside. There was a rumbling quake like none he'd heard here yet, and Bob knew that it meant the rain was returning, and that it was going to be a hell of a storm.

When the thunder had faded out and he felt himself growing jittery, he returned his focus to the door and swallowed hard. Then, he heard what sounded like clawing coming from the other side. His mind could have been playing tricks on him, but that seemed unlikely. He knew what he'd heard, and it was the type of scratching sound that could have been made by a rat, along with numerous other things.

Things like zombies…

There were zombie body parts down in the cellar, and Bob was becoming a little paranoid. It was as simple as that.

Another great eruption of thunder made him nearly jump from his skin.

"Fuck it!" he shouted and opened the heavy cellar door.

A mouse ran out at him, speeding between his spread feet and disappearing somewhere into the shadows of the basement.

"Fucking shit!" Bob shouted, picking up his feet like he was dancing a jig and nearly falling over from the surprise. His heart felt like it was about to leap out of his chest. He took a second to calm himself and then he started down the cellar stairs.

The lights were still on from earlier when he'd laid out his new goodies, yet his goodies were not laid out quiet like they had been. A hand was at the foot of the steps. One of the heads had rolled away from the other. The brain with the eyes was a few feet from where it had been. There was a trail of slime between it and where Bob had earlier set it.

He would have blamed the mouse, but that critter had been only a portion of the size of the brain. There was no way it could have pushed or rolled it that far.

"Someone has been down here…" he whispered, looking at the scattered zombie parts. "McDougal." He breathed with sudden fury.

It made sense, he thought. McDougal could have come down here when Bob was helping Ethel throw away her old clothes and the shoes that he had worked so hard to sabotage. There had been plenty of time for the old man to scatter all of the pieces around, but it didn't make sense as to why he would have done such a thing to begin with.

A thump came from behind him and he turned to see the hand that was at the foot of the steps was now rested on the bottom step.

"What the fuck?" Bob whispered. Then, as if responding to him, the hand jumped upward by the force of its fingertips, leaping upon the next step. Bob stumbled backward, startled, and stepped on the hair of one of the two decapitated heads. Looking down at it, he watched as it hissed at him angrily and then snapped at the air with its teeth and jaw.

Bob let out a yelp and stepped back again to avoid being bitten. The head began to roll away from him, toward the steps.

His watched in utter disbelief as the head clamped onto the bottom step with its teeth and then thrust itself onto the next step. The head was a third up the stairs and out of Bob's sight before he finally stirred from the shock. At that point, the hands and the foot, along with the second head, were also pulling themselves up the stairs, leaving Bob alone with a few random parts and a brain with eyes that seemed to stare right at him. The lung and hearts were the only parts that didn't seem animated or functioning.

The brain and its eyes were the most singularly disgusting thing he'd ever seen. He sneered at it as it stared at him – wide-eyed... unblinking. The brain pulsated... It was hideous. Bob wanted to puke, but he realized that he had more pressing matters at hand. He had to stop the other appendages and the heads from reaching the top of the stairs. He had to seal them into this cellar until he could figure out – or at least begin to understand – what was going on.

As he climbed the stairs, he watched the head pull itself off the last step and onto the basement floor. Bob was too late.

In his rush, he tripped and nearly fell up the last few steps, but he managed to steady himself enough to lunge out into the basement, on guard and in pursuit of the runaway zombie bits.

To his left, he watched a hand inch away into the shadows by the washer and dryer. Straight ahead, the foot ducked beneath the basement stairs as a head was attempting to bite its way up the first step. In every corner, body parts moved and hid – blending with the darkness and clutter of the damp basement.

Lurching forward, he jumped for a hand… or a foot – he wasn't sure which one. It slipped away as soon as he made contact and then ran across the room on its fingers. Definitely a hand, he decided as he chased after it.

He could hear the storm outside grow with tremendous force. Its heavy winds rocked the house with their gusts, and for a moment, Bob stopped chasing the animated body parts and stood, worried that the house may collapse atop him.

The wind died down for the moment, and when Bob was convinced that he was not going to be toppled by an old, crappy farmhouse, he looked again for his scattered collection of zombie parts. Now, everything seemed to be in hiding. Nothing moved around and nothing could be seen.

"Fuck," he said in a grunt and took a deep breath. "Okay, you little shits. Enjoy your new home, because I'm locking you in this basement."

He knew he should have stayed down there and continued his search for them, but he needed a moment to collect himself and to survey the storm outside. Thusly, Bob hurried up the stairs and looked at the basement door. It was partially ajar, but he considered it could have been him that left it that way. Stepping into the great room, he closed the door behind him.

On the table near the stairs, he noticed one of Karen's leather pouches. She'd always called them her change purses, but Bob knew she kept her cigarettes in them also. Bob was fully against smoking. He'd seen the bad of it. But he had pieces of zombies running around in his basement and his nerves had been on edge since the moment he killed his wife – even more so since his mother arrived.

Curiously, he checked the leather pouch, finding two cigarettes and a lighter inside. He took one of the cigarettes and the lighter and stared at them in his hands. He'd never smoked a cigarette before. He wasn't even sure how to light one. But he knew that when Karen smoked, she was always less of a bitch and a little bit calmer than when she didn't. She'd hid the smoking from him for years now, but he'd always known. He could smell it on her... on her flesh and her clothes. On her breath and in her hair. He considered that smell as he put the butt of the cigarette in his mouth, struck the lighter, and lit it. He blew out the first puff without inhaling. Sniffing the air, he thought again of Karen. The smoke reminded him of her scent and, for a moment, he missed her.

He took another drag, inhaling this time. He coughed hard and quick, nearly collapsing to the floor from the sudden fire in his lungs.

When he could sort of breathe again, Bob stubbed the

cigarette out on the end table, deciding he never wanted to go through that again. Whatever high Karen had gotten from the nicotine just wasn't worth it to him.

What Bob needed to calm his frazzled nerves was a drink – a sip from his magical refilling bottle in the library.

As he approached the library door, he heard a knock come from behind him, accompanied by the sounds of thunder booming in the sky and heavy rain pounding against the windows and exterior walls of the house.

Someone was at the front door.

"What idiot would be out in this mess?" he huffed as he turned toward the door. Then, the answer became obvious to him. It was likely McDougal. The old man picked the strangest times to come by, but this time, Bob did not mind. He wanted to have a talk with McDougal… a *serious* talk.

His steps became quicker as he approached the door, and as he opened it, his vision was blinded by a great flash of lightning, and the sound of his mother screaming from her room upstairs filled his ears. He wanted to turn his head toward the stairs in regard to Ethel's screech, but as the lightning faded and his vision cleared, he found that he could not move. Temporarily paralyzed through shock and bewilderment, Bob stared at Karen, soaking wet, naked as the day she was born, and staring bitterly at him with her one good eye.

"You threw a screwdriver into my eye," Karen told him in a tone that made him shiver from head to toe, awakening him from his sudden paralysis and allowing him to take a frightened step back.

Part III

Then – 1: Chariot, Tennessee

She folded the shirts just the way that her boss told her to. They were neat and tidy, ready for the door to unlock and the shop to open. She looked around. Everything was spic and span for the new business day.

"It's five 'til," Rosemary told her from the register, where she counted down the drawer. "Go ahead and open up, Karen."

"Sure thing."

It was company policy that all employees dressed in the clothing that Marcus Bennett sold, and Karen felt especially fashionable today as she unlocked the front entrance and turned on the neon open sign. The company provided its employees with a clothing allowance – three outfits a week, every other week each month. Before working here, Karen's choices of outfits depended on which pair of old jeans went with what ratty old t-shirts. Now, she had more clothes than she had closet space.

This was definitely the best job she'd ever had.

Marcus Bennett designed and sold fashionable clothing for fashionable people – both women and men, although Chariot's outlet catered primarily to female clientele. There was a section for men, but it was a quarter the size of the women's section. On a Thursday, like today, the shop would be slow until just after lunch, and by the time Karen's shift ended, the place would be hopping. While she wished that her shift was busier throughout, she was glad to be on days, as she'd hated working evenings and nights at her last job.

She was redressing a mannequin when the jingling of bells signaled the opening of the door and the first potential customer of the day. Karen looked over to the register where Rosemary had been, but her boss was nowhere in sight. Looking to the customer, she felt her heart skip a beat.

He was handsome, even if in a slightly geeky way. His features were stunning – dark hair and eyes to match, even if his eyes were somewhat masked by a set of black framed glasses. His body was perfect; at least, it looked like perfection beneath his formfitting t-shirt and tight Tommy Hilfiger jeans. His glasses complimented the confused look on his face as he glanced at the clothing around him.

Despite knowing it was her duty to approach him and offer

assistance, Karen watched him instead for a moment as he browsed through a couple of racks of women's clothing, obviously hunting something for someone else. Finally, when she knew she had to do her job or risk losing a customer, she stepped toward him with a smile on her face.

"Welcome to Marcus Bennett," she told him, and he smiled when he saw her. "Can I help you find something?"

"Yeah…" he replied in a tone that was as uncertain as his expression was when she'd watched him search the racks. "I've got a job interview this afternoon, and I realized I don't have anything nice to wear." He paused, swallowed, and looked again at the clothing in front of him. "I may not be in the right shop though."

"We have men's clothing too," Karen told him in a reassuring way. "Just not as much of it as we do women's clothing. Follow me. I'm sure we can find something to really make you stand out."

She led him to the men's section, which took up the far wall and the racks and shelves immediately around it. There, she began searching through blazers and button-down shirts.

"What kind of job are you interviewing for?" she asked as she looked for a few items in various styles to try.

"It's a job with a tech company," he replied, almost bashfully. "I'm applying for a software design position. If it happens, it could be really big for me."

"That sounds fantastic," she told him and chose a light tan blazer with a pale blue shirt. "I don't think you need a tie." Then, looking him over, she added, "Maybe a bowtie."

"A bowtie?" he questioned, grinning with inquisitiveness.

"It's classy, and it's not *too* business formal." She took slacks that complimented the blazer – having guessed his size by only a glance at him – and then choose a soft blue and cream bowtie to finish it off. Handing the ensemble to the customer, she added, "Go try these on. We'll see how you look."

"Yes, ma'am," he replied, still grinning but this time it seemed different to her. It was more charming than questioning, and she felt her heart skip that beat again.

She returned to her work with the mannequin while her customer ventured to the dressing room. A moment later, Rosemary reappeared, returning from a visit to the break room.

"I needed more coffee," she told her, and Karen grinned.

"Wait 'til you see my customer," she replied, giddily.

"We have a customer already?"

"He's hot." Karen nearly giggled as she said it, but she held it back.

"Where is this hot customer?"

"Changing."

While Rosemary helped her finish off one mannequin's

wardrobe and begin on the next, Karen found herself distracted by thoughts of the handsome stranger and his tech-job interview. Tech work brought in a lot of money, she thought. If he was single, he was truly a catch.

She heard the dressing room door open and stepped from her mannequin work to check out the customer as he approached. He looked as perfect as she thought he would.

"Is it a good fit?" she asked him, walking up to him and checking the length of the jacket and slacks. She glanced to Rosemary, who was watching with a dropped jaw – obviously also enamored by the customer's hotness.

"It fits great," he replied. There was a tinge of excitement in his voice. "How do I look?"

She looked him over again and smiled. She wondered if her face showed that she was blushing. "You look fantastic. Like a winner."

"I feel like a winner," he said. "Ring it up and clip off the tags. I'll wear it out."

"You got it," she told him and then looked down at his feet. His sneakers were worn and clashed completely with the outfit. "But not until we get a new pair of shoes on those feet."

Marcus Bennett had a small line of men's shoes that were stunning, and it was easy for Karen to find the right style to compliment his outfit.

At checkout, she learned that his name was Robert and she wished him good luck on his interview. When he stepped from the shop and the door closed behind him, she heard Rosemary gush.

"That is one delicious specimen," Rosemary said in an adolescent-like sigh, making a clicking sound with her tongue afterward.

"Yes, he is," Karen replied, wishing she'd made a move on him. But, he was just another customer on just another day, and she had work to do. She'd have to meet her Mister Right some other day.

With that thought on her mind, the bells jingled as the door opened again and four giddy, giggly women in their early twenties entered – loudly and with enthusiasm. The handsome man and his easy-to-assemble sale were gone. Karen's *real* work for the day was about to begin.

Then – 2

Friday was her last shift for the week, and on Saturday, she slept in – having spent Friday night with Rosemary at a club called Rambler's Inn, drinking until they were shitfaced and trying unsuccessfully to pick up guys with slurred speeches and sloppy body moves.

Now, as she awoke at eleven a.m. and drug herself out of bed to make coffee, she regretted every moment of it. She ached from a hangover. She didn't feel like she would be sick, but her head throbbed and the light from the kitchen was near-blinding.

As the coffee brewed, she lit a cigarette – feeling a bit better as the nicotine helped her headache to ease. Shortly thereafter, the first cup of coffee pushed her even closer to normality. Before she knew it, she had finished the pot of coffee, smoked three cigarettes, and endured two full episodes of some cheesy streaming sitcom.

Awake enough to shower, she cleansed her body, washed her hair, and shaved her legs. After dressing, she called Rosemary to see if she wanted to do a late lunch, but her manager-slash-friend had a prior commitment at a baby shower.

Karen understood and decided a day of shopping and a late lunch alone sounded just fine.

She decided to have soup and a sandwich at YOLO – Chariot's most popular of its three cafés. She ordered a triple espresso with a shot of caramel, deciding that there was no harm in a little extra caffeine to give her a boost for shopping. It was Saturday, after all. Certainly there were sales galore going on nearly everywhere.

She recognized the jingling of bells as a customer entered, but this was not Marcus Bennett and she was not on duty so she paid little attention. It wasn't until the customer began placing his order that Karen's attention was truly piqued. The voice matched that of Robert, her customer from Thursday morning at the shop.

Coyly, she looked over at the counter and grinned. Yep, it was Robert. She recognized his physique through his formfitting t-shirt and the name brand blue jeans. She liked the way the jeans held his muscular ass, and as he paid and turned around, she found that she had been lost in his beautiful bottom, staring intently at it.

Robert smiled when he noticed her, and she smiled in return – hoping he hadn't noticed her staring at his ass.

"Hey," he said with a wave from across the room.

Karen waved back, but she didn't speak. Robert's order was ready, and aside from his beverage, it was in a to-go bag.

She'd briefly considered inviting him to join her for lunch; she wanted to know how his interview went – if his outfit had helped him nail it – but he obviously had other plans.

Regardless, he took his bag and beverage and approached her, stopping short of sitting down.

"How's it going?" he asked her with a chipper voice.

"I should be asking you that," she replied. "How did the interview go?"

"Nailed it," he replied, blushing as he smiled. "Thanks for remembering. The outfit helped, I think. That's all because of you."

"So, you got the job?" Her smile was one of pride. She knew that outfit would kill, and she'd been right.

"I'll know on Monday, but it seems pretty certain." A buzzing sound broke into the conversation and Robert shifted. "That's my phone. I've got to go. It was really good seeing you again."

"You too," Karen replied. "And good luck with the job."

She exhaled a sigh of dreamy goodness as he walked away from her toward the exit – his butt cheeks shifting with perfect buoyancy through each step.

Ten minutes after Robert's departure, Karen finished her meal and left the café, climbing into her car and driving to the Chariot town square. There, she hunted for a parking place – a struggle, as the square was more active with shoppers than she'd seen it in ages. She knew Marcus Bennett would be busy today too, so she decided to stay far away from it. She wanted a relaxed day, and if she walked into her workplace and they were slammed, she knew she'd have to help out.

She liked her job, but she also liked her time off.

Two... maybe three hours passed. She lost track of time, and of funds, as she racked up a few high bills and accumulated several new outfits and accessories. While Marcus Bennett gave their employees a clothing allowance, and while she loved the clothing that she acquired through that allowance, she also liked to splurge on things that were *not* Marcus Bennett from time to time.

As the hours passed, Karen became hungry again. She'd worked up an appetite doing all of that shopping, and she wanted something a bit heavier than the light lunch she'd enjoyed at the café. She drove to Stovetop – a meat and three on the east side of town. There, she enjoyed a country fried steak with an order of mashed potatoes, coleslaw, and green beans. She had sweet tea to drink, and it was the sweetest she'd tasted in a long while.

After dinner, she smoked a cigarette in her car and drove to the multiplex, where a new comedy was showing that she'd been aching to see – *Happiest Day*.

In the theatre's lobby, she saw Robert again, but this time she kept her distance from him. He was with a woman around

Karen's age, but skinnier and a little prettier. They were at the concessions counter ordering popcorn and drinks. She waited until they departed the counter to approach the concessions, but when they entered into the room showing *Happiest Day*, Karen paused in her steps. She considered turning around and leaving the theatre all together – just to avoid confrontation, however pleasant it may have been. Yet, as the thought hit her head, she saw Robert step back into the lobby – alone – and notice her immediately. He approached her with swift, somewhat excited steps, and Karen prepared herself for another quick hello and goodbye from this handsome but obviously attached man.

"Wow!" Robert said, walking up to her with a smile that Karen had nearly memorized. "You're everywhere today."

"Hey, Robert. It's good to see you again," she replied with a pleasant, controlled tone.

"Please, call me Bob. Everyone does. Everyone but my mother, anyway!" He laughed and cleared his throat. "So, what movie are you here to see?"

"Oh, um…" she acted as if she'd forgotten – which, really, she just didn't want to tell him – and fumbled with her ticket stub. "*Happiest Day.*"

"Another fantastic coincidence," Bob replied. "It's my cousin's birthday today and that's what she wanted to see."

"Cousin?" Oh, how wonderful the world was beginning to

seem again.

"Yeah. It's her sixteenth birthday today. Thought I'd treat her."

Sixteen? Karen thought, astounded. The girl looked twenty at the youngest.

"Would you like to sit with us?"

Bob's question made her heart do that funny beat-skipping thing again and she felt her pulse quicken. She was about to respond when her cellular went off in her purse. Startled by it, she nearly dropped the purse as she reached in for the phone.

"Excuse me," she told Bob, answering the call.

"Emergency!" Rosemary pleaded from the other end.

"What's wrong?" Karen asked, turning her back to Bob to focus on the call.

"I'm broken down with a flat about ten miles out of town," Rosemary explained. "I was driving home from the baby shower when my tire popped."

"Oh, Rosemary, that's awful. Are you okay?"

"Yeah. A tow truck is on its way out, but because of the hour, it'll be morning until the tire is repaired. Can you come get me?"

Karen paused and looked over her shoulder at Bob, who watched with concern. She'd been thrilled at his offer of spending the next ninety minutes or so with him and his cousin, but

Rosemary was her closest friend, and she couldn't leave her stranded on the side of the highway. After telling Rosemary she was coming to her rescue, she hung up and turned to Bob to apologize.

"You don't have to say a word," Bob said, holding up a hand as he smiled. "I completely understand. Go save your friend."

"Thanks, Bob," Karen replied, backing away – albeit slowly. She hated having to leave this perfect opportunity – this perfect moment – but she was glad that he understood.

"You're a good friend," Bob added as she approached the exit. "That's kind of hot."

Karen's pulse quickened again and she smiled from the flirtatious comment. Then, waving goodbye, she stepped from the theatre and walked to her car.

Then – 3

The third time she ran into Bob, it was nearly three weeks later and it was late on a Friday night. They met at a bar; neither had brought a date nor a friend. Rosemary was pregnant and couldn't drink, and Bob was celebrating the completion of a new app's beta stages at his new job.

After a few drinks, Karen went down on him in the restroom, and he went down on her in the parking lot. In the car, they fucked like wild rabbits, and in his apartment, they made sweet, passionate love.

In the morning, she awoke in his arms, earlier than usual for a Saturday. For a while, she lay naked in his embrace, savoring every moment of his strength and warmth. Then, while he slept, she helped herself to his shower, donned his bathrobe, and made a pot of coffee.

The smell of the freshly brewing coffee woke Bob, and he came up behind her in the kitchen. A few minutes later, after they both reached climax, they sat at the table for coffee and conversation.

Karen wanted a cigarette to go with her coffee, but she sensed that Bob did not smoke, and she didn't want to offend him. Instead, she utilized him as her nicotine and soaked in every word that he said.

They made love two more times before lunch, and at one o'clock, when Karen had slipped back into the clothes she'd arrived in, she bid him goodbye. He offered to drive her back to her car, but she opted for a cab and blew him a kiss from the curb as her ride approached.

Once she'd claimed her vehicle and arrived home, she changed into some fresh clothes and called Rosemary.

"You're shitting me!" her pregnant friend said in a tone of astonishment. "Was it as good as I think it was?"

"It was the best sex I've ever had," Karen admitted. "He's hung like a horse and built like a brick shithouse. I've never had anyone know how to please me in bed like Bob."

"I'm so jealous. Johnny hasn't touched me since he knocked me up."

"Maybe he's afraid sex would hurt the baby."

"I think he's more afraid of the fact that he got me pregnant in the first place."

"How's the new job?" Karen asked, shifting the conversation. Rosemary had been fired from Marcus Bennett a week ago for bitch slapping a rude customer.

"Well… it's not Marcus Bennett, but at least it's a clothing store." It hadn't taken Rosemary long to find work. Her new job was at a discount clothing shop called The Thrifty Barn.

"Can you do dinner tonight?"

"No… Johnny has asked me out for a romantic dinner. I think he's going to ask me to marry him."

"Oh, wow!" Karen exclaimed through a whisper. "Are you going to accept?"

"Fuck, no!" Rosemary laughed. "He's only doing it because I'm pregnant. I do *not* want to be saddled with that man for the rest of my life."

"I'd marry Bob in a heartbeat," she confided with a shy giggle.

"Hell, *I'd* marry Bob in a heartbeat!" Rosemary added in a cackle. "He's a stud."

"He fucks like a beast but he talks a lot about computers and technology and stuff."

"That can be forgiven." There was a beeping sound and Rosemary grunted. "Johnny's trying to call in. Let me get back with you later."

"Smooches," Karen told her and ended the call.

She lit a cigarette, made herself a drink, and killed the afternoon watching old movies and wishing she'd just spent the day at Bob's instead of coming home. She thought of calling him, but she didn't want to seem desperate. She'd *just* seen him, after all.

At around eight o'clock that night, the original *Night of the Living Dead* aired on one of the movie stations. She hadn't seen it since she was a child. Back then, the movie had terrified her. Now, she found it laughable. The idea of zombies, of all things, being able to exist, much less cause all of the destruction that they brought... Watching them, she took note of how slowly they moved and how, if the victims just ran, they could have easily escaped them. It was silly, unrealistic, and completely unbelievable.

She found a rerun of *Beverly Hills: 90210* and settled back with her secret fantasy crush on Luke Perry's hot character Dylan.

TV's Dylan and her Bob were completely different types of men, and yet, Karen found them to be similar to one another. They were both hot; that was for sure.

When she took a moment to think about it, that was about all the two had in common, but it was enough. Besides, Bob lacked Dylan's attitude and sarcasm, which undoubtedly worked to her advantage. Bob seemed like the kindest, most fun guy in the world, and she really liked him.

Aside from that, the sex she'd experienced with him had been the best of her life, and she craved more. She stood and turned off the television, retreating to the bathroom where she took a second shower for the day. Then, she dressed in her sexiest outfit and an overcoat, set on returning to Bob's apartment, where she would seduce him and experience more of the best sex she'd ever known.

Yet, just as she slipped on her hottest pair of high heels, she heard a knock at her door. Her first thought was that it was Rosemary, there to tell her about how Johnny had proposed and how she had rejected him. Then, she considered that possibility to be unlikely, as Rosemary always called before coming over.

Cautiously, Karen left her bedroom and approached the door. It had no peephole, so she leaned in close and asked, "Who is it?"

"It's Bob," she heard as a reply. Karen perked at the response. "You left something at my house."

"Oh?" Karen asked as she unlocked and opened the door. "What did I leave?"

"Me," he said, stepping inside in nothing but a long, open trench coat with the most massively inviting hard-on Karen had ever seen.

With no further questions, Karen shut the door behind him.

Then – 4

Three weeks later, Karen felt uncomfortable while on the toilet. There wasn't a bit of blood, and her period was over a week late. Over the last couple of days, she'd also been sick to her stomach when waking in the morning. This morning, she called into work over it. Stephanie, her current manager at Marcus Bennett, had not been pleased and asked for her to return tomorrow with a doctor's note.

At the doctor, she learned that she was pregnant. That both excited her and made her fearful. Rosemary had, indeed, rejected Johnny's marriage proposal and immediately thereafter eliminated her pregnancy. Karen was excited over knowing that her pregnancy was caused by the most perfect man she'd ever met. The fear came over the concern that Bob would react more like Rosemary than like Johnny in this situation. She was afraid that he would not be warm to the idea of being a father, especially so soon in a new relationship. Karen knew that Bob liked her – a lot – but she didn't know if he loved her. If he didn't love her, what were the chances of him loving a baby brought in by her?

She had to tell him; she had no choice. Eventually, she would begin to show, and at that point, there would be no denying it. It was best, she thought, to be upfront about it. So that Friday while they dined at Flapjacks for a breakfast style dinner, she broke the news to him.

"You're what?" he asked with eyes wide from shock. Karen swallowed through a knot in her throat.

"I'm pregnant," she replied. The words felt like breathless nothings escaping her lips, as if she had not spoken them at all. Yet, as Bob folded his hands before him, she knew that she had indeed said them, and that he had heard them.

"That is…" he began, visually choosing his words, "the most *amazing* thing I have ever heard." He smiled at her, and she felt her heart flutter.

"Do you really mean it?" she asked. She was nervous – so nervous – and she wanted so much for him to be receptive to the idea. She didn't want to have to pull a Rosemary. She didn't want to abort the baby, and she didn't want to have to raise it alone either.

Bob was smiling so hard that his cheeks were turning pink. Behind his glasses, a tear began to fall. "This is the best news I've ever heard," he whispered, fighting back a full-fledge cry. "I – I've always wanted to be a dad… and it's with *you*! God… I love you, Karen." He reached across the table and wrapped her hands with his. "I love you so much."

It was everything that she had wanted to hear, and the moment she opened her mouth to respond, they both began to cry tears of joy. Bob kissed her hands, and then he stood, walked over to her, and sat beside her in the booth where he kissed her more tenderly than ever before. She was so happy – the happiest any woman could have ever been. She had the perfect man, and they had created a life within her.

When the kiss broke, Bob remained beside her but looked down instead of at her. Karen could feel that something was wrong. There was something new on his mind – something that worried him, and now it worried her.

"What is it?" she asked, taking his hands. "What's wrong?"

"I – I've got to tell my mother," he said, looking at her. "It's no big deal though."

"We can tell her together," Karen offered, realizing this was Bob's first mention of his mother. Of course, he *had* a mother, she thought. Everyone had a mother at some point – even her. She just hadn't thought of Bob's mother. Yet, she was suddenly excited to meet her. "I'm sure she'd want to meet me. I mean, I'm carrying her grandchild, after all."

Bob smiled at her but his eyes shifted from her quickly. After a silent moment, he told her, "My mom's a very… old school woman. Set in her ways."

"She won't approve that I'm pregnant because we're not married?" Even though she asked the question, she wasn't surprised by this. Older people were usually somewhat reserved or conservative, in her experience.

"It's not just that," Bob continued, pulling his hands away. "My mother is going to be super-pissed that I got a girl that she hasn't *met* pregnant."

"We've only been dating a few weeks though."

"That just makes it worse," he said, surprisingly chuckling through the comment. "But you know, Mom's just going to have to deal." He took her hand again and Karen felt hopeful once more. "Sure. We can tell her together. We can have brunch on Sunday at my apartment and we'll spill the news."

"Brunch sounds great," Karen replied, excited within but showing very little of it on the exterior. She was thrilled that she was going to meet Bob's mom. Her own mother had passed some time ago, along with her father, and Karen had no family to speak of remaining. She missed that mother-daughter interaction and was eager to see the mother-son interaction between Bob and... "What's your mother's name?"

"Ethel," he replied and grinned. "It's the worst name in the world, but she loves it."

"It's... interesting. Old fashioned."

"It's hideous. It's like that lanky girl in the comics. What's her name...? Jughead's girlfriend."

"Ethel?" Karen asked, giggling.

"Yep," Bob smiled and leaned into her. "That's the one." Then, he kissed her... tenderly... lovingly. It was a blissful kiss, one that made her melt into the booth and created an invisible unity around them. It was fantastic.

When the kiss broke and they'd finished their meal, taken in a movie, and had a little fun, Bob dropped Karen off at her apartment and retreated to his. For the rest of the night and all day on Saturday, meeting Ethel was all Karen could think about.

Bob was such a wonderful man, so she imagined Ethel was even more spectacular. Despite having an old-fashioned name and beliefs, she was surely an impressive, caring woman to have produced a son of those same qualities.

Saturday afternoon, she shopped for a present to give to the grandmother of her unborn child. At a gift shop called Such and Such, she browsed a few aisles of cheap knickknacks, expensive collectibles, and hideous mass-produced junk. It suddenly felt impossible to choose a gift for this woman whom she'd never met. She didn't want to show up with something generic and she couldn't get too crazy with it either.

"Hi," asked the sales clerk from the counter. "Can I help?"

Karen approached the counter, glanced at the clerk's nametag, and smiled. "Hi, Olivia. I sure hope you can. I'm meeting my boyfriend's mom for the first time tomorrow, and I'd like to give her a gift."

"You'd like to buy her approval of you," Olivia said, bluntly.

"What?" Karen questioned, baffled and thrown off.

"You're giving her a gift for the first time while meeting her. Is it your way of thanking her for her son?"

"No, of course not." She was feeling offended, but she was also second-guessing. "I mean... not like that. I'm not *thanking* her for giving birth to my boyfriend."

"Is it an exchange? A gift from you in exchange for her son?"

"No... it's nothing like that." Karen took a breath and looked at Olivia, who stared back with a deadpan emotionless expression. "Where is all of this coming from, right here?" She waved her hands around in front of her. "What is this?"

"I just need to know the circumstances to be able to suggest a gift," Olivia stated and smiled.

"I need the kind of gift that someone would bring to the host's home during a brunch." Karen was agitated and somewhat dumbfounded by the absurd questioning. She hoped this specific – if still off-base – reply would help.

"Why didn't you say that to begin with?" Olivia asked as she stepped from behind the counter. She went to the window display and took a potted purple orchid, carrying it directly back to the register and ringing it up. "$24.14."

"It's beautiful," Karen noted, and it was. In fact, it was perfect – just what she was looking for, only she hadn't realized it until now. She passed over her credit card, signed the slip, and enjoyed a green tea gelato at the shop's tiny café.

At home, she placed the orchid in the kitchen beside the sink, under the glow of the lamp over the stove in hopes that it would still be alive tomorrow. When she awoke Sunday morning and checked on it, it was indeed alive and she was thrilled. Karen had never had much luck with plants, but she'd managed to keep this one alive for a full night and it would soon have a new caretaker.

Into her second cup of coffee and the start of a fresh cigarette, her phone rang. It was Bob and she answered with a warm but scratchy voice – still sleepy but glad to hear from him.

"Good morning, handsome," she told him and then sipped her coffee.

"Good morning, gorgeous," Bob replied. His voice sounded a bit rushed. "Last minute changes, I'm afraid."

"Oh, no…" Karen sighed. She'd somewhat been fearful of this happening. "She doesn't want to meet me. I had a feeling…"

"No, it's not that at all," Bob continued. "But she can't do brunch. Instead, we're having supper… at her place."

"At her place?"

"Yeah… she lives just down the road from me, so no worries. I can pick you up, or you can come here and then I can drive us over."

"What time?" Karen had felt alright about meeting Ethel at Bob's apartment, but she was a bit intimidated about having to meet the head lioness on her own turf.

"Around four-thirty at my place and we'll head over from there." He paused, and Karen wondered what he was thinking about. "Look, I'm manscaping so I should go, but I'll see you at four-thirty, okay."

Manscaping, Karen thought, licking her lips. *Mmm.* "Sounds great."

They ended the call and Karen finished the cigarette and her second cup of coffee, thinking all the while about what all Bob was manscaping and excited over the thought of exploring his body later to find out… *after* meeting Ethel.

When it came to dressing for the occasion, she was thankful to have the extra time, as she hadn't planned her outfit in advance. She was not short on clothing by any means, but this made for the problem of being inundated by options and choices and assortments of ensembles. She didn't want to appear too bland, but she didn't want to look even the least bit slutty either. She assumed Bob would wear jeans and a t-shirt, but Karen wanted to stand out just a bit. To appear as if she took the time to choose just the right clothes – which was exactly what she was doing.

She decided on a lavender silk blouse with white Capri pants and lavender heels to match. She wore a strand of pearls around her neck to compliment the pants and shirt. The pearls had belonged to her mother, and she felt like this was the perfect opportunity to wear them.

At four o'clock, she began grew anxious… more nervous than she had been. She considered calling Rosemary for some reassurance, but she realized she still hadn't told her that she was pregnant. She didn't want to have to tell Rosemary *and* Bob's mom all in the same day, so she held her angst inside and dealt with it alone. A few minutes later, she climbed into her car and drove to Bob's apartment building, knocking on his front door at 4:29.

Bob greeted her with a kiss and a squeeze of the ass. She handed him the orchid and he set it on the table beside the door.

"Bob, what do you think…" she began, but his lips kept her from saying more. As he kissed her, he ran a finger between her thighs, sending chills across her skin. In a minute flat, they both wore their pants around their ankles as Bob took her from behind. She felt him release inside of her, and she loved it. She was already pregnant, so those worries were gone. She worked to clench out every drop.

The second Bob pulled out, he said, "We should get to Mom's. She must be wondering where we are by now."

While Karen understood what Bob was saying, she didn't really think it should have been the *first* thing out of his mouth after filling her with his spunk.

It turned out that Ethel's house was closer than Bob had let on. By *not far* from his apartment building, what he should have said was *three buildings down*.

Still, even though it was close enough and even though she had insisted they could walk, he drove her there, worrying something might happen to the orchid or the unborn baby otherwise.

At five to five, they rang Ethel's doorbell, and less than half a minute later, she answered.

Instantly, Karen was worried all over again.

"You must be Karen," the stern-looking woman said through a smirk as she looked Karen over.

"It's a pleasure to meet you, Ms. Granger," she replied, handing the orchid to Ethel.

"Put it by the sink," Ethel said in lieu of taking the plant. She walked back into the house, leaving the door open for Karen and Bob to enter.

The house had been built in the fifties and hadn't been redecorated or renovated since the seventies. The furniture in the living room, albeit dated by decades, still had plastic coverings over it, protecting it from dirt, spills, and dust mites. Ethel, herself, was dressed simply in an old flowery blouse and black slacks. She wore slippers on her feet and thin-framed glasses upon her nose. Her lips were lined in black and otherwise as red as a whorehouse's open sign. Her eyes were also lined in black with too much light blue eyeshadow and too thin penciled-on eyebrows. She held a glass of wine in one hand and the television remote in another.

"We'll find an educational program," she noted as she handled the clanky remote. Karen thought the television was from the eighties, at the latest. At least it had a color picture... and rabbit ear antennas. "Television rots the mind, you know. Robert's father bought this for us years ago, but we've rarely used it. I prefer books, and I've instilled that trait in my son. I'm sure it's my influence why he's become so intelligent and successful."

"Dad used to watch westerns on it," Bob noted and left it at that.

Karen felt the strength of her uncomfortable feeling grow. What kind of woman didn't watch television? She would have pinned Ethel as a soap opera addict.

There was not even the scent of food in the house. Karen peeked into the dining room as she crossed over to the sofa. The table was not set, but it was instead loaded up with hordes of shopping bags and packages.

"Good to see you, Mom," Bob said with a smile as he and Karen sat across from her.

"Thank you for welcoming me into your home," Karen added, feeling she should make an attempt at conversation. "I love the wallpaper," she noted, looking at the tacky paisley design. "Is it original to the house?"

"This was my mother's house," Ethel told her, although she kept her eyes on the television. She'd found a nature show on PBS. "I inherited it when she died."

"Oh, I'm so sorry…"

"Everybody dies," the older woman noted, looking directly at Karen now. "It's a fact of life, dearie."

"I – I suppose everyone *does* die… eventually, I mean."

"So," Bob injected, "what's for supper? I'm starved."

"I thought we'd order Chinese," Ethel replied and glanced at the clock on the wall. "It should be here soon. It's Robert's favorite takeout food, isn't it, sugar?" Karen didn't like the way that Ethel was looking at her son, or the way she blew him a kiss. It made her feel a little dirty, in a bad way.

"I love it," Bob responded. Karen wondered if he was as uncomfortable with Ethel's demeanor as she was.

The food arrived ten tense minutes later, and they ate at a small table in the kitchen near a window. No one spoke during supper, which drove Karen crazy. She didn't know what to say or how to strike up conversation with this thin-lipped, tight-faced woman, and Bob wasn't offering any assistance in the matter. Perhaps silence during supper was a tradition in this household; she didn't know, but it was making her more uncomfortable by the minute.

Finally, she couldn't take it anymore. She cleared her throat, propped her elbows on the table, and looked at Ethel as she ate. After the briefest moment of this, Ethel caught her gaze and returned the stare.

"Have you always lived in Chariot?" Karen asked her through a smile that she hoped showed she was trying.

"No," the woman replied, lowering her eyes to her plate and taking a bite of food.

"Really? That's interesting. Where did you move here from?"

As Ethel chewed, she was silent. She was eating rice. There was no reason for her to be chewing so much, but Karen assumed she was thinking of her answer… choosing her words. She held her smile as she awaited a reply.

"Mom's parents moved here a couple of years after Mom married Dad," Bob explained, injecting an answer into the dense silence. "Mom and Dad stayed in West Virginia where Dad's coal mining job was."

"Robert was four when his father died," Ethel continued, which disturbed Karen. She hadn't expected the woman to say a word. "There was a cave-in at the mine he was working in. He and seven others died that day. It was a terrible thing, and we don't discuss it. Do we, Robert dear?"

"No, Mom," Bob replied through a breath. "We don't discuss it." He looked at Karen and she smiled at him. "A few months after the accident, my grandparents offered to take us in, and we moved in here with them. Gramps died of a heart attack when I was nine, and Grammy died suddenly in her sleep one night the next year."

Ethel sneered at him and Karen caught the look. It made the hair on her arms stand up.

Clearing her voice and sipping her wine, Ethel turned her sights back to Karen and smiled. Ethel's smile reminded Karen of a witch up to no good.

"And where are *you* from, dearie?" the woman asked in such a way that it made Karen's skin want to crawl right off her body.

"Right here," she told her, holding her smile although it felt like it was frozen to her face. "Born and raised."

"And your parents. What do they do?"

Karen cringed at the question and lowered her eyes briefly to the table. Then, looking at Ethel once more, she said, "My parents died in a wreck a few years back, but my dad was a factory worker and my mom cleaned rooms at a hotel."

She noticed Bob shift in his seat. They had never discussed her parents before. She wondered if the news came as a shock to him.

As if fully unaffected by what she'd just been told, Ethel added, "And what do *you* do for work?"

"I work at Marcus Bennett," she replied.

"A clothing store. That explains the expensive wardrobe. They *must* give you a clothing allowance."

"Mom has an eye for fashion," Bob added. Karen was thankful for his injection, as it distracted from Ethel's cutting insult.

"I have an eye for a lot of things," Ethel remarked and then sipped her wine.

Deciding she'd waited long enough to share the news, Karen could hold back no longer and blurted out, "I'm pregnant with Bob's child."

Mid-sip, Ethel paused in her drinking. Mid-bite, Bob stopped chewing. Karen remained smiling, deciding this was happy news and everyone should have been smiling, but everyone was not. Only she.

She caught Bob's stare – a pleading, terrified stare that screamed *what did you do?* The look on Ethel's face was a look of stone. Expressionless, while still bitter.

Slowly, Ethel lowered her glass, swallowed, and smiled. After a moment, she spoke. "Surely, you're mistaken, dearie," she told her in a tone that Karen knew she would never forget. "Perhaps one of your *other* men impregnated you. I'm sure it will be tough to narrow down, but I assure you, it wasn't my Robert. My Robert is a good boy, aren't you, dear?"

Karen looked to Bob, her smile still plastered on her face, although she felt its freeze beginning to melt. The shock of what Ethel had just said to her was beginning to wear off and she quickly became both offended and pissed.

"Mom, I don't think that's a very…"

"That's your problem, Robert," Ethel interrupted. "You don't think. You're just like your father in that way. Never using your noggin. If you'd used your noggin, you might not be sitting here right now having this conversation with me, would you?"

Bob lowered his eyes and shook his head. Karen could see his face turning a bit pinkish. "I love Karen," he whispered, and even though Karen could hear him, she wondered if the same could be said for Ethel, as his voice was so low. "That's my baby." He was nearing tears. She could see them welling up behind his glasses. "She's having *my* baby, Mom."

Ethel was silent as she looked at him. It was now apparent that she had heard him, and from the look in her eyes, she didn't like what she'd heard.

"If you'll excuse me," she said after a long silent moment and stood from the table, taking her glass with her. "I must refill this."

Even though the bottle of wine was there in the kitchen with them, Ethel carried her glass into another room, out of sight, but where she could be heard sobbing and then screaming as if she was in absolute agony.

"I thought she'd be excited!" Karen claimed in a hushed tone to Bob, who was just sitting there, eyes closed, shaking his head.

"Well," he replied, looking at her through exasperated eyes, "she's handling this better than I thought."

"Noooo…!" they heard Ethel squeal, followed by more heavy, threatening sobs. "Please, God, no!"

"This is *better*?" Karen questioned. She'd never heard such wailing before. "She sounds like you stabbed her and left her for dead!"

"That's probably how she feels," he admitted to her and began to stand. Karen put a hand on his forearm, freezing his position.

"Let me check on her," she told him, standing in his place. "I caused this mess. Let me talk to her."

Bob tried to protest but Karen wouldn't allow it. Instead,

she stepped from the kitchen and into the living room, where she found Ethel standing at the edge of the hallway with her forehead resting against the wall as she cried.

"Ms. Granger?" Karen whispered softly as she stepped toward her. "Is this all really that necessary?"

Ethel stopped sobbing and looked at her with the most ruthless, wicked stare Karen had ever seen. She had been wrong before, she decided. There was no way in hell that Bob had gotten his humor, looks, kindness or compassion from this woman. It all had to have come from his father.

"How dare you come into my house, tell me such horrible things, and then tell me how to behave?" Ethel questioned, taking a step toward her. Karen began to respond, but she was cut off. "You have no idea what atrocities that young man in there has suffered over his lifetime. You could not *begin* to know what I have had to help him through, hold his hand through, comfort him through… You think you can just waltz into my son's life and steal him away from me? Well, you're mistaken! I am Robert's best friend. He needs his mother at the forefront of his life, guiding him… holding him. You…you will only cause him trouble and heartaches. You're a mess who got knocked up and now you want to take my Robert down with you, but I won't allow it. No way, dearie. I love my son too much to let him fall into your clutches!"

Karen, fighting tears of anger, opened her mouth to

retaliate – to tell Ethel off just as she'd just been told off, but instead, she told her, "Don't you ever fucking call me *dearie* again or I'll smack that lipstick right off your tight little face."

"Don't you threaten me, or I'll make sure my Robert never sees you again."

Karen swallowed, trying hard to not actually slap the woman. Just as she was about to respond, Bob came into the room.

"Everything okay in here?" he asked, standing on the threshold and looking at Karen and Ethel with a cautious gaze.

"Oh, Robert, dear. Everything's just perfect," his mother said, strolling over to him and wrapping her hands around his waist. She pulled him in close for a hug and then kissed the nape of his neck. "Don't you worry about your old, widowed mother." She kissed his chin, his cheek, the corner of his lips... Bob seemed to be smiling, but Karen wasn't sure he looked happy.

"Karen, are you okay?" he asked, but Karen was rendered speechless by Ethel's twisted display of affection. With a simple shrug of the shoulders, she gave her reply.

What she really wanted to do was point out the most obvious case of Jocasta Complex she'd ever seen. Ethel was touching her son in ways only a lover should, and it was beyond disturbing. It was chilling and horrid.

"I think we should be heading out, Mom," Bob told her, pulling away from her physical connection. "Karen and I both have to work in the morning."

Karen sighed, relieved that Bob had found an *out* for them. This house... that woman – they were more than she could take, and she didn't want to spend another minute there.

"Oh, Robert, dear... you'd leave your sweet momma all alone, especially after memories of your father's *tragic* death were brought up and placed in the forefront of my lonely mind?"

Karen thought she'd be sick. Ethel was literally pouting for her son to stay with her, and worse yet, she was playing the widow card. Deciding that it was time for her to intervene, she marched up to the mother-son pair and took Bob's hand, leading him a step away from Ethel.

"It's been an... experience meeting you, Ms. Granger, but we really must go now," she said, leading Bob to the door. "Please, enjoy the plant."

"But –!" Ethel began, but Bob cut her off.

"I'll see you soon, Mom! Thanks for supper!"

When the door shut behind them, Karen felt a great relief. Ethel had been much worse than she'd imagined, and she was thankful to have simply made it through.

"I don't think your mom took the news very well," she told Bob as he drove them back to his apartment.

"I think she handled it pretty well," he said in a smirk. "You should have seen how she behaved when she found out I lost my virginity."

"Oh, lord! I can only imagine."

"I thought her head was going to turn into a volcano and lava was going to start spewing out of her."

Bob laughed at his comment and Karen laughed along with him, thankful for this light moment after a torturous evening.

Once the car was parked and they were inside Bob's home, Karen stripped him naked, tied him up, blindfolded him, and then punished him in ways he'd never before experienced for putting her through such an evening. He'd been a naughty, naughty man, and he had to pay. While she punished him, she managed to work in a compliment on his manscaping job. He was smooth as silk in all the places that mattered.

Then – 5

When the memory of her first meeting with Ethel felt like no more than just that – a memory – Karen once again began to relax into her new relationship. On the Tuesday that marked their fifth week of dating, Bob picked her up from Marcus Bennett for lunch and treated her to a delicious meal of sushi and Saki. From there, he drove her to the courthouse, where he asked her to marry him in the parking lot.

"I've never been in love with anyone like I am with you," he told her, presenting her with the most beautiful diamond ring she'd ever seen. "Please, Karen. Marry me. Right here; right now. Let me be more than a father to our child. Let me be your husband and make you the happiest woman in the world."

"Oh, Bob…" she whispered as he slid the ring onto her finger. "Yes… oh, yes!"

They married in front of the Justice of Peace and they had sex immediately thereafter in the courthouse's janitorial closet. Aside from a mishap with a broom, it was the most exciting sexual moment of her life – the first copulation between her and her new husband.

Happily together and newly married, Karen moved into Bob's apartment, letting hers go and placing her furnishings in storage.

As handsome and wonderful as Bob was, he was a terrible homemaker. The apartment was a scattered, dusty mess. With the combination of their incomes and the cost of only one apartment instead of two, Karen found that she could afford to take a few days off to give the apartment a facelift. As a two-bedroom, it was bigger than hers had been, which was fantastic, considering the fact that her clothing and accessories had *not* gone into storage.

In a few days' time, Karen had managed to get the place shipshape. With Bob's approval, she disposed of the old furniture in the living room and the bedroom and replaced it with brand new pieces that better fit their unity.

Karen was considering how to decorate the nursery when it happened. She felt a sharp, sudden pain in the pit of her stomach and was floored by it. Unable to stand from the stabbing feeling in her gut, she pulled herself across the floor to the bathroom, where she climbed atop the commode and pulled down her pants. She felt a release similar to pee but much different also. Looking down between her legs into the toilet, she saw the red of fresh blood.

She didn't need a doctor to tell her what was happening. She *knew* what was happening. She could feel it; she was miscarrying. Her child was dying… or dead, and there was nothing she could do about it.

She began to cry… began to sob. Hysterics at first, and then silent sobs filled with mournful pity and loss. Finally, as she wiped herself and flushed the commode, she took her phone from her pocket and called 911. Then, while blood continued to flow from her, she passed out.

When she opened her eyes again, she was on a hospital bed, connected to IVs and machines. Bob was in the room, asleep in the chair across from her. A nurse was checking her pulse.

"It's good to see you awake," the nurse told her with a bright smile that illuminated her dark skin. Karen noticed her dreadlocks. They were long… beautiful. "My name is Crystal. I'm the nurse on duty for the next few hours."

"Hi, Crystal," Karen said in a weak voice. She felt dizzy, woozy, and hungry. Despite all of those things, her child was at the heart of her thoughts. "My baby…?"

Crystal's smile softened and her eyes were sad. "I'm sorry," she whispered, sympathetically touching Karen's shoulder. "You suffered a miscarriage. I'm afraid your child has died."

Karen felt tears well up in her eyes again, but she nodded her head to show that she understood. She knew it was true the moment it happened. She'd just needed to hear it.

"Does he know?" she asked, looking at Bob – beautiful as

he slumbered.

"Yes, Mrs. Granger," Crystal told her. "We called him as soon as you arrived at the hospital. He's been here at your side ever since."

Karen smiled a bit. It was all she had the strength for.

"What time is it?"

"Just after three in the morning. You should consider going back to sleep."

"I feel so hungry," she admitted, but she didn't know how true the hunger was. Perhaps she just felt... empty.

"You'll get a warm breakfast in just a couple of hours. I'm going to hit this little button right here and help you rest."

Karen watched as Crystal walked to one of the IVs and lifted a controller. "Wait..." she began, but almost the second the button was pressed, she felt no pain, no hunger, no nothing as she drifted once more to sleep.

This was the case for two more days until the hospital released her with orders of bed rest at home. She'd lost more blood than she'd thought during the miscarriage and had hit her head when passing out. She had a slight concussion, and they explained it would take a few days for her to get her strength back.

Bob took this time off from work as well, catering to her every need. For the most part, their relationship had been fueled by sex, but now, she was seeing a different side of him. He was caring, attentive, loving, and understanding. Instead of trying to seduce her, he brushed her hair at her bedside or massaged her feet or shoulders. Even though she'd never really enjoyed being read to, he read to her from one of her favorite books, and then he read to her from one of his favorite books. The way he handled the voices of the various characters amused and entertained her.

He also cooked for her and helped her bathe in the tub, even though she could have handled that one on her own.

When Karen was well enough, she and Bob both returned to work. Though she wore a smile upon her face, inside, she was devastated over the loss of her child. She'd grown used to the idea of motherhood. She'd been looking forward to it, and it had been the whole reason Bob had married her. He still loved her; he'd reiterated that to her multiple times in numerous ways since the miscarriage happened. Still, she felt incomplete now, like a part of her had been stripped away... which it had been.

As she helped some young woman find an outfit for lunch with a new beau, she considered Ethel's reaction to the miscarriage. Bob never outright told Karen what his mother had said, as he had walked over to her house to tell her in person, and when he returned three hours later, he was shaken, pale, and had very little to say. He had immediately showered, put on his pajama bottoms, and gone to bed.

That alone let her know Ethel's reaction had fallen beyond

even the darkest shadows of bad, and she promised herself to never make him talk about it with her unless he brought it up and wanted to. She'd asked him how it went when he arrived home, and his only response had been, "I love you."

"I like it," she heard her customer tell her, stirring her back to the here and now. "Ring it up."

"You got it," she muttered and took the three items up to the register to complete the purchase.

This was how every day seemed to be for a while. Yet, whether she began to realize it or not, over the next several weeks and into a few months, her depression from the miscarriage lessened. By Thanksgiving, Karen was back to her normal self. By Christmas, she wanted to hang herself.

"I can't do this!" she screamed through her crying as she beat against the mattress of the bed. Bob stood in the doorway watching her, but as kind and loving of a husband as he was, she knew he could do little to soften her mood, and he knew it too.

"I'm not going to let you hurt yourself," he told her in a calm, compassionate tone. "We'll try again."

"We've *been* trying again!" she shouted and then threw herself facedown into her pillow, sobbing heavily and letting her voice sink into a mournful moan. "I just want to die!"

"That's crazy talk," Bob said, finally entering the room and climbing onto the bed beside her. "Look. We may not have the family that we thought we'd have right now, but we *are* a family, and I love you. I love being with you and spending my life with you. If we have a child, that will make our family so much more wonderful, but please stop believing that what you and I share isn't important... that we're an incomplete family, because we aren't."

She lifted her head from her pillow and looked through tear-stricken eyes at Bob, whose face was tearstained as well. She rolled over onto him, placing her head on his lap, and felt a bit of calm as he stroked her hair and held her.

He was right; she knew this. They would keep trying until they finally had their child, and in the meantime, she would do her best to be content and appreciative of what she had – a loving husband and a cozy apartment.

Come spring, the cozy apartment was filled with brown boxes, all labeled with the names of the rooms they were to be moved into. Bob had received a large promotion with Milton Enterprises and he and Karen were being relocated to a town named Deerborne in Connecticut.

"Are you sure we can afford this?" Karen asked him, looking around at all of their belongings confined to boxes. "I mean, the apartment is $800 a month. We're buying a two-story house with a $1500 a month mortgage."

"Of course we can afford it," he promised her as he kissed her on the cheek. "I'm making the upward part of six digits a year now. We can afford pretty much anything we want."

"But Connecticut?" she countered. It had never been a place on either of their living wish lists. "What about your mother?"

"I thought you'd be happy to be moving far away from Mom." He smiled and pulled a light jacket on over his t-shirt. "Think about it. I only have to be in the office twice a week this way. The rest of the time, I can be home with you."

"But then how will I have an affair with the milkman if you're home in the mornings?" she replied with a coy grin.

"I'm sure you'll manage somehow, dear," he chided, kissed her full on the lips, and helped her into her jacket. "I'm going to miss this apartment though. We've had some good times here."

"We sure have," she thought, reminiscing. Then, she grabbed his crotch and squeezed. "Care for one more good time?" She began to tug down the zipper.

"I'm all for a good time," Bob answered, tilting his head back as Karen lowered herself to her knees and brought him to full attention.

A few minutes later, Bob climbed into his car and Karen climbed into hers. The movers arrived shortly thereafter, and even though Karen and her husband left first, their belongings made it to their new home over a day before they did.

Within a week, the boxes were unpacked and the furniture

had been placed in its proper rooms. Bob was spending his first day at the new Milton Enterprises headquarters, learning the ropes and meeting new associates. Karen decided she'd earned a free day, and so she drove the ten-minute drive to Deerborne's shopping district and became acquainted with Connecticut fashions and trends.

She also did something Bob had told her she didn't need to do. She applied for jobs at four clothing boutiques. The fourth shop – an upscale store called Monique's – interviewed her on the spot, and twenty minutes later, she walked out with the sales associate job.

Bob had been right. She was feeling alive again. She was feeling more like the old Karen, and this new, fresh start at life was certainly helping. Having a new job was like the sprinkles on an ice cream cone – extra and delicious.

She treated herself to a latte at a café called Ironwood – a strange name but worth checking out. There, she considered how she would tell Bob that she'd taken a job. Surely, he would understand why she needed this. She needed something to do, aside from sitting around a gigantic house in the suburbs all day. Besides, Bob was primarily working from home now, which meant he needed some peace and quiet during the day.

That was how she'd explain it, she decided. She'd play it up to his benefit, not to mention that it would give her some extra spending money without having to tap him for cash every time she turned around.

Truth be told, if this Connecticut thing worked out, she hoped to be able to save some of her new income to open up a shop of her own. Not a clothing shop; she'd done enough of that to enjoy the work but not want to call it her own. Perhaps a bookshop, or an antique shop. Both of those ideas appealed to her, and as she finished her latte, she began to think up business names.

"So, what do you think?" she asked Rosemary, having called her to bounce her plans and ideas off of her.

"I think that's great!" her friend exclaimed. She sounded a little drunk or high. "I'm *so* jealous of what you have with Bob. He really did turn out to be the full package, didn't he?"

"Yeah. Yeah, I guess he did," Karen confessed.

"I mean, he's handsome, well-built, and has money. What more could a woman ask for?"

"I'd say a big dick, but Bob has that too," Karen said in a laugh.

"Yeah, he does!" Rosemary added – accidentally – and fell silent after she spoke.

"What did you say?" Karen asked her in a whisper, hoping that she'd heard wrong.

"I said… I bet he does."

"That's *not* what you said."

"Now, Karen... don't get mad, okay. It was early on. I mean... you'd only been dating a few weeks, and you made him sound *so* tempting."

She couldn't believe what she was hearing. Bob had fucked Rosemary. The color drained from her face and she fell into a state of shock while the realization of what she was learning settled in.

Rosemary made an attempt at explaining how it had happened, but Karen didn't want to hear it. Rosemary was supposed to have been her best friend. So was Bob. She'd never felt so betrayed.

"Take my number out of your phone, Rosemary," she told her former friend, trying hard to control her voice, as she was in a public place. "I never want to hear from you again."

"But, Karen..." Rosemary began. Karen ended the call before she could continue.

As she sat in the café and set her phone down on the table before her, the commerce, chitchatting and bustle of the activity around her continued, but to Karen, time was frozen. At a standstill. Nothing around her existed. Nothing she believed existed. She was alone in a universe that had, bit by bit, begun to destroy her.

She stood from her seat and exited the café, feeling rushed, flushed, and faint. In her car, she paused to catch her breath and steady her heart rate. Then, when she cranked the car, she drove straight home and waited on the sofa for Bob to return.

Then – 6

For eight weeks, Karen called room 109 at the Deerborne Inn her home. She'd refused to spend a single moment alone with Bob in that house, knowing what he'd done with Rosemary and likely with countless other bimbos. He'd admitted to having sex with Rosemary, and he'd said it had only been one time. Karen didn't believe him. He'd also told her that Rosemary had been the only one he'd screwed around on her with. She hadn't believed that either.

Bob began to court her all over again in an attempt to salvage their marriage. He had flowers delivered to her hotel room door daily, and four times since the split, they'd had lunch at a diner near the hotel – only meeting in public places with other people around. It was the only way Karen could guarantee their meetings wouldn't turn into brawls.

Bob surprised her one afternoon at her job at Monique's by showing up with a dozen red roses, a teddy bear, and a balloon with a honey bee that said *Bee Mine*. It had gotten a chuckle out of Karen, but it hadn't gotten Bob out of the doghouse.

Finally, one afternoon as she was getting off from work, she began walking to the car when she saw Bob standing in the alleyway across the street from her, staring at her with a smile, wearing a trench coat. When she noticed him, he opened the trench coat, showing her his chiseled, naked body and the hungry erection attached.

It had been a while since Karen had been with Bob in a sexual way – or in any way, for all it mattered – and she tried unsuccessfully to resist his temptations. The display reminded her of when he'd shown up at her door wearing the exact same thing, and how she'd experienced sex beyond sex with him that night.

As she began to grow wet between the legs from the memory of sex past and the promise of sex in the present, she crossed the street, backed Bob further into the alleyway where the shadows cascaded and hid them, and with soft moans and deep thrusts, Bob and Karen began to rekindle their marriage.

Even though she moved back into the house, Karen did not forgive him right away, and she knew she would *never* forgive Rosemary. She gave up her job at Monique's, deciding she needed to be home when Bob was home to keep an eye on him. She also made a point to get to know the people at Bob's office – everyone from the secretary to Bob's superior. She was not going to allow him to screw her over twice.

As for working from home, Karen did not make it easy for

Bob. She decided that, as long as his sexual appetite was satisfied, Bob had no reason to cheat on her, and so she made an effort to fuck him at least once a day, every day, unless he just couldn't get it up from exhaustion. This constant sexual activity brought about a new light in their rocky marriage – Karen's second pregnancy.

This new light also brought with it a new darkness. Upon learning of the pregnancy, Ethel sold her house in Chariot at a good profit and bought the house next door to Bob and Karen's Deerborne home.

"You've got to be kidding!" Karen said in response to the news.

"Nope... I wish I was," he replied, but she wasn't sure if she believed him. "She'll be moved in next week. She's flying in the day after her stuff and car are delivered."

"This is bullshit!" Karen spat, not taking fondly to the news that her wicked mother-in-law was moving in next door. "That's too close. *Way* too close. Can't you talk to her? Talk her into a house on another block maybe? Or somewhere in the city?"

"It's done," he replied, and it wasn't what she wanted to hear. "I hate it too, but she's signed for the house, and she paid for it outright. She owns it. There's nothing we can do."

"How can she afford to do that?" she questioned, baffled.

"She gets a big check every month from the mining company dad worked for when he died, not to mention the inheritance from my grandparents. Mom never had to work a day in her life. Selling her house in Deerborne only added to her nest egg."

"I still don't know how she *has* any money. All she does is shop."

"Hey, now…" he told her, letting his voice go stern. "She only buys things on discount." He smiled. "Besides, she's sure to be a big help when the baby comes. She can help out, run errands, whatever."

"You're so positive in your thinking. Always believing the best… not to mention she has you wrapped around her thin little pinky." Karen grunted, grinned and considered her comment as her husband glared at her with a smirk. "Speaking of my dear mother-in-law, I've always wondered… How does she stay so skinny? She eats like crap."

Bob mostly ignored the comment but offered, "She *does* buy toilet paper in bulk." He winked and returned to his home office to work.

Ethel's move to Deerborne caused a fresh rift between the couple, but the promise of a new baby worked like glue to hold them together. Ethel had, indeed, been by often to 'help' Karen with anything she needed, or at least that was how it always came across to Bob. For Karen, the woman was a living nightmare. Anything Karen wanted to do, Ethel had a million reasons on why her ideas wouldn't work, and why *hers* would. Although Karen chose to try and keep the peace by not verbally telling her husband how much she loathed spending time with his mother, she was often temperamental about it and would fret, gripe, or yell over the littlest things – things that normally wouldn't have irritated her.

Karen chose a room in the house for the nursery and began to decorate it, painting all of the walls a vibrant yellow with stencils of cute animals all about. Ethel eventually seemed to realize that things were going to be done how her daughter-in-law wanted, and so she did her part to actually help by hiring a carpenter to build a bassinette and crib in whatever style Bob – and Karen – wanted.

The act shocked Karen, but Bob merely said, "That's my momma."

Karen shook her head at him, but she did not counter him, as it *was* a generous offer – one she had graciously accepted. Perhaps there was another side to Ethel after all. A side Karen just had not seen yet, likely due to Ethel's jealously over Bob.

* * * *

She survived her first trimester with flying colors, but at the start of the twelfth week, Karen felt an all too familiar pain wrench in her gut and send her back to the hospital. She was unconscious as they removed the tiny, dead being from within her, and when she awoke, she felt like she was dead too. She may as well of been dead. She'd managed to create another life, and then lose it before it ever had a chance to see the world.

Bob's concern had been immediate, and as soon as Karen was released from the hospital, she was checked into a rest home where she had continuous support and counseling for her depression.

Highly medicated, Karen met with two specialized psychiatrists every other day, and she took part in random crafts, group meetings and events. Anything to help make the time pass. Bob visited her every third day when visitors were allowed. Once a month, he brought Ethel with him, but she spent most of her time flirting with the staff.

In just under three months, Karen went home, where she wore a smile on her face and pretended that all was right with the world. She'd stopped taking her medication at the rest home two weeks prior, having faked swallowing them every time they were administered. Now, she had a prescription for them that she filled but did not use.

Nothing was the same as it had been, Karen realized as she settled back in to the house. Bob, although still working some from home, spent more time at the office, and Ethel made a habit of popping in from time to time to check on Karen, which just made things worse.

"You must be starving," the mother-in-law told her as she burst through the front door with a key Bob had made for her. "Heaven knows you probably haven't had a decent meal in weeks!"

"I made a sandwich for lunch," Karen commented. She then sighed at Ethel's presence.

"That's what I mean! A sandwich… You need *strength*, Katharine!"

"Karen," she corrected, shooting the old woman a little side-eye.

"Whatever…" Ethel walked to the couch and patted Karen's shoulder on her way to the kitchen. "The fact is, you need to get healthy and strong as soon as possible. What is it they say? Third time's a charm! Time to get up off that couch and get your ovaries nice and strong before it's too late."

"Too late?"

"Why, yes, dearie." Ethel's voice rose as she wandered through the kitchen and left Karen's view. "You're not getting any younger! In no time, you'll be all dried up and your eggs will be like brittle raisins!"

Karen wondered if Bob would notice his mother's disappearance if she was to go into the kitchen and kill her. Then again, she could see Ethel was at least trying to be useful, although she couldn't seem to check her insults at the door. Besides, the old bat had a point. If Karen was ever to get pregnant again, she and Bob needed to start trying before it was too late. She wasn't worried about menopause; she was much too young for that. Her ovaries wouldn't dry up for many years to come.

She was worried about her and Bob. Somehow, she didn't believe their marriage would survive this time... not without a baby.

Days... weeks went by without Bob attempting anything sexual toward Karen. Perhaps he was afraid of hurting her. Perhaps he was giving her time to recover. Perhaps he just wasn't interested anymore, which was okay in a way. She didn't feel all that interested in him either. Twice in a three-month period, he asked her to perform oral on him, and although she obliged, he'd climaxed neither time.

While their marriage still existed, Karen felt it crumbling. She didn't think Bob was cheating on her again. She could find no signs of it, yet she remembered seeing no signs when he'd fucked Rosemary back in Chariot. When she would call is office, he was there. When he'd get off from work, he'd be home within the hour.

She felt like he was being faithful, but she also felt like that was making him miserable.

"What are you looking at?" she asked, walking into the bedroom to find him propped on the bed, looking at a sheet of paper.

"Our old list," he told her, handing her the paper. "The one where we both wrote down our top five places to live."

"Look," she said, smiling and pointing at Bob's list. "You listed Hong Kong as your top pick."

"It's a technology super-city," he replied, beaming through a smile.

"Well, *that's* never going to happen. I don't think I want to learn a whole new language at this point in life."

"But you chose England," he scoffed, taking the paper back and pointing to her list. "That's another country."

"But they speak the same language."

"If you can call it that. I can barely understand a word they say."

"That's because you just don't listen."

She smiled. He smiled in return. There was a moment, a glow of warmth that built into the room – something that Karen hadn't felt in quite some time. Bob set the paper down on the bed beside him. Karen lowered herself down on top of him, and just like that, a match was struck again as the couple made sweet, passionate love for the first time in a long time. This time, Bob not only finished, but he completed rounds two and three, bringing Karen through the loops of orgasmic ecstasy with him.

Then – 7

Bob's salary continued to increase and Karen grew used to being a stay-at-home wife, but she didn't thrive in it. Bob began traveling a lot, to conferences and such, which gave her some time alone to plan her future bookstore. Yes, she'd made a decision and she was excited for it. She'd told Bob of her plans, and he'd agreed to help finance it to get her started. She was going to call the bookstore Chariot Books, in honor of her hometown, and she'd sell new books – mostly indie – to the eager readers of Deerborne.

In their fourth year in Deerborne, her store closed after eight months of business – or the lack thereof. It had been a disaster, averaging only a small handful of customers a week – few of which actually bought anything. She'd tried hosting readings, events, and book clubs, but the people of Deerborne simply were not literate. They had money and no need to read or to better themselves through literary culture.

She and Bob never did quite get back into the swing of things. They stopped trying to have a child. Karen stopped wanting to put herself through the pains of losing a baby, and Bob seemed to just grow tired of Karen all together. This brought about an emotional vacancy in their marriage. There were no more heartfelt discussions, no romantic gestures, and intimacy was a thing of the past. They were broken, and nothing they tried could fix them.

"You're home from the office earlier than usual," she noted as he walked into the front door, placing his briefcase and a box of items onto the floor in front of him. "Bad day?"

"Worst day," he corrected, walking over to the bar counter at the far end of the living room and pouring himself a drink. "They fired me," he said after the first deep swig.

Karen looked at him, blankly through blinking eyes. "What?" she asked in disbelief.

"The bastards fired me!" he spat, taking another drink. "*Me*! Their top director of creative design."

"What'd they fire you for?" she questioned, perturbed but trying to remain calm.

"Oh, they'll be lost with me." Bob was fuming. He poured himself another drink. Chugged it. Refilled the short glass. "They'll see. They won't know what's their ass and what's their motherfucking face." In a deep gulp, he drank the vodka down.

"Bob," Karen asked again, standing from the couch, "what did they fire you for?"

He shifted in his step and poured another drink. Nervously, he sipped it and held the glass, looking from Karen to the floor.

"They said I stole the coding for our new shopping app," he

told her, and he drank.

She could not believe what she was hearing. Bob was a technological genius. She knew that for a fact. He had no reason to steal from another company, or from anyone. There had to have been a misunderstanding – a piece of the puzzle they just hadn't placed yet.

"You told them you didn't do it, right, Bob? You told them?"

"Of course I told them I didn't do it…" he paused, drank, paced. "But they have proof… so they fired me."

"Wait." Karen took a deep breath – not wanting to scream, but knowing it was coming. She held it back, albeit barely. "You *did it?*"

Bob set his glass down and rushed to her, taking her gently by the arms. Looking deep into her eyes, he said, "I had to, baby. I *had to*. I had to have something ready in time for our launch, and I had nothing. *Nothing*. I mean, it's fucked up that they even caught me."

Karen sighed, shook her head, and averted her eyes from his. "How'd they catch you, Bob?"

He released her arms and walked away, back toward the bar where he refilled his drink. "It was a fluke, you know." He took a sip, swished it around in his mouth a little, and swallowed. "I have a buddy – *had* a buddy – over at GenyTech and he needed my help with something and I needed his help with something. I helped him out; he got me the coding. What I helped him out on backfired; he ratted me out. End of story…"

"What did you help him with that backfired?" She couldn't believe she was even asking the question. This whole conversation – it was the last thing she'd ever expected to happen.

"A job interview. He wanted to leave GenyTech. I put in a good word for him with the heads at Milton and they interviewed him. They just didn't like him. When they told him he needed more cutting edge ideas like their boy Robert Granger had, he laughed in their faces and then threw me to the wolves."

"Pour me one of those," she told him and drank the glass straight down as soon as he passed it to her. "What do we have in savings?"

"Not much. We lost a ton of money on the bookstore, and because I was fired for theft, I lost everything that came with the job."

Karen began to feel the desperation of the situation sink in. She was so angry and scared all at once that she didn't know what to say or do. "How will we be able to keep this house? Pay our bills? Eat?"

"It'll work out," he told her, pouring her another drink. "I'll find another job. I've got years of experience. It shouldn't be hard. I've got a few connections. I'll make a few calls."

Karen drank down her second glass of vodka and felt a headache emerge. The headache was not caused by the alcohol though. It was caused by Bob and the dire situation he'd just landed them in.

She wasn't stupid, but she imagined Bob was if he thought he could go right out and find another job after being fired from one for stealing from another company. No one would trust him to not do the same thing to them, and if they did, she thought they were pretty damn stupid too.

She left the living room and went to the bathroom, where she took a hot shower. There, she tried her best to relax and wash her cares away, but it was to no avail. Bob had officially ruined them, and if he didn't find a way to keep them afloat, she'd have no choice but to leave him and move back home to Chariot.

Karen slept in their bed while Bob crashed in the guest room. He'd wanted to share their bed, but she wouldn't allow it. If she had, they'd have been up all night fighting. That was a guarantee.

When she woke again, Bob was already up and dressed, ready for the day.

"There's no time like the present," he said, straightening his tie as he walked to the front door. "Next time you see me, I'll be a man with a brand new job."

She didn't respond, and when he left, she had her coffee

and a cigarette and began her day.

Karen considered going back to work and tried to return to her old job at Monique's, only to learn there were no open positions. Day after day, Bob left the house with the intention of getting a new job. "Today's the day!" he'd say as he left, and when he returned, he did so in the manner of a beaten and broken dog.

By the end of summer, their funds were depleted. They couldn't get any more loans, and they'd run out of stuff to sell.

"Can't you just ask your mom for a loan?" she pleaded, but Bob would not hear of it.

"You know how my mother is. If she was going to lend us any money, she'd have done it by now."

"What are we going to do?" She slumped down onto the floor, feeling absolutely defeated.

"The only thing left to do is sell the house," Bob told her, looking down at her from a few feet away.

"Sell the house?" she questioned, staring up at him. "Where will we go?"

"Well… she may not give us any money, but Mom would be happy to give us shelter. We could live with her for a while."

"No!" She stood, as to show how adamant she was on her stance. "Absolutely not! I refuse to live with your mother!" She censored herself, burying the urge to list her reasons why. Instead, she added, "We're adults, Bob. We should be able to live independently from parents."

"I don't see what choice we have," he countered, raising his voice a hair as if to get his point across. "Otherwise, we'll be on the streets and sleeping in the cars."

"Then we'll sell my car." She didn't want to say it, but it came out anyway. It was a far better option than living with Ethel. "We can make a few grand to get us through for a little while."

The few grand got them through a few weeks, but the bills kept coming and the situation grew grimmer. Eventually, Karen had to concede defeat and agree to let Bob put the house on the market. When it sold, it sold for less than they paid for it, leaving them homeless and with less than they'd expected to start fresh on. Once they were caught up on bills, there was only around eighty grand left in the bank, and Karen knew that wouldn't get them far.

"We've got less than a month until the new owners move in," she told him, pacing the nearly empty living room floor. There was still furniture, but nothing of value anymore. "Any idea where we will go?"

"Actually, yeah," he replied, smiling as he opened the laptop – the only piece of technology, aside from their cell phones, left in the house. Bob pulled up a website and showed Karen the closed listing for a recently sold farmhouse somewhere on the English coastline. The house and its property sold for just over forty-five thousand American.

"Wow," she whispered, looking at the image. "That place looks dreary. I can't believe they got that much for it."

Bob looked at her, smiling, but his smile seemed like a nervous one.

"No..." she breathed, her eyes growing wide and her jaw falling slack. "Bob, please tell me you didn't..."

"You said you wanted a fresh start!" he exclaimed and pointed at the image on the website. "And, what was the top spot on your list of places to live?"

"England..." she admitted, begrudgingly.

"And guess where we're moving?"

"I hate you."

"No, you don't," he replied and kissed her on the cheek. "You love me. It's just things have been hard. But I promise you, when we get there, you'll see. Everything will be great again."

She sighed and looked at the image of the farmhouse with nothing but water behind it. She knew better than to judge a book by its cover, and so she agreed to give the farmhouse and the move to England a chance. She and Bob had suffered some rough times, but they'd had some really great times also, and if this move would help salvage that, she'd give it a try.

She had to.

"What about your mother?" she asked him, walking into the kitchen for a bottle of water. "What does she think about you moving so far away from her?"

"She thinks it's great. She said it will give her a place to visit and travel to from time to time."

Karen looked at him with a stern gaze. Having lived next door to Ethel for these last few years had nearly driven her crazy. The woman was the worst person that she knew. If the move to England offered Karen one thing, it was the knowledge that she would be in another country, far from her wicked mother-in-law. She would have to make sure that, if Ethel ever visited, she would make her stay with them as uncomfortable as possible.

Over time, Ethel's treatment of Karen had not only grown worse, but the way the woman treated Bob had deteriorated as well. Now, as if she had been saddled with the worst daughter-in-law in the world, Ethel had grown bitter toward Bob, sending him from one end of the emotional rollercoaster to the other every time they saw one another. In Karen's eyes, Ethel now saw Bob as a worthless nobody, which wasn't very far from how Karen felt about him.

Perhaps this move would change that. She didn't think it would, but she hoped it would. It was Bob's last chance to fix this mess he'd gotten them in, and she would allow him to try. After all, what choice did she have? She'd considered returning to Chariot, but even though she'd have been away from Bob, she'd have been closer in proximity to Rosemary again, and that option was no option at all.

If she saw Rosemary again, there was no telling what she would do to her. One thing, she knew…whatever she did to her would be excruciatingly painful.

Still, even though she was agreeing to try this new venture with Bob, she was angry that he had not consulted her first before purchasing the property. With her luck, the house was going to be the worst thing she'd ever laid eyes on, and she prayed she was wrong. At least, she considered, she would be surrounded by new culture and neighbors and… lots and lots of water.

She walked back to Bob and looked closer at the photo. She could see the house, some property, a couple of outbuildings, and then nothing but water.

"Are there more pictures?" she asked, looking for thumbnails to choose from. "I'd like to see photos of the area around the house and inside."

"Looks like we'll both have to be surprised. That's the only photo they uploaded for the listing." Bob tapped the photo on the screen. "The description says it's a pretty big place though. A lot of rooms, basement, attic… a boat house. Maybe we can get a sailboat."

Karen liked the idea of a sailboat, but the grayscale photo of the farmhouse made her cringe. It was like something out of an old Hitchcock flick. "The photo's not even in color."

"No… it's in color. It was just a very gray day."

"A gray day, indeed."

Fortunately, they had each renewed their passports the prior year because the next thing Bob told her nearly sent her over the edge.

"We leave in three days. We've got enough left in the bank to have the rest of our stuff shipped and to buy a new car when we get there. And we'll fly. I know you love to fly."

She didn't love to fly; not at all. He would know that if he had paid attention to her the few times they took trips together. Her silence on the flights… the way she gripped the armrests of her seats. The valiums she took before boarding and during… The idea of being thousands of miles above ground always terrified her.

She ignored the urge to counter him on this and focused on the other part of this life-altering news. Three days… that was a rush if she'd ever heard one. Granted, most everything was already packed and ready to load up, but *she* wasn't ready yet. She felt like she was going blindly into this next phase of her life, and she was scared.

"Think of it," he told her, closing the webpage and the laptop, "at least we'll be somewhere where we can start fresh. I can get a job there. I'll be somewhere new and word won't have reached them about how we got into this situation to begin with."

"Let's hope so, Bob," she said, eyeing him sternly,

"because this English farmhouse is our last chance at healing our marriage." Her head swirling, Karen left the room and retreated upstairs, where she laid down, trying to get a grip on this new bombshell that had been dropped on her, and took a long, restless nap.

Part IV

Day 6 – Karen

From above rang an incredible boom from the heavens, echoing down to the earth below. With the great boom came the thunderous clouds, the lightning, and the rain. Shielded away from sight by the darkness the storm created, the moon took its stance in the sky, allowing nighttime to begin.

A bolt of lightning, so blindingly bright, escaped one of these tremendous dark clouds and plummeted with swiftness through the drops of rain, shooting straight into the rocking sea. There, as it began to surge through the saltwater, it struck a figure… a being… a corpse, and it rippled throughout that corpse, spreading its electric magic from the top of the head to the tip of each toe.

Where there had been darkness, Karen opened her eye to a powerful beam of light that felt like an explosion – one that sung through her head like a chanting siren and blistered through her veins like a singeing inferno. She opened her mouth to scream, but she could not make much of a sound. Frantic, her arms and legs flailed about, but they were trapped – wrapped in soft vines and seaweed.

I'm underwater, she thought and gasped for air despite her realization. Only water came in and her immediate instinct was to panic. In a struggle, she fought against the vines that bound her, fearing the inevitable – that her lungs would fully fill with water and she would drown. She didn't know precisely where she was or how she'd gotten here, but she had to free herself. She had to reach the surface and breathe before it was too late. Before she died…

She suddenly grew still. Only able to see out of one eye, she looked at the dark area surrounding her. She was most certainly in the sea, and even though she knew it was impossible, she believed that she was somehow already dead. It didn't matter how much water filled her lungs. She had already taken her last breath.

Unable to bring anything into her lungs but water, she discovered that she no longer required air to function. She calmed, letting her body float just above the sea's floor, and she began to untangle herself.

She wondered how she came to be here, and why she was naked. She tried to remember, but her mind was so dark – like a castle with all of the lanterns extinguished for the night. All she could see were foggy images that faded in and out – flashes of a place... a man... a hellish existence that she hoped hadn't been hers. Where was her memory? Why could she not remember what had happened to her? If she was in the sea, had she been in a boating accident? What was her name?"

Karen... she thought as a name came to her. It felt right... familiar. *Yes... my name is Karen.*

She couldn't pull anything else – only the name, and even though it was familiar, she still wasn't sure it was hers. Everything seemed so unclear and distant. It was liken to a dream... a very bad dream.

Something felt strange in her right eye. Slowly, she brought her hand to it and felt with her finger. There was a hole there where her eyeball should have been. While this explained her impaired vision – seeing only through her left eye – it terrified her and made her panicky again. Just as she was about to pull her hand back, she felt something inside her eye socket touch against her finger. She grabbed it and began to pull. Little by little, she tugged on the slimy, slick object and pulled it out of her. When it was fully retracted, she saw the object was some type of eel or other frightening sea creature and was around eight inches long.

Shocked and scared by the discovery, she released it. The creature was quick to escape and disappeared into the dark of the sea. Karen was not so quick to recover from the moment. She floated in her position, feeling paralyzed by everything she was experiencing. Finally, after waiting countless time for some other disturbing thing to happen to her, nothing else happened and she let her tension subside and relaxed as best she could.

Her neck hurt, and she popped it – snapping it into place and sending a sharp jolt of pain straight up into her brain. All at once, it was like her whole life began to cycle in front of her and she remembered. She remembered it all… She remembered being a child again and she remembered the tragedy of losing her parents. She remembered wearing fantastic clothes and marrying the man of her dreams. She remembered two pregnancies, two miscarriages, and a mother-in-law from hell. Then, Karen remembered a farmhouse, and she remembered Bob, flailing his arms about in anger and flinging a screwdriver into her eye. She remembered backing up and tumbling over the railing, crashing down to the first floor where everything went black.

Bob, she thought, tasting something bitter in her mouth but figuring it was just the memory of him and not the stench or rot of death.

Karen knew Bob pretty damn well. Somehow, ever since arriving at that godforsaken farmhouse, she'd known he was going to kill her, and accidentally or not, he had done it. Then, if he did what she thought he did, he rowed her out to sea and dumped her body like chum for the sharks.

She was suddenly thankful that no sharks had found her, as her body seemed pretty much intact, aside from feeling cold and blue and missing an eyeball.

That son of a bitch, she thought, and with a push back of her arms and legs, she began to swim upward toward the surface of the rocking sea.

It was storming as she surfaced, but she didn't mind it. She didn't find it a threat anymore. *Let it rain*, she thought, swimming instinctively toward the southeast. A bolt of lightning struck so brightly that, for just a glimmering moment, it illuminated everything around her. There, a few hundred yards ahead, she saw the farmhouse beckon to her. She hoped that Bob was awake because she was coming home.

About a hundred yards or so away from the shore, she felt an incredible sensation come over her. She could actually smell Bob from this distance. She'd have known his scent anywhere. Bob was definitely home. She could practically taste him.

Karen swam with all her might toward the house, pushing against the harsh waters and waves. More than a time or two, she was pushed under, and several times, she was pulled back, but she persisted.

She would not be stopped. Not by nature, and not by Bob. Yet, there felt something very *unnatural* about nature at the moment, and it was proving to be a force to be reckoned with.

She dove beneath the upper layer of water, to where the force of the current wasn't nearly as strong. There, she was able to move at a greater speed toward the house. Not having to surface for air came in handy and bought her some time. However, when she did surface and attempted to breathe, she found that her lungs were full of water, and she coughed up all she could.

She reached where the water crested against the foot of her land and she walked onto it with quiet steps and a cautious eye. The earth squished between her toes. She surveyed her surroundings. A bolt of lightning helped her see that no one was around outside with her, and so, she moved away from the water and the outbuildings and ventured up the slippery driveway. At the top of the hill, she took steady, almost timed steps toward the house. Lightning flashed behind it and then above it, displaying it with such illumination that it seemed to be welcoming her home.

Karen did not know exactly how she was alive or why, but she knew that some power beyond her own had brought her back from the dead, and she was thankful for the opportunity. After all, it gave her one more chance to confront that deadbeat husband of hers.

She walked up the steps to the front door and stood before it. Raindrops leaked onto her from the porch roof.

"I hate this fucking house," she said, having drawn a breath just to speak. It was painful, she discovered, but it was worth it to know she still had a voice. Likewise, she learned speaking was the only thing she'd needed to breathe for thus far.

As the thunder rolled, the rain pounded, and another surge of lightning illuminated the sky around the desolate farmhouse, Karen beat against the front door with four heavy knocks.

She waited a moment. She could smell him inside. He was close – perhaps at the far side of the great room – and she listened for his footsteps. She was ready for him. She was going to tear him apart. Rip him limb from limb… shred his miserable remains all throughout this hideous house that he bought. She hated him with such fury that she would bring that wrath down upon him so strongly that his ancestors would feel it.

Shit, she thought, listening as he stepped to the door and grabbed the knob. Suddenly, her mind went blank. She didn't know what to say or do. She froze up, but she was still pissed.

The door opened and she saw Bob for the first time since falling over the railing. He looked well, which made her even madder. While the premeditated actions of her anger failed her, her speech was quick to return.

Taking a labored breath, "You threw a screwdriver into my eye," Karen told him in her most bitter tone, looking at her husband as he took a panicked, cowardly step backward.

"You…" Bob whispered. His voice was shaky and barely

present as it quivered through his lips.

"How dare you?" she continued, stepping through the threshold, soaking wet and covered in seaweed, into the living room. Karen had no idea how she looked, and she didn't care. She was too pissed to care.

"How... how is this possible?" Bob asked, backing up to the far wall beneath the upstairs hall. "I watched you fall and break your neck."

"You dumped me in the goddamn sea," she told him as she crossed the room toward him.

"You're supposed to be dead," he retaliated, although his retaliation came from a voice that was stunned.

She stopped short of him by just a few inches, close enough to slap him hard against the cheek.

"Ow!" he exclaimed and put a hand to his scolded cheek, rubbing it.

"How dare you?" Karen repeated and drew another large, labored breath. If she could have still cried, she would have. "After all we've been through. After all the times I've stood beside you when you've fucked things up... including moving to this dump! And you not only kill me, but you dump me in the sea? What the hell is wrong with you, Bob?"

Bob watched her with wide and wild eyes as she chastised him, and she could see he was sweating. He was nervous and scared, perhaps so scared that he was terrified. That gave Karen a taste of satisfaction, but it was only a taste.

"And why am I naked, Bob? Where are my clothes?"

"Clothes?" he asked, mumbling the word. "You – you had clothes on when I dumped your body. They must have been torn from you by the water." He swallowed. He was trembling. Karen had the upper hand on him and she intended to utilize it.

"You could have called the police instead of dumping my body, you know."

"Called the police? Are you insane?" He smiled that nervous smile he got from time to time. A crackly chuckle escaped him. He was shaky and looking anywhere but at her. "They'd swear I did it on purpose. A screwdriver? Right in your eyeball? A broken neck from a fall over a railing? We'd lost everything and I'd moved you here, away from everyone. They'd think that was a pretty good murder plot, Karen."

"You're right," she concluded, nodding her head. "It does sound like a pretty good murder plot, doesn't it?"

He was quiet for a moment, studying her. She could feel his eyes searching her single eye, as if hunting for something. "What are you implying?" he finally asked. She could sense the desperation in his voice.

"I'm not *implying* anything. You brought me here to kill me." Every time she spoke, she had to draw another breath. That seemed to be the most painful part of this physical transition for her. Through her one eye, her vision was better than ever. Her sense of smell was also heightened. It just seemed like every breath made her have to reawaken her lungs all over again. She hoped that this would pass once they got used to being active again. Otherwise, she figured she'd end up talking a whole lot less from here on out.

"I brought you here to try to fix us!" he yelled, fuming. Karen could see his fear transform into anger right before her eye. "And I fucked that up too!"

He sighed, grunted through his angst, and slipped away from where Karen had his back to the wall.

"I need a minute," Bob told her and walked to the front door, opened it, and stepped out into the dark storm. The door slowly shut behind him.

Just then, Karen heard a shrilling scream summon from upstairs – the scream of a woman.

"That fucker," she said under a forced breath and walked to the stairs.

"Help!" shouted the unknown voice, and this desperate plea took Karen's bomb of anger and lit its fuse.

She didn't know how long she'd been dead, but she felt like it hadn't been more than a few days, and already Bob had another woman in the house.

"Over my dead body," Karen grunted and began up the stairs, hurrying her way to the top.

On the second floor landing, she looked over at the railing from which she'd tumbled and then to the door of the guest room Bob had been working on. She sniffed the air, pinpointing the scent of this *other woman* to that room.

Like a savage dog, she marched to the door, turned the knob, and threw it open.

There, she saw her mother-in-law standing on the bed, hopping from one foot to another as a severed hand tried to jump onto the bed with her.

"You!" Karen said in a shocked, disgusted tone.

Ethel caught her gaze and looked at her, screaming in sheer terror at the sight of her.

"You fucking bitch…" Approaching Ethel made something new happen inside of Karen. It made her stomach growl with a hunger she'd never known and one that she found nearly impossible to fight. She considered this new kind of hunger as she stormed toward Ethel. The hunger's primal nature won over her moral sense of right and wrong, but Karen actually didn't consider it a win at all. She considered it a compromise, as her savage cravings wanted her to tear into Ethel and devour her, while her human nature distinctly wanted Ethel Granger dead.

Like a lioness, she leaped upon the bed with her mother-in-law, throwing the stunned woman down to the mattress.

"What happened to you?" Ethel asked through her fear – her voice quivering with emotion. "Why are you so hideous?"

"Hideous?" Karen replied, offended by Ethel's choice of last words. "I hope you taste like jerky."

"What?"

Karen opened her hungry mouth wide and bit down into Ethel's neck with such quickness that the woman had no chance of dodging her. Ethel screamed again as Karen fed on her, but when she reached her throat, the scream was cut off.

She could feel the life leave Ethel's body as she ate her flesh and sipped thirstily on her blood. It was amazing how delicious the old woman tasted... how good it felt to swallow down her chewy flesh and suckle on her warm, sweet blood as it pumped from her veins like the most perfect fountain. It was a delightful sensation for Karen, who not long ago would have fainted or been sick just to have witnessed such a display. But she didn't care about the old Karen right now. That Karen was dead, and this Karen was hungry.

As she fed, her hunger began to subside and she became lost in the magical tranquility of her new diet. She'd never tasted a meat so naturally salty and oily. No glass of wine had ever tasted as good as Ethel's blood.

The moment Karen decided to pop one of Ethel's eyeballs

into her mouth, she glanced behind her to see Bob watching from the doorway, looking a bit bluish-green in the face. Shocked. Disgusted.

"Oh, my god…! Karen. What have you done?" he asked, rushing into the room and to Ethel's side. He took her hand to check her pulse. "You *ate* my mother!"

"She deserved it!" Karen spat her words at him through a mouthful of gore. "The bitch said I look hideous!"

"You *do* look hideous!" Bob exclaimed, frantically pulling at his hair. "Have you looked at yourself?"

It occurred to Karen that, no, she had not looked at her reflection since rising from the bottom of the sea. She swallowed her food and stood from the bed, feeling the heat of Ethel's blood race down her naked flesh. She might not have been a beauty queen, but damn it, she was certainly a runner up. Determined to prove to Bob – and to herself – that she was not hideous, she crossed over to the full-length mirror near the dresser and took a cold, hard look at her reflection.

She wished she could cry. She wished that more than anything at this moment. While she could not cry, she could still scream, and she took a deep, labored breath, releasing it in a shrilling tone that sent Bob backing up to the doorway.

"Look at me," she said through a tearless sob. "I *am* hideous…!" Over the course of time that she had been dead and under water, Karen's skin had taken on a pale blue coloring. Her remaining eye was nearly completely white, her lips were brittle and chapped, and she was missing part of an earlobe. There were gashes and cuts all across her body, none of which had begun to heal because the flesh had been dead when the incidents occurred.

She saw that she was no longer Karen Granger, the beautiful young woman that had the whole rest of her life still ahead of her. She was no longer the woman that could have left her husband and found someone better - someone that would have loved her. Now, she was a walking, talking... *breathing* corpse made of rotting flesh, savage hunger, and shrilling screams.

"Why is this happening to me?" she asked, turning and looking at her husband with a deeper sadness than she'd ever felt.

"I – I don't know..." he whispered. "You've become one of *them*."

"One of *them*?" she questioned, wondering what he was talking about. "One of *what*, Bob?" She felt like he was withholding important, valuable information from her – like he knew something about her condition that she didn't – and it ticked her off.

Bob swallowed, looking between her and Ethel's body. He looked frantic, scared, and in utter disbelief. "You ate my mom!" he repeated, gesturing toward the dead woman as if to prove his point. "What the fuck do you *think* I'm comparing you to, Karen?

You're a goddamn zombie!"

She looked at him, blankly, and blinked her good eye. Then, she shifted her position from one foot to the other and wiped a smear of blood from her mouth. Finally, she took a deep, forced breath and replied, "What did you just call me?"

"A zombie!" he shouted – belligerently, Karen thought. Bob took a deep breath, and in a calmer tone, he added, "You're a zombie, Karen."

"How am I a zombie?" She took a step toward him, and he took another step back. "And how would you know this anyway?"

"Um… it's common knowledge that when someone rises from the grave, they're a zombie! Duh!" Like a bitchy teenager, he smacked his forehead on the *duh* and began to chew on his thumb nail.

"In movies, sure," she countered, "but this is real life, Bob, and people don't just rise from the grave."

"You *ate* my mother!"

"She deserved it!" she yelled, repeating her earlier response.

"I know!" he yelled back, this time shocking Karen with his answer. He looked at her and shook his head. "You ruined a perfectly good thing when you killed her, you know?"

"A good thing? What? So she could cradle you against her bosom at night or make sure you've cleaned your privates properly in the bath? I don't know exactly what god-awful things your mother did to you, Bob, but you can't defend her. I know how she used to look at you… used to kiss you like she was trying to get to third base."

"I'm not defending her," he said, walking up to Ethel's body and sneering at it with spite. "I wanted to kill her myself."

"Excuse me?" she asked, dumbfounded. This was not what she'd expected to hear him say. Just a wee bit, hearing it pleased her as well as confused her.

"I was planning on making it look like an accident," he continued, sitting on the edge of the bed beside the body. "Aside from the sale of her house in Deerborne and what was left of the money from the sale of her Chariot property, she was well-set. Add in the money from my father's accident and the rest of her inheritance from her parents… well… Mom was worth a fortune."

Karen's eye grew as she listened. She couldn't believe what she was hearing.

"It would have been perfect. I'm an only child. I would have gotten everything." He shook his head at her again and looked at the floor. "*We* would have gotten everything."

"What *we*?" Karen wasted no time in her response. At first, she'd begun to think that she'd just ruined a perfect thing – a way to get rid of Ethel and to get out of their dire financial state – until Bob reminded her of something. "I was already dead when you planned this, Bob. When this all was going down in your head, I was at the bottom of the sea, tangled in weeds. Where did this *we* come in at?"

"You were, yeah," he said, admittedly, "but now you're not. Had you just not *eaten* her..."

Out the corner of her eye, Karen saw the hand reemerge and cross over to Bob, trying to sneak past him and escape out the door. Bob also noticed it and stood from the bed, scooping the hand up and holding it like it was a pet.

"What's the deal with *that*?" she asked, eyeing the hand.

"Long story," he said, tucking it under his arm. "I'll fill you in later. I'm just... exhausted."

She looked at Ethel's body – the face and neck mostly devoured. Then, as she considered the area in which they lived, she had an idea. "Bob?" she asked, stopping him as he walked to the door. He looked at her questioningly.

"Yeah?"

"I'll make a deal with you," she began, walking up to him. This time, he did not back away.

"A deal? What kind of deal?" His eyes were doubtful and his expression rang with a thousand uncertainties and questions.

"What if I can still make Ethel's death look like an accident?" She smiled. Her eye grew wide again, only this time with hope.

"You ate most of her face," he reminded her. "I don't see how you can make that look like an accident."

"But if I can?"

"Okay, I give... What do you want in return, *if* you can make Mom's death look like an accident?"

"I want for you to help me look less hideous," she told him, her eyes lowering to the floor.

She thought he would return with a jab – a smartass reply – but all he said was, "Let me take care of this roaming hand and I'll be right back. We can talk about it."

His words gave her hope in this darkly shadowed moment of her existence. As he and the hand departed for the stairs, she returned to the mirror and looked once more at her naked reflection, illuminated under the dull bedroom lighting. She stared at the cuts and gashes, at the hole where her eyeball was... at Ethel's blood covering large areas of her bluish flesh. She didn't know if she would ever look like her old, living self again, but she was praying for a miracle and hoped – for once in his life – Bob could come through for her.

* * * *

While she was certain the essence of greed flowed through Bob's veins during their conversation, it was the essence of vanity that entrapped Karen. She found Bob to be very understanding as they discussed her situation. After all, it was because of him that she was in this shape to begin with, and he admitted more than a few times how stunningly beautiful she had once been.

"I'd love for you to be beautiful again," he told her, looking her in the eye. She felt the honesty swarm from him. "I mean, you'll never be the head-turner that you once were, but I still think you could be pretty fucking hot if we put some effort into this." This wasn't the romantic Bob that he used to be. Karen assumed that – like the old Karen – the old Bob was dead and gone as well. At least, figuratively. She wanted to punch him for the comment, but she fought against the urge.

"What will we do about the eye?" she asked him as she poked her finger into her eyehole. "I can't just go around with an orbless slit like this." She took a labored breath to sigh. They still hurt, but she was getting used to it.

"A glass eye?" he proposed. "Like Sandy Duncan?"

"No," she said, shaking her head. "If it gets off just a little bit, it would look weird. Everyone would stare at it and it would become a whole big thing... How about an eye-patch?"

"Like a pirate?"

"I think they're sexy." She grinned at the idea, and Bob did as well. "Rock stars wear them too."

"Name one," Bob challenged.

"Madonna," she noted.

Bob smiled and shifted. "Name one."

She was about to remark that she just had named one when she caught his crude joke about the Material Girl and the phrase 'rock star.'

"You're still a dick, you know," she told him instead.

"Sure. It's only been a couple of days."

Bob took the time to explain to Karen what he had learned from the journals and boxes in the library. Karen, in turn, told him what she remembered about being in the cellar with the spell book and the pentagram on the floor. With his information together with hers, they managed to piece together a decent amount of the puzzle, but there were still gaps that Karen was uncomfortable with. They decided that, tomorrow, Bob would venture into town if the road was clear enough to get supplies for Karen's beautification process, and when he returned, they would sort through the rest of the journals and boxes in the library to try to get to the bottom of the mystery.

"Now," he said, looking at her with a sharp stare, "how do you intend to make Mom's death look like an accident?"

"I'll take her out to sea tonight," she replied, considering her plan as she spoke. "I'll make sure she washes up to shore a few miles down the coast."

"And what would she have been doing in the water to begin

with?"

"It's storming pretty hard out there. Perhaps I returned home and Ethel and I got into a huge argument. She stomped off outside, needing some fresh air – like you did earlier. She could have slipped on the hill and fallen down into the water pretty easily. With the thunder and rain, we'd never have heard her scream." She cleared her throat to try and loosen its stiffness and the strain of speaking and then took another hard breath. "We can report her missing. Call it in when she doesn't come back. When they find her, they'll know something was feeding on her. They'll assume it was some fish or shark or something. They'd never suspect a person having had her for supper." She licked her lips and then smiled, naughtily.

"Do you really think it will work?" he asked, and she could tell that he still had a thousand questions. "I mean… if we say that you and Mom had a dispute and then she ended up dead in the water, they'll probably look at you – or both of us – as a suspect."

"The solution is simple," she replied, leaning over Ethel's body and looking at her handwork where the face once was. "If anyone comes to investigate, I'll take care of them."

"What do you mean by *take care of them*?"

"I'll kill them," she said after a breath, looking at Bob again. "Maybe I'll eat them too. Who knows? It will depend on how hungry I am at the time."

"If they think we're suspects – and especially if their investigators disappear while visiting us – we won't get Mom's inheritance. You realize that, right?"

"Well..." she said, thinking. Bob was right. She hated to admit it, but if they were considered suspects, the plan would be for naught. "What if I've been out of town? Maybe staying in the city because we've been having marital troubles? Do you think they'll find *that* believable?"

"I think anyone would find that believable," he told her and smiled.

"Then that's what we'll do. I'll dump Ethel, and then stay out of sight in my room for a day or two. That'll give enough time for you to report Ethel's disappearance, her body to be discovered, and for me to make my return home afterwards."

"And while you're in hiding," Bob continued, "we can work on that beautification process we were talking about." He took her hand, and she nearly pulled away out of habit, but the contact felt comforting for a change.

"I'd like that," she whispered, smiling. "A lot."

Karen stopped to think as Bob looked away from her, over to the corpse of his mother.

"We should get her in the boat," she said, considering the plan. Bob looked at her again and she recognized the guilty grin on his face. She sighed, which hurt but she no longer minded, and then she shook her head. "What did you do, Bob?"

"About the boat," he began, and then he proceeded to explain his paranoia when the boat returned home and how he burned it.

She was disappointed, but somehow, she understood. "Okay, then. At least help me get her out of the house. I'll take it from there." Her eyes roamed and she noticed the crib and baby supplies that had been here when they first arrived. "The nursery stuff is still here," she said in a somewhat sad tone. It reminded her that if she even wanted to try and have a child again at this stage in her life, it would likely not happen. "I thought you would move it all out when you started getting it ready for your mom."

Bob looked around at the items and shrugged. "I intended to," he admitted, "but there was a lot going on. I mean, well, I had *you*, of course. I had to dump your body and clean up the mess. McDougal kept sneaking around. That man's the most suspicious fucker I think I've ever met. We'll talk about that later though... Then Mom showed up and the room wasn't ready. You know how this stuff goes."

He was rambling. Karen used to hate it when Bob rambled. Now though, she didn't seem to mind. As strange as the realization felt, the sound of his voice made her feel alive... *truly* so.

They wrapped Ethel's corpse in the bedding and then Bob dragged her down the stairs. From there, he pulled her through the great room and out the front door, laying her flat on the porch floor.

"Do you need help getting her to the water?" he asked, and even though she was thankful for the offer, she refused.

"No... I got this." She thought Bob looked exhausted and realized that – even if he had slept over the last few days – he had not gotten a bit of rest. "Why don't you get some sleep? We can figure out everything else that we need to figure out tomorrow."

"Are you sure you don't mind?"

"Positive."

As Bob retreated inside to his bedroom, Karen began to drag Ethel down the slippery, muddy hill. It was still raining, but it was no longer storming.

Pulling the body behind her, Karen led it into the water, where she continued to pull it across the slick, slimy sea floor. She followed the course of the island's structural embankment for what felt like minutes, but perhaps it was hours, as Karen no longer had a sense of time. She had no need to resurface for air, and if there had been any underwater predators there with her, they did not make themselves known. She assumed that, by being dead of the flesh, neither she nor Ethel made for very attractive meals anymore.

When she felt like she had traveled far enough away from the farmhouse to ensure it looked like the water had swept Ethel away, she resurfaced and brought Ethel up to the shoreline. She could see a small town in the distance, asleep during the late hour.

Surveying the area, she took note of a tugboat not far from her, docked. She went to it, pulling Ethel along with her, and dragged the corpse to the boat, the bottom of which was covered in seaweed and vines that had become entangled around the fan blades. Removing the wet sheets from Ethel's body, she loosely attached the corpse to the seaweed and loose vines, making it look like Ethel had simply washed into them instead of having been placed there.

Karen took the sheets with her as she returned home. By the time she stepped out of the water again, she could see a sliver of color coming over the horizon. The rain had stopped and morning was soon.

In the house, she climbed the stairs, discovering that her room was no longer her room. Bob had claimed it, and he was asleep in her bed.

Her body... her mind... everything about her was exhausted. She hadn't the strength to wake him up for a fight. It would have to wait until later. For now, she needed rest.

She returned to the room that Ethel had used and climbed onto the bed – wet and stained from the old woman's blood. As she lay down, she felt strange... weird. Everything around her was beginning to fade in and out, as were the sounds of the creaky old house. Just as she caught a glimpse of the sun rising through the window, her eyes slipped shut and everything went away.

Day 7 – Bob

The rain had stopped, the sun was out, and the road was clear and passable. Bob stretched and felt his back pop with the release of a yawn. He made coffee, feeling foggy-headed through the first cup. Last night – actually, all of yesterday – felt like a weird dream to him, and for a moment, he wondered if Karen had actually returned or if his mind had just been playing tricks on him.

With his second steaming cup of java, he headed back upstairs and opened Ethel's door. His mother was no longer there, replaced with a sleeping Karen on her bed.

Bob smiled and shut the door, deciding to let her rest until he returned from town with supplies for her beautification project.

Content now that last night had actually happened, he went to his room, stripped, and stepped into his private bathroom, where he bathed and shaved.

On the drive into the city, he considered the events of yesterday – the slaughtering of the zombies, Karen's return, and her feasting upon and killing his mother. Yesterday had been a productive day, and he appreciated Karen taking care of the body.

Still, he worried that his chances of inheriting Ethel's fortune were now gone. Even as good as Karen's plan was, it still didn't sound feasible. There could still be suspicions over how Ethel ended up dead in the sea. Yet, he knew he had to trust his wife. What other choice did he have? If he didn't, she'd probably eat him.

His dick throbbed with the thought.

The city was busy and traffic was heavy as Bob entered into town. He had not made a list of what he would need, but he'd seen *Death Becomes Her* more than a few times and remembered Bruce Willis's character mentioning the use of spray paint to make his corpses look beautiful, so Bob's first stop was at a hardware store. He purchased a variety of spray paints in a few different fleshy tones. He also grabbed a sharpie and some small tubes of acrylic paint in various colors.

From there, he drove to a costuming store, where he bought nonprescription contacts the color Karen's eyes had been before her death and a patch for the open eye socket. He also bought make-up and, just for shits and giggles, he bought Karen a *Corpse Bride* costume.

At a tavern, he ate heartily while he drank two mugs of a local lager. He considered getting a carryout order for Karen, but he remembered that the food of the living was no longer part of her diet. As a zombie, she required living human flesh. Keeping her well fed would be a chore, he realized, and he was not looking forward to the process.

He wondered if she could still drink though, and at a wine store, he bought a bottle of merlot for them to share later.

It surprised Bob as to how considerate he was being over Karen. The tension and anger between them had been so strong for so long that it felt like those feelings were an eternity old, but last night's plot to stage Ethel's body had been the first conversation they'd had in weeks where they had not fought with one another. It had actually been pleasant, and it reminded him of how things had once been between them. There had been a time when he and Karen were madly in love. They'd been passionate, excited, and had made love at every open occasion. Bob knew he had been the one to ruin their love affair. He'd stolen from one company to improve his standings with another, and it turned around and bit him on the ass.

There had also been the affair. That had been the harshest of the breaking points in their marriage, he figured, and even after what he had done, Karen still took him back. He hadn't meant to even have the affair. It had just happened. He'd been out one night, drinking with a coworker at a bar. The coworker went home and before Bob could leave, there was Rosemary, liquored up on the stool beside him. They had a couple more drinks together, and then they banged in the parking lot. It had seemed so new and fresh – a distraction from life – and it became a habit. Up until the move to

Deerborne, he and Rosemary saw each other at least once a week, all behind Karen's back.

If he were still in Chariot, he felt like he could have killed Rosemary right then and there. Perhaps that would have evened out things with Karen. Perhaps he could have fed Rosemary to her. He thought she might enjoy that.

There were the miscarriages too. They'd taken a major toll on their marriage. Karen barely recovered from the first one, but she was never the same after the second. He knew that she still wanted a baby. Hell, he still wanted one too. But after the miscarriages, the job termination, and the affair, things got so bad between them that they just stopped trying.

Now that she was a zombie, he knew that they would never have a child of their own. The happy little family that they'd hoped for would never be, and that made Bob more than a little sad. In so many ways, he had failed the woman that he'd loved the most – as a husband, as a potential father, and as a man.

Part of him was amazed that she hadn't attacked and eaten him the second that she saw him. Another part of him was thankful that she hadn't, while a third part knew that he would have deserved it.

This thought brought a new question to his active brain. Karen seemed to have so much in check. She could speak, she could smile and move somewhat normally, and she still had emotions. The creatures he'd seen on his property the other night – the ones that he'd slaughtered yesterday – had seemed more like the creatures from Longfellow's notes, yet even they had held some human tendencies. For instance, one of them had sucked his cock instead of biting it off. That proved there had been some humanity left in the creatures. Otherwise, Bob's dick would have been nothing more than a snack to Louise.

Karen, along with certain traits of those other zombies, gave Bob a new image of what the living dead were capable of. They were not these slow moving, brain hungry creatures from the original *Night of the Living Dead*. They weren't those super-fast savages from *28 Days Later* either. Karen was still an intelligent being. The only main differences to Bob seemed to be the fact that she was dead and that she ate people... or at least that she ate Ethel.

The thought of Ethel sent shivers down his spine as he drove out of the city and toward home. She had been his mother – granted – but she'd made herself become much more than that in his life. At times, she had been his best friend, his worst enemy, his sibling, his teacher, and – yes – his lover. He had wanted to kill her years ago, back when he had been a young teenager, and he'd wanted to do it ever since. She'd helped develop Bob into the man he was – a pathetic excuse for a human being. He was glad that Karen had taken care of her for him, although he still wished that she hadn't eaten her. That had the potential of making things messier for them, and they were already in quite a mess.

"I can't believe she's alive…" he whispered as he drove, thinking of his wife. "Or something like alive, anyway."

When Bob killed Karen, he panicked – true – but then he grew used to the idea. After a bit, the knowledge that he'd taken his wife's life had no longer bothered him. It had, in turn, filled him with a feeling of power. It was what had finally convinced him that he'd had to get rid of his mother once and for all. In all of his years, Bob had never so much as started a fistfight with another person, and he'd suddenly become a coldblooded killer. This scared him – more than he wanted to admit. He'd become a completely different person over the last few years, and especially over the last few days. Suddenly, he did not like himself, not even a little bit.

Karen's return was, he decided, a sign from a higher power, telling him that it was not too late for him – for *them* – and that he still had a chance to fix things with his wife and to become the good person that he once believed himself to be.

Turning down his road, he was excited to be returning home to Karen. He was excited at the chance to get to see her again, to hold her again, to kiss her again… He was thankful that she was not still dead in the water – that she had returned to him and that she hadn't eaten him like she had his mother.

Despite the immense marital problems they were facing when he killed her, he now felt a love for her that was renewed within him, and he was eager to share that love with her.

Slamming on his brakes, he brought the car to a squealing stop in the road as he came to the house with the zombies that he'd visited yesterday. It and its barn were engulfed in flames.

"What the fuck?" he breathed, staring at the blazing fires. With both structures on fire and neither close enough to the other for the fire to have easily spread, Bob knew this was arson. The ground was too wet for this to have been anything else. They were being burned on purpose, and Bob believed that he had something to do with it. "Someone knows their little zombie secret is out," he said, smiling at the display. "Well… they're not going to burn *all* the evidence. My basement is literally *crawling* with more."

As he neared closer to his house, he thought of how he should have gotten Karen flowers while he was in the city. Then, he wondered if somewhere he could have purchased human-flavored chocolates. He imagined she would have loved those.

Parking the car, Bob realized just how excited he was. He worried that he might have been reading too much into their brief moment of not fighting with one another, but he was hopeful, to say the least.

Unloading the packages, he considered how lucky he was to have been given a second chance like this – a chance at happiness with a woman that he truly loved.

Yet, that woman was a walking, talking corpse, and he realized this as well. What if she began to turn more savage as time went on? What if she began to turn into one of those movie zombies? Would she turn on him and eat him? He suddenly understood Longfellow's concerns that were logged in his journal entries.

Although hopeful for reconciliation with his wife, Bob was not certain how much he could trust her. He *did* kill her after all, even if it had been an accident. Certainly, she was holding a grudge over that. For the moment, she was calm. He just had to keep her that way – remind her of how much they had once loved each other, and how they could be like that again.

Entering into the house, he wondered what kissing her would be like... what sex with her would be like. Would she be cold and clammy inside? Would her tongue be like a reptilian's tongue, cool and slithery?

He stopped thinking about it, as the idea of it all was beginning to turn him on, and he had to focus on making Karen beautiful again before he could switch the focus to freshly exploring her insides.

"Karen!" he called, setting the packages down on the floor near one of the chairs and looking around. The house was quiet and just as he'd left it earlier. In fact, he thought it was *dead* quiet.

"Karen?"

Bob imagined that the transformation from living person to corpse to zombie had likely put a strain on her, as when he'd left, she'd been asleep. She had to be exhausted, he figured, but it was mid-afternoon and time for her to wake up and become beautiful.

"Karen!" he yelled as he climbed the stairs toward the room in which she rested. "Rise and shine!"

He paused at the closed bedroom door and listened. Not a sound emerged from within. He'd hoped she would have been awake and ready, but he didn't mind waking her. If he did it sweetly enough, perhaps it would help direct her toward loving him again.

"Karen?" he questioned again, twisted the knob, and pushed open the door. A creak escaped it, low and impending.

There she was, laid out over the bed, her eyes shut, sleeping peacefully like she hadn't a care in the world. She looked like she hadn't moved a bit.

Softly – almost timidly – Bob crept over to her and sat on the edge of the bed beside her. He looked at her for a moment, exploring her face with his eyes and imagining how he and Karen would soon revive her beauty. He was excited – giddy like a schoolboy – and as he reached for her arm to stir her, he wondered if he should have made her a pot of fresh coffee first.

"Karen," he said, gently nudging her arm. "Wakey,

wakey!"

Nothing. Not a movement or a sound. Not even a *hmm* to question what he wanted or why he was disturbing her. A little less gently, he nudged her shoulder, and then he began to shake it a little.

"Karen?" he asked, trying again. Raising his voice just a bit, he repeated, "Karen!"

He looked for a sign of breathing... checked her pulse. Listened for a heartbeat. Nothing let him know what was happening, which he figured made sense, as she was deceased.

"This is like waking the dead," he muttered, not noticing the pun or humor in his words. However, as the words slipped from his lips, he realized something that he considered tragic, and it saddened him more than he could have imagined it would. Karen was, indeed, dead. Not zombie dead, but dead like she had been before rising from the sea. "No..." he pleaded, feeling a tear begin to trail from his eye and down his cheek. "My poor Karen."

He stroked her hair and caressed her cheek, looking at her through heavy eyes and a heavier heart. When he initially killed her, he had not truly mourned her, aside from panicking over the fact that he was the cause of her demise. He'd otherwise been thankful to be rid of her. Now, he found that he missed her and loved her, and he wasn't ready for her to go again.

"It must have been a fluke," he whispered, standing from

the bed. "Temporary." He turned around to face her. She looked peaceful, which brought him a tinge of comfort, but she also looked terrible. He couldn't just dump her in the sea again. She didn't deserve that. Not twice, especially. She deserved a proper burial here on the hill, but she deserved to be buried looking like Karen – not like a zombie. Not like she'd been stuck at the bottom of the sea for three days.

As a last courtesy to the wife that he'd once loved and had begun to love again, he decided he would follow through with Karen's beautification project – just like she had wanted – before he would bury her. Bob hurried downstairs and collected the supplies, including the *Corpse Bride* costume, and carried them back up to where *his* corpse bride rested. With Karen dead again, the irony of the costume's joke was no longer funny to him. Instead, it seemed biting and much too cutting for humor. However, the gown was lovely, and it would serve as a beautiful burial dress for her.

"You'll be beautiful again," he promised, looking at her bluish, wounded naked body. "I'll make sure of it."

Bob began with foundation – a spray paint the tone closest to Karen's natural skin color – and he began to spray a thin layer all over the front of her body. Once the first layer was complete, he noticed he could still see some blue shining through, and so he applied a second, much heavier coat of paint.

"Look at that," he said with a smile, admiring his handiwork. "Not even a mole or a pore. This covered all those cuts pretty good too. Man… I'm *so* good."

Once the paint was dry, he flipped Karen over and repeated the process until the only things on her body *not* beige were her hair and lips – both up there and down there. After the skin-coloring, he began to work on her make-up, using a black sharpie to define her eyebrows and serve as eyeliner around her unscathed eye. He then took some rose-colored paint and painted little circles of blush on her cheeks, to add some life to her. He used the same color on her lips, accidentally moving the brush outside of the lip-line, making her lips seem larger and puffy.

"Shit," he said, and he considered wiping it off and starting fresh, but what did it matter? No one was going to see her but him, and when he buried her, not even the bugs in the ground would notice his makeup mistake.

With the costume make-up he'd purchased, he applied a heavy dose of blue eye-shadow, caking it onto both her top and lower lids. It was a bit heavier than how she normally wore eye-shadow, but since he would be putting her in the ground, he wanted it to last and stand the test of time. Then, when one day the water eroded the hill and someone happened to discover her, they would think, 'Man, that's one hot dead chick!'

He pulled open her eyelid, which had seemed stuck at first

but eventually budged, and put the contact onto her eye. Then, he lowered the lid back into place. Over the injured eye, he placed the pirate patch she'd wanted so much.

Bob took one last look at Karen's naked body. He spread her legs and stared at her vagina, wishing he'd had the opportunity to explore it, but without Karen being alive during the process – in one manner or another – he could not bring himself to violate her body.

"We were supposed to have our second chance," he told her as he dressed her in the *Corpse Bride* gown. He began to cry, but he did not sob. Instead, as the tears trailed down his face, he pushed through with his task until Karen was fully dressed and ready for her burial.

Taking a step away, he gazed at her and smiled. Bob's make-up skills were not the best, and his painting skills were even worse. She looked like a mannequin that had been turned into Raggedy Ann and put on display at a bridal shop. Yet, to Bob, she was the most beautiful woman that had ever walked the earth. He found her breathless – even more beautiful than when they'd met – and he missed her more than he could bear to admit. He hated that he had to bury her, but again – it was better than just dumping her in the sea a second time.

It had taken time to recreate Karen's luscious beauty, and as Bob glanced out the window, he saw that it was dusk. Soon, he figured, he could start digging the hole. With the fires blazing just a half mile down the road, he didn't want to risk being in the middle of an illegal burial if someone came to investigate and ask questions.

As if he had summoned the act, there was a heavy knock at the front door. It startled Bob – made him nearly leap from his skin. He glanced toward the doorway, to Karen, and then to the doorway again. The knocking persisted, and he exited the bedroom – hesitantly – and shut the door behind him.

"I'm coming," he announced in a high tone as he took the stairs step by step, with intentional slowness. He had to calm himself from the shock of the knock, as he could not seem suspicious in any way. After all, his wife was dead upstairs on a bed, dressed in a costume wedding dress from a popular movie and made up with spray paint and sharpies. He would surely be locked up if that was found out, and he doubted it would be in a prison. An insane asylum sounded more appropriate to him.

The knocking was still persisting as he reached the front door. He unlocked it and opened it, finding McDougal awaiting him; not an investigator.

"Ya fuckin' bastard!" the old man told him as he barged into the house. "Ya cocky, arrogant, entitled, selfish fuckin' little bastard!"

"Good to see you too, Mr. McDougal," Bob replied,

stepping aside from the heated old man. McDougal's mood was out of character, but it was not unsuspected. Bob imagined this arrival of the former caretaker would bring about some much needed answers. He shut the door and followed McDougal into the great room.

"How could ya kill 'em?" McDougal asked, looking at Bob with angry, tear-filled eyes.

"They were *zombies*!" Bob exclaimed, almost laughing at the question. "It was only a matter of time before they ate me!"

"They would have never eaten ya," McDougal countered, eyeing him with fierce intention. "I fed them every single night when they awoke. They would never have eaten *anyone* in this house; they haven't in years! I had seen to it that those days were over!"

"I guess you're the one that burned that house and barn then, right?" Bob was finally starting to feel like he was closer to understanding this whole weird mess. He needed to press McDougal for more information, and while the old man was angered, the information would be easier to obtain.

"I had to! Oh, ya left a mess... a goddamn mess!" He cleared his throat and looked around, searching for something. "Where is my lovely Ethel? I've come here to take her away from ya – to keep her safe. Ya be a violent, terrible man, Mr. Granger. *Terrible*!"

Fuck! Bob thought at the mention of his mother. He had to think quickly, but he was starting to reel from the *violent* comment. He'd killed *zombies*, for Christ's sake. Surely, that didn't count as being violent *or* terrible.

"Mom's not here," he said, technically not lying. "I haven't seen her all day. She went out last night… she said she was going out with you."

There it was. The alibi and the set-up he'd been looking for. By framing McDougal, he would be off the hook if his mother's death was deemed not an accident or an aquatic attack.

He wanted to smile, but he knew better than to do so as he asked, "What did you do with my mother, Mr. McDougal?"

They exchanged stares. McDougal's turned from angry to confused, and then his old eyes brightened as he exposed a devious smile.

"Ya killed her, didn't ya?" he asked Bob, taking a step back. "Ya killed yer own mother."

"No, old man. *You* killed her. You took her away from here yesterday, and there's no telling what horrible things you did to her. You probably fed her to your little zombie friends."

"Ya have no proof of anything yer sayin'!" McDougal shouted as he turned red in the face. "Especially about the living dead."

"Oh?" Bob perked again, feeling the upper hand. "Is that

really what you think? Well… do I have a surprise for you? Wait here. I'll be right back."

"Where ya be going off to? We're not done here!" McDougal stomped his cane to the floor, showing his adamant protest.

"I'm going to the basement, and when I return, you'll see that I've got more on you than you think."

"Ha!" the old man laughed, shaking his head. "There's nothing down there but some old tools an' a clunky washer an' dryer. I know every inch of this house like the back of my hand."

Bob held up a finger to him as he approached the basement door. "Just wait. Hold on. When you see this, you'll eat those words."

As he began down the basement stairs, slamming the door behind him, the sun went away for the night and the moon and stars replaced it in the sky. Bob could hear his acquisitions stirring – the scattering of severed hands, feet and heads. Once McDougal saw his little collection, he'd know he was fucked and Bob would have him right where he wanted him – taking the fall for Ethel's murder.

Day 7 – Karen

It was like a tug and a snap, and suddenly, she was no longer traveling through a paradoxical universe, lacking in rhyme or reason. Instead, she was surrounded by darkness, with no sounds and no movements.

Then, there was a tinge of sound – muffled at first... voices... someone shouting followed by the slamming of a door. She tried to open her eye, but it felt sealed shut. She also tried to move her body, but it was stiff as a board. She managed to wiggle a finger and felt something crackle all around it. Then, she wiggled more fingers... her toes... her nose. Her mouth opened rather easily, but something cracked around the edges of her lips, jaw-line, and cheekbones.

She had to focus on nearly every area of her body, beginning with her hands and feet and working her way up. Once her hands and arms were loosened, she pried open her eyelid. The other, she could feel, had a patch on it.

With her mouth open and her eye open, Karen took a deep, painful breath, fully returning to *life*.

It took some effort to stand from the bed, and when she crossed to the mirror, she nearly screamed. Dressed in a tacky outfit off of a costume store rack, she looked worse than she had when she died again. Her body had been spray-painted all one color, and the thickness of the layer was cracking and crumbling with her every movement.

Her face looked like a clown's face – an ecstatically happy clown that had been turned into a doll, perhaps. She tried to wipe it off with her hands, and only then did she realize that it wasn't make-up. From the chipping, it looked like a lot of paint. Bob had also used some kind of ink on her – perhaps sharpie. It had long dried. Only the eye-shadow appeared to be legit make-up but it was so thick that it would be hell to remove.

She knew it was Bob that had done this. No one else could have made her look worse than she had been when they started on her.

"That son of a bitch," she muttered, staring with disbelief at her reflection. "That idiot!"

More paint chipped away from her face as she spoke and worked the muscles around her mouth. Bits of blue and white – her skin's true current tone – showed through the cracks and gaps in the paint. She wanted to cry; she wanted to cry more than anything in the world, but she could not. She couldn't make tears anymore.

Bob did this to her; surely, he could undo it. She didn't care who he was arguing with downstairs. Whoever it was, she could take care of them.

"If he doesn't fix this," she whispered from a painful draw of breath, "I'll kill him."

Each step – every movement forward toward the door – was a brittle one, as the paint began to further crack and crumble, falling to the floor in chunks and dust. She opened the door – slowly and soundlessly, avoiding even the slightest creak – and stepped into the hallway. Descending the stairs, more paint began to chip away – chunks, fragments... bits and pieces flaking away like scales from a shedding snake. The hem of her dress flowed behind her as she stepped down to the main floor and into the great room. There, she stopped as her eye fell upon McDougal.

There was a rumble in her tummy as she saw him – the wicked old man that she hadn't trusted since she first laid eyes on him. The man who had seen her naked, having had no business wandering alone anywhere near her bedroom to begin with. Oh, yes... she thought he would make the perfect meal.

His back was to her as he looked over the décor. She considered creeping up slowly behind him, but she decided to just get it over and done with. Quickly, like a lioness, she hurried to him, leapt upon him when she was just a few feet away, and tackled him to the ground.

When he landed, he shouted, and when he turned his face

to see who had attacked him, he whispered, "I knew it..." just as Karen opened her jaw to bite off his cheek.

"No!" she heard a shout – a familiar one... Bob's voice – cry out from behind her and she paused just before her clownishly painted lips met with McDougal's meaty cheek. She looked back at Bob to see him stepping from the basement with a large closed box in his arms. He kicked the door shut behind him. "Don't eat him, Karen! We need him."

"Need him?" she asked in a grunted, hungry tone, and looked back at McDougal. "Need him for *what*?"

"You want to know why you're like this? Well, he's the only person that can give us any kind of answers. If you eat him... you'll never know."

She stared into McDougal's eyes. They were filled with fear, and yet, the old man was smiling.

"He's right, ya know," he told her as she loosened her grip on his arms. "If ya kill me, ya will never understand what all has happened to ya, and ya'll never be able to fully appreciate the rare beauty of this gift that ya've been given."

"Gift?" she questioned, huffing... snarling... growling. Karen glanced to her husband, who set the box on the floor and stepped up behind her. "I should rip out his goddamn throat."

Bob knelt down beside her and placed a hand on her shoulder. She almost pulled away, but she didn't. "I have a better idea."

"It better be an improvement over this paint job," she told him, forcing the words to rise above her savage hunger. "Later, we're going to talk about this clown-mannequin job you did on me."

"I thought it looked great," he admitted, grinning. "Before it started to chip, I mean."

Karen lifted off of McDougal and stood, taking a step away. "What do we do with him?"

"I have some rope in the box. I was going to tie him up and make him talk."

"I like that plan… That's a big box for rope."

"It's not the only thing in there."

The box moved a little and a thump came from inside. Karen got the gist of what he was saying. She remembered the hand from upstairs and was certain that was what was in the box.

"I'm hungry," she said, loud enough to make sure McDougal heard as well as Bob.

"How about, every time we think he's lying, you can eat one of his fingers."

"What?" McDougal asked. His eyes were wide.

"What about when we run out of fingers?"

"You can eat his toes," Bob told her, adding, "and when those are gone, you can eat his cock and balls."

"Mmm… I haven't had cock and balls yet."

"I bet you'll love them."

"No…" McDougal pleaded, shaking his head as he climbed up to his feet. "No, ya will not be enjoyin' me cock an' balls!"

"Then you'd better tell us what we need to know, or by the time my wife here is done with you, there will be nothing left of you but bones."

"Tie him up, Bob," Karen directed, walking toward the closed library door. "If I get any closer to him right now, he's done for."

McDougal did not put up a fight as Bob bound him to a chair with three long pieces of rope, but the old man's scent was making Karen's mouth water, and she had to look away from him to suppress her primal cravings. She hadn't gotten to eat much of Ethel before Bob walked in, and then she had died again. This was her second time returning from the dead, and it was a tiring process that seemed to make her hungrier each time. She prayed it would not happen again.

"We want to know *everything*," Bob told McDougal, standing in front of him with his hands upon his hips. "We want to know how my Karen became a zombie, we want to know everything about this Longfellow guy, and we want to know why in the hell you were taking care of that flock of undead in the old house and barn."

"Ha!" McDougal laughed, not even fighting against the ropes. "Ya think ya can make me tell ya what ya want to know? If she eats me, ya'll never know a word. I really don't see how ya have an upper hand in this, Mr. Granger."

"I don't have to kill you," Karen said, turning to him and approaching him, "to satisfy my appetite." When she reached him, she leaned to him and bit onto his right ear, ripping it from his head and chewing it up. The ear tasted strange, like old meat that had been sitting out. McDougal screamed from the pain. Blood spilled from the open wound. She licked at it, like it was a refreshing drink after an hors d'oeuvre. The taste was a bit different than Ethel's blood though. Even at Ethel's age, her blood had tasted fresh and sweet. McDougal's was bitter.

"Bloody fuck!" the old man shouted as he attempted to pull up one of his hands to cover the wound. The ropes were tightly secured.

"Do I start on your fingers now?" Karen asked him, wiping her lips on the polyester sleeve of her tacky gown. The fresh red was a stark contrast to the dress's shiny white coloring. "Or do I go straight for your groin?"

"I'll talk!" McDougal yelled, cringing in pain and trembling in his seat. "I'll tell ya what ya wanna know." Karen caught his stare and locked hers with it. He winced, as if anticipating another violent attack, but she repressed the impulse and simply licked her lips instead; she wasn't sure if she truly *wanted* to eat more of this man, but she would if she had to. "There is a book... I believe ya know the book, Mrs. Granger," he continued. His voice was strained and hoarse – either from the pain of his injury, the loss of blood, or from fear. Perhaps it was from all of the above. Karen wasn't sure, and she didn't care. She remembered the book he was referring to, and so she nodded her head in agreement. "Ya read from the book. Ya spilled yer blood onto the pentagram. Ya did this to yerself, Mrs. Granger. No one else did it to ya."

Karen looked at Bob, who was staring angrily at the old, bound caretaker. "Then undo it. Get the book and make her normal again."

"I couldn't if I wanted to," McDougal huffed, wincing again from the pain that throbbed through his fresh wound. "It's gone. It had to go."

"What do you mean *gone*? Where is it?"

"In flames," he replied, managing a laugh to follow. "Burning in the house with the remains of *yer* senseless slaughter. It had to go. It was the only way to end all of this."

Karen expected Bob to retaliate but she had not expected him to punch McDougal with such force that it sent the old man and his chair down to the ground.

"I said *undo it*!" Bob screamed in such great infuriation that it made Karen cringe. She'd never heard him sound this hysterically angry. "Make my wife human again!" He was fighting for *her* and she realized then and there that Bob, despite having made her up to look like a terrifying porcelain doll, loved her again, and perhaps he had always loved her. But now, she could see and feel it again.

"I *can't*," McDougal shouted in return. "What's done is done. I have destroyed the book."

"Then get another fucking book!"

"They certainly don't grow them bright on yer side o' the pond, do they?" he asked Bob, cocking an eyebrow at him. "There be only *one* book, lad. And now, its flesh and words are ash and dust." McDougal laughed again, and this time it was a more diabolical laugh than before. It worried Karen. There was something about the old man that she still did not trust. "Many lives have ended in this house, and many others have been reborn in it. It is a chaotic cycle of life and death, and then life all over again. But every time life is reborn, others must die to feed it. Isn't that right, Mrs. Granger?"

He looked at Karen again and she took another step back. He was right; she knew this, but she didn't want to admit it – not to the man who seemed to know so much for a living, breathing person.

"The book was created thousands of years ago, when an

angel fell to Earth – cast away from Heaven for being beloved above God – and was reborn a serpent. From the skin of its decaying angelic form and the scales that the serpent shed, pages were crafted and a book was bound at the serpent's request by his greatest follower, Cain.

"It is said that from the blood of Abel," McDougal continued, "the words the serpent whispered were written into the book by Cain's hand, complete with symbols and shapes that would invoke and evoke great powers that would prove the fallen angel's stature as a god, for the powers held within could have only been told and given by a true god – one with such powers that it would force the humans to realize this serpent's true abilities and put him on a throne greater than the one who had created him."

"You speak of Lucifer?" Bob asked, almost laughing through his reply. "Seriously? You're going to sit here and give us a fucked up Bible lesson?"

"He's an old man, Bob," Karen intervened. "He's probably got Dementia or something. You should just let me eat him. We could put him out of his misery and I could enjoy a good meal, all at the same time." She knew calling it a *good* meal was a stretch, but it would be a meal nonetheless. Her hunger was painful.

"Certain spells in the book have been used throughout history in efforts to thwart power, to take power, and to hold financial control," McDougal added, obviously ignoring Karen's comment. She, however, noticed that his accent had changed since speaking of the book. He no longer sounded like a seaward sailor. Instead, he sounded educated and old beyond his years. This change mystified her. "Perhaps the most intriguing and well-known use of the spell book – the earliest recorded use – was the one that defined and developed the most popular of modern Western religions.

"Centuries ago, there lived a young man who had built a following for peace throughout the kingdoms that he traveled. A poor man, his influence was in his speech and ideas, and his ideologies spread so far and wide that they managed to reach the keeper of Lucifer's spell book. This keeper, along with his own coven of dark-minded minions, sought after the peaceful guru, hoping to partner with him in an attempt to reach his followers with their message of power, coyly intertwined with his message of harmony.

"By the time they found the young man, he was on a cross, being crucified for his disruption of a king's reign. The bookkeeper and his coven were approached by their own king, once more in serpent form, and given their instructions. When the night grew black as coal and the guards surrounding the three crosses had fallen into slumber, the coven murdered the guards, taking their bodies into the night and covering them in sand. The occultists who remained at the crosses continued to carry out Lucifer's orders by encircling the young man's cross with a pentagram and chanting in unison around him.

"'What are you doing?' the young man asked them through a strained voice, looking down at them with tearstained eyes and a crown of thorns cutting into his head. 'Giving you eternal life,' the bookkeeper replied and took a knife, slicing into the bottom of the young man's foot. While the man winced from the pain, his blood dropped down to the pentagram, soaking into it as the ritual completed.

"By morn, the young man had died on his cross, and three members of the coven and the bookkeeper took shelter in a nearby cave, waiting for the young man's body to be delivered and entombed. For three long days, they waited with the body, without food or water, ensuring its safety as the ritual reached completion. On the third night, a terrible storm came to pass, and the young man's eyes opened as life returned to him.

"The coven and the bookkeeper, weak and malnourished as they were, managed to slide away the boulder that had sealed the tomb and depart through the dark of night, unseen and unheard. In the morning, when the young man's followers returned to his tomb and discovered it open, they found that the young man had returned from the dead, and a miraculous, glowing angel was standing beside him – showing the followers the true might of his power. Even then, however, it had not been done with perfection.

In fact, there are no recordings of the spell ever being done perfectly…

"Until it finally worked on me," McDougal concluded, beaming brightly through the words.

"Worked on you?" Karen asked, laughing in his face. "Impossible. I ate your ear. You bleed. You're as naturally alive as Bob, here."

"The spell worked on me," the old man added, "because I never died before the end of the third day. I am one hundred and eighty-seven years old, Mrs. Granger, and I have never had to see the blade of the reaper's scythe."

"Longfellow…" Bob breathed. Karen could hear the shock in his voice.

"That is *Doctor* Wilfred Longfellow to you, my good man. Now that I have answered your questions, untie me."

"Oh, fuck no. You've got some talking to do. Why did I die again when the sun rose?" Karen asked. He may have answered some things – much of which she didn't buy – but she had plenty more questions for him, and he was going to answer them, whether he wanted to or not.

"Jesus Christ stood in that tomb with the sun in the sky only because of Lord Lucifer's angelic touch. I am able to live during the day because I never died to begin with. You, my dear, fall under a different category. Mrs. Granger, you may only walk at night."

Bob walked over to the cardboard box and lifted it in his arms. From within, something moved around, bumping against the sides. He carried the box to Longfellow, setting it upon the old man's lap.

"What is this?" Longfellow asked, staring from the box to Bob and then to the box again. "What is in there?"

"Something else that I imagine can only *walk* at night," he replied and opened the box for Longfellow to see. "Your family."

Longfellow's eyes grew wide, wrapped in horror as he stared down at the animated head, hand, and foot of one of his kin. The head hissed at him, and Longfellow shouted in shock. "Thomas…!" He looked at Bob and quivered. "How dare you?" he demanded, spitting at Bob while he took the box from his lap. "How dare you keep him like this? Trapped in a box? Nothing but appendages and a head! My dear, poor nephew… Where is your mercy, Mr. Granger? Where is your humanity?"

"Where is your dark angel now?" Bob replied, closing the lid on the box and carrying it over to the fireplace. Kneeling, he lit some kindling wood and began a fire. "I'll tell you where he is. The same place these fuckers are going. Hell." Before Longfellow could protest the action, Bob shoved the box and its reanimated contents into the fire, letting them burn. Then, he turned back to the bound man and grinned. "You said it yourself, didn't you? In your journals? Burning them is the only way."

"When they're already dead," Karen said, answering for Longfellow. Once more, she crouched down beside the old man. "When they're still alive, I'm sure there are plenty of other ways."

"What are you doing?" Longfellow asked her, fear ripping through his voice like the wind through a tornado's rampage.

Bob sighed and nodded. Karen didn't know if he had any more questions for Longfellow or not, and even though she, herself, may have still had a few to ask, she no longer had the desire to know the answers.

She took in deep Longfellow's scent, growled in the pit of her gut, and licked his old, plump cheek.

"I did what you asked!" he pleaded, tugging at the ropes that bound him. "I answered your questions! Free me!"

"Wait..." Bob whispered, looking at the desperate man. "I have one more question."

"If I answer, will you release me?" he begged.

Karen caught Bob's stare as he exchanged a glance with her and then nodded at Longfellow. "Sure. You have a deal."

"What is it you ask?"

Bob eyed the old man. Karen crossed her arms as he asked, "How did *you* come to have the spell book to begin with?"

Part V

The Book – 1

June 5, 1882: Port of Piraeus

On a cargo ship returning from Greece, the young man hid amongst the remaining crates – each recently emptied of their contents. No one had seen him slip onto the ship. It happened at night, while the crew was celebrating their hard work with libations at a local bar. With few men left aboard to watch the ship, it had been easy for Sander to slip on and quickly find shelter.

Tucked under his arm and wrapped in a fine red cloth was the item that he was sworn to protect. It had been given to him three years prior, passed into his hands by a woman whose face had been hidden by a niqab and only her green eyes could be seen. Her eyes had held warning, and as she handed him the book, square in the middle of a busy marketplace, she had whispered to him, "You have been chosen," in her native Egyptian tongue.

Holding the book, he had understood every word, even though he'd never spoken nor heard the language before.

The book had been given to him just as he carried it – wrapped in the same red cloth that protected it from both the notice of others and from the elements. He hadn't known at the time what the book was – or that it was even a book wrapped up – until much later that night, when he was squatting in the dark shadows of an abandoned, crumbling stone structure, lit only by the brightness of the full moon. There, he unfolded the cloth, revealing to him the book built of flesh and scales and penned in blood.

He could hear a whisper in his mind as he opened it. In fact, it seemed like many whispers, all chanting the same words to him but not unison; their voices flowed unsteadily over one another. The language of both the whispers and the script in the book were foreign to Sander. A poor man with no family, he had been free to travel as he had wished, and he'd made the most of the ability, hitchhiking and stowing away as he saw fit, seeing cities, villages, and islands that he would have otherwise only dreamed about. Yet, in all of the places he'd visited, he'd never heard words like the ones in his mind and he'd never seen writing like what was in the book.

When he closed the book, the voices silenced, but Sander's curiosity eventually gained the better of him, and with time, he began to understand the whispers that chanted in his mind and even the words on the pages. He began to feel the book's power, and he began to understand what the woman in the marketplace had meant with her words. He'd been chosen to protect the book – to ensure its safety and prosperity – and while doing so, he was also in control of the book's powers and infinite wisdom.

For the first year that Sander was in possession of the book, he practiced only the spells that the book itself opened to for him. He learned certain things that made his life on the streets a bit easier – like how to convince people to give him what he wanted just by a certain stare and a whispering of three wicked little words. He also found that, when put in different orders, the wicked words did other things as well, including forcing the person they were spoken to into taking their own life or willed to take the life of another.

Sander had only used that power a few times – once accidentally as he learned what happened when the words were spoken that way, and three other times when he'd found himself in grave physical danger.

During the course of that first year, as long as he protected the book and used it how it wanted to be used, he not once had to worry about food, shelter, wine, or women. The book had provided all, and all he'd had to do in exchange was keep it wrapped in the red cloth and at his side, and to only utilize the powers it wanted him to utilize.

In the second year of his possession, his curiosity began to grow again and Sander forced the pages of the book to open to a new spell for him – one that he had not learned the written translations for or the correct pronunciations of the words for. Casting the spell had proved disastrous, causing a great quake to cascade across the land, trembling into the ocean and stirring the sea with a fierce, mighty vengeance. Shortly thereafter, thousands of dead aquatic creatures washed ashore to a land where thousands more humans had also perished.

Sander and the book had been spared, and he had been the only person left alive for several miles in all directions.

The great quake had been a warning to Sander – one telling him to not abuse the book's powers. For months after, Sander respected the book's warning, studying only what he was allowed, until one day the book opened to a new page – one that, when Sander performed the spell, showed him a glimpse of the future.

Through the vision that materialized before him, he saw glimpses of buildings – the Vatican, a great tunnel, and a courtyard. Then, he saw men in black cloaks – six of them – walking through the darkness with their faces lowered in the shadows. Finally, he was shown the vision of his own murder and the theft of the spell book by orders of the Pope.

For six weeks, Sander passed the time by evading these cloaked figures, encountering them almost daily as he fled for his life and for the safety of the book.

Now, huddled with the emptied cargo crates of the ship, he hoped that he had evaded them for good, as he was crossing from the Port of Piraeus to the Port of Southampton and – aside from jumping ship – there was nowhere left for him to hide.

He felt the book vibrate in his arms and he unwrapped it from its cloth, wondering what it needed him to know. He opened the cover and listened as the whispering voices filled his head. The pages of the book began to flip before him, finally stopping on a familiar spell – one that would allow him to see the future – or at least *a* future.

"Here?" he asked in a whisper, looking around him to make sure no one could hear. "It's too risky to do this here."

The whispers grew louder in protest and their boom within his head brought pain. With the pain came tears, and with those tears came submission.

"Okay," he pleaded against the torment, "I'll do it."

The whispers lowered and the pain subsided as Sander performed the spell.

A new vision appeared before him – one of a middle-aged man standing in the courtyard that Sander had seen in the earlier vision. He saw himself passing the book to the man and then fleeing quickly away.

"No…" Sander whispered, shaking his head in disbelief. "I

won't do it. It's too soon. I have so much still to learn from you."

He knew what passing the book on meant. The hooded collectors from the Vatican were eventually going to find him, and they were going to kill him. He had to pass the book on before it fell into their hands.

He remembered again the Egyptian woman with the stunning green eyes and the rush she had been in when passing the book to him. He imagined she had been in a similar situation as he. Perhaps the hooded men had been after her too, and perhaps after passing the book onto him, they had caught her... and killed her.

The idea made him shiver. He wasn't ready to die. He was ready to *live*. He had this brilliant, mystical book right there in his hands. He had powers – unbelievable powers – right at his fingertips. Surely, with the power of the book, he could defend himself against the Pope's bandits. He'd managed to outmaneuver them thus far. He was young... agile. He was witty and not at all dumb. What Sander didn't know from books, he made up for in street smarts.

"I won't..." he repeated, closing the book and silencing the whispers. Wrapping it in its red cloth, he added, "You can't make me. I keep watch over you, and I won't turn you over. Not to the man in the vision. Not to the collectors. Not to anyone." Holding the book close to his chest, he rested his back against a crate. "I belong to you... and you belong to me."

The Book – 2

June 18, 1882: Port of Southampton

Over the course of thirteen days, Sander used the book and its powers to his benefit. On his second night aboard, he read a spell from the book that implanted a memory of him into the minds of everyone aboard the ship. The next morning, they all believed that he was part of the crew, and they treated him as if they'd known him for a while.

He ate with the crew, drank with the crew, cut-up with the crew, and he slept in the bunks with the crew. It was a perfect cover for Sander until the ship docked. As he and his book stepped off, the spell dissipated and he was wiped from the memory of everyone that had been placed under it.

Yet, even as the sun shown down with a positive disposition and the area around him was crowded with workers, pedestrians, merchants, and shoppers, he could see the six black cloaked figures awaiting him at the end of the dock.

Barely twenty-six years of age, Sander was an agile young man, and he took off with the speed of light – or the speed of desperation – into the crowd, hoping to lose the collectors. The only way they could have found him, he realized, was if they had seen him board the ship. Either way, *how* they knew he was there did not matter. What mattered was the fact that they knew, and that they were after him and his book.

Through his heavy sprint, he tried to recall a spell to set the collectors off his course, but his mind was frantic and trying to remember what he had learned was failing him. There was no time to unsheathe and open the book... no time to stop and search for a spell. He just had to run until he knew he could pause for breath and hunt for some magic phrase or another to save his skin.

Sander glanced behind him. They were not right on his tail, but they were there, several paces behind him... not rushing, but moving at a swift enough pace to keep him in their sights.

He had to find some place to hide. Some place where the collectors wouldn't be able to sniff him out. Up ahead, he saw a tunnel – a mine, perhaps, and he rushed to it, hoping that somewhere within its darkness he could possibly hide.

The tunnel did, indeed, lead to a mine, and while the workers were busy with pickaxes and shovels, they paid Sander no attention, and he slipped into their dimly lit darkness with ease. Sander had to travel downward for a bit, and when he reached a flat area again, he found a fork in the mine – two more tunnels leading off to the left or the right. He began to turn toward the one heading left when he felt the book vibrate in his arms. A warning, he knew, and so he chose the path to the right instead.

There was no light here. Sander traveled with blind caution, although he kept his pace as quick as he could manage. Several meters down this path, the only footsteps he could hear were his own. If the collectors had followed him into the first initial tunnel and the mine, they had not followed him down the right wing of the fork. He slowed his pace, catching his breath as the oxygen was thinner here, and thanked the book for sending him in the correct direction for safety.

"See," he said, clutching the spell book tightly to his side as he walked, "you do love me." He chuckled, but his humor was brief as the ground opened up beneath him – a cave-in – and caused him to fall into the new mouth. The ground in this new opening was smooth and slick and he slid and skidded down it, feeling himself twist and turn in so many directions that it became dizzying. He clutched the book to his chest, holding it before him as if it would safeguard his journey.

Eventually, this downward sloping tunnel began to grow wetter until it opened into an underground pool, dumping Sander into it. He could barely breathe as it was – the oxygen had grown much too thin – but he took in what air he could before plunging into the murky water.

Fully submerged, he opened his eyes and looked upward,

seeing the glow of what looked like daylight not too far away. He realized that time was of the essence as he swam, and so he hurried as fast as he could, surfacing above the waterline just as he felt he couldn't hold his breath any longer.

He gasped, sucking in a fresh breath of air. Ahead, he could see only the sea. He turned around and saw a beautiful manor with a lush garden and an inviting courtyard just beyond the shore. He was out of the mine and it's darker than night tunnels, but he was also right where the book wanted him to be.

"I know what you want me to do," he told the book as he swam to shore. Stepping onto the slightly sandy, slightly rocky terrain, he added, "I won't do it though. I won. I've lost the collectors – *again*, might I add? – and now I can stop, rest, and form a plan. Your vision was wrong. I am your keeper."

The book vibrated as he approached the finely kept lawn with lush gardens and cascading waters flowing from exquisite fountains all around. Whoever lived here, Sander suspected he was a very wealthy, fortunate man.

There was nobody in sight – no one in the courtyard up ahead – and he grinned to himself, content that another part of the book's vision had been wrong.

Confident, feeling alive and cocky, he began to spring toward the courtyard and to the house that lay just beyond it. Only then did the notice a man stand up from a crouched position, earlier hidden from Sander's view by the beautiful flowers and plants of the garden.

The man noticed him and smiled, although his eyes were a bit surprised, as were Sander's. He slowed his pace as he approached the courtyard, and with the intention to stop, he let his gaze drift from the prominently dressed man to the house behind him. There, he saw the six cloaked collectors, approaching the courtyard from the opposite side.

"Impossible," Sander huffed to himself. He had outran them – *out-swam* them – and yet, there they were.

There was no time to spare, and there was nowhere else to run. The book vibrated in his clutches once more and he knew what he had to do. He had no choice in the matter anymore, if he'd had any choice to begin with. Picking up his pace again, he rushed up to the man, pushed the book into his hands, and whispered, "Έχετε επιλεγεί," Greek for *you have been chosen*.

Sander gave the man no time to question him as he rushed by him. He knew he couldn't let the collectors near the man and the book; he had to lead them away – as far from this place as he could – so that the book could survive, even if *he* couldn't.

The Book – 3

He held the strange, cloth covered item with curiosity, but he had no opportunity to ask what it was, or to inquire as to whom the young man was that gave it to him. As quickly as it was handed to him, the boy whispered something strange – foreign – to him and ran. Even though he'd never spoken a word of Greek, the moment he held this package and the words were spoken, he understood what the young man told him. Still, the message was cryptic, and he watched the boy until he departed toward the east side of the property. Then, he noticed the six hooded figures chasing him.

Doctor Wilfred Longfellow was an educated man of forty-one, and he knew that if the object had been given to him while someone was in pursuit, said object had to have been of importance.

Longfellow was a doctor of medicine, and currently, he was on a most wonderful house-call, visiting an old colleague with a touch of pneumonia. He'd been here for three days now – a terrific break from his own house on the hill a few hours away. He missed his family, yes, but he was thankful for the serenity that this job offered.

Over the course of the days, his colleague's health had improved, and this evening, Longfellow was set to return home. He would miss this place, but now, with the strange appearance and then disappearance of the young Greek man, and with the gifting of this unusual and seemingly forbidden object wrapped in fine red fabric, he felt he would be taking a mystery home with him.

Under the shade of a fine gazebo, he unwrapped the object and stared at it – at first in curiosity, and then in horror. It was a book – that much was for certain – and it was the most hideously crafted book he'd ever laid eyes on. The covers and binding... even the pages seemed to be made from some poor creature's skin and another's scales. It vibrated from his touch and he pulled his hands away, letting the book fall from his lap to the ground. There, the book ceased its vibrations, almost tempting him to lift it again.

"What are you?" he asked it, staring down at its ugliness.

He thought of the strange boy that had pushed the book onto him. Young, fit, and rushed. He thought of the hooded men. They meant no good; that was for sure.

Perhaps, he considered, the book was meant for his colleague – Lord Samuel Jameson, who was resting at this hour, asleep from the medication.

The book looked old – ancient, even – and it was likely of irreplaceable value. If it belonged to Jameson, then the man was due it. Longfellow lifted the book again and stood. Thankfully, it did not vibrate this time. He left the red cloth on the bench in which he had sat, deciding that once an item was unwrapped, there was no point in rewrapping it. Jameson would appreciate it the same either way.

Lord Jameson was known for being a collector of the strange and unusual. His entire estate was a testimony to it. Statues from around the world were strategically placed across the grounds and gardens, and the inside of the manor was like venturing though the grandest museum in the world. There was an entire wing dedicated to African ceremonial masks and tools, but Longfellow had only ventured there once. The items had felt haunted to him – or enchanted, as ridiculous as it sounded.

Longfellow carried the book into the well-decorated manor, nodding to the maid as she dusted off an urn as large as she was.

"A new artifact has arrived for Lord Jameson," he told the maid with a smile. "I shall deliver it to him personally. Please, however, alert the staff. The artifact was delivered in such a rushed way that it strikes concern with me."

"Concern, sir?"

"Yes. You see, as soon as the book was handed to me, the young delivery boy rushed off. He was being chased by six hooded men."

"Six? Oh, this artifact must be o' value. Usually, when someone tries to steal one o' the Lord's treasures, only one person is sent."

"Well, there were six this time. Please see that they do not disturb Lord Jameson."

"I'll ask Arthur to release the hounds. They'll see to the problem."

"Thank you, Miss Hartwell."

Holding the book under his arm, Longfellow ascended the stairs and walked down the long, dark hallway. He considered knocking on the door at the end of the hall, but if Jameson was still asleep from the medication, he wouldn't have heard a knock. Instead, Longfellow opened the door and entered into the large master-suite of the manor, unannounced. Across from him at the far end of the room, he saw Jameson lying atop the plush mattress of his four-post bed, sound asleep.

"Poor man," Longfellow noted as he approached him. "I do hope he makes a full recovery. Still, he'll be glad to see that... *whatever* this is has arrived for him."

He placed the book atop Jameson's chest where he would be pleasantly surprised to see it upon waking. It slowly rose and fell with his breaths. Then, deciding to leave him to his slumber, Longfellow departed the room as quietly as he'd entered and return to his own temporary chambers to finish packing for his return home.

He hadn't brought much with him to Southampton. A few changes of clothing, his grooming essentials, his briefcase, a few books, and his medicine bag. He had a few suits in this room on reserve for when he needed them. After all, he and Jameson had known one another for decades, having spent their formative years schooled together. He had visited Jameson so frequently over the years that this room was always reserved specifically for him.

Through the window of his room, he saw his carriage arrive just as he finished gathering his belongings. Tomlinson, the butler, appeared in the threshold of his room.

"Your buggy is here, Doctor Longfellow," the man announced and, without needing to be asked, took Longfellow's bags. "As requested, the grounds man has released the hounds. The six men in hoods appear to be long gone, Sir." With a nod of the head, the butler departed the room.

"Thank you, Tomlinson. I'll be down momentarily," he told him as he followed him from the room. "I'd like to say my goodbyes to Lord Jameson and leave further instructions for medication at his bedside."

"Very good, sir." Tomlinson walked down the hall, toward the finely crafted staircase. Longfellow thought it made his stairs at home look as base and ordinary as they could be.

Once more, Longfellow ventured down the long, dark hallway, passing by numerous closed, lifeless doors as he approached the master suit. This time, he knocked on the door, but received no response.

"The old chap should be rising by now," he noted before entering. Opening the door, he stepped into the room, letting the door close halfway behind him. "Jameson, you silly old goat. I'm departing now. Won't you wake long enough to bid me goodbye?"

There was no answer, and so he approached the bed with slow, soft steps. Jameson had been more than half recovered before taking his afternoon dosage and drifting off to sleep. He should have been stirring by now.

"The house is on fire!" he joked, nearing his friend. "There's been an invasion and the military is here... France has come to take away all of your expensive artwork!"

None of his attempts to scare Jameson awake worked, and so he decided on another tactic; he would stir the man with a gentle shake of the arm.

Yet, when he reached the bed and looked down at the man, it was Longfellow that was shaken. To say that Jameson was dead would have been an understatement. The man looked sunken – hollowed – with his eyes open and the orbs rolled back with only the whites showing. His mouth was drained and stretched into the most wretched opening Longfellow had ever seen. The entire body was white, shriveled... like his very life had been sucked out of him.

In his years of medical profession – no; in all of his *life* – Longfellow had never seen anything like this. Why, just an hour or so ago, the man was alive and on the mend. He looked healthy. Now, he looked as if he'd been dead for centuries.

The book was still on his chest, right where Longfellow had left it. It didn't seem possible, but something about the book made Longfellow more uneasy – as if the book, itself, was the cause of Jameson's death.

He didn't know how a mere book could suck the life out of someone's body, but he truly believed the book was responsible. If that was the case, then the book was invaluable to medical sciences. He had to take it, to study it... research it. Coyly, he looked behind him to ensure no one was watching and then took the book and tucked it away into his briefcase. After a deep breath, he cried out for help.

When the inspector arrived, they asked Longfellow for his medical advice on the matter, to which he replied, "A reaction, I presume."

Hoisting the blame of his old friend's death on an allergy to the medication, Longfellow and his newfound research departed for home, having closed the case to the inspector's satisfaction.

The Book – 4

His wife Marissa, along with his nephew Thomas and niece Charity, awaited his return with open arms, even though the hour was late when Longfellow finally returned home.

"You must be famished," Marissa told him as she stepped aside to let him enter into the house. "I've kept a plate on the table for you."

"Did ya bring us anything, Uncle Wilfred?" asked Thomas with an eager grin.

"I missed you so much, Uncle Wilfred!" added Charity.

Thomas and Charity were the children of Longfellow's sister Mary. Mary and her husband had died in a tragic boating accident two years prior, and as the closest relative, he took over custody of their children.

"Nothing this trip," he told the children, "but tomorrow, we shall all go on a nice picnic!" The children's eyes lit up, and so did Marissa's.

When the children and Marissa had retired for the night and he had pleasured both himself and his wife, Longfellow retreated to his library, where he documented the events at Jameson's manor in his journal. On his desk beside his quill pen and inkwell lay the book – a wicked mystery that gave him chills every time he glanced at it.

He wrote of Jameson's illness, of his treatments, and of Longfellow's own experience in the courtyard, when the young man rushed up to him, drench from the sea, and pushed the book into his hands before leading a band of hooded men on a curious chase. Then, he wrote of the book itself, detailing its description and how it seemed to have claimed his dear friend's life – something he had ensured not to tell the inspector.

When his entry was complete, he closed his journal and opened the side drawer of the desk, grabbing for his bottle of scotch. Pulling it free, he groaned at the fact that it was empty – drained from his last encounter with it.

"I really could have used that drink," he noted, setting the bottle atop the desk and staring at it with sad, tired eyes.

Before him, the book began to vibrate. Longfellow nearly jumped from his skin. He had not yet opened the book since bringing it home, but now as it set there on his desk, trembling before him, the temptation arose. Reaching out with a shaky, nervous hand, he touched the cover and opened it.

His mind filled with the sounds of a thousand whispers, all chanting to him in a language he could not comprehend. The shock of their chants nearly sent him from the chair to the floor, and it caused a slight ache to overcome his temples. He watched the pages of the book begin to flip – swiftly like with a strong wind – and then suddenly stop.

The whispers in his mind somehow began to make sense to him as he looked at the script on the page. It felt like a tomb of secrets was being opened up to him, and as his fingers touched the book, he could feel its power. Longfellow did not know precisely what was happening, but as the hint of new power surged through his fingertips, he was no longer afraid. Instead, he wanted to understand. He wanted to know what it was that this book was promising him – offering to him – and he wanted to embrace it.

The whispers silenced as he began to read aloud the words on the page. When he was finished, nothing happened and the whispers returned. He tried again to the same result. On the third attempt, he changed his pronunciation of the unusual words and letters, and when he finished reciting the spell, his scotch bottle replenished right before his eyes.

"Impossible…" he whispered, taking his hands from the book and letting the whispers fall away. He picked up the bottle and observed it… uncorked it… sniffed it. It looked like scotch. Hell, it smelled like scotch. Better yet, it smelled like the same expensive scotch that had been in this bottle previously.

Curiously, he tasted it, and miraculously, it *was* the

expensive scotch that he enjoyed so much. Longfellow drank deeply, finishing half of the bottle before he set it back down on the desk. The power of the liquor hit him hard and fast, but it was not a bad buzz. If anything, it made him giddy and more relaxed… happier.

"Why, you are quite the book, aren't you?" he asked the spell book, stroking it with his index finger. "If you can make things like that happen, you and I are going to get along just fine."

The book vibrated from his touch, and when he pulled his fingers back, the pages flipped backwards with great speed and the cover shut as the book closed itself.

"So, I presume this one miracle is all for tonight?" he asked the book as he took another swig of his scotch. "That's quite okay. I'm certain you have much to teach me, and I vow to you – I am an avid, attentive pupil."

The book vibrated once more, as if recognizing what he'd just told it, and then it stilled again.

Drunk and eager with anticipation, Longfellow began logging his most recent discovery into his journal, documenting the great power that the book had just displayed to him.

The Book – 5

Some would have called it a miracle, certainly. Others would have referred to the great power of the book as witchcraft. Doctor Wilfred Longfellow decided that both descriptions were accurate. While some of the book's abilities certainly seemed like miracles – refilling his scotch, building up his medical clientele to the likes he'd never seen, and causing his thinning hair to grow again – others had not been so innocent.

Into his sixth month of possession of the book, Longfellow had seen it only as a companion to his whims – a granter of wishes and a provider of the otherwise impossible. Yet, as he rode his buggy home from a house call late one night, his horse struck a little girl just a mile or so away from his property.

Longfellow knew most of the people in the area – if not all of them – but this was the first time he'd ever seen this child, and there were no houses on this stretch for her to have belonged to.

She was badly injured from the collision. She'd run out into the road when his buggy approached, and her presence had spooked his horse. The horse, in retaliation, trampled the small girl, causing great damage before Longfellow was able to control the beast.

"It's okay," he told the girl as he scooped her into her arms and loaded her up in the buggy. "Hang in there, sweet girl. I'll save you. I'll fix this."

She was bleeding all over, and Longfellow assumed there were internal injuries too. She wasn't conscious, but she had a heartbeat… albeit a weak one.

When he arrived home, Marissa, Thomas and Charity were all asleep, and the house was quiet. He brought the little girl inside, cradled in his arms, but he did not trust to work on her in the great room. He needed a quiet place – a place where he would not disturb his family. They didn't need to see the mess this girl was in, and if he couldn't save her, they didn't need to know what had happened.

He carried the girl down to the basement and then into the cellar. There, he laid her flat on the stone floor while he returned upstairs to retrieve his medicine bag and a medical book from the library. When he entered into the library, the spell book was vibrating from within the drawer he kept it tucked away in. After gathering his other items, he took the book also – as if beckoned by it – and returned to the cellar.

One by one, he laid out his tools and some medicine for her pain. He was going to inject the medicine when he noticed the most tragic possible circumstance had happened. During his trip upstairs, the child died from her injuries.

"No..." he whispered, feeling as his heart skip a beat and his skin turned clammy. "No... this cannot be. Please..." Even though it had been an accident, he had, indirectly, killed the little girl. It had not been by his hand, but it had happened – both by his animal and on his time. "I'm so sorry," he told the child, stroking her hair and her bloody cheek. "This shouldn't have happened."

We can save her, he heard the voices whisper into his mind as the book began to vibrate beside him. The words slithered through him as if spoken from a serpent's tongue. It was the first time Longfellow had heard the voices speak in unison. *We can return what has been taken...*

As the voices spoke to him, Longfellow became afraid of them... of the book again – just like he had been when he had retrieved it off of Jameson's withered body. It was the book's tone this time. It was the offering of the impossible. The book had yet to fail him a single time, so he had to trust it. What other choice did he have? He was desperate. A child was dead because of him, and if there was a chance he could make it right, he had to take it.

"What do I have to do?" he whispered. The words trembled from his throat, even though he wished he could have suppressed them.

Through the whispers, the voices relayed preparation

instructions to him in an ancient language that he had learned to mostly understand. The book also opened up to a new ritual, offering a visual to aid in the instructions. These instructions required him to draw a pentagram on the floor and place the child atop it. Then, he had to ensure some of the child's blood was dripped onto the circle with her. There was plenty of blood already, and so he did not have to concern himself with that part.

Once Longfellow finished the preparations, he heard a great storm begin outside – something he'd never heard from within the cellar. He could hear the howling of the wind through the trees, the roar of the thunder from the heavens, and the crashing of the water in the sea just beyond his home. While it was a remarkable experience, it was also a frightening one. The house was only thirty years old, but he feared such a storm would destroy it.

Still, Longfellow knew he had to trust what was happening. He had to put his faith into the book, as he had to try to save the girl… to save his immaculate reputation from becoming that of a killer.

Taking the book in his hands, he recited the ancient words on the page, using full intention in his voice. When he was finished, he heard the storm die down and everything went calm. The book vibrated once before shutting in his hands.

He set the book down and looked at the little girl, kneeling down beside her. He checked her pulse, her temperature, her heartbeat… The spell had not worked. The girl was still dead.

"What is this?" he asked, looking at the book. "What has happened? Did I make a mistake? Did I say something wrong?"

He took the book again and tried to open it to the page of the spell, but it would not budge. He couldn't even open the cover. Somehow, it was locked – letting him know he was not to use it again at the moment.

"But it didn't work!" he shouted, letting his voice rise. "She's still dead! Help me, goddamn it!"

The book remained silent and closed. It had bested Longfellow – failed him. Or he had failed it. Whichever was correct, he was uncertain, as the voices were not whispering to him right now. They were, instead, treating him like Marissa when she was in a pissy mood; they were giving him the cold shoulder.

Now, he didn't know what to do. He couldn't save the girl's life – not with medicine and not with magic. She was gone. He was responsible. His heart sank deep inside of him as he began to sob. He cried for the child, and he cried for himself. He did not know what was going to happen from here on out, but he knew things would never be the same for him. Once word leaked out, his career and reputation would suffer, even if he wasn't charged.

Yet… there were important circumstances that he had to keep in mind. For instance, he was the only person that knew what had happened to the little girl. He was the only one that knew she had been trampled, that she had been brought to this house, and that she had died here.

While the idea made him sick, Longfellow knew there was only one solution. He had to get rid of the body. He had to remove all traces of this girl from his house, his buggy... from his life. She had to be destroyed – buried or dumped in the sea. Then, and only then, would his life retain any morsel of substance.

He would need something to wrap her in, he decided, and taking his tools, bag, and books with him, he returned the items to the library and headed to the front door. There were some items in the shed, he remembered and thought they'd be perfect to wrap the corpse in.

Just as he was about to open the door, he heard Marissa call to him from the stairs.

"There you are!" she exclaimed and rushed down to him, wrapping her arms around him in an embrace. He prayed she would not notice the child's blood on his clothing. "Are you just getting in? The most awful storm just passed through here."

"Yes," he whispered, nodding his head. "The storm seems to have departed now."

"It was quite frightening." She kissed his cheek and broke the embrace. "Come up to bed with me. I don't think I can fall asleep without you."

Longfellow swallowed through his nervousness. "I'll be right up," he said and offered a forced smile. "I just want to take off these clothes before going upstairs. My client... got sick on me. They're disgusting."

"You're my husband," she noted as she climbed the stairs. "I am your wife and I love you. I'll clean those up in the morning. Come on to bed. I'll carry them down to the basement in the mornin'."

He wanted to protest, but it would have done no good. If he tried, he knew he would have trapped himself in a web of lies. Once tangled in a web, only terrible things began to happen. That was the case with spiders and their prey, and that was the case with liars and their fibs. He had to keep what he told Marissa to a minimum, or else the figurative spider would devour him like a snack.

Begrudgingly, he followed his wife upstairs, stripping off his jacket, bowtie, and shirt before ever reaching their bedroom.

The Book – 6

While some spells worked instantly, others took time to take effect. Longfellow learned this in a most shocking and horrifying way.

Between clients, his nephew and niece, and his wife, there had been no time to take care of the young girl's remains, and she had been left in the cellar to rot. Longfellow prepared himself for the stench, wearing a surgical mask over his face as he descended the cellar stairs with heavy cloth in tow – ready to wrap the body for dumping.

The hour was late and, without their knowledge, he had given Marissa and the children something to help ensure they would sleep. He'd hated doing it, but he had to get rid of the body before it became more of a problem. He knew what a mess bodies made when they started to decompose, and he wanted to avoid as much of that as possible.

Fortunately, he thought, the cellar was nice and cool, and the floor of it was even colder. With any luck, it had helped to preserve the body long enough for him to dispose of it.

Yet, when he reached the bottom of the stairs and held his lantern before him, he let out a terrified scream – thankful that his family would not awaken due to it. When he last lay eyes on the little girl, she had been dead... cold... a cadaver. Now, she was standing upright in the middle of the cellar, looking at him through white eyes and snarling lips.

"What in God's name...?" he whispered, but the second the words left his lips, the young girl was upon him – attacking him like a savage beast in the jungle.

It was a struggle of strengths – his against hers, which was surprising to Longfellow. The violent girl was incredibly strong, much stronger than any child should have been. He fought against her, managing to thwart the approach of her nails and the constant chomping of her jaw as she tried to bite him. He managed to force her to the ground, pinning her down with his knees as best he could. Still, she snarled and snapped like a wild animal.

"Stop it!" he shouted, holding her head down to the floor. "Stop it!" Then, he began to beat her head against the floor, hoping to still her – to keep her from biting at him. When she still fought against him, he beat her head harder against the floor, eventually crushing the skull. He felt the brain smoosh from the impact.

All was still for a minute. Quiet. The whole world stopped. Was time even ticking? Longfellow didn't know anymore. He didn't know what just happened either. She had been dead, and then... she wasn't. She was reanimated – alive – but the little girl had changed somehow. She had been different. Something terrible had happened to her. Something that he hadn't intended or wanted. He'd just wanted her alive again – but healthy, like she had been. This... this creature...it was not what he'd hoped for.

The book, he thought, standing from the girl's remains – now twice dead – and trying to calm himself. He was shaking uncontrollably.

He remembered thinking that the book had failed him when he'd performed the ritual three days ago, but he'd been wrong. The spell had just taken time. The book had not failed him, but somehow Longfellow had failed the book. This couldn't have been the spell's intended outcome. What was the purpose of bringing back the dead if they were brought back as savages?

He considered going immediately upstairs and retrieving the book to find out what he had done wrong, but the body was much worse off now than he'd left it before and it had to be taken care of. It had started storming again at sundown, and it was too muddy and wet for him to dig a hole. He'd have to wrap and dump the body into the sea, and so that was exactly what Longfellow did.

By the time that he had cleaned up his mess and changed out of his wet clothes, the sun was rising and the storm had cleared. In the library, as he drank from his magical bottle of scotch, he took the spell book from the drawer, and looked at it.

"Please," he begged of it, stroking its scaly, fleshy cover. "Please… tell me what I did wrong. That… that *creature* I faced… That was not the same little girl that I left down there before. Something had happened to her – something… awful."

The book vibrated before him – the first time it had done so since closing after the last ritual. Then, the whispers returned, filling his mind with so many thoughts – dark thoughts in foreign languages of times long past – that it made him dizzy and he began to bleed from the nose.

All at once, he fainted, falling from his chair and tumbling down to the ground. When he opened his eyes again, the grandfather clock was striking the eighth hour and he could hear the pitter-patter of children's feet descending the stairs.

He sat up with a jolt, feeling the pain of a hangover sweep over his head. He could hear the children in the great room, and he knew it was only a matter of time before one of them, or Marissa, checked the library to see if he was in there. The headache would have to be dealt with later. His first priority was putting the spell book back in its drawer and out of sight.

Just as the book was placed inside and the drawer was slid shut, he heard a hand on his doorknob and the door slowly began to open.

He'd expected Marissa, but it was Charity who poked her head in to see him. She wore a grand smile on her face and it helped to lighten Longfellow's disposition.

"Uncle Wilfred!" she exclaimed, rushing into the room. "I had the best dream last night!"

"You did?" he asked, catching her as she leapt into his arms. She felt heavy to him. "What did you dream?"

"I dreamed about a pony," she told him, hugging him close. "She was small and pretty."

"Why, *you* are small and pretty," he noted, touching her button nose. "Perhaps you dreamed about yourself *as* a pony."

"Well, *that* would be queer!" the girl exclaimed with a giggle and then leaped from his grip. "Come on! Aunt Marissa has made toast with marmalade, and she even boiled some eggs!"

"She *did?*" he replied, watching her as she hurried to the door. "You tell your aunt I shall be there momentarily."

"Yes, sir!" she answered and left the library, pulling the door to behind her.

Charity was a treasure, he thought as he took a breath, feeling the force of the hangover loom over his body. Charity was young, innocent... kind. Like the girl that he killed had been, he presumed. He could not imagine anything like that happening to Charity, and it made his heart hurt for the family of the child he'd only hours ago dumped into the sea.

Then, he reminded himself that the dead girl had not been the same little girl when she'd come back to life. She'd changed, and for the worst. Her second death had been necessary.

There was still a thought in the back of his head as he took his scotch from its hiding place, seeking the hair of the dog as a cure for his hangover. The thought was of the ritual itself and of the words that he had spoken. It had been his first time performing the ritual, and he was set on the idea that he'd done something wrong. That he had misspoken a word or not utilized enough of the girl's blood on the pentagram.

If he ever had to attempt the spell again, he decided, he would do so with more caution, more patience, and he would work harder to ensure the correct pronunciation of the words. As the words were written from an ancient, foreign tongue, it was a struggle for him to learn at the irregular pace the spells and whispers were presented to him.

That was something else he vowed to work on. He would have to work with the book more, listen to the voices harder… make better sense of what they were telling him. Sometimes, they were clear as day. Other times, the whispers were so separated from one another that they were nearly impossible to focus on and realistically hear.

He had to grow closer to the spell book so that it would open up for him more. They needed to develop a stronger bond together – one that would encourage the book to trust him further and teach him its secrets at a more consistent pace.

Taking one more swig, Longfellow felt the headache subside and left the library to clean up and join his family for breakfast.

The Book – 7

Over the course of several months, the spell book proved stubborn to Longfellow, only opening when for him when it wanted to, and only opening up to spells he'd already done before.

For four days, he had the house all to himself. Marissa had taken the children to visit her cousin Alice in Southampton for the week, and so he had intentionally not scheduled any appointments during her time away. Instead, he decided to dedicate the time to further studying the book and to try and get it to teach him to view more of its offerings than just the ones it had been allowing.

Currently, the book sat atop his desk, opened to a spell he'd performed numerous times. Once more, he did it just to please the book. It was a vision spell – one that allowed him to see into a familiar place without actually visiting it. He could see clearly his old friend Jameson's former home, which was now the residency of his nephew, a twenty year old scoundrel who was currently in the bed Jameson died in, making love to three women at once.

Longfellow blinked the vision away, having seen much more than he'd intended.

"That was an indecent use of this power," he told the book, feeling shame over what he just saw. "Have you nothing of value left to teach me? The parlor tricks have grown old, my friend, and I have grown impatient. An impatient pupil is a reckless pupil, mind you."

Just then, he heard the sound of a horse-drawn buggy from out his window. Glancing out, he saw the approach of Mrs. Burnett Collard, wife of Samuel Collard, the banker.

The book began to vibrate violently as the buggy stopped in the drive. Longfellow attempted to grab it and put it away, but something new happened when he touched it – it burned his fingertips. The book did not want to be moved; it made that obvious. Instead, its pages began to flip and it landed on a spell that it had shown him only once before – the spell he'd used to bring the little girl back to life.

Looking out the window again, Longfellow took notice of the fact that Mrs. Collard had coached her own buggy to his residency, as neither a driver nor Mr. Collard was with her. He heard the whispers return to his mind, telling him that it was time to try again… that she was the one.

As she approached the front steps, he turned from the window and left the library, shutting the door behind him. What the book was asking of him was madness. Mrs. Collard was an upstanding woman in the community, and she was a dear friend of

Marissa's as well. He couldn't bear to hurt the dear woman… he *wouldn't*.

Just as she began to knock on the door, Longfellow answered it, smiling pleasantly and hoping that the shock of her arrival and the desires of the book were not written across his face.

"Mrs. Collard," he began in a somewhat cheerful manner. "What an unexpected pleasure this is. I am afraid, however, that Marissa is away at her cousin Alice's for the week."

"I am actually here to see you, Doctor Longfellow," the woman said as she pushed past him and entered the house. Her voice had always been chipper during conversation. Now, it sounded strained – worried.

"Is something the matter?" he asked, shutting the door behind her.

"I'm afraid it's Mr. Collard," she told him in a fretful tone. "You see, he's terribly sick, Doctor Longfellow. He needs your help. Please, won't you return with me? Why, he requested you specifically."

"I really wish I could, but you see, Mrs. Collard, while Marissa is away I have taken some time off, and I am involved in some very deep research. Important research that I just can't break away from. It could save lives, you understand."

Mrs. Collard was quiet for a moment as she considered his words. Then, she blinked and nodded, finally whispering, "Yes…

yes, I see."

"Perhaps Doctor Andrews could be of assistance. He's a decent, well-educated physician."

He began to walk the woman back to the door when she stopped again and faced him. "Some medicine, maybe? I think it's influenza that has stricken him. Or a touch of pneumonia. Oh, please, Doctor Longfellow. There must be *something* you can do."

Longfellow sighed and considered her request. He decided he could safely send her away with a bottle of tonic for her husband and instructions on how it was to be administered. If it would get her out of the house so that he could concentrate, it would be worth it.

"Give me a moment," he said, smiling and nodding his head. "Of course, I have some medicine I can send home with you. I'll write down the instructions also."

"Oh, Doctor Longfellow, that's wonderful," Mrs. Collard said, beaming brightly at his announcement.

"My bag is in my study. Please, wait here a moment and I'll retrieve it."

Leaving Mrs. Collard in the great room, Longfellow retreated once more to the library to fetch his medicine bag. Yet, the second the door closed behind him, the whispers returned to his mind and they were much louder than before. The sound of them floored him, and he held his hands over his ears hoping to muffle them out, but it did nothing to lessen the deafening pulsations that riddled through him, from them. His nose began to bleed from their pressure.

That moment, the book slid off of the desk and landed before him, still open to the spell he'd used on the little girl. The book was being persistent, and it was not going to relent until he agreed to do what it asked. Feeling defeated and left without any other option, he told it, "Fine... I'll do it."

All at once, the whispers silenced and Longfellow was able to regain his wits. He stood upright and wiped the blood from his nose. Then, he walked to his medical bag and pulled out a reflex hammer. Holding the hammer behind him, he returned to the great room.

Mrs. Collard's back was too him, and even though he knew the door had made a sound when opening, he approached her with timid, soft steps. He didn't want to do this. It wasn't something he was *choosing* to do. It was something he was being made to do, and that made it all the more difficult.

"Did you find what you were looking for, Doctor?" she asked. Longfellow quickened his pace.

"Yes... I have just what you need, Mrs. Collard." He had to do it quick – before she turned around and looked at him. He didn't want to face her when he did it. Yet, as he pulled up the hammer and began to lower it onto the back of her head, Mrs. Collard turned around and the hammer crashed hard against her nose, breaking it on contact.

Mrs. Collard screamed as she tumbled backward, and Longfellow panicked. Dropping the hammer, he tackled her to the ground and wrapped his fingers around her throat, squeezing as hard as she could. She fought against him, struggling under his grip and the pressure of his body. He locked her down with his knees, like he had done with the girl in the cellar, and he continued to choke her until her eyes opened so wide that they were bulging from the pressure and she stopped fighting against him. He continued to choke her for another few minutes to ensure that she was dead, and then he checked her vitals just to make sure.

Once he was certain that Mrs. Collard was no longer among the living, he stood, wiping the blood from his hands onto his pants. He was shaky, nervous, and sick to his stomach, but he had to hold it together. This was the first time he'd committed an actual murder – the little girl had been an accident – and he was certain that his soul was damned.

He took the book from the library and carried it with him as he dragged Mrs. Collard's body down the basement and into the cellar. There, he propped her against the wall as he chalked out the pentagram and prepared the ritual. He could hear a storm beginning to brew outside.

"This is nothing personal," he told Mrs. Collard as he laid

her out in the center of the pentagram. "I don't have much choice in the matter, you see. It's this, or the book won't let me rest. Surely, you understand."

Mrs. Collard did not respond, nor had Longfellow expected her to.

He remembered the little girl and the shape that she had returned in. He had partially blamed her savageness on the possibility that not enough of her blood had been spread out over the pentagram. In order to remedy this, he ventured into the basement, found a small but sharp piece of metal, and used it to cut into Mrs. Collard's wrist. With a wound opened, he squeezed until more than enough blood – he hoped –spilled out onto the pentagram.

More cautiously than before, he took the book in his hands and recited the spell. He paid special attention this time to each word, hoping to recite the words the best that he possibly could.

Once he was finished, the book snapped shut and fell from his hands, refusing to open again.

He stared at Mrs. Collard's dead body in the center of the pentagram, waiting for something to happen. A twitch. A blinking eye. A breath... anything. As the minutes passed, he saw nothing – no changes to her demeanor. She was dead, plain and simple.

Longfellow then remembered the young girl and how it had taken some time for the spell to take effect. He decided to leave

Mrs. Collard just as she was for the day and check on her tomorrow. Perhaps, if he was lucky, she would be revived and less savage than the little girl had been.

* * * *

Early the next morning, Longfellow remembered Mrs. Collard's horse and buggy. He rode it out a few miles away from his house and then turned it back with a quick snap of the reins, intentionally causing the horse to jerk hard and fast, forcing the buggy to unhitch, topple and wreck. He allowed the horse to flee, and he managed the long walk home, leaving the wreckage of the buggy for someone else to find and investigate. He checked on Mrs. Collard when he returned home. She was as dead as she'd been the moment he'd killed her. He decided on a shot of scotch before curling up in bed to sleep off his exhaustion.

When the next afternoon came and Longfellow finally woke and returned to the cellar, Mrs. Collard was still very much dead. Throughout this day, he checked on her repeatedly, and each time he was met with the same results. During this time, he drank heavily from his enchanted bottle of scotch, emptying it just to see it refill again.

Through much of the third day, he slept – passed out from sheer drunkenness. He awoke early in the evening, sprawled out naked on his lawn with his shoes on and covered in mud. Had it not been for the thunder warning of an approaching storm, he would have slept all night too, he figured as he stood and walked down the hill to the shoreline where he cleaned away the mud and relieved his bladder.

As he stepped inside his house, the sun was setting and the storm was beginning. Rain began to fall at a tremendous speed, and the sky grew black with both the night and the dark clouds that joined it. He watched the storm unfold through the great room's window, but when a blindingly bright bolt of lightning struck the ground just a few meters away from the porch, he stepped away.

In his library, he drank from the bottle again, deciding he needed a *clear head* before checking in on Mrs. Collard again. He did not bother dressing. There was no one to see him. Mrs. Collard was dead, and Longfellow was certain that she'd still be dead when he went down to visit her.

He carried the bottle of scotch with him to the basement and took one more sip before setting it temporarily on a shelf. Then, he picked up a sturdy axe – just in case.

When he opened the cellar door, he found Mrs. Collard standing there, waiting on him. She had the same evil white eyes as had the young girl before her, and also like the girl, she snarled when she saw him. Then, as Longfellow took a step back, Mrs. Collard hissed and lunged forward at him.

With a single, lucky swing of his axe, he sent Mrs. Collard's head traveling across the basement, landing at the foot of the stairs. The body collapsed in front of him, but it did not die. Instead, as he continued to back away, it began to crawl toward him, blindly.

He turned to flee and noticed that the head was upright and staring him down. It, too, was still alive. While it hissed at him and tried to chomp at him, he could hear the body shuffling up closer behind him. Beheading the creature had not killed it. He considered the young girl and how he'd bashed her head into the floor. After that, she'd stayed dead.

"The brain," he whispered, struck with the sudden realization. "I must kill the brain."

Just as Mrs. Collard's hand grabbed onto Longfellow's left leg, he lifted up his axe and brought it down hard on her decapitated head. As it split through into the brain, her body fell limp and its grip on his ankle loosened. He pulled his axe free from the head and took a step up the stairs, shaken from the experience. He stared at Mrs. Collard's body and then to the decapitated head and let the axe slip from his fingers to the ground. Then, after reminding himself to breathe, he flew up the basement stairs, slamming the door shut behind him.

"Fuck!" he shouted, utilizing a word he'd used rarely before. He was near tears, completely distraught by what he'd just witnessed. "That was *not* what I wanted!"

Bitterly, fearfully, angrily, he stormed into the library and took the book from the drawer. He was going to yell at it, but he decided it needed to be punished instead, and so he threw it to the wall as hard as he could, letting it slide down to the floor. It began to vibrate when it hit, and the whispers returned in a mind-shattering way. They caused his body to feel like it was on fire and his head to feel like it would simply explode.

When he could not bear anymore of this torture, he begged for the book's forgiveness, and the burning sensation, as well as the pressure inside of his head, dissipated away.

It took Longfellow a bit to gather his strength back, and then he was able to pick himself back up off the ground. He went to the book and took it, returning it to its drawer. Then, as he stepped from the library and headed toward the staircase to lock himself away in his room, he heard a knock at the door.

He froze. He was in no shape to see anyone, and he was expecting nobody. Also, it was storming outside and the hour was a bit late for casual company.

As the knocking persisted, he walked to the door and stood before it. Swallowing through a knot in his throat, he opened it to find Miss Juliette Wells, a neighbor from a half mile or so down the road. He had not heard a buggy approach and, peering out into the yard behind her, he saw that she had arrived on foot. She was soaking wet and staring at him in shock. Only then did he remember that he was still naked, less his shoes. Quickly, he covered himself with his hands.

"Miss Wells," he said through a cough, blushing in the cheeks. "What an unexpected surprise."

"Pardon me, Doctor Longfellow!" she exclaimed, looking away. "I wanted to inquire if you'd heard anything about the buggy accident up the road earlier this week. I've not been able to rid it from my mind, and no one seems to know a thing. I had hoped you or Marissa might have heard something about it, but it appears I have arrived at a bad time."

"No, not at all," he told her, although he secretly agreed with her. "Mrs. Longfellow is out of town at current, but please, do come in." He stepped aside, and with one hand still covering his crotch, he gestured for her to come into the house. Hesitantly, she entered. "Now, tell me about this… buggy accident."

Miss Wells, as attractive of a young woman as they came and even more enticing soaking wet, tried to face him again but looked right away, unable to make eye contact.

"Actually, please… excuse me for a moment. I was just… preparing a bath when you arrived, and I needed something from downstairs… so I put my shoes back on. I shall return momentarily after I become a bit more… presentable. Would you care for something to dry off with?"

"I am quite fine, thank you," she told him, barely looking at him. Her cheeks were rosy as she blushed.

He began up the stairs when, halfway up, he wondered if Miss Wells was watching him. Glancing back, he saw that she was, although she looked away the second she was noticed.

Longfellow was not sure why, but the fact that she had been watching him climb the stairs naked made him smile. It also made another part of his body show excitement, and so he hurried on to his room to dress and suppress.

When he returned to the great room a few minutes later, he found his library door open and Miss Wells inside. She was leaning over his desk, reading over the journal entries that he'd left open after his last notations – the entries about Mrs. Collard... or the corpse of Mrs. Collard, rather.

She looked up at him as he entered – her face torn in an expression of shock. She backed away from him as he neared her, pinning herself against the window while holding her hands before her.

"You nosy little snit," he told her. "I really wish you hadn't done that." He was nervous again. She knew what he'd been up to, which meant she knew too much. Her expression showed everything. She was trembling... scared. She knew what Longfellow was capable of now, and so he had no choice but to demonstrate those capabilities on her.

"Please, no," she pleaded, and as he grabbed his quill pen from atop the desk and began to stab and slash her with it, she began to scream. She slid down the glass of the large window, to the floor where she held her bleeding gut and looked up at Longfellow with tears in her eyes. Before she could open her mouth to speak or scream again, he slit her throat and let her tumble forward to die.

Instantly, he could hear the whispers return and he could almost feel the vibrations from the book. It was an opportunity to try again – to master this cursed spell so that the book would let him move on to another. The storm outside began to grow again in both strength and sound, becoming a roar as Longfellow dragged Miss Wells out of the library and to the cellar.

This time, after the ritual was completed, Longfellow chained Miss Wells to a post, ensuring she would not be meeting him at the top of the cellar stairs later. Now understanding that it took three days for the ritual to complete, he secured the cellar door and abandoned the basement area so that he could tidy up the house before his wife and the children returned from Alice's.

The Book – 8

    Miss Wells had been just like the other two – a savage, beastly creature that he'd had to put down. Also like the others, he'd had to destroy her brain in order for her to die again. He left her remains in the cellar for quite a few days, and when he returned, he discovered that her bashed and beaten brain had slowly begun to regenerate itself. Killing the brain had not actually killed the curse of the spell. Longfellow discovered that it had, instead, temporarily disabled the creature while a unique healing process took over. The brain, however, was the only thing that seemed to heal from this process, but that was all it took, he knew, to reanimate any part of these creatures.

    The remains had to be burned – turned into ashes and dust. It was the only way to truly get rid of them, he realized as he thought about Mrs. Collard and the young girl – both of which he had buried at sea. He considered the possibility that they would heal, and when they did, their remains would likely return to bring havoc upon him once more.

    He burned Miss Wells late at night, far off in a field a

quarter mile away from the farmhouse while his family slept. The smell from the burning flesh was atrocious – much worse than anything he'd ever been in contact with. He had smelled burning flesh before, having been the physician signing off on many a cremation in the past. This smell, however, was much worse. It smelled inhuman and unearthly... so foul that it made him sick to his stomach and lightheaded all at once.

When he was certain all of the body would burn away, he left the scene and returned home, feeling as if he was going mad. When he went to bed, he did not sleep. During the next day, he stayed locked in his study, ignoring both the enchanted bottle of scotch and the flesh-bound book that was rumbling to be released from its drawer. Instead, he focused on his journal entry, documenting every moment that had evolved since his last notations – the ones that Miss Wells had unfortunately stumbled upon through her snooping.

He managed to keep up his stubborn silent treatment toward the book for quite a while. He also understood that this silent treatment was being *allowed* by the book. Otherwise, it would have just sent the voices to deafen him and force him into submission like it had before. He got that, but he still felt like he had earned the break from it.

During this time, Longfellow's beloved wife Marissa began to suffer an occasional dizzy spell – something that was new for her since returning from her sister Alice's home. At first, the signs of sickness were few and far apart. Marissa would have a dizzy spell while kneading dough or tending to the children. Sometimes, she would awaken from a full night's sleep as if she hadn't rested at all, exhausted. As the weeks passed, she became bedridden with a fever that Longfellow could not cure. She was losing a dangerous amount of weight, and her senses were leaving her. The situation was dire, and he devoted every waking moment to trying to save her. His book, his patients, and often even his niece and nephew went ignored.

He called in the assistance of a colleague who specialized in rare and unusual illnesses. Not technically a doctor, Mr. Randall Potter had dedicated his life to traveling the world and studying various diseases and natural remedies. Mr. Potter had been a close acquaintance of Longfellow for many years, and Longfellow needed an expertise that only he could provide.

"What seems to be the trouble?" Mr. Potter asked upon arrival. He arrived solo by buggy, and after being informed of the circumstances surrounding Marissa's illness, he immediately went to the bedroom to tend to her.

Longfellow, however, retreated to his study – exhausted from tending to his wife. What he needed, he felt, was a drink. He sat at his desk and eyed the drawer that held his magically enchanted bottle of scotch. He knew that taking a drink from this bottle would end his silent treatment toward the book, and he wasn't certain that he was ready for his quiet time to be over. But the quiet time had not been peaceful time, and the strain on his mind needed to be relaxed.

"You win," he caved, opening the drawer. He took out the bottle and uncorked it. "I give up. I need this." Heavily, he drank. Instantly, he felt relief.

Also instantly, the book began to vibrate within its drawer and the whispers made themselves present in his mind once more. Almost mechanically, Longfellow took out the book and set it upon the desk. It opened to an all too familiar spell and he thought he would be sick.

"Please, no," he begged, shaking his head as he sank within himself. "Don't make me do this again... not now. Please, not now."

The whispers turned to howls inside his thoughts, ravaging him with their wicked desires. Demanding he to do as they ask. He had no choice in the matter, as always, and he stood from the desk, uncertain of how to proceed or who he was to kill.

As he opened the library door and stepped out into the great room, he was met by Mr. Potter.

"I've never seen anything like it," the man told him, beaming from ear to ear.

"What is it?" Longfellow questioned, desperate for some

good news.

"Marissa seems to have made a full recovery, just like that." He snapped his fingers for effect as he told Longfellow the news he'd been yearning to hear. "I was in the process of examining her and, all of a sudden, a great change overcame her. It was like she was a new, fully revived version of her old, wonderful self."

"My Marissa..." he grinned, overwhelmed with relief. He looked at the staircase and then back to Mr. Potter. "Where is she now? Still in her bed?"

"She's in the bath chamber, freshening up. The children wanted to join her, but I sent them to bed. I hope you don't mind. I was afraid they would have exhausted her again."

"That is perfectly alright. Will you be staying the night?"

"No, I'm afraid I must be going. I have quite a ride ahead of me, and the hour is already growing late."

"Please, then, allow me to escort you to your buggy."

On the walk from the door to the horse and buggy, Longfellow and Mr. Potter exchanged light chitchat while Longfellow extended his gratitude to the man for aiding in his wife's swift recovery. Then, as Mr. Potter began to step into the buggy, Longfellow retrieved a large stone from beside his feet and slammed it hard onto the side of Mr. Potter's head, killing his longtime friend.

"I'm sorry, old friend," he told his dead colleague. His wasn't nervous this time, but his voice held a mournful tone as he spoke. "It's this book, you see… I have no power over what it makes me do."

With a smack to the horse's back hip, the animal reared up and took off with the buggy in tow, hurrying far away from the house without its master. Convinced that the shadows of the night would conceal Mr. Potter's body for the time being, Longfellow returned to the house, where he met his wife at the foot of the stairs and kissed her with more passion than he could last remember showing her.

Longfellow was no fool. The moment he learned of Marissa's recovery, he knew that Mr. Potter had played no role in healing her. The book had made Marissa ill, and the book had taken her sickness away. Had she died from the illness, Longfellow realized it would have been his doing, as it had been his silent treatment toward the book that had led to the illness in the first place.

With Thomas and Charity asleep in their rooms, Longfellow made love to his wife atop their dining room table, and then again in front of the fireplace. By the time they were through, Marissa was exhausted again – this time from something far more fun than an illness – and she was ready for bed. Longfellow, however, still had work ahead of him, and thusly sent her to their room ahead of him.

"Will you be late?" she asked him from the top of the stairs.

"Only an hour or so."

Mr. Potter was heavier than Mrs. Collard or Miss Wells had been, and he had been a struggle to pull through the house and into the cellar without making much noise. There, Longfellow performed the ritual for a fourth time, hoping – praying – that he had finally gotten it right. As he had with Miss Wells, he chained Mr. Potter's body to the post and locked him in the cellar.

"What were you doing down there all that time?" Marissa asked him as he stepped from the basement. He was shocked to see her, as he thought she was asleep. He assumed the storm that always seemed to accompany the ritual had kept her awake.

"Considering a conversion," he told her, being forced to come up with something on the spot. "I am considering moving my study down there." He hated to lie, especially to his wife, but he knew he had to keep his darkest secrets hidden from her.

"To the basement?" she replied in astonishment. "For heaven's sake, why?"

"The library… it's so cramped in there that I have trouble spreading out my research."

"Cramped? It's the second largest room in the house. You have it filled with so much stuff that it just feels small to you." She smiled and touched his shoulder. "Why don't we do this? Tomorrow, I'll help you clean that mess up in there, and it will feel like a whole new space to you. How does that sound?"

"Help me clean up?" he asked. He couldn't fathom what she might discover.

"Of course! We can organize and sort, burn old rubbish that you don't need any more… that sort of thing."

The idea sounded positively awful to Longfellow – the worst thing she could have suggested.

"That sounds wonderful," he lied again, shrugging his shoulders with a fake smile plastered over his face. Then, he pulled another magic trick from up his sleeve. "However, I was hoping to spend time with you tomorrow – and with Thomas and Charity too."

"Oh? Do you think they could help us? It *would* be a good idea to include them in chores more often."

"I was thinking more along the lines of a day away from this place. Surely, you're ready to stretch your legs a bit after your illness. We could take the buggy into town and spend the day at the market and soaking up some local color. But, if you would rather spend the day cleaning and sorting…"

Marissa agreed to the day in town. Taking the family into town bought him enough time before he retired to bed that night to gather up anything incriminating and move it down into the basement, safely out of sight – including the spell book and all of his journals since discovering the book. Marissa got to feel the joy of helping him sort and organize, and Longfellow got to keep his secrets hidden away for a bit longer.

Two nights later, a storm came upon the area, and it was just like the storms that had come when the others awoke. Once Marissa and the children had retired to bed, Longfellow injected them with something to keep them asleep and ventured down to the cellar, ready to inspect his latest reanimated creation.

Killing the people had been the worst part of this, but checking to see what had happened to them after the spell took effect was definitely the scariest, he thought.

Mr. Potter, like the others, was awake and awaiting him. His eyes were white. His flesh had a blue tint to it. The gash on his head from the rock was open and had not scabbed over. A strand of thick, gray drool dangled from his mouth and ran down his chin.

He looked at Longfellow, and Longfellow returned the stare. He expected Mr. Potter to growl or snap at him at any moment, but the reanimated man simply watched him instead.

Then, quite suddenly, Mr. Potter took a deep, forced breath and parted his lips. "Long…fellow…" he croaked in a tone that sent shivers up the doctor's spine.

He had said his name. Mr. Potter had *actually* said his name. This was a vast improvement over the others, and yet, he did not feel as if he had fully succeeded in the ritual. While Mr. Potter had managed to speak three syllables, he still looked and sounded as if he had been dead for three days.

Before Longfellow could reply to him, Mr. Potter continued. "Must… eat…"

"Must eat? Oh! You're hungry?" Now *this* was an improvement over the others. Not only could Mr. Potter speak, but there was the chance that he was hungry for *actual* food. "What would you like? Bread? There is some pork jowl in the kitchen."

"Must… eat… *you*!" With that final word, Mr. Potter began to behave just like Miss Wells and Mrs. Collard, and even the little girl. He tried to rush at Longfellow, but he was stopped inches away as he reached the end of the chain. He snapped at him, snarled at him, tried to rip him apart… He was hungry; that much was for certain. The horrifying part of it, Longfellow realized, was that he was hungry for living, human meat… another failed attempt. "Must… *eat*!"

Shocked, dismayed, and terrified, Longfellow rushed from the cellar and up the stairs, through the basement, and up to the great room, where he leaned against the door after shutting it… to catch his breath and calm himself. No matter how many times he experienced this, it never seemed to get less scary for him. Each time, he was in mortal danger, and each time, he had to put an end to his reanimated experiment. What made it worst for him was that

Mr. Potter was a longtime friend – the closest Longfellow had been to any of his subjects thus far.

He needed to write – to document this incredible yet tragic event – and so once he gathered his wits about him, he retreated back down to the basement, grabbed his current journal, and then hurried to his freshly cleaned and organized library. Yet, once he sat down in his chair and dipped his pen into the ink, he paused.

Mr. Potter's speech was a great advancement over Longfellow's three prior attempts at the spell. Even though the creature was still savage, perhaps his state would improve. He considered the other three specimens; he had killed each of them within moments of discovering they had turned. Perhaps this savage hunger would dissipate over the course of a few days. Perhaps the reanimated cadaver would eventually seem more like the old Mr. Potter again, given enough time and patience.

He put the pen back on its stand and closed the journal without writing a single word. He decided he needed more time to observe Mr. Potter before logging his findings. As the man had been one of Longfellow's greatest friends, he felt he owed him that much.

The Book – 9

By the end of April 1884, Longfellow's research had led him to the following theories about the undead. It took three days for the spell to take effect, after which the subject could live each night, but it died again each day. This led him to the belief that only the living may walk during the day, and the dead were reserved solely for the night.

Longfellow also learned that, while some subjects such as Mr. Potter and a young inspector by the name of Anderson managed to retain aspects of speech and memory, their savage hungers remained present. They required human flesh to live – *living* human flesh. Four times for Mr. Potter and twice for Inspector Anderson, Longfellow ventured out to find them a random stranger to feast upon. Each time, he ensured that Marissa and the children had been drugged into a deep sleep, as to not be awakened by the screaming of the meal.

Finally, he learned that the physical state of the subjects could not be changed once they were reanimated. However they looked when they came back to life was how they stayed. Only damage to the brain was repaired – a phenomenon that he'd learned with Mrs. Collard but still could not explain.

For every new piece of information he discovered, Longfellow found himself desperate to learn more – to find a cure through this wicked spell that would end death as mankind knew it, that would right all of his wrongs by providing a true service to humanity… life after death. *True* life. Not an *afterlife*.

Without showing further progression or promise, Mr. Potter was burned two weeks after his initial death, while Inspector Anderson was burned only five days after his. Both burnings happened during the day, while the subjects had once again died from the curse of the spell.

While the days, weeks, months and years flew by, Marissa again became direly ill – this time from a human ailment and not one inflicted on her by the book. Longfellow, seeing his wife slipping away before him, strongly believed that he was closer to mastering the spell and could save her. When she died suddenly while pouring herself a glass of water, Longfellow rushed to revive her.

He performed the ritual with such practiced perfection that it impressed even him. Then, after chaining her to the post, he visited her every few hours to ensure her body stayed cool to avoid decay. He brought with him a cold, wet rag every time, wiping her down from head to toe, desperate for her to return to him with the same beauty she'd had at her death. The only wound on her body was where he'd had to cut her for her blood to spill onto the pentagram, and he still hated the fact that the wound would remain present after she awakened.

When the spell again failed to produce more positive results and it was obvious that his Marissa would never *truly* return to him, he had to burn her and he felt the largest part of himself die along with her.

Longfellow explained Marissa's absence to his niece and nephew by telling them that her illness had required her to be moved to a location in Southampton where there was a specialist making her all better. By winter, the children had grown accustomed to life without Marissa, but Longfellow had not. The holidays took a toll on him, and he smothered Thomas to death in his sleep, desperate to perfect this damned ritual that had failed to cure his wife.

Even though Thomas had come back with the same ailments and savage hunger as the others, Longfellow found that he could not burn him. He hadn't the heart to do so, as Thomas was only a child and reminded him of the little girl that he'd had to destroy at the beginning of all of this. Not to mention that he and Charity were all he had left.

Longfellow logged in his journal that he had burned Thomas nonetheless, as a precaution should his journals ever be discovered. Then, keeping the reanimated boy alive in the cellar, he fed him daily chunks of meat from neighbors and townsfolk.

Shortly thereafter, he strangled sweet Charity and performed the ritual on her too. Once again, the results were the same. While she still looked human, she was as savage and hungry as the others. Unlike Thomas, Charity was able to mutter some words of recognizable English. For instance, whenever she saw Longfellow, whether it had been an hour or a day, she'd mutter, "Uncle... Wil... fred..." in a raspy voice that Longfellow could tell brought her pain.

"This is the third one this week," Longfellow told her as he fed her in the cellar when she woke. "You eat so much more than any of the others."

Charity looked at him with white eyes and a big, bloody smile as she replied, "I am... a growing... girl..."

That had been both the cutest and most tragic comment that she could have chosen, he thought as watched her suck the meat off of some harlot's thigh. Next to her, Thomas snacked on an arm.

These experiments – this dire need to perfect this blasted spell – became both an obsession and a thorn in Longfellow's side. Giving up his medical practice in lieu of research, he spent years focusing his complete attention on finding new subjects to experiment on while hunting down food for the existing ones. Over time, he had managed to train them like dogs, letting them know not to bite the hand that fed them. He was able to unchain them and let them wander the grounds, stretching their legs and having just a taste of what their former lives had offered them.

The problem arose when daylight would come and his subjects would die again, scattered all over the property and in the woods. Longfellow eventually solved this dilemma by purchasing a house with a barn just down the road from his own. There, he trained his creations to look at the new property as their home and to return their every morning before the sun rose so that they could slumber safely through their repetitious deaths. Each evening when they awoke again, he would feed them and release them out onto the grounds, growing fond of them as if they were more than subjects – more than pets. He began to look at these creatures as a new sort of family, and he began to love them.

During the midst of World War I in 1916, Longfellow met a woman by the name of Louise while he was out hunting food for his savage kin. Her buggy had lost a wheel on her journey, and she was helpless to repair it herself. Longfellow, being her gentleman savior, repaired the wheel the best he could, and he grew fond of Louise through conversation.

"I love afternoons in the spring," she told him as he twisted the wheel to make sure it would hold. It did not. "I suppose it's a good day to be on a walk," she continued, and he knew that she saw his mishap. He tried again. "If it's no use, please do just tell me. I'm glad to ride my horse home. It wouldn't be the first time, I might say. This buggy is older than I am, and it is always having problems."

"Have you considered an automobile?" Longfellow asked her, twisting on the wheel again. This time, it took. "They're the latest fashion, you know."

"So I've been told. They are also quite handsomely priced, are they not?"

"Surely a woman of your beauty could persuade her husband to get her one."

"And what makes you presume that I have a husband, Doctor Longfellow?"

"Why, you're much too lovely to *not* have a gentleman in your life." He chose his words carefully, finding her beauty to be a pleasant distraction from the rest of his existence.

She blushed and smiled and looked away for a moment, but as she stared off into the nothingness of the distance, her smile dissolved. "I do have a gentleman in my life," she confessed finally in a tone that smoldered with concern. "He's a darling, handsome boy named Nathan, and he's off fighting in the war." She turned and looked at him, smiling again even though she had tears in her eyes. "He writes to me all the time, so I know he hasn't forgotten me. So I know he's okay... He sends me photographs too, sometimes. I just know he'll be coming home soon."

"I'm certain he will." Longfellow grinned at her, and the two continued their conversation for a good twenty minutes longer before they parted ways.

That night, while Longfellow's creations roamed the land, the book allowed him to try a new spell – surprisingly at his request. He received confirmation of its success two weeks later, when he was out and about hunting human prey.

It was in town while he was selecting some vegetation from the local market that he saw Louise for a second time. Her face was tear-stained. Her eyes were red.

"Louise," he called as he approached her. "What is the matter?"

"My Nathan…" she sobbed, sniffling through the name. "Oh, my poor Nathan!" Louise broke down, collapsing in Longfellow's arms. He held her close. Comforted her.

"Tell me what happened," he whispered calmly into her ear. "It will help you heal."

"He – he was shot by his own commanding officer," she explained. He could tell she was having trouble holding back her sobs. "In the forehead. In his sleep. No reason… After he did it, they say the officer didn't even know what had happened. That he'd been in a blackout."

While he comforted her, while he held her in his arms and promised her everything would be okay, Longfellow smiled. The new spell had worked. Her precious Nathan was dead, and perhaps with the right amount of comforting, Longfellow could persuade her to be his.

The age difference between him and Louise was rather large, but he was not bothered by it. She was a young, beautiful woman, and he had become depressed and morose due to his lack of living female companionship. She made him feel young and alive again, and she gave him something to focus on, aside from raising the dead. As their friendship developed, one afternoon of tea and chitchat led to another and so on, and he felt like she was beginning to feel the same spark for him that he felt for her.

As they sat together on the sofa and chatted, Longfellow decided to make his move. He placed a hand upon Louise's knee, and he was more nervous about it than he'd been about anything in a while. She set her teacup and saucer down on the side table and looked at him with wondering eyes and slightly parted lips. Those lips made his mouth water, and unable to resist the temptation, he leaned in and kissed her.

His kiss was returned with a slap to the face and the sound of shock.

"Doctor Longfellow!" she exclaimed, standing from the sofa. "What has gotten into you?"

"You, my love!" he announced, albeit desperately. "We cannot fight our love for one another any longer." He stood and took her hand. She tried to pull away, but he wouldn't let her, keeping a firm grip. "Just kiss me. Tell me you love me!"

"What?" she shouted, turning her face from his as he moved in for another kiss. "No!" She pushed him away, forcing her hand from his, and tried to run for the door.

Longfellow was not going to let her go. It had been too long since he'd felt this way, and even longer since he'd felt himself inside of a beautiful woman. He needed this, and he knew how she felt about him. He had paid attention to their conversations and the subtle hints that she'd dropped. She loved him, and she needed this too.

He wrestled her to the floor, turning her over to face him. Pulling up her dress, he tried to control her legs and kiss her all at once, but she was still struggling against him. He had to make her stop. She had to be calm and take it. If she just took it, she would love him.

"Stop fighting me," he told her through gritted teeth, putting his hand over her mouth. Immediately, Louise bit it.

"Whore!" he shouted, slapping her for the bite. "How dare you?" He slapped her again and noticed she was crying. *Good*, he thought, slapping her once more. *She needs to cry. To feel.*

He lessened his weight on her and gave her an opportunity to settle down, but when she tried to wrestle away again, he grabbed her by the hair and began to beat her head into the floor.

Now, all of a sudden, she looked like the little girl, and he had to kill her to keep from getting attacked. Fearful, he began to bash her head down harder, more forcefully and swiftly with every push.

Soon, the little girl – who now looked like Louise again – did not fight against him anymore. The body lay limp below his, and in a state of confusion, Longfellow slid off of it and stood. He looked down at the blood coming from the back of Louise's head and began to cry.

"What have I done?" he asked himself in a quivering voice. His whole body trembled. "Oh… what have I done?"

Then, he saw it. It was slow… shallow… but Louise's chest was rising and falling. She was breathing, which meant she was still somehow alive. Outside, a familiar storm began to brew.

He knew what he had to do. It was the only way he could save her… that he could keep her. Hurriedly, before the life could have another chance to leave her, he carried her body down to the cellar and performed the ritual.

One moment after the ritual ended and the companion storm outside dissipated, Louise took her last breath and died.

During her three-day hiatus into death, Longfellow found her home and cleared it out of her personal belongings, making it look as if she had fled town. He killed her horse after leading it into the woods, and he burned her buggy with it. Of her belongings, he took only what he thought she might have taken if she had run off – a few garments, some mementos from around her humble dwelling, and her correspondences and physical memories of her romance with Nathan.

When Louise rose from the dead, she was Longfellow's moment of perfection. She was still beautiful – with the exception of the back of her head from where he'd beaten it into the ground. She could still speak also, and unlike the others, she could hold intelligent conversations with him. Best of all, she somehow had no memories of what had happened to her, only that Longfellow was her friend.

Quickly, through postmortem persuasion, Longfellow convinced her to become more than just his friend. He hungered for her in a way that he hadn't felt since Marissa, and while there were still some similarities with the other undead creatures, Louise was a step above.

The similarities were notable, however. First, like the others, Louise died again each day the second the sun rose, rising again each night with the conclusion of the sunset. Secondly, while she was well-spoken, attractive, and kind, she still required the flesh and blood of humans to survive. These two things seemed to be an inescapable constant with this damned ritual, but despite them, Longfellow was pleased. The third issue with her reanimation was that, while her brain healed from being bashed in, nothing else on her did. If she cut herself, broke a bone, or chipped a tooth, the wounds became permanent. There was no healing any injury or ailment. Because of this, he took special care of her.

Aside from being a good companion and lover, Louise proved to be a good role model for Charity, who clung to her almost the moment she awakened. Thomas had not been so warmly inviting to her though, and he acted out by throwing tantrums of murder and destruction.

Even as the living dead, Charity began to recognize Louise as a mother-figure, whilst Thomas looked at her more like a replacement for his former mother figure, his aunt Marissa, who had long ago met with the fire. Longfellow found this intriguing – especially in Thomas, whom he looked at as one of the most primitive of his current collection of walking dead. It showed that, somehow, Thomas still recognized the aspect of family and the emotions of love and jealousy – love for his missing aunt and jealousy or resentment over her replacement.

While Thomas refused to bond with Louise, Charity took to her with as much excitement – albeit a primal, savage excitement – as a young girl could have. Longfellow's hope now was that Louise – his miracle of miracles – could work with Charity to help return the child to more of a normal, stable condition and state of mind.

For quite some time, this experiment seemed to work. While the book finally opened up to some new, simpler spells for him to try his hand at, Louise began helping Charity speak more fluently again. This accomplishment was an astounding one to Longfellow, who basked in the progress of his ever-evolving family.

Overtime, Charity's progression seemed to hit a plateau where it just stopped. Longfellow thought that it seemed like her brain simply could not process any further new development, as it had only grown in mass just so much before her death. In other words, it was 'all full up.' Around the same time, something began to happen to his dear Louise. While she would be fine one moment – doting and loving – the next moment, she would turn into a whole other person, throwing fits... throwing furniture. Shrieking in such high pitches that he'd had to cover his ears and sometimes leave the house completely just to block it out. At one point, she began screaming the name of her former lover as she hunted through the house, looking for Nathan until the memory eventually passed and left her mind completely. When fits like those would occur, a thick black liquid would secrete from her nose, and each time, it set her back another step, slowly making her more like the others. To Longfellow's despair, she began to regress into a hungry, primitive animal.

It was inexplicable, he thought as he tried to figure out what was happening to her and why it was happening. It was heartbreaking as the transition progressed, and eventually, one night when the sun had fully set, Louise awoke just like all of the others had when first reanimating from the spell. The woman that Longfellow knew and loved was gone. Instead, he had just another savage pet to hunt for and feed. For a second time, the love of his life had been turned into an animal, and Doctor Wilfred Longfellow became a broken man.

The Book – 10

In June of 1919, Doctor Longfellow had a sudden realization. He had grown old and was continuing to age quickly, while his family was not aging at all. They were remaining just the same, day to day, and when he eventually died, they would all be left alone to fend for themselves. At night, they would be fine – able to protect themselves under even the most threatening of situations. During the day, however, they were prey, and there would be no one to watch over them and ensure their safety.

There was, of course, only one solution to this problem. He had to perform the spell on himself before he died to ensure that he was alive to take care of those that needed him the most.

The great storm arrived as he performed the much-practiced ritual, slicing his hand to squeeze out fresh blood onto the pentagram. As he lay flat on his back, he repeated the incantation that he knew so well. Once finished, he stood, feeling a bit unchanged – unsure if it would work without him dying within three days' time. Then, quite suddenly, everything went black as he lost unconsciousness.

When he opened his eyes again, he was still in the cellar, and he soon realized that not much time had passed since he passed out, as it was only the next morning. On this second day, he experienced the most excruciating headache he'd ever known — worse than any the book had given him. It grew worse throughout the day, spreading throughout his body and making it nearly impossible for him to move. He felt like he was dying, and so he spent the rest of the day in his bed, waiting for the Reaper to come for him… waiting to die and to return as a savage.

However, on the third evening, a familiar storm once again came to his land – powerful and dangerous – and at night, he felt *it* hit, surging through his body with electric waves. Awakening his senses. Filling his body with more energy that he'd ever known. It was an amazing experience for Longfellow, who felt reborn during this transformation. When the storm subsided, he didn't feel savage at all, nor did he crave the flesh of another human or the instinct to attack.

He looked at the wound on his hand that he'd created to supply blood for the pentagram. It began to heal right before his eyes.

The phenomenal realization that he had finally succeeded in performing the ritual correctly dawned on him, and it made him the happiest he'd ever been. He knew that he would never age again and that any injuries to his body would eventually heal. He understood also that there would be drawbacks to living theoretically forever. For instance, those that he knew would always die around him, unless he, himself, saw fit to change that with the help of the book and its demonic properties.

A bit of regret fell over him as he realized this was what the book had been after him to do the whole time. The little girl had been alive when he'd brought her home and the book took notice. It had wanted him to do the spell when Mrs. Collard and Mr. Porter first arrived. When Marissa went sick, it had tried to force him to use it in order to heal her, but he had misread the book's intention. He'd believed it had wanted him to sacrifice his colleague Mr. Porter in exchange for his wife's health. Perhaps, Longfellow considered, Marissa would still be alive and well, had he only performed the ritual on her before she dropped dead of her illness.

Now that he had been given the gift of eternal life, Longfellow made it his life's mission to continue taking care of the ones that he had damned into being undead. He would care for Thomas and for Charity, and he would care for Louise. He would care for the half dozen others that he had transformed and not burned away, and he would care for anyone that he was forced to revive in the future.

For the rest of the day, Longfellow celebrated with his enchanted bottle of scotch and a meal fit for a king. That night, he slept like a baby, dreaming no dreams but finding when he awoke that he'd had the best rest of his life.

Two hours later, the book began to vibrate with such intensity that it stirred him from his breakfast in the dining room, summoning him into the library.

When he entered the room, the entire desk was violently shaking from the book's vibrations. He hurried over and slid open the drawer, taking the book out to calm it.

"What is it?" he asked, holding the book before him. "Is there something new for me to learn, now that I have mastered the spell of eternal life?"

He heard the whispers in his thoughts, striking chords of warning and distress. Then, as if the library dissolved before his very eyes, he saw a vision materialize – one of the young boy that he'd met many years ago. The one that had passed the book on to him.

He watched the boy's journey with the book. He now even knew the boy's name. Sander. Uncertain of what this vision meant, Longfellow sighed.

"Yes, I know the boy," he told the book, nodding in effect. "I remember him well."

The vision began to change from the frivolous young man utilizing the powers of the book to one of Sander fleeing from six beings in black hooded cloaks.

"I remember them as well," he noted, observing the display. "They chased after young Sander when he gave me the book. It was quite a spectacle, I might add."

From there, the image changed yet again, showing now Longfellow with the book, choosing its hiding place in the desk drawer.

"I remember that day, also. Those were the days of the simple spells. The ones that made me rich and prominent before I gave up the practice to focus on raising the dead. Ah... the good ole days."

Now, the image flashed to a scene Longfellow was not familiar with – one that had him in a similar situation as Sander. One that had him fleeing from the six men in hooded cloaks, running down a crowded dock. The image then changed to an explosion.

"Impossible..." he whispered, shaking his head. "It has been thirty-seven years since you were handed over to me. Those men have not once come here in search of you."

"If you wish to remain our keeper... If you wish to live forever," the whispers told him in their ancient language, *"then you must first die... one way or another..."*

He understood the whispers clearly, and he knew what he had to do.

Over the next several hours, he prepared for this new,

unexpected change in his life. He did not want to lead anyone out here to his sanctuary of the undead, so he hopped into his brand new Richardson cycle-car and drove into town. There, he rented a small boat at the dock, paying only for the day, and then loaded up a case of common chemicals that, when ignited, would cause one hell of an explosion.

The urgency of the spell book's vibrations let him know that the hooded men were in the vicinity, and that the time had come to fight or flee.

Longfellow had spent over three decades of his life attempting to perfect one single spell, and now that he had eternity on his side, he was not going to let six strangers take it all away from him. Thusly, he chose to fight... *and* to flee.

For nearly an hour, he hunted through the afternoon crowd, seeking the hooded men that he'd once caught a glimpse of at his friend Jameson's home. Finally, as he was about to question the book for assistance, he turned around to find the collectors approaching him. While he had been hunting him, he discovered that they had been right on his trail.

This surprised him, but it did not derail him from his plan. With the book clutched close to his chest, he began to run, knowing the hooded men would follow.

Glancing back, Longfellow saw his notion to be true. Although they were not running, they were moving swiftly, breezing through the crowds of people with ease. As old as he was, the newfound energy of his transformation made it easy for him to gain a good distance on his pursuers, and he set the course to lead them back to the dock and the boat that awaited him.

Quickly untying the boat from the pier, he climbed aboard and pushed off, allowing it to set out into the water a few meters before he began to row. When he felt like he was a safe distance away but still close enough to the pier to see what was happening, he stopped rowing and saw the hooded men appear at the pier's edge, watching him drift away.

Longfellow waved at them. Smiled. Then, he lifted the case and showed it to them as he opened it up. He set the case down and held up the spell book also, making sure that they could see it. Then, he held up a pack of matches.

He watched as one of the hooded men tried to lunge into the water after him, but the collector was held back by two of the others.

Perfect, he thought as he clutched the book under his arm and took a match from the pack. With delicateness, he struck the match and grinned once more at the men as he dropped the flame into the case of chemicals.

The chemicals, mixed with the intense heat of the flame, worked together to form a small quivering within the case. Then, all at once, they exploded into such a mighty inferno that the flames shot high into the sky to be seen for miles away. When the fire died down, the boat was destroyed and Longfellow was long gone – presumed dead and lost at sea.

Part VI

Day 7 – Bob

"What is happening to your head?" Bob asked Longfellow as he stared in grotesque shock.

"What do you mean?" the old man asked, shifting as much as he could in the chair. "I can't really touch it to find out, you know."

"I see it too," Karen added, looking closer. "It's the area where I bit your ear off."

Longfellow laughed heartily at the comment. Bob and Karen backed away. "It's starting to grow back. Because the ritual was performed on me while I was still living, and because I never died before the three-day completion period ended, my body regenerates at a tremendous speed." He looked at Karen and grinned. "Don't you wish you could say the same thing, my dear?"

"This is all *your* fault!" Karen shouted, marching up to him again. She wanted to rip his face off. Instead, she slapped him with a hand of fury.

"I did not make you go down into that cellar," he sharply countered. "*You* read from the book. *You* bled onto the pentagram. *You* passed out in the middle of it. You did this to yourself, dear, and perhaps you too would have a healthy body that regenerated itself if your loving husband here hadn't killed you before the spell was complete. If anyone is to blame for your condition, it's the two of you."

"I'd eat you right now," she told him in a slow, detesting voice, "but you'd just fucking grow back!" She slapped him again and stepped away.

Bob needed to intervene, but he was stunned by two things – the ear growing back on Longfellow's head, and the story the old man had just shared with them. Longfellow had shared so much information and answered so many questions for him that it made his head spin. Still, it seemed for every answer, he had more questions that he wanted to ask. For instance, he wondered how Longfellow had survived the boat explosion, and he wondered – if he had learned so much from the book – why he wasn't using a spell against them now.

Instead, he asked, "Did you ever see the hooded men again?"

"By now," he replied, "those men are dead, and any

modern search for me will show that I am dead too." He pulled against the ropes that bound him and groaned. "If you're not going to kill me, could you at least untie me?"

"Fuck you!" Karen spat.

"Fine…" Longfellow whispered as he sighed. "Then I'll just have to do it myself."

With a recitation of three foreign words Bob had never heard before, the ropes fell from Longfellow and the chair, letting the old man stand freely, unbound. *Well*, Bob thought, backing away further, *there goes my question about using magic against us…*

"I haven't managed to stay alive this long by letting my guard down," Longfellow continued, wiping off his shoulder as if it had gathered dust while he sat. "Now, we are going to handle this situation the easy way. I had been saving this for dear Ethel actually. I found her a suitable replacement for my Louise. But you had to go and ruin that too, didn't you, Mr. Granger?"

"What? No!" Bob exclaimed, confused in the moment. "Karen's the one that ate her!"

"Bitch deserved it," Karen added.

"There is an incantation I learned early on to implant a memory, or to remove a memory," Longfellow told them, rubbing his hands together as he contemplated it. "In a moment, you, Karen Granger, will be just another one of my undead pets – loyal to me in the ways that Louise was loyal to me... at least, until you go feral." He looked at Bob and winked. "And you shall be her supper."

Bob and Karen looked at each other with intense expressions. Bob couldn't believe what the old man was telling them. At any moment, Longfellow could simply recite a series of words, and their lives would be over – or in Karen's case, further changed forever.

Sure, Karen had read from the book and performed the ritual without even realizing she was doing it, but Bob was the reason she was in this zombified state and he knew it. He couldn't let Longfellow keep her like a pet in a field for the rest of her existence. She didn't deserve that. No one did, he thought.

Karen was his wife, for better or for worse. Until death do they part...

"I won't let you change her... throw her scraps every day like you did your other *pets*," he told Longfellow, approaching him. "She's my wife and I love her, and I'll be damned if I'm going to let you ruin our lives together."

Again, Longfellow laughed. This time, more heartily than before. He looked at Bob and shook his head, making a tsking sound with his tongue.

"I'm afraid you've already done that yourself, Mr. Granger," he replied, crossing the room and warming his hands by the fire. "Just as you did your research on me, I too did mine on you. I learned an interesting amount, I might say. I learned of your thievery at your former job and of your termination. I learned about your affair with your wife's closest friend. I even learned about Mrs. Granger's terrible miscarriages. All of those things must have caused such a severe strain on your marriage."

"How do you know all of these things?" Karen asked; her eyes shifted between her husband and her new enemy.

"Let's just say your mother-in-law was a wonderful conversationalist. She hated you very much, Mrs. Granger."

"The feeling was mutual." Karen walked from the great room to the basement door and opened it.

"Where do you think you're going?" Longfellow asked her, taking a few steps toward her.

"I need a goddamn cigarette," she snapped – literally, she snapped at him – as she stormed down the basement stairs.

"I figured she'd given up the habit for good when she died," Bob told Longfellow with a shrug of the shoulders. "Who'd of thought the nicotine would still have that big of a hook in her, even after death?"

"It's a nasty, terrible habit," Longfellow agreed, nodding his head.

"She should be the spokeswoman for the Cancer Association. She could do the commercials looking like a zombie and be like, 'I smoked cigarettes and look what happened to me!' or some shit like that, you know." Bob fidgeted and looked to the floor, chuckling at the visual he'd just given himself.

Longfellow also laughed, but it was short-lived.

A moment later, Karen's footsteps could be heard as she ascended the stairs. While Bob saw Karen's approach, Longfellow did not, and it was not until the head of an axe connected with the old man's neck that he knew she was there. By then, Bob knew it was too late.

"Fuck you, asshole!" Karen shouted as she retracted the axe and then swung it again into Longfellow's neck. She did not give him a chance to respond or to react before decapitating his head and letting it tumble to the ground. Even with his head grounded, his body stood; his arms flailing about. Dark blood sprayed all over as she began to chop off his mobile limbs, hacking through his body with great force and intention. When the body fell, she continued her vengeful carnage. Bob watched her, feeling like he was watching the maddest psychopath imaginable. For a moment, he wondered if there was any of Karen left in her body... in her mind. She chopped and hacked away pieces of Longfellow with a speed that spoke of determination and urgency as much as it did anger.

When she was finished and took a step away, Bob felt sick as he looked at her handiwork. Karen... the walls... the furniture… Bob… everything was covered from the spray of Longfellow's ancient blood. Longfellow, in turn, was chopped into at least a dozen massive chunks of old fatty flesh and bone, with bits of meat flung here and there by the power of the axe's blade. The old man's head sat propped against the library door, blinking and moving its lips, but unable to speak. If he couldn't speak, Bob realized, he couldn't perform magic.

"Regenerate *that*… you lousy fucker!" Karen yelled and walked over to the head, crashing down upon it with the butt of the axe. The head popped and splattered like a busted watermelon.

Bob backed up to a wall and slid down it, crouching over the floor with his face in his hands. While that had been the bravest thing he'd ever seen Karen do – *ever* – this whole scenario was also rather terrifying.

"Jesus Christ, Karen," he said in a voice that was barely there, "couldn't you have just eaten him."

"No…" Her tone was hoarse and somewhat animalistic. "He was already dead… like me." The axe slid from her hand and dropped to the floor. "I like my meat fresh, and his blood tasted a little funny."

He looked up… looked around him. Every memory in this house – every single last one of them – was a tragic memory. Murdering Karen… Karen eating Ethel… McDougal being Longfellow and then being chopped up into chunks… Not to mention everything Longfellow had done in this house – all of the people that had died here or were kept here as animalistic, savage pets. This was a house of horrors, and it made Bob hate himself for ever bringing Karen here in the first place.

"We have to leave this place," he told her as he slid back up the wall and stood. "This house... it's cursed... haunted, Karen. I love you so much and I still treated you so badly. Then, I moved you here, to friggin' Zombieland, and look what happened. I not only pushed you away from me, but then I killed you too."

He began to cry and wanted to tell her he was sorry, but he didn't deserve to say the words because he felt he didn't deserve her forgiveness. He deserved to be eaten instead, he decided, and he began to strip away his clothes.

"What are you doing, Bob?" she asked him, looking at him with a wondering eye. The patch over the other one dripped with Longfellow's liquid remains.

"I know you're hungry," he told her, forcing the tears away as he stood tall and naked, trembling from fear-filled nerves. "Please... eat me. I deserve it, Karen. I deserve to die for what I've done and how I've behaved, and I want you to be the one to kill me... by eating me and satisfying a hunger that I helped create."

Karen said nothing at first, but she stared at him with a cocked eyebrow and a twisted, tight mouth. Then, she smiled and crossed over to him, gently touching her cool hand to his warm cheek.

"What is wrong with you, Bob?" she asked him, nearly chuckling but suppressing it. "I don't want to eat you. We've both done some pretty terrible things. Besides, I feel pretty vindicated from chopping up McDougal."

"Longfellow."

"Whatever. The point is, I love you too." She kissed him and took a soft step back. "It took being turned into a zombie and being faced with a worse man than I thought you were to realize it, but you defended me against that old coot. You stood up for me. You even tried to make me pretty again, even though you thought I had died again for good. You did a shit job, but you tried, and that means a lot."

"You really think I did that bad a job?" he asked her, his mood lightening. "I think you look pretty hot."

"It's the eye-patch, isn't it?"

"Mm hmm," he remarked and started to smile again. "It makes you look like a sexy pirate bride."

"A sexy pirate bride *zombie*?"

"Now *that's* even hotter."

Bob took Karen by the hand and pulled her down to the floor, where his wish of having sex with her as a zombie came true, even if it was in a nest of Longfellow's body parts and a pool of his blood.

When they were finished and he lay on the floor, naked and spent, Karen excused herself and headed for the kitchen. He watched her take her cigarette pouch from the stand by the stairs – something she didn't do when retreating to the basement earlier. Bob had caught that, and that's why he wasted time with Longfellow through small talk – to buy her some time.

He heard the kitchen door open, meaning she was outside, on the small porch, smoking her cigarette just like she used to do before he killed her. It made him smile.

A few minutes later, Karen returned and curled up beside him. Bob was in heaven. He had a wife that loved him again. He'd just had terrific sex. The cares and trials of the day seemed to melt away. Then, as Karen stretched, he felt a slight jab in the side of his neck, and suddenly, his eyes fell shut and his world went black.

Day 7 – Karen

While smoking her first cigarette since rising from the dead, Karen took notice of Longfellow's car. Postmortem, the nicotine seemed to have no effect on her, but utilizing the old habit still made her feel a bit better. Strolling toward the car, she thought of everything that she and Bob had just endured. Murder... cannibalism... betrayal and secrets. In a week's time, they had gone through more tumultuous circles than anyone she knew. Their lives had forever been changed, and although they felt their old love for one another again, she knew that they could never go back to who they were before all of this began.

Longfellow had been murdered... No. Longfellow had died in 1919. *McDougal* had been murdered. As had Ethel. Karen, herself, looked like a mannequin that had been painted by a child and then left out into the sun to crackle. If an inspector came around looking for her and Bob or to ask questions about Longfellow or Ethel, Karen knew she would be a dead giveaway for the 'something's not right here' feeling.

There was also Karen's well-being from here on out to

consider. She required fresh human meat for food, and she needed to eat daily, she imagined – just like everyone else. That was savagery, she knew, and she neither wanted to hunt down some poor soul every day nor eat him up like a witch in a gingerbread house. She also couldn't ask Bob to hunt her food for her. It wasn't right or fair to him, even if he *had* killed her.

Her appearance was also still an issue for her. Her wounds would never heal. She would never look alive and healthy again. Once upon her life, she had been beautiful and she had relished in it. Now, she was something different entirely. She was, by all definitions, a monster. Perhaps her dress was fitting after all, she thought. She felt like a bride of a Frankenstein and perhaps she was one, having risen from the dead with a great surge from a bolt of lightning. Either way, her days of being accepted by those on the outside were over. She was doomed to spend the rest of time in hiding. Eventually, she figured, it wouldn't matter. If what had happened to Louise happened with her, she would turn feral and not remember a bit of her former life. She wouldn't care. She'd just be hungry… always, eternally hungry – her nights spent hunting.

Nights and days… they were another subject all together. Karen loved the sun and the warmth of its rays upon her flesh. She loved spring and summer, and even fall and winter, and she loved how the seasons changed. She considered that she would never see another sunrise, sunset, or sun period. No more rainbows. No more spring flowers and blue jays. No more summertime cookouts by a pool or picnics in an overgrown garden. There were no more days for her. She was dead during the day – every day –for the rest of her existence.

To only live at night was, indeed, for the dead, she thought as she leaned against Longfellow's car and took a drag from the cigarette. Smoking hurt, as it required breathing, but she didn't mind so much because it seemed to help her put her new world in perspective.

A creature of the night that could never be seen by man – at least by any human that wished not to be eaten... she was, indeed, a wild animal. A predator. She was savage, and she could feel that savageness within her as her stomach growled for sustenance.

She walked around the car and opened the door, sitting in the driver's seat. It felt so long since she'd been in a car... only it *hadn't* been long at all. Her old life seemed so far away. It truly had been another lifetime.

Beside her, she saw Longfellow's briefcase. Curiously, she flicked her cigarette to the mud and opened the case. There, various documents, notes, and charts were stacked and bundled together. There were also a few items from the man's days as a physician, and she found one of them interesting enough to take.

She carried the item back into the house, holding it close to her body and hidden from view. She saw Bob on the floor, right where she'd left him, basking in the afterglow of sex. She smiled at him and went to him, crouching down beside him and then curling up in his arms. Through the guise of a stretch, she brought a syringe down into her husband's neck, injecting him with a drug that put him instantly to sleep.

When she was certain that he was out, she stood and took his hands and dragged his body up the stairs to the master bedroom, where she laid him out on the bed. She kissed his cheek, his lips... she kissed each of his closed eyes, and then she covered him with a blanket.

Back downstairs, she walked over to Longfellow's crushed skull and looked at the brain. It had already regenerated and was building a new skull from scratch.

In the basement, she saw the remains of Bob's reanimated collection of severed appendages, including a brain with both eyes still attached. It seemed to watch her every move as she walked around, uncertain of what she was looking for.

"Don't stare at me like that," she told the brain and its zombified eyes. "Be patient."

Finally, she chose her tool – a large half-full gas can. She returned to the basement stairs, pouring gasoline along them as she ascended them. Then, in the great room, she let the gas trail to Longfellow, where she soaked his remains, and then up the stairs to the bedroom, where she soaked the blanket and sheets, along with Bob.

Once she was out of gas, she stepped back outside and smoked another cigarette, looking up at the sky as it began to change hues and lighten for a new day. It was beautiful, she thought as she took a drag off her cigarette. Different shades of black and blue... hues of orange and red... It was the closest she'd ever get to seeing a sunrise again, and so she basked in it while she could.

She began to feel tired, like the trials of the day were weighing on her. But Karen knew that it was more than that. It was a similar feeling that she'd experienced at the end of her first night, before she died again.

Returning to the house, she smoked inside and glanced out the window to see the sky grow a little bit brighter. Then, with heavy steps, she walked up the stairs and retreated to the bedroom, where she climbed into bed next to Bob. Cuddling up beside him, she rested her head on his shoulder and took one last drag from the cigarette, flicking the butt in the air, across the room.

As it landed, the sun appeared and Karen died. The butt landed on the trail of gasoline – just as Karen had hoped – and its cherry ignited an inferno that spread throughout the house. As it spread, Longfellow's regenerated brain burned away, as did the rest of his remains. The severed body parts and the brain with eyes in the basement also met their ends; Karen had believed they'd earned their release. Longfellow's journals and mementos – memories of his past and the horrors he had dedicated his life to – all went up in flames.

As the house burned, so did Bob and Karen, painlessly as they slumbered together in eternal rest, finally at peace with one another and with themselves through the rekindling of a love once thought lost. Through this house of horrible secrets, satanic rituals, and the living dead, they found each other again, and as their bodies burned, they did so with a fire that was created purely out of love.

Epilogue

When the Smoke Cleared

The fire that destroyed the home belonging to Bob and Karen Granger burned for three days and nights. Unlike the zombies that had been created within it, the house did not revive. When the smoke cleared, all that remained of it was rubble, smoldering ashes, the skeletons of furniture, and tall brick chimneys. Only one area of the house had not been affected by the fire; that place was the cellar – built deep in the ground and made of stone and cement.

Long ago, the rumors of the house and the land spread. Tales of disappearances, murders, cover-ups, occultism, and even zombies made their rounds, and no one much dared to venture down that way anymore. They hadn't in decades. Thusly, the fire burned without notice or interruption.

As for the house up the road that Longfellow torched

before confronting Bob, it had been gutted by the fire. It was a danger to anyone and anything that neared it. Yet, six men in black hooded cloaks stood in front of it, surveying the damage.

One by one, they approached the entrance. Four stood guard, two on either side of the open doorway, while the other two entered the house and searched. In the very center of the house, they found what they were looking for. The Book of Lucifer, completely untouched by the flames.

When the two collectors stepped out of the house, they found their four associates slaughtered, dead on the charred porch floor.

They looked around and saw the assailant – a kindly old woman in a simple black dress with a ruffled collar. Her white hair was pulled back into a bun, and her thin-rimmed glasses were perched atop her button nose, perfectly in place. She wore black slippers for shoes, and the whites of her stockings could be seen below her dress's hemline.

"Good afternoon, gentlemen," she began, smiling a friendly grin and taking a soft step toward them. "My name is Madame Howell, and I would greatly appreciate it if you would hand the book over to me."

They looked at her through their dark eyes, shadowed from the brim of their hoods. Then, they looked to each other for a moment, as if pondering her request. Finally, as they looked to

Madame Howell once more, the one holding the book tucked it into his cloak and both men took a defensive stance.

"Now, gentlemen," Madame Howell continued, still smiling sweetly, "surely, we can settle this like the civilized adults we are. Otherwise, things could get a little nasty. I *just* got this dress yesterday and I would hate to scuff it up already."

One of the men drew a knife six inches long from within his cloak, while the other simply pounded his fist into the palm of his hand. Slowly, they approached her, but Madame Howell did not back away.

Instead, she held up a hand to them and whispered, "Fly and flail."

With a flex and an extension of her fingers, the two collectors did just that. By an unseen force, they were sent flying back through the air, flailing helplessly until they crashed feet away, against the remaining structure of the house. The structure, in turn, began to crumble down over them, covering them.

The collectors tried to climb out from the rubble, but as they lifted their heads up through the mess, Madame Howell twisted her hands like she was spinning a ball, and the necks of both collectors snapped, killing them instantly.

The wind began to blow around Madame Howell as she walked toward the dead collectors. Merely by lifting her hands, she elevated the bodies from the rubble and then laid them down in front of her. She then extended her left hand, and with great focus and power, she pulled the spell book out from within the collector's cloak.

"Hello, there," she said in an accent that was a mixture of many different lands. "My name is Madame Howell, and I am your new keeper."

The spell book vibrated against her touch and the whispers greeted her with their usual clamor. Madame Howell, however, was able to silence them – to rid them from her mind and hold control over the situation.

"Not with me, you don't," she chided, holding the book under her arm. "We will have none of your head games. I am not your ordinary, run of the mill bookkeeper. There is nothing you can teach me that I don't already know."

The book vibrated again, a warning to Madame Howell, even if she had managed to block out the whispers and could not hear what it had to tell her.

"I have vowed to keep you safe," she continued, walking down the narrow, winding road, heading toward the end of it where the remains of a house overshadowed by irrepressible tragedy and horror sat as a pile of ashes and debris. "I will ensure no one ever hunts for you again, and if they do, I will make sure they don't find you."

Once more, the book vibrated – another warning gone

unheard.

Approaching the remains of the old farmhouse atop the muddy, receding hill, Madame Howell set the book down and focused on the destroyed structure. With the chanting of a few short words and the wave of a hand, all of the debris and remains of the house disappeared – all but the cellar built into the hill. There, in the secluded safety of the old cellar, she placed the book on the floor and sealed the room up tight. Once back on the hill, she rebuilt the ground and flattened it out where the house had been, trapping the cellar deep beneath the soil. In place of the house, she used her powers to grow a tree – a massive tree that would hold a bounty of fruit all throughout the year, despite the season or weather.

When she was content that her duty was over and that she would never have to deal with Lucifer's book again, Madame Howell walked down the hill to the two sheds, dematerializing them as if they'd never existed to begin with. Then, kicking off her shoes and pulling off her knee-high stockings, she dipped her feet into the sea and sat on its murky shore.

The sun was setting. It was the Madame's favorite time of every day – when the sky was painted in an array of colors, all of which would slowly transform into a pitch-black night.

As darkness fell, she stood from her resting place and stretched her legs. She looked to her tree – a tree that offered a fruit once considered forbidden – and she smiled. With her work done and her mind relaxed from the serenity of the sea and sky, she walked back toward the road.

Lucifer would be proud of her, she figured. Not only was the book safe, but she had eliminated the Vatican's collectors and ensured that all signs of what had happened on this land were gone.

All but the small farmhouse with the barn. There, she recalled, the dead bodies of the collectors still rested, as well as the remains of the house and barn.

There was not even the cooing of an owl to be heard as she approached the ruins. Just like with the house by the sea, she made this one and its barn dematerialize, leaving the land empty for future natural growth. Looking at the six bodies that remained, she snapped her fingers and each of them burst into flames, burning at a rapid pace until nothing of them remained but ashes that blew away with the breeze.

Free of her bookkeeping duties, and with all traces of Doctor Wilfred Longfellow and his mess gone, Madame Howell decided it was time to leave this place and rest.

A sound from behind caught her attention. Turning toward it, she glanced at a young girl just before the child leapt upon her and began to claw at her throat and face. The sudden savagery of the moment was so excruciating for the Madame that she could not focus on a spell to defend herself. With beastly quickness, the child ripped out the Madame's throat just as a scream began to escape her painted lips.

In a moment, Madame Howell collapsed to the ground and the light faded from her as the creature – a girl once known as Charity, forever a child and forever a monster – ate her flesh and drank her blood until she'd had her fill. Then, standing with satisfaction, the girl darted into the dark embrace of the woods, leaving behind the land of her former home and the remains of her delicious and unexpected supper.

"One makes mistakes; that is life.

But it is never a mistake to have loved."

~ Romain Rolland ~

About the Author

When the muses speak, Jae El Foster writes, and he has been doing so for nearly twenty years, tackling some of the most intriguing genres out there. Delivering fresh, incomparable tales of horror, science fiction, and romance – sweet or spicy – he pens with seasoned skill the tales that his muses deliver to him. Follow him on Instagram @jaeelfoster, on Twitter @jaeelbooks and 'like' him on Facebook at www.facebook.com/authorjaeelfoster to keep up with upcoming releases, contests, events, free reads and more. To view all of his works with DCL Publications, visit his author's page at www.thedarkcastlelords.com/authorjaeelfoster.

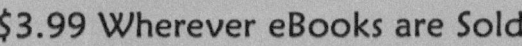

DCL Publications, LLC

http://www.thedarkcastlelords.net

Find our books at any fine online retailer.

www.ingramcontent.com/pod-product-compliance
Lightning Source LLC
Chambersburg PA
CBHW020917020726
47495CB00002B/229